MURDER IN AN ITALIAN PIAZZA

Books by Michael Falco

MURDER IN AN ITALIAN VILLAGE

MURDER IN AN ITALIAN CAFÉ

MURDER IN AN ITALIAN PIAZZA

Published by Kensington Publishing Corp.

MURDER IN AN ITALIAN PIAZZA

MICHAEL FALCO

Kensington Publishing Corp.
kensingtonbooks.com

KENSINGTON BOOKS are published by

Kensington Publishing Corp.
900 Third Avenue
New York, NY 10022

All Kensington titles, imprints, and distributed lines are available at special quantity discounts for bulk purchases for sales promotion, premiums, fund-raising, educational, or institutional use. Special book excerpts or customized printings can also be created to fit specific needs. For details, write or phone the office of the Kensington Special Sales Manager: Attn. Special Sales Department, Kensington Publishing Corp., 900 Third Avenue, New York, NY 10022. Phone: 1-800-221-2647.

KENSINGTON and the KENSINGTON COZIES teapot logo Reg. US Pat. & TM Off.

Library of Congress Card Catalogue Number: 2025936283

ISBN: 978-1-4967-4219-3
First Kensington Hardcover Edition: October 2025

ISBN: 978-1-4967-4221-6 (ebook)

10 9 8 7 6 5 4 3 2 1

Printed in the United States of America

The authorized representative in the EU for product safety and compliance
is eucomply OU, Parnu mnt 139b-14, Apt 123
Tallinn, Berlin 11317, hello@eucompliancepartner.com

This book is dedicated to all the Brias of the world. The women who share their love, their strength, their wisdom, and their laughter with everyone around them. They make life better and a bit more joyful. Here's to them!

Big thanks to the entire Kensington team for publishing number sixteen! What a ride it has been. From vampires to werewolves, from romantic comedies to murderous mysteries, we've done it all. And thanks to my agent, Evan Marshall, who's been there since the beginning.

La vendetta all'inferno ribolle nel mio cuore.

The vengeance in Hell boils in my heart.

Prologue

There was something in the air. Bria couldn't quite place what it was, but she knew it was about to change her life forever.

Standing on her balcony waiting for the sun to make its appearance, Bria inhaled deeply and welcomed the familiar scent of sweet lavender and citrus. This morning she noticed the homespun fragrance was sprinkled with a faint touch of sea salt from the Tyrrhenian Sea far below, that lazily caressed Positano's beaches with each ebb and flow. She drew in another breath and smiled. Even after living in this little slice of paradise for almost two years, Bria still found the smell—and the village itself—intoxicating.

As the sun slowly rose to illuminate Positano's distinctive landscape, Bria surveyed her new homeland and her smile grew wider. She stood in awe and couldn't imagine a day when she would take the view for granted. The vertical panorama was truly a masterpiece of man-made structures and nature's own whimsy. Jagged rocks, winding roads, lush foliage, and a collection of square, sun-bleached buildings that together created a spectacular vista that was unmatched and envied.

Through the centuries, the seaside village had invoked both terror and desire from those who cast their eyes upon her. She had lured sailors, explorers, refugees, hedonists, and tourists, some stopping briefly, while others, like Bria, put down roots. As the owner of Bella Bella, one of the village's newest and most popular bed-and-breakfast, Bria Bartolucci was now a local, one of the Positanesi. But even for her, the village still held surprises.

She watched a cloudless blue sky materialize before her eyes and heard the cry of an unseen gull. The sky was empty, the land was unchanged, the village was awakening as it did every morning, but something was different. Bria could feel it in her bones, in her mind, and, most of all, in her heart.

Alone, Bria blushed. The village hadn't changed, she had. Yes, there was something new and exciting in the air, but it hadn't originated from an outside force, it had been given life from within Bria herself. She could feel it seeping out of her pores, wrapping itself around her, encircling her with a lightness that almost lifted her off the ground. The feeling was that much more exhilarating because it was something Bria didn't think she would ever feel again.

It was love.

Chapter 1

Springtime in Positano meant that beauty could be found everywhere throughout the village. This year, it also meant that *amore* was in the air.

After years of witty banter and friendly camaraderie, Enrico and Mimi turned their friendship into a romance. Both in their sixties, both widowed, both local business owners, Enrico Taglieri, the man behind Flowers by Enrico, and Mimi Lanacello, the woman who owned the village's only bookstore, A Word from Positano, had started dating. The sight of the new couple casually holding hands or Mimi wearing a brightly colored flower in her short, gray hair that everyone knew had been put there by Enrico's hand made it impossible for even the most cynical not to smile.

On the younger end of the spectrum there was Rosalie and Michele. It had taken them a while to find their footing, but the village's most colorful boat owner and most recent mechanic had finally found their way into each other's arms. The jury was out, however, if they had made their way into the village's heart.

Since Rosalie Vivaldi was a beloved fixture in the community, its members were overly protective. Although Michele Vistigliano had ties to one of Positano's longtime residents through his *zio* Paolo, his murky past prevented him from earning the village's complete trust. While everyone was rooting for the couple, they were not entirely convinced Michele was worthy of being Rosalie's partner.

There was no question, however, as to how the village felt about Positano's latest "it" couple—Bria and Luca. The unanimous decision was that theirs was a perfect match. The B and B owner and the chief of police had flirted, bickered, and solved crimes together all the while trying to deny the attraction that was so obvious to everyone else. When they finally gave in to their feelings, their friends and family were so excited that some wanted to turn the event into a national holiday. Neither Bria nor Luca wanted their love to be officially commemorated, they simply wanted to enjoy each other's company as they embarked on their journey as a couple. A journey that often included other passengers.

"Do we really have to go?" Luca stood near the front door of Bella Bella, his head tilted to one side, his forehead furrowed, his shoulders slumped forward. He more closely resembled a bratty toddler than the forty-one-year-old man he was.

"*Uffa!*" Bria threw her hands up in the air. "I've told you three times already, yes, we really have to go!"

Luca pouted and pressed the back of his hand against his forehead. "*Dio mio!* I think I may be running a slight fever."

"I don't care if you have malaria and spread it to everyone in the restaurant! You're not getting out of this double date!" Bria grabbed her clutch from the dining room table and stomped toward the front door. "*Andiamo!*"

"Malaria isn't contagious, by the way."

With the dexterity of the champion fencer that she was, Bria spun around, slapped Luca in the shoulder with her clutch, kissed him on the lips, turned, and walked out the door.

"Now, *andiamo!*"

* * *

By the time Bria and Luca entered La Cambusa, a trendy restaurant steps from Spiaggia Grande Beach, to meet Rosalie and Michele, their playful lover's spat was completely forgotten. They were smiling and holding hands as they greeted the maître d' who led them out to the balcony. But when they saw how miserable Rosalie and Michele looked, their smiles faded.

Sitting in a chair next to Rosalie, Bria feared the worst and instantly thought Michele had done something to break her best friend's heart. Bria was half-right. Rosalie's heart was broken, but not because of anything Michele had done. It was thanks to another man.

"*Zio* Nazario died," Rosalie announced.

"Oh no!" Luca sat in the chair next to Bria, who didn't say anything, but placed her hand over his. "When?"

"Last week," Rosalie replied.

"Why didn't you tell me?" Luca cried.

"I just found out now." Rosalie held up her cell phone. "We both got a group text a few minutes ago."

Luca pulled out his phone from the inside pocket of his black linen blazer and quickly read the message. "He died peacefully in his sleep, two months shy of his one hundredth birthday." He quickly made the sign of the cross and then brought his index finger to his lips so he could kiss it. "*Dio lo benedica.*"

Bria reached out to clasp Rosalie's hand. "I'm so sorry, I know you loved him very much."

"He was our favorite." Rosalie turned to Michele. "Nazario was my father's older brother. He didn't have any children and treated me and Luca like his own."

"It wasn't easy for Nazario back then, being gay, even though no one in the family cared," Luca explained. "Papa was so sad when he moved to Rome."

"When we found out he was living with Pierre, we were thrilled," Rosalie added.

"Except Papa," Luca corrected. "He didn't care that his brother loved another man, he was furious that he didn't settle down with an Italian."

"That sounds like your papa." Bria laughed.

"They stayed together for decades until Pierre died, but whether he was single or in a relationship Nazario always made time for us," Luca explained. "He took us on trips, wrote us countless letters and postcards from all the places he visited."

"Sounds like he was rich," Michele commented.

"Why would you say that?" Bria asked.

"A single man without children who travels a lot most likely has a lot of money," Michele surmised. "Like my *zio* Paolo—well, without the travel."

Bria nodded her head in agreement despite feeling there was something about the tone of Michele's voice that she didn't like. It was crass. Michele sounded as if he was more interested in the man's wealth than the man. Possibly because Rosalie had already read him the rest of the text message.

"We need to attend the will reading tomorrow," Rosalie announced.

"Tomorrow?" Bria repeated. "*Before* the funeral?"

"They already had the funeral," Luca said. "According to this text, the lawyer tried to reach us but couldn't find our contact info until just now."

Michele raised his bottle of Peroni. "Here's hoping he is rich."

"We'll find out tomorrow," Luca said.

"Where are they having the reading?" Bria asked.

"At the lawyer's office in Ozzano dell'Emilia," Luca replied.

"Where's that?" Michele asked. "I don't think I've ever heard of it."

"It's in Bologna, but unless you're a history buff, there's no real reason to know of the place," Luca replied. "It was once called Claterna, the Pompeii of the North. It's a historical site, but the government funding ran out and the site was never fully excavated."

"We better make this a quick dinner, you two will have to get up early tomorrow," Bria said, picking up her menu. "It's about a seven-hour trip to Ozzano."

"It might be worth it," Michele said. "He could have left you his entire fortune."

"He could have a fortune, or he could be penniless," Luca said. "We won't know until we get there."

"Maybe you should go alone, Luca," Rosalie said. "I have two big tours this weekend and Mariana can't handle them on her own."

"Maybe your boyfriend could step up and help you out," Luca suggested.

"I would," Michele replied. "But Paolo needs me in the garage."

"Plus Michele gets seasick," Rosalie added.

"You're dating a woman who lives on a houseboat, and you get seasick?" Bria asked.

Michele smiled sheepishly and shrugged his shoulders. "What are the odds, right?"

"*Non preoccuparti*, I'll find someone from one of the other crews," Rosalie said. "Maybe Imperia can spare an extra yachtsman."

"Let's raise a glass to *Zio* Nazario," Bria said. "Go pay your respects, find out what he left you in his will, and then hurry home."

Luca grinned. "You can't bear to be away from me for one night, can you?"

Bria grinned back. "I'm not thinking of myself, Positano can't survive without its chief of police."

"It's just overnight," Luca said. "What can possibly happen in such a short time?"

Bria looked at Luca as if he had forgotten the fatal events that had befallen Positano ever since she'd arrived in the village.

"You must have a very short memory," Bria replied.

The next morning when she answered the knock at her front door, she realized bad luck had already arrived. It was never a good sign when the mayor of Positano popped up unexpectedly before eight a.m.

"Dante," Bria said. "What brings you here . . . so early?"

Brushing past Bria, Dante walked into the house. He then spun on his heel to face Bria, his arms outstretched, his foot upturned, and bowed slightly, looking more like a jester in a castle than a mayor in a B and B. "Can't I pay Positano's most celebrated business owner a friendly visit?"

"You can." Bria gave the door a little swing so it shut with a bang. "But you never do unless you want something."

A high-pitched chuckle filled the air and Bria thought Marco had run into the room. When her son didn't appear, she realized the sound was coming from Dante.

"Bria, Bria, Bria, this is why we would make such a wonderful couple," Dante stated. "You understand me."

"On the contrary, Dante, I don't," Bria said. "I don't mean to be rude, but I have a busy day ahead of me. What are you doing here?"

"I have come here to share some exciting and confidential news since you and I have such a particular relationship."

"We do?"

Smiling obliviously and ignoring Bria's question, Dante continued. "I wanted you to be the first to know that Positano is going to have a very special visitor."

"Who's coming to visit?"

They both turned around when Marco burst into the room from his bedroom, his schoolbag hanging off his shoulder, his black hair flopping on his forehead, and Bravo inches from his feet.

Marco gave Bria a quick hug and then stared up at Dante's face. "And don't you know you shouldn't have chocolate gelato for breakfast?"

Bria couldn't prevent herself from gasping. She had been dying to ask the same question ever since she'd opened the front door, but as a thirty-three-year-old woman she understood it would be impolite to make such a comment. A nine-year-old boy wasn't bound by the rules of social decorum.

Self-consciously, Dante touched his upper lip. "*Certo che no,* my chef prepared my usual Tuesday morning breakfast consisting of a soft-boiled egg, grilled prosciutto, and a grapefruit cut into thirteen squares."

"Then why do you have a chocolate moustache?"

Self-consciousness was replaced by pretense as Dante gestured dramatically at the dark line underneath his nose. "*Mio caro ragazzo,* my moustache is the height of fashion."

"*Figo!*" Marco cried. "Then I must be very fashionable because I always get gelato on my mouth when I eat."

"I visited Dr. Frangipani at his new clinic and noticed he was sporting one," Dante said. "He is such a trendsetter that I decided to try it for myself. Doesn't it suit me?"

Marco looked up at his mother and asked, "*Sì*, Bria, what do you think?"

Bria gasped again. Her son was growing up much too fast.

"Marco, basta, Giovanni is waiting outside to take you to school." Bria knelt down and kissed Marco on both cheeks, unable to hide her smile. "And my name is Mamma."

"I know that . . . Bria!" Marco grabbed his lunch bag from the dining room table and ran toward the front door with Bravo right behind him. "*Ciao,* Dante."

"*Ciao,* Marco," Dante replied.

The moment they left, Bria felt the need to wrap up the impromptu meeting. She didn't mind being alone with the mayor of Positano and she didn't dislike Dante, but his comments had made her become aware that he was acting more like a spurned romantic suitor who had lost Bria's hand to his rival. Or as Rosalie liked to call Dante, the man whose heart Bria destroyed.

"I didn't know pencil-thin moustaches were back in style," Bria commented.

"Another reason you need to let me take you from this village," Dante cooed. "I could show you the most fascinating, mesmerizing things."

Fifetta had taught Bria that one of a woman's most powerful defenses when caught in an awkward or uncomfortable situation was the ability to change the subject. It was motherly advice at its most practical.

"Tell me, Dante, who is coming to visit?"

"I've piqued your curiosity, haven't I?" Dante replied. "Would you like to try and guess? We can make a game out of it."

"I don't have time to play games, I have a business to run."

"I do love the huskiness of your voice when you get stern."

"Dante, tell me!"

It was Dante's turn to let out a little gasp. He clutched his throat, took a deep breath, and finally revealed the name of Positano's special visitor. "Carlotta Incantaro."

Bria recognized the name, but it took her a second to remember why. "The opera singer?"

"Not just any opera singer! The world-famous soprano."

"I haven't heard of her in years."

"Because she hasn't sung in years," Dante said. "She's coming out of retirement to sing one more time right here in the Piazza dei Mulini, the night before *La Festa della Mamma.*"

"That's this weekend!" Bria cried. "Why hasn't Annamaria been spreading the news all throughout the village?"

"Carlotta wants it to be a surprise," Dante explained. "Of course I begged and pleaded, but she refused to do any publicity for the concert. She wants it to be simple, a diva singing at sunset for unsuspecting tourists."

The tightening Bria felt previously returned, this time not in her chest, but in the pit of her stomach. It was a telltale sign that she suspected danger or at least that someone wasn't telling the truth. An opera diva coming out of retirement to sing unannounced and just for the fun of it didn't make sense.

"Why now?" Bria asked. "And why here?"

The pencil-thin moustache lengthened eerily as Dante smiled. "Always suspicious."

"Always deflecting," Bria replied. "Answer my questions."

Sighing heavily, Dante threw up his hands. "I cannot keep secrets from you, Bria, I truly cannot. Carlotta is sharing her incredible singing talent once again to celebrate her daughter's wedding."

"Her daughter's getting married here?"

"No, in Lake Como in June."

"Then why is Carlotta singing in Positano in May?"

"Carlotta hasn't sung in public for almost a decade and wants to perform a small concert first to overcome her fears."

Bria had no desire to prolong the conversation, but Dante, as usual, was talking in circles. "Why would a famous singer be nervous to sing in front of friends and family at a wedding?"

"Because her daughter, Ombra, is marrying Armando Puccia, the only son of Pietro Puccia."

Once again, Bria recognized the name, but this time was unable to place it. "Why do I know that name?"

"I'm sure Marco talks about him all the time," Dante replied. "Pietro Puccia is one of the most famous soccer players who ever lived."

"That must be it, Marco must have watched him play on TV."

"Only if it was a replay of a very old game, Pietro retired decades ago and is now a billionaire businessman, thanks to his tech company, which means this will be the wedding of the year. I'm surprised you haven't heard about it."

"I've been busy working and I don't really pay attention to those things," Bria said. "I understand why Carlotta would be nervous to get back on stage, but why sing here?"

"Because this is where her career started."

Bria thought she knew all the landmarks in Positano, but obviously one had slipped by.

"We don't have an opera house."

Dante's high-pitched laughter once again filled the room. "When she was a young student, Carlotta would sing in the Piazza dei Mulini for the money people would throw in her hat." Dante pressed a hand to his heart, and it looked as if he was trying to shed a tear, but he only managed to look constipated. "Now she wants to pay back the village."

"What a beautiful story, wait until Luca hears."

Dante stiffened and his moustache shrank. "Luca is an opera fan?"

"I don't know, but he loves soccer so he'll be excited to meet this Puccia."

"It brings me no joy to disappoint our chief of police," Dante lied. "But Armando's father won't be attending. He's too busy with their businesses and social engagements. The concert in the piazza will be a very small affair."

"I'm sure it will still be a thrilling event no matter the size," Bria said. "Thank you for letting me know."

"It was my pleasure."

Dante reached out to grab Bria's hand and she fought the urge to pull it away from his grasp. Luckily, Giovanni entered and Dante's hand shot up to his mouth.

"*Scusi,* Sister B wanted me to remind you that Marco will be staying after school for practice," Vanni announced. "*Ciao,* Dante, I think you have some dirt under your nose."

Dante's cheeks turned red and he opened his mouth to speak, but started to cough instead. It took him a few moments to compose himself. "Bria, I trust you'll keep our secret private and not share it with the hired help."

"I think he means me," Vanni whispered.

"Your secret is safe with me," Bria replied.

"*Buona giornata,*" Dante said.

The second the front door closed after Dante left, Vanni turned to Bria with a perplexed expression. "What was that about?"

"*Mi dispiace,* I must keep my promise." Bria grabbed her bag that was hanging off a chair at the table. "But once I tell Annamaria, the entire village will know."

It was rare that anyone could *outgossip* a gossip. Which is why Bria felt empowered on her walk over to Caffè Positano. It was silly, but it brought a beaming smile to Bria's lips.

She rounded a corner of Viale Pasitea, the main road in Positano that started at the top of the mountain and moved in a long, curved path down to the beach, and felt her pace quicken as she got closer to her destination. When she arrived at Caffè Positano, however, Bria thought she might need to salvage a friendship instead of sharing some gossip.

Sitting at a table in the corner of the café, Annamaria and Mimi were not only arguing, they were also practically screaming at each other. In an attempt to defuse the situation, Bria did what countless other peacekeepers—and fools—had done throughout history. She willingly walked into the lion's den.

"*Salve signore.*" Bria sat in a chair in between them. "Isn't it a beautiful day?"

"It's humid," Mimi growled.

"And overcast," Annamaria gruffly added.

Bria eyed the clear blue sky through the window and realized she had her work cut out for her. "I've heard the most incredible news that I'm dying to share! We're about to have a very special visitor."

"Is another bitch coming to town?"

Bria was shocked by the vitriol in Mimi's voice. She had only heard that sound once before from Mimi when the bookstore owner was enraged that Luigi Brugnaro, the mayor of Venice, had banned some children's books that told stories about nontraditional families, including one about yellow and blue circles that are so close they become green. Now it appeared that Mimi and Brugnaro had something in common—they were both responding irrationally.

"Are you talking about Carlotta?" Bria asked.

"Do you know any other *cagna* dropping in for a visit?!"

"Mimi, *per favore,* you have to calm down," Annamaria said.

"Calm down? After what she did to me? And to my family? Never!"

"You know Carlotta?" Bria asked.

"She's my cousin!"

"Your cousin?" Bria cried. "I've never heard you speak of anyone so harshly, especially family."

"Carlotta isn't family."

"You just said she was your cousin."

"Sharing the same blood does not make someone family," Mimi confirmed.

"Science would disagree," Annamaria interjected. "But that was a long time ago, Mimi."

Mimi pounded her fist onto the table and pointed her finger at Annamaria. "*Blasfemo!* How can you say that when you know what she did?"

"*Naturalmente,* what you told me Carlotta did was terrible," Annamaria agreed. "But Mimi, you have to let it go."

"Never!"

Bria felt like she was sitting in between her mother and sister during one of their legendary arguments. She didn't know who was right or who was wrong, but she wanted to get to the heart of the matter. Even though she was disappointed that the women already knew Carlotta was coming to Positano and presumably why, Bria was energized because now she needed to find out what terrible, unforgiveable act the diva committed against Mimi's family that would cause her friend to fly into a fury. Mimi was so eager to tell the story one more time, Bria didn't even have to ask.

"Ludovica was a much better singer than Carlotta and that vixen knew it! Carlotta deliberately caused my sister to miss her audition for the Royal College of Music and destroyed her music career," Mimi explained. "Carlotta went on to stardom and my sister had to settle for a life that was beneath her.She died of a broken heart knowing she had been denied the chance to use the gift God had given her."

Bria desperately tried to think of something to say that could soften Mimi's rage or at least not further ignite her wrath. She glanced over at Annamaria, and when she saw the fear in her eyes, Bria knew Annamaria was thinking the same thing: there was no way to corral Mimi's hatred.

"I swear to you both right here and now that I will make Carlotta pay for what she did," Mimi hissed.

Bria understood how Mimi felt. If someone had hurt her sister, Lorenza, as severely as Carlotta had hurt Ludovica, Bria would want revenge, too. She knew that such a feeling was a basic human response. The problem was Bria also knew that when a woman held a grudge for decades, the result could be terrifying.

Chapter 2

Hours later as she walked to pick up Marco at school, Bria still couldn't shake the feeling that something bad was going to happen. Despite the warm breeze that swirled around her, Bria shivered. She understood Mimi's desire for vengeance, which meant she also understood the lengths Mimi might go to settle the score. What she didn't understand was why Imperia was standing next to Sister Benedicta at the gates of St. Cecilia's Grammar School.

As she was about to greet her mother-in-law, Bria was overcome with a greater sense of panic. The only reason Imperia would be at Marco's school was if something bad had happened to Marco. Bria couldn't hide the fear in her voice as she spoke. "Is Marco all right?"

"He's fine," Sister Benedicta assured. "He should be out in a few minutes; Sister Caterina is giving them a special lesson."

"*Grazie, bene.*" Bria sighed deeply. "I thought something was wrong."

"Because I'm here."

Imperia ran a bloodred, well-manicured nail through her black hair, tucking some strands behind her ear to expose a glittering amethyst-and-diamond earring. If Bria wasn't still trying to shake off the fear that refused to detach from her body, she would have laughed out loud at Imperia's ostentatious display. It perfectly illustrated how odd she looked standing next to a nun.

Imperia smiled. "Isn't that right, Bria?"

Instinctively, Bria began to formulate a lie in her mind—nothing elaborate, just a white lie that would not validate Imperia's comment. Then she paused. She and her mother-in-law did not have the warmest of relationships—between them lay friction, discourse, and mild animosity—but recently Imperia's icy demeanor had begun to thaw, allowing the women to enter a new phase, one where their family bond could be fully realized. In order for that to happen, there also needed to be truth.

"Yes, it is."

While both Bria and Imperia smiled at the honest reply, Sister B's olive complexion turned white. Bria could tell the nun feared she would be in the crosshairs of an uncomfortable exchange of words. She needed to put the sister at ease.

"It's nice to see you, Imperia," Bria said. "But I didn't expect to see you today."

"Naturally, maternal instincts kicked in when you saw me standing outside Marco's school," Imperia replied.

"Exactly," Bria replied. "But if there isn't anything wrong, why are you here?"

"I came to talk some sense into Dante, and I never miss an opportunity to spend time with my grandson."

"It's heartwarming to see that Marco is surrounded by such a large, extended family," Sister B said. "Not all of the children are so lucky."

"I have a plan for how Bartolucci Enterprises can help with that," Imperia said.

"Really?" Sister B clasped her hands together. "Perhaps I could arrange for you to speak with Mother Superior."

"She and I have already spoken," Imperia replied. "This is something that you'll be able to help us with."

Sister B appeared stunned by the comment. "Me?"

"False modesty is unbecoming especially in a sister, Sister," Imperia teased. "You know you've become a pillar of this community as much as Bria has."

It was Bria's turn to appear stunned. She opened her mouth to protest, but Imperia cut her off.

"What did I just say about false modesty?" Imperia chided. "It's a woman's greatest weakness. For centuries men have demanded that women know their place, and I agree, especially when that place is at the top of the pyramid."

Bria saw the surprise in Sister B's eyes and knew that it matched her own. Bria did feel she had earned the village's trust and felt she had become an *il locali,* but a pillar? Before she could utter a protest she knew Imperia would undoubtedly try to refute, she was saved, quite literally, by a bell.

Among the group of children, who were all wearing the same navy blue and gold school uniforms running out into the courtyard, there was one little boy who had pieces of Bria's and Imperia's hearts woven into his. Nothing Marco could ever do or say would sever the inextricable ties that bound him to these two women. Bria and Imperia knew it and Marco, while not comprehending the full meaning of unconditional love at his age, understood that these two women—along with Fifetta, of course—were the center of his world. He might have fun with Tomaso and his other friends, he learned soccer tricks from Giovanni and Luca, he even laughed uncontrollably with Rosalie, but these three woman, especially Bria, made him feel safe.

"Mamma! *Nonna* Imperia!" Marco's beaming expression suddenly turned sour. "Did I do something wrong?"

"Like mother, like son," Imperia remarked.

"Nothing's wrong, *mio piccolino,*" Bria said. "*Nonna* was visiting a friend and wanted to see you."

"I thought you said *Nonna* didn't have any friends," Marco replied.

"Marco!" Bria cried.

Imperia's roaring laughter drowned out Bria's admonition, but didn't stop Sister Benedicta from summoning divine intervention by making the sign of the cross. Once again Bria was speechless, but luckily Imperia wasn't waiting for her to respond. She was too busy admiring her grandson.

"I see you've inherited your grandfather's sense of timing." Imperia bent down and hugged Marco fiercely. "Don't ever lose it."

"What friend did you come here to see?" Marco asked.

"Dante."

Bria had already seen the look in Imperia's eyes earlier in the day. Her eyes bore the same anger she had seen in Mimi's. Bria didn't need to hear anything more to know why her mother-in-law wanted to speak to the mayor.

On the walk back to Bella Bella, Imperia ranted and raved about how terrible a decision it was to allow Carlotta to return to the village. Usually, Bria tried to spare Marco from hearing such negativity, but she could tell by the tone of Imperia's nonstop monologue that it would be worse if she asked her to stop or tried to veer the topic of conversation to a happier subject. Truthfully, Bria found Imperia's uncharacteristic venting to be quite entertaining.

"I remember once she sang at La Scala—when you're a little bit older, Marcolito, and can truly appreciate the majesty of opera, I'll take you there to see *La Traviata* or *Il Barbiere di Siviglia*—but I will never, ever subject you to *Die Meistersinger von Nürnberg*."

Imperia walked into Bella Bella so grandly, it was as if she was making her first entrance in a celebrated opera. She flung her purse onto the dining room table, spun around to face an amused Bria and a slightly perplexed Marco, and continued her story.

"That poor excuse for an opera is almost five hours of German screeching, and Carlotta screeched the loudest," Imperia recalled. "By the third act I had a splitting headache."

"Is that why you don't want Carlotta to come to the village?" Marco asked. "Because she'll give everyone a headache?"

"*Si, mi nipote.*" Imperia raised her silk-blend skirt an inch so she could bend down to look Marco in the eyes. "Remember, Marco, a woman who makes your head hurt cannot be trusted."

"Mamma made my head hurt once," Marco replied. "She was swinging me around like the baby seagull in *La Gabbianella e il Gatto.*"

"*The Little Seagull and the Cat,*" Imperia sighed. "*Mio angioletto,* I gave you that book when you started school."

"I know, Papa used to read it to me all the time," Marco replied. "Mamma was swinging me around like Papa used to, but she isn't as strong and she dropped me on my head."

It had finally happened. Bria heard Marco talk about his father and it didn't bring tears to her eyes, it didn't fill her with melancholy, it only made her smile. She looked over at Imperia and saw that her mother-in-law had not yet made such a transition.

Hearing Marco talk about Carlo still brought Imperia pain. Bria only had to look at her son to understand why. As deeply as Bria had loved Carlo, the feeling paled in comparison to the unconditional, unexplainable love she felt for her son. Bria knew that until the day Imperia died, the thought of Carlo would bring pain. Sometimes the pain would be cradled in a smile or accompanied by laughter, but it would still be pain, nonetheless. It was a mother's burden.

"I think it's time for a little boy to do his homework," Bria said, knowing this time that Imperia would appreciate a change of subject.

"I will," Marco said. "Right after Bravo and I have our afternoon snack."

Bria looked around the room, suddenly noticing the silence and the lack of one very special canine. "Where is Bravo?"

"He's right here!"

They all turned to the front door and saw Bravo bounding into the room followed by Giovanni, who was holding a bag of groceries. Instead of racing toward Marco first, Bravo surprised everyone by greeting Imperia. Once again Bria was reminded of how sweet her dog was. He could sense that Imperia needed a little comforting.

"*Ciao, mi dolce ragazzo.*" Imperia inched up her skirt even farther this time so she could kneel on the floor and pet Bravo properly.

"We were out of a few things so I took advantage of the quiet and ran down to Palatone to get some groceries," Vanni explained.

"Did you get more Lotte pies?" Marco asked.

Giovanni took in the scene and sensed that his entrance was an interruption.Why don't you come with me into the kitchen and find out for yourself?"

"That means Vanni wants to get me out of the room so you and *Nonna* can talk about adult stuff," Marco said, wearing a very unadult grin.

"*Esattamente!*" Vanni cried. "*Adesso vieni,* and bring Bravo, too."

"Come on, Bravo," Marco said. "Time for us to go."

He ran toward the kitchen, but halfway there, turned around and shouted, "Don't leave without saying good-bye, *Nonna!*"

Imperia didn't respond verbally but merely nodded her head in agreement. Bria turned away and gave her mother-in-law a few moments to collect herself before resuming their conversation. Although Imperia had talked quite a lot about Carlotta, she hadn't shared anything that would explain why she hated the woman as much as Mimi did. Bria wanted to find out why the opera diva had so many enemies and had learned from experience that Imperia appreciated the direct approach.

"Why do you hate Carlotta so much?"

"Because she's a fraud." Imperia sat at the table and Bria joined her. "She puts forth an air of sophistication and class, but I know the truth."

"Would you mind sharing it?"

"We were both contestants in the Miss Italia contest, which as you know I won, but Carlotta won the talent competition."

"I assume she sang."

"Most of us at that time did, but Carlotta was by far the best. Mind you, this was before she added the flourish and contrived phrasing that became her trademark. Then, her voice was still pure and honest, nothing like the real Carlotta."

Imperia poured herself a glass of orange juice from the carafe in the center of the table and took a few sips as Bria patiently waited for her to continue her story.

"Right before the evening gown competition, Carlotta cut my dress into shreds."

"*Oh mio Dio!* How do you know she was the one who did that?"

"She waltzed out of my dressing room waving a pair of scissors in the air," Imperia explained. "Subtlety was never her forte, which is why she was perfectly suited for the opera."

"How did you win if you had nothing to wear?"

"I had packed a spare gown in the false bottom of my suitcase," Imperia replied. "Even back then I knew how vicious women could be."

Bria marveled at the fact that even as a teenager, Imperia had the savvy to own a suitcase with a false bottom.

"It was a cruel, malicious act that I may have forgotten if she didn't also try to steal my husband from me."

"Guillermo?"

"I've only had one husband."

"What did she do?"

"We were on a business trip in Athens and she was there preparing to play another tortured woman at the Greek National Opera, but she was mainly on the hunt for a rich suitor because her last one dumped her for one of the chorus girls." Imperia smiled at the memory. "I burn easily so I stayed inside while Guillermo basked in the sun on the beach. When I went to join him later, Carlotta was practically draped over his body."

Imperia paused to take a breath and allow the dramatic tension to build. "Guillermo was loyal, but he was a flirt and he did enjoy the attention. Carlotta followed us around for a few days until finally he grew bored of her. One night at dinner, I went to speak with some friends from Rome and when I returned to the table, Guillermo was laughing in her face. She turned red and ran out the moment she saw me."

"Why was Guillermo laughing?"

"Because Carlotta suggested they run away together after her final performance that night."

"She actually thought Guillermo would run away with her?"

"Carlotta Incantaro has always been desperate and desperate women are dangerous," Imperia declared. "That's why I tried to persuade Dante to cancel this concert."

"You weren't successful?"

"I'm not sure if you've noticed, but Dante often likes to travel down a darker path."

Bria nodded in agreement. "I have seen his new moustache."

Imperia rolled her eyes and shook her head, clearly agreeing with Bria's assessment of Dante's latest cosmetic change. "A facial hair fiasco. But regarding Carlotta, I told him that if he didn't cancel this ridiculous concert, he needs to be prepared for the consequences."

"What do you mean?"

"I honestly don't know what I'll do if I see that woman again," Imperia seethed. "I know it's been many years, but she and I have unfinished business!"

Imperia's raised voice attracted the attention of the others in the kitchen and as she was preparing to leave, Marco and Bravo ran back into the room. Despite overhearing the venomous tone of his grandmother's voice, Marco wasn't afraid. On the contrary, he seemed to find her as amusing as Guillermo had once found Carlotta.

"*Nonna!* You always make me laugh when you get so serious," Marco said. "Like you're going to kill somebody."

"Marco!" Bria cried. "Your *nonna* would never do that."

"I know," Marco said. "But she looks like she wants to."

Imperia smiled, but Bria could tell that this time it wasn't genuine. "Another thing to remember about women, Marco, is that you never know what they're really thinking."

Imperia kissed Marco on both cheeks, said good-bye to Bria, and patted Bravo on the head.

"Come on, Bravo," Marco said. "It's time to do our homework."

Giovanni entered the dining room as Marco ran after Bravo who was already in his room and plopped on his bed. "Will you be okay without me for a while?"

"*Certo, perché?*"

"I'm going to help Rosalie."

"Rosalie isn't here, she's still in Bologna at the reading of the will."

"That's why she needs help."

"*Scusa,* Vanni, I don't understand."

"I'm going to help Mariana on the tour if that's okay," he explained. "Unlike Michele, I don't get seasick."

"*Che carino!* Yes, go, we'll be fine."

After Vanni left, Bria realized they weren't fine; in fact, no one was. In the span of a few hours she had already learned that Mimi and Imperia hated Carlotta and wanted revenge against her. Who knew who else harbored ill will toward the opera diva? And who knew what lengths they'd go to in order to make Carlotta pay for the things she had done to them? The trepidation Bria felt upon hearing that Carlotta was coming to Positano was not unwarranted. Somehow Bria knew that this woman was going to bring devastation to the village with consequences that would last much longer than the memory of a memorable performance.

Bria typed out a quick text on her phone and sent it to Luca: **Hurry home, trouble is brewing in paradise!**

Chapter 3

By the time Bria finished preparing dinner the following evening, Rosalie and Luca were back from their trip and sitting around the dining room table. While Luca appeared refreshed from the quick foray to northern Italy, Rosalie looked like she had walked the entire way there and back.

"I got a rock!" Rosalie exclaimed.

"You did not," Luca protested. "*Zio* Nazario left you his entire collection."

"Of rocks!" Rosalie looked around the table and searched the faces staring back at her—Bria, Vanni, Marco, even Bravo—for support, but all she saw were people trying not to laugh and a dog trying not to get caught stealing a biscotti.

"Luca got a villa in a ski resort and I got rocks!" Rosalie cried. "How is that fair?"

"It might not be fair," Luca said. "But it does make sense."

"*Sei pazzo?*" Rosalie screeched. "How does it make sense?"

Luca popped a slice of tomato and mozzarella into his mouth. "*Zio* always said you had rocks in your head."

Bria stifled her laugh, and even Marco understood it was probably best to keep quiet, but Vanni ignored any social protocol and burst out laughing.

"You think that's funny?" Rosalie asked.

"As a matter of fact I do," Vanni replied, still laughing.

Rosalie rested her chin in the palm of her hand and after a few seconds of mulling it over agreed with Vanni. "It is funny. Plus, I'll have my own bedroom in the villa so I guess it turned out all right."

"The villa probably has so many bedrooms, you could use one to house your rock collection," Marco added.

"That's not a bad idea," Luca said. "There are so many bedrooms you could have your own, too."

"*Figo!*" Marco cried. "Is there one for Mamma, too?"

Bria had to turn away because she saw Luca's ears start to redden. "Yes, I do believe there's room for your mamma, too."

"*Bene!*" Marco cast a smile in Bria's direction, warming her heart.

She knew that he was too young to understand all the details of her burgeoning relationship with Luca, but he was also old enough to know that something had changed between the two of them. Bria didn't feel a need to explain the details to Marco mainly because she didn't really know what those details were herself. But she was thrilled to see that Marco and Bravo loved having Luca around and thoroughly enjoyed his company.

Bria caught a glimpse of Rosalie staring at her cell phone with an irritated look on her face. She was definitely not enjoying her brother's company. Maybe it was because the man she really wanted to be spending time with wasn't present.

"Rosalie, why don't you invite Michele over for dinner?" Bria suggested.

"I just sent him another text, but he hasn't responded," she replied. "He must be working."

"On dry land, of course," Giovanni chided.

Rosalie managed a smirk in response. "*Mi dispiace tanto, scusami,* thank you for helping Mariana the other day. I have a check for you."

"*Non essere pazza,*" Vanni replied. "You are not going to pay me, I did a friend a favor."

This time Rosalie managed an easy smile. "*Grazie.*"

"Now you owe me," Vanni replied.

Rosalie's smile turned to genuine laughter, which quickly faded when she saw who was standing at the front door. "What are *you* doing here?"

Nunzi was used to the cold reception she received from Rosalie so it didn't bother her. A true cop, she had learned long ago not to take anything that anyone said to her personally. She merely smiled and tipped her cap. "*Bentornato.*"

"That doesn't answer my question," Rosalie replied.

"*Ciao,* Nunzi," Bria said, ignoring her friend's rude comment. "Come in and join us for dinner."

"Maybe Nunzi is here on official business," Marco said.

"I am," Nunzi replied.

"What's wrong?" Luca asked.

"Nothing, but I knew this would be the first place you'd come after the reading of the will and I wanted to talk to you about security measures for the upcoming concert."

"What concert?" Rosalie asked.

"I didn't even get a chance to tell you," Bria said. "An opera singer is coming to the village to perform."

"Why does a singer need security?" Marco asked.

Luca faced Marco and spoke to him respectfully, not in a patronizing tone or as if he was trying to placate a child. Bria loved him for it. "We always like to have security measures in place whenever there's an outdoor event, and since Carlotta is a famous opera singer, it's even more important."

Marco thought about it for a second and then nodded in agreement. "That makes sense."

"I just found out about it this morning from Dante," Luca said. "We can talk about how to protect Carlotta from overzealous fans later, but right now I'm starving. Nunzi, sit down, *mangia.*"

"*Grazie.*" Nunzi sat down between Luca and Marco and took off her hat. She leaned to the side to place it on the floor against the leg of the chair, and when she sat up straight she saw that everyone was staring at her. "What's wrong?"

"*Caro Dio!*" Rosalie cried. "What on earth did you do to your hair?"

The question was rude, but not unwarranted. Nunzi had highlighted her brown hair with blond streaks, which Bria felt was a vast improvement over the policewoman's naturally drab color. But Nunzi—or more precisely her hairstylist—had also cut her hair to a chin-length bob and had given Nunzi bangs.

On any woman over the age of thirty, bangs were risky. On a woman with a strong square-shaped face, who almost never wore make-up, bangs were a mistake. Instead of softening Nunzi's look, the bangs only hardened it. Bria wondered if Nunzi had sought out makeover advice from Dante.

Despite the severe change, it was clear by the smile on Nunzi's face that she liked her new look. And if a new hairstyle made Nunzi happy, who was anyone to judge?

"I think you look terrific," Bria said.

"So do I," Vanni added.

"You do not!" Rosalie chastised. "You're just saying that because you're afraid Nunzi will arrest you."

"Again," Marco added as he took a bite out of a fried meatball.

"I mean it," Vanni protested. "Nunzi, I think this might be the first time I've ever seen you smile. It looks good on you."

Despite their longstanding antagonistic relationship, Bria could tell that Vanni's comments were genuine. Nunzi appeared to agree because her smile grew wider. "*Grazie,* Vanni. I know it's a big change, but I like it."

"Which is most important," Luca said.

"So tell me, boss, what did your uncle leave you in his will?"

"A villa near the Swiss border," Luca replied.

"*Nizza!*" Nunzi replied. "What did he leave you, Rosalie?"

Rosalie jabbed her fork into a meatball and breathed in deeply through her nostrils.

Marco leaned over and whispered in Nunzi's ear. "That's kind of a sore subject at the moment. You should drop it for now and ask her again after she's eaten."

"You, Marco, are a wise young man," Nunzi said.

"No more talking, *mangia,*" Bria announced. "I think we're all going to need to keep up our strength to get through the next few days."

The next morning started as it typically did at Bella Bella. Clear blue skies, warm temperature, a soft breeze that carried with it the scent of the sea, and a stranger at the door. Ever since Bria started running the bed-and-breakfast, she was used to greeting people she had never met, but this morning the stranger was a bit stranger than usual.

"*Ciao*, I'm Bria. May I help you?"

"Yes, I have reservations."

The man looked like he'd come out of a time machine that had departed in the late 1980s. He was tall and thin and had light brown hair that looked like it had been blow-dried to add extra height and body. He was wearing a burgundy dress shirt under a tan linen sports jacket and pleated linen pants in the same color. When the man extended his right hand to Bria, she noticed that the gold chain link necklace he was sporting was identical to the bracelet dangling from his wrist. She also noticed the man was wearing thin, black gloves.

People rarely wore gloves in Positano because it was almost always warm. Some winter evenings could get cold, especially if the wind was blowing, but there were few tourists at that time of year. She couldn't imagine that anyone traveling to the village or the entire Amalfi Coast would ever think of packing a pair of gloves. Except this man.

"I'm Fiorello Sanzari," the man said. "I reserved two rooms."

Bria grabbed her tablet from the bench near the front door where she had left it earlier and searched for his name in the reservation list but came up empty. "I'm so sorry, we're fully booked and I don't see a reservation for a Fiorello Sanzari."

The man's deep olive complexion started to fade to a much paler beige. "It must be there, I know I booked two rooms."

"Vanni!" Bria called out. "Did you take a reservation for a Fiorello Sanzari?"

Vanni came out of the kitchen and walked toward the front door scrolling through his cell phone. "No, and I don't see that one came through the website."

"*Oh caro, oh Dio mio!*" A small bead of sweat started to appear on Fiorello's brow and, interestingly, on the sides of his long aquiline nose. "It must be there, it simply has to be, I received an e-mail confirmation."

"*Fantastico!*" Vanni cried. "Do you have a confirmation number?"

"*Sì, sì, certo.*" Fiorello took his phone out from the pocket of his sports coat, but instead of using it to find the information Vanni requested, he hit his forehead with it. "*Mi dispiace!* I booked the reservation under a fake name."

"Why would you do that?"

"I didn't want there to be a crowd waiting."

"Are you famous?" Bria asked.

"Me? No."

She looked at Vanni who shrugged his shoulders. "Then why would there be a crowd?"

"For my companion—she's the famous one."

Finally it dawned on Bria who this man was. Or at least who the man's companion was. "You must be traveling with Carlotta Incantaro."

"Yes! I'm her pianist, Fiorello, but I made the reservation under Giacomo Lancia."

Bria scanned the reservation list and there it was, proof of the fake name. "*Certo*, reservation for two rooms under Signore Lancia. *Benvenuto.*"

"*Grazie! Scusami un attimo, per favore.*"

Fiorello ran out of Bella Bella as quickly as he had arrived, leaving Bria and Vanni to stare at each other in bewilderment. Before they could start to ask each other questions or comment on how odd Fiorello seemed, he reentered, held the door open with his foot, and extended his arm to the open entranceway. A full twenty seconds later, Carlotta emerged looking as if she were stepping onstage to take a final curtain call after a ten-minute standing ovation.

For a woman who, according to Fiorello didn't want to draw a crowd, Carlotta was doing a very bad job. The singer may have been retired, but by the way she was dressed, Carlotta Incantaro was still a diva.

Her hair was pulled back away from her face into a large bun that sat at the back of her head. It was the color of the sand on Spiaggia Grande Beach and perfectly complemented her copper complexion that appeared to be partly natural and partly a product of worshipping the sun. Her make-up was minimal, but the eyeshadow, rouge, and lipstick were in shades of rust and orange, giving her the aura of a sundrenched goddess.

She wore a turquoise blouse with long flowing sleeves and slim white pants that showcased a svelte figure. Her turquoise-and-gold sandals had a three-inch heel that filled Bria with both envy and fear because she loved wearing high heels but knew from experience that they were not Positano-friendly footwear. Bria had a closet full of fancy dress shoes but almost always grabbed her beloved espadrilles whenever she needed to walk around the village. Carlotta either had better pain management skills than Bria, didn't know better, or didn't care how she felt, only that she looked good.

Her jewelry appeared to be expensive costume pieces—Bakelite bracelets, turquoise drop earrings, and a gold metal choker that should have clashed with her free-flowing outfit, but actually worked as an anchor. The only expensive piece of jewelry Bria noticed was a large lapis lazuli ring that she wore on her right hand. It was a large stone set into a braided gold band. Against the white and turquoise, the radiant blue color popped.

Bria wanted to applaud. She knew exactly what Carlotta was doing and she admired her. The opera singer was in her sixties, many years since she had reached the pinnacle of her career, but she wasn't invisible, she was still vital, still filled with life, and she was going to make sure the world knew it. Carlotta was also the antithesis of the stereotypical image of a female opera singer; she wasn't cherubic nor did she have a large bosom, she was powerful and strong, like a former athlete, which she basically was. Singing opera took not only natural talent, but intense training and physical stamina. It was not for the weak.

"You've done it again, Fiorello." Carlotta beamed. "This place is sheer perfection."

"*Grazie mille,* Signora Incantaro," Bria said.

"My daughter and her fiancé are staying at Villa Magia," Carlotta explained. "But I couldn't stay there."

"Why not?" Bria asked. "Magia is magnificent, one of the best hotels in the Amalfi Coast."

"My face and my voice are instantly recognizable in a place like that." Carlotta walked in a circle surveying the room. "When I'm singing I can't have distractions. I need to be somewhere provincial, dull, where nobody would expect someone as famous as me to be. Someplace like right here."

Bria could sense that Giovanni was about to defend Bella Bella's honor, and although she was grateful for his instinct, she didn't want to start an argument that might end up with Carlotta leaving and cancelling her concert. Luckily, Fiorello intervened, sounding as if he had been hired to do publicity for the B-and-B.

"All the online reviews for Bella Bella were raves," Fiorello remarked. "Everyone loved the location, the staff, and especially the food. You'll be very happy staying here."

Carlotta waved a hand in front of her dismissively. "I won't be happy until this is all over."

"Isn't this a happy occasion?" Bria asked.

When Fiorello spoke he extended his left arm forward in front of Carlotta as if to block her from responding, his black-gloved hand inches from her mouth. "What Carlotta means is that the days leading up to a performance are always stressful, but it's worse now because it's been several years since she's sung in public."

"Ten to be exact."

Fiorello turned to Giovanni, who had made the comment, and literally examined him from head to toe. "Are *you* a fan?"

"Who isn't?" Vanni responded. "Signora Incantaro, it's an absolute pleasure to meet you."

Vanni extended his hand to grab Carlotta's and she recoiled in horror as if he was going to stab her. "I am not to be touched by anyone, is that understood?"

"Yes . . . yes, of, of course," Vanni stuttered.

"The worst thing about singing to the public is that the public has to be there." Carlotta stepped farther toward the living room area. "Now where is my room? I'm suddenly tired and I need to rest."

"It's right upstairs," Bria said, pointing toward the third door from the staircase. "Do you have any luggage?"

"Of course I have luggage, it's right outside," Carlotta spat. "You are quite beautiful, like a young Claudia Cardinale, but not nearly as smart as she was."

Bria had been lucky because ever since they opened they hadn't had any difficult guests. Some were needier than others, some had food allergies that had to be accounted for, but they were all pleasant and didn't cause any problems. Carlotta's outburst startled her and Vanni so much that they couldn't immediately respond. And if Carlotta demanded one thing, it was immediate attention.

"Do you expect me to carry my luggage in by myself?" Carlotta asked. "Fiorello, is this like that place in Switzerland where I had to do everything for myself?"

"Carlotta was scheduled to sing at a Red Cross fundraising benefit, but they subscribe to an all-hands-on-deck policy," Fiorello explained. "It turned out to be a very short visit."

Vanni walked toward the front door. "I can get your luggage."

"I'll help you," Fiorello said, following Vanni outside.

That left Bria alone with Carlotta. Or so Bria thought.

"*Dio mio, aiutami!*" Carlotta cried. "Get that thing out of here!"

Bria turned in the direction Carlotta was pointing and immediately understood her concern. She assumed Carlotta must have thought Bravo was a stray who'd wandered into the house from the street. "Don't be afraid, that's my Bravo."

Carlotta's disgusted expression didn't change. "It's a . . . *dog!*"

"The best dog in the whole world." Bria bent down and patted her knee. "Isn't that right, Bravo?"

Carlotta once again recoiled in fear as Bravo bounded over to Bria. She stood behind an armchair and used it as a blockade between her and what she considered to be four-legged danger. One look at Bravo, tongue dangling out of his mouth, almost as long as his drooping ears, and anyone could tell he was harmless. Carlotta, however, would need some convincing.

"I think it's destiny," Bria said. "You of all people must love hearing people yell bravo."

"When my fans want to express their adoration for me, they shout *brava*, not bravo," Carlotta hissed. "Now get that thing out of my sight!"

Marco ran in from outside and was followed by Vanni and

Fiorello, each carrying several pieces of matching red leather luggage. The men looked concerned, but Marco looked angry.

"Bravo's not a thing!" Marco yelled. "Bravo's Bravo!"

"I don't care what it is, I am allergic to dogs!" Carlotta pivoted and pointed a finger at Fiorello. "How could you have made such a mistake?"

"I'd like to know that, too," Bria said. "Bravo's photo is right on the landing page of the website."

"I saw that," Fiorello replied. "But on the reservations page it states that Bella Bella is listed as *not* pet friendly."

"That's because there's already a pet on the premises," Marco stated.

"I . . . I . . . I'm sorry," Fiorello stammered. "I must have missed that when I was making the booking. I . . . I must have been distracted."

"I don't know what is wrong with you lately, Fio, but your head has been in the clouds," Carlotta seethed. "How many times do I have to tell you that *sorry* is unacceptable, like that filthy thing."

"I just washed Bravo yesterday," Marco protested.

"That doesn't mean it's clean!" Carlotta roared. "Either that thing goes or I do."

Despite the possibility of jeopardizing the concert, Bria found it to be a very easy decision to make. "Bravo is family and this is his home."

Carlotta gasped. Bria imagined it was one of the few times someone told Carlotta she couldn't have what she wanted. "Then I will let everyone know that you couldn't accommodate me, the woman who has come here to sing to the people of Positano!"

"And the people of Positano welcome you with open hearts."

Everyone whipped around to see Enrico standing in the doorway holding a beautiful bouquet of red petunias that perfectly matched Carlotta's luggage. Upon seeing Enrico and his offering, Carlotta paused. Her eyes grew wide and she grabbed onto the back of the armchair to steady herself. She opened her mouth to speak, but no words came out. She inhaled deeply, then exhaled with the same intensity as if she was trying to remind herself how to breathe.

"Who . . . who is this madman?!" Carlotta shrieked.

"Carlotta," Enrico started. "I . . ."

"My throat closes when it's bombarded by unnatural scents," Carlotta said. "Why is everyone trying to kill me?!"

"Forgive me, Signora Incantaro," Enrico said in a voice that was thick with embarrassment. "There's nothing more natural than the smell of freshly cut petunias."

With a flourish, the sleeves of her blouse flying around her, Carlotta turned away from everyone. "Get those flowers and that animal away from me!"

"She wants us to kick Bravo out just so she can breathe," Marco said.

"Bravo can stay with me," Enrico said.

"I can't ask you to do that," Bria said. "It's too much of an imposition."

"*Che dici?* It's only a few days and Bravo comes over all the time already," Enrico replied. "Marco can visit whenever he wants. It's the perfect solution."

Bria stared at Enrico and could sense there was something wrong with him. His offer was not out of place; ever since she and Marco moved to Positano, Enrico had been like a doting uncle, always checking in, making a fuss, sharing his wonderful spirit. But as she peered into his eyes she noticed a sadness. Carlotta was being thoughtless and unkind and Enrico was a sensitive man. He was also proposing a solution to her problem, so maybe Bria should quit analyzing and accept.

"Marco, is this all right with you?" Bria asked. "Bravo is as much yours as he is mine."

"*Va bene,*" Marco replied. "I can go with them now and help Bravo settle in."

"*Mi scusi,* signora, *per I fiori.*" Enrico bent his head forward and hid the flowers behind his back. "I only wanted to welcome *la signora* back to our humble little village."

Carlotta's fury softened upon hearing Enrico's apology and she finally turned around. "*Grazie*. Now that you've done that, please go."

Enrico met Carlotta's eyes and bowed dramatically before escorting Marco and Bravo outside.

"*Ringrazio Dio!*" Carlotta did her best impersonation of a grande dame and walked toward the stairs. "I'm going to my room now and I do not want to be disturbed. Fiorello! When you see the chef give him my special diet."

"I'm the chef," Vanni announced.

Carlotta swooned and grabbed the railing to steady herself. After a moment, she began to ascend the stairs, fist held high, as she continued to bellow, "If my daughter doesn't appreciate what I'm doing for her, I swear before God right now that I will kill her with my bare hands!"

Carlotta slammed her bedroom door shut behind her and for a few moments there was silence. Without looking at each other, Bria and Vanni turned to face Fiorello for some kind of explanation of Carlotta's actions.

"Carlotta is one of the best sopranos who has ever lived, but like most exceptional artists, she's insecure," Fiorello explained. "Those insecurities have heightened now that she's older and has been out of the spotlight for several years, but believe me, it's worth a few days' discomfort to hear her sing. Listening to Carlotta is like hearing the voice of an angel."

The voice that screeched from the upstairs bedroom sounded more like an angry banshee than an angel. It was a voice, however, that would not be ignored.

"*Fiorello!*"

"Coming, signora!"

Fiorello raced up the stairs, ran to Carlotta's door, knocked twice, entered, and shut the door behind him. Bria and Vanni braced themselves for more shrieking, but there was only silence. Perhaps Fiorello was the angel and not the other way around.

"I think my mother-in-law was right about Carlotta," Bria said.

"What did she say about her?" Vanni asked.

"That having her here would be something we'd all live to regret."

Chapter 4

Most every morning Bria was serenaded by a European robin. The species of bird, native to Italy, could be found throughout the Amalfi Coast especially in gardens like the one Bria had on her balcony, which was small, but robust and colorful, thanks to Enrico's endless supply of seeds and Giovanni's constant pruning. Petunias, roses, lavender, and even some sunflowers created a vibrant and inviting visual and aromatic minipanorama that birds couldn't resist.

One particular robin, which Bria had christened Rosso, since the Italian word for robin was *pettirosso,* had started becoming a frequent visitor a few months ago. He would arrive early most mornings to greet Bria with a song and start her day off on the right musical note. The high-pitched chirping with its staccato break that softened into longer held notes was the perfect alarm clock. This morning Rosso had company.

The scream blended in with Rosso's chirping splendidly. The richness of the sound with a hint of vibrato complemented the bird's bright trill. It was only until the scream became more of a throaty cry did Bria wake from her dream and realize Rosso's singing partner wasn't another robin, but a guest. Unfortunately, the only guest who could rival Rosso's vocal artistry was a certain opera diva.

"Nooooooo!"

No one else but Carlotta could make a sound that was as ear-shattering as it was delightful. Bria lay in bed and wondered if Bravo had somehow gotten back into the house. She knew the front door was locked, but wouldn't put it past a homesick Bravo to figure out how to unlock the door without any human intervention.

Bria threw off the covers, threw on a robe, and threw her unflattering image a disgruntled look when she passed the mirror. She wanted to stop and brush her hair or apply some lipstick, but Carlotta's screams were getting louder. If she didn't investigate immediately, the police would soon be on their way. There was no way she was going to let Luca see her in this condition without the memory of a sleepover fresh on his mind.

She grabbed her cell phone from her dresser and once she was out in the main downstairs area, Bria realized she had been right and the screams were coming from Carlotta's bedroom. Bria couldn't believe the other guests weren't already complaining, but then realized the only other guest at the moment was Fiorello. The couple from Mexico City checked out last night and the travelers from Holland weren't expected until this afternoon. Luckily, Marco was blessed with a child's ability to sleep through an explosion, so the only ones awakened by Carlotta's screeching were Bria and presumably Fiorello. Unless her pianist had become immune to Carlotta's ungodly sounds.

"Carlotta!" Bria ran up the stairs two at a time. "I'm coming!"

Manners be damned, Bria opened the bedroom door without knocking and saw a sight that perfectly encapsulated the relationship between the singer and her accompanist. Carlotta was pacing the floor, waving her arms frenetically, one fist clutching her cell phone, as she repeatedly screamed "No!" at the top of her lungs. She was wearing a long, black silk robe with a floral pattern in pink and green and her blond hair was worn loose and hung past her shoulders. She looked like Madame Butterfly with a dye job contemplating her famous exit.

In contrast, Fiorello sat, hands clasped, head bowed, fully dressed, in a chair in the corner of the room. Except for the jacket, he appeared to be wearing the same clothes as yesterday including the thin black gloves. He looked like he was in a confessional or a meditation class. Whichever it was, he didn't seem disturbed by Carlotta's performance. Bria, on the other hand, had had enough.

"Carlotta!" Bria shouted. "Please stop shouting, you're going to wake the whole village."

As if she finally got her cue, Carlotta whipped around and pointed a finger at Bria. "The whole village *should* be roused so they know what kind of travesty awaits them."

Bria took a deep breath. Italians were known to be dramatic, and her family had its fair share of drama queens starting with her sister, Lorenza, but unless Positano was in danger of sinking into the Tyrrhenian Sea or if every bottle of limoncello had suddenly been stolen, there was no need to disturb their sleep.

"Could you be a bit more specific and describe this travesty?" Bria asked.

"The concert has been ruined!" Carlotta declared.

"I told you I would fix everything," Fiorello replied. "As I always do."

"How are you going to fix this?" Carlotta asked. "How can I sing without a piano?"

"This is about a *piano?*" Bria asked.

Finally, Fiorello looked up. "I received a text early this morning advising that the piano may not arrive in time for the concert."

"I'm sure there's a piano somewhere here in the village that you could use," Bria suggested.

Carlotta's response was primal. Her eyes were wild, her body hunched forward, her voice gruff. "It's the only piano I trust!"

"It's the one Carlotta used for years when she was performing. It's coming from France and then by ship, and there's been an issue with customs," Fiorello explained. "But as I told Carlotta, I have a backup plan."

The sound that escaped Carlotta's mouth was like a balloon popping. "I will not sing in public while you play an electric piano! Mozart would rise from his grave and avenge such an act of heresy! I know that neither one of you can possibly understand what is at stake here but one of you better damn well make it right. Until then I must have my privacy!"

A part of Bria empathized with Carlotta as she watched her slam the bathroom door behind her, another part of her wanted to throttle the woman for being so ridiculously histrionic. Bria was not a singer nor had she ever made a living as an artist, but she did study painting at Rome University of Fine Arts, which meant she understood the creative process. She knew how important it was to have the right tools to create art, whether that was a painting, a sculpture, or a piece of music. Carlotta trusted this piano and it helped her feel secure during a performance. Luca's text had the opposite effect on Bria.

"Is something wrong?" Fiorello asked.

"It's a text from Luca; he needs to see me immediately at Villa Magia."

"That's where Ombra's staying. Is anything wrong?"

"I don't know, but he says I have to bring you with me. Let's find out."

Built in the eighteenth century as a watchtower to warn residents when dangerous Saracen pirates were approaching the shoreline, Villa Magia had since been transformed into one of the largest luxury hotels on the Amalfi Coast. Perched on the cliffside, the hotel had breathtaking views of the sea and the surrounding landscape and was a flight of stairs away from Fornillo Beach. Over the centuries, various owners have added two pools, two upscale restaurants, a spa, and wellness center to the original structure, as well as round-the-clock concierge service. A building that started life as a means to keep out intruders, Villa Magia was now one of the most inviting places in all of Positano.

Walking through its terracotta archway trimmed with a ribbon of ivy, Bria wondered if she could apply the same adornment to Bella Bella. Rows of lush green ivy would look terrific against the hot pink façade. She would have to remember to speak to Enrico and see if he could work his magic to the front of her home like he did in the back.

On their way over, Luca sent Bria another text telling her to meet him in Magia Bistro, the smaller and more casual of the two restaurants at the villa that catered to the pool and beach crowd who wanted a light lunch, snack, or a cocktail as opposed to a full gourmet meal. Bria didn't think the Bistro opened so early, but figured Luca had been able to pull some strings.

"Bria, Fiorello, thank you for coming so quickly." Luca then extended his arm to the couple standing next to him. "This is Bria Bartolucci, owner of Bella Bella where Carlotta and Fiorello are staying. Bria, this is Ombra Incantaro and her fiancé, Armando Puccia."

Bria's eyebrows involuntarily rose as she took in Carlotta's daughter and future son-in-law. They were proof that opposites, indeed, did attract. Bria thought the couple looked odder than Imperia and Sister B, and between the two pairings Bria wasn't sure which was the more inappropriate.

Physically they were disconnected. Ombra appeared to be about five foot six, but since her shoulders were hunched and she was wearing ballet flats she could've been taller. She looked to be about thirty, though it was hard to tell because she wasn't wearing any make-up, and although her arms were thin, she wore a beige shift dress that made it impossible to tell what the rest of her body looked like. Ombra must have taken after her father, however, because she had none of Carlotta's features. She had long black hair that hung to her shoulders, dark eyes, pale skin, and a prominent nose. As far as her personality went, she could have been timid, well-mannered, or just tired at this early hour, but she didn't seem to possess any of the energy, passion, or flair that her mother exuded.

Armando actually bore a much closer resemblance to Carlotta, not necessarily in physical appearance, but attitude. Even though he was slouched in a chair, his arms crossed in front of him, he looked more alive than Ombra did at the moment. His index finger was tapping against his side, the veins in his hands and forearm twitched, and his toes, peeking out from his black leather sandals, flexed and curled, in rhythm. He sat still, but his body wasn't.

Despite online sources stating his age as thirty-five, he appeared younger. He had thick brown hair, smooth olive skin, and blue eyes with long, feathery eyelashes. His polo shirt and linen trousers couldn't hide his muscular frame, but it was his aura that made Bria think he could more comfortably orbit Carlotta's world than Ombra. Bria didn't need to be told that Armando was wealthy and confident, he exuded rich-boy swagger.

Physical differences aside, Bria got the sense that they didn't want to be in each other's company. It was early and they could both be tired, but they were engaged and allegedly in love. They weren't touching or glancing at each other. In fact, the only evidence that made Bria think that Ombra and Armando remotely resembled being a couple was that they were in the middle of an argument.

"My mother must have that piano," Ombra said, her voice breathy and light, another trait she clearly didn't inherit from her mother.

"Fiorello can play the electric keyboard," Armando replied, in a booming voice that would make his future mother-in-law proud. "That's why he brought it with him, as a backup."

"Absolutely not!" Even when she shouted, Ombra sounded more like the wind than thunder.

"The electric piano isn't able to create the kind of sound Carlotta needs for her concert," Bria interjected.

Armando looked up, and when he gazed at Bria a sly smile slowly formed on his lips. "I see Carlotta's brainwashed you already."

"Bria understands the needs of an artist," Fiorello said.

"And I understand the needs of a master manipulator," Armando replied.

Both men looked like they were poised to escalate their comments into an argument but were silenced when Ombra's cell phone pinged. When she immediately began to type a text, Armando sighed and shook his head. "You should marry your phone instead of me, you're always on that thing either texting your mother or your wedding planner."

"*Scusi,* I want everything to be perfect." Ombra didn't look up from her phone when she spoke, and she reminded Bria of how Fiorello had acted in Carlotta's room. "You know this wedding is very important to my mother."

"Sometimes I think I'm marrying her instead of you," Armando quipped. "First we had to push up the date and get a new venue, then we had to make time for this concert, and now we have to deal with a missing piano when I should be having breakfast in bed."

"My mother needs this concert in order to sing at our wedding," Ombra shared. "It was your Papa's idea after all."

Bria realized Luca had been right about remaining quiet and letting people talk. It really was the best way to pick up clues and learn more about people. Bria had no idea what kind of relationship Ombra had with Carlotta, but it was interesting that she referred to her as *my mother* while she called Armando's father *Papa*. It was a small detail that could mean nothing, but it resonated with Bria. Probably because she always called Fifetta

Mamma, the same word Marco used for Bria. Each family was different and the monikers they gave each other didn't necessarily define their relationships.

"Papa isn't happy unless he's controlling every detail of my life." Armando suddenly rose and Bria realized he was taller than she had thought, a little over six feet. "Maybe I should call him because clearly the police are incapable of doing their job and solving this problem."

Bria saw the subtle shift in Luca's body language. His head was tilted back, his chin jutted forward, lips pursed, and she knew he was incensed by Armando's comment. She was about to remind Armando that Luca was the one who called them here so he must have news to share when Nunzi entered the room.

"Nunzi!" Luca cried. "Were you able to resolve the issue?"

Despite the recent modification to her appearance, Nunzi's professional demeanor had remained the same. When she spoke, her voice was its usual unemotional monotone and didn't even attempt to capture an ounce of Luca's energy.

"I spoke with Julien, the captain of the ship that's carrying the piano, and there was an error on the insurance certificate, but I was able to rectify the problem and get it through customs," Nunzi said. "The piano will arrive on time."

Luca turned to face Armando. "Looks like the police were able to solve the problem after all."

"*Grazie mille!*" Fiorello shouted. "That is a relief."

Ombra closed her eyes, inhaled deeply, and then started typing on her phone. "Yes, it certainly is."

"*Grazie,* Nunzi," Luca said. "I'm sure this will make Carlotta very happy."

The sound of her voice emanating from Ombra's cell phone proved to the contrary.

"Do not tell me something else has gone wrong!" Carlotta bellowed.

"I have you on speaker, Mother," Ombra replied.

"What?!" Carlotta shouted. "I told you never to do that!"

"I . . . I'm sorry, but it's okay, I have good news," Ombra replied. "The police have gotten the ship through customs and the piano will arrive on schedule."

"*È magnifico!*" Carlotta cried, her voice finally shifting to a more positive tone. "I told you, Ombra, God is watching over us."

Bria smiled because that was something her own mother would say. Ombra was not as pleased.

"Why must you always bring God into things?!" Ombra yelled. "I told you to leave Him out of this!"

Bria couldn't tell if Ombra was devoutly religious and objected to the idea that God would help in a trivial matter or if she wasn't spiritual at all and bristled at the mention of a higher power. Whatever it was, Ombra was not happy with Carlotta's word choice, but by the singsong sound of Carlotta's voice on the other end of the line, it appeared that she didn't take her daughter's comment seriously or, more likely, had ignored it altogether.

"*Grazie infinite!* Fiorello, please come back so we can practice. I am filled with so much joy I cannot contain myself! I must sing!"

Carotta began to sing, and just when her voice was rising to hit an impossibly high note, Ombra jabbed her phone and Carlotta's voice disappeared. The change in the atmosphere of the room was immediate. Uncontrollable energy was replaced by stillness. Even when she wasn't present, Carlotta commanded a room.

After a few moments, Ombra's tiny voice broke the silence. "*Grazie,* Nunzi, you have no idea how helpful you've been."

"As your fiancé pointed out, it's all part of our job," Nunzi replied.

Nunzi's subtlety was not lost on Armando, who responded

by chuckling and shaking his head. "If I may be excused now, I'd like to have breakfast before another Carlotta crisis interrupts my day."

Without waiting for a reply, Armando left the room. And without being asked to join him, Ombra nervously smiled at everyone and quickly followed her fiancé.

"I should get back to Bella Bella as well," Fiorello said. "I don't want to keep Signora waiting."

"Fiorello . . ." Bria started.

"Please call me Fio," Fiorello interrupted. "Most everyone does."

"*Prego,*" Bria replied. "Fio, *perdonami*, but I have to ask, why are you wearing gloves?"

Fio blushed a little and held up his hands, still clad in the thin black gloves he was wearing when he arrived at Bella Bella. "As a pianist my hands are my tools. If I were to bruise them or get cut, I wouldn't be able to play, and if I can't play, Carlotta can't sing since she refuses to have any other accompanist but me."

"You must be exceptional," Luca said.

Again, Fio blushed. "There are many who are better than me, but an accompanist to an opera singer is more than a piano player; they are another limb, they breathe at the same time, they feel the same emotions, they almost become one with the singer."

"Then Carlotta's lucky to have found you," Bria said.

"I'm the lucky one." Fiorello shook his head definitively. "She has given me more than you could possibly know. Now if you'll excuse me, Signora awaits."

Bria watched Fiorello leave and noticed his pace quicken. Up until that moment, he had been quiet, not really partaking in the conversation, but listening to it. Now he was filled with energy because Carlotta gave him a purpose, she gave him life.

Another less positive thought entered Bria's mind. Carlotta

also controlled Fio, and no one, no matter how loyal or dedicated, truly wanted to remain under another person's thumb. At some point, there would be a breaking point, a moment when they would no longer want to remain submissive, when they would demand the roles be switched. If Bria's theory held true, there was a very real chance that Fio would rebel and Carlotta would be the one paying the price.

More than ever, Bria couldn't wait for this concert to be over.

Chapter 5

Almost any night in Positano would be perfect for an outdoor concert, but it seemed like the elements had conspired together to turn the village into an even more extraordinary venue than usual. The sunset was an entrancing blend of pink, red, and purple, like a watercolor painting hovering over the sea. The evening air was balmy and aromatic, brimming with natural fragrances, and there was a mischievous breeze that would suddenly make an appearance and startle the skin, then disappear leaving bodies wanting more. It was as if the Sirens themselves had returned with an even more seductive vendetta. Thanks to the fountain they had.

In the center of the piazza was a local landmark that had simply become known as the Sirens' Fountain. No one could remember who built it or how long it had been there, but it commanded the space. Bria stood on the steps of Piazza dei Mulini, and despite the warmth and electricity in the air, she shivered. Mythology could sometimes feel all too real.

Legend had it that sea nymphs known as the Sirens lived on three small rocky islands off the coast of Positano, now known as the Li Galli islands. The locale was a frequently photographed tourist attraction, but according to folklore the Sirens had one mission, which was to lure sailors to their deaths using the only weapon they possessed: their voices. The myth was interpreted as a way to illustrate the dangers of sailing, but Bria wondered if it could be more than a fable and closer to a premonition. Ever since she heard that Carlotta—a woman blessed with a powerful voice—was coming to Positano, Bria felt a sense of danger lurking in the shadows. Now, in the presence of the three intertwined Sirens that rose from the center of the fountain, their sculpted mouths opened wide, torrents of water rushing out of them like infinite screams, Bria wondered if she had been right. Had Carlotta brought evil to their village?

Then again, maybe Luca was right about what he always said about Bria, that she allowed her imagination to formulate her opinions. What evidence did she have that the night would turn into a disaster of mythological proportions? Only that a tempestuous visitor had come to the village unexpectedly bringing with her an odd trio of traveling companions and was loathed by at least two people Bria knew. Based on her brief encounters with Carlotta, Bria suspected there could be others besides Mimi and Imperia who wanted to see the opera singer suffer public humiliation for her past deeds, if not seek revenge.

"*Uffa!*" Bria cried, shaking her head and pulling the apricot-colored pashmina tighter around her bare shoulders. "I think Luca might be right about me after all."

"If you're thinking that you're the most beautiful woman in the world, then I'd say you were right."

Bria was smiling before she turned around to face Luca. He really did have the most exquisite brown eyes she had ever seen. Shimmering and multishaded, his eyes reminded her of a small table her father built for her when she was a little girl. The patterns of the grain in the tabletop's wood caused the color to shift slightly from dark walnut to copper to sandy brown. A collage of color just like the one she was staring into.

"Or perhaps you're thinking about something else I said

that wasn't as flattering," Luca added in response to Bria's silence.

"*Scusi,*" Bria whispered, noticing how dry her throat suddenly felt. "*Stavo sognando ad occhi aperti.*"

"Daydreaming? At this time of night?"

"It's a woman's prerogative to dream about a handsome man whenever she gets the urge."

Luca's face morphed into mock indignation. "Who is this handsome man who's distracting my girlfriend?"

Another smile formed on Bria's lips. She had never really been someone's girlfriend before. She dated in high school and college, but never seriously, and when she met Carlo, she knew immediately that she wanted to be his wife. Technically, she had been Carlo's girlfriend for a short time before he proposed, but she never felt like one. She had always considered girlfriends to be temporary, interchangeable, but now that she could be classified as one, she understood the meaning of the word. Luca wanted the world to know that he and Bria were connected. Bria wanted to make sure that Luca knew she understood.

When she spoke, her voice was still a throaty whisper, but it was no longer dry. It was rich with promise and desire. "I'm looking right at him."

By the way his eyes widened and bore into hers, Bria knew he was genuinely surprised by her comment. Bria may not have a lot of experience being a girlfriend, but she knew the number one rule—every once in a while, throw your boyfriend a curve. It was something she was going to have to remind Rosalie.

Ever since her best friend began dating Michele, Bria had uncharacteristically kept her comments to herself. She knew that Rosalie understood Bria had reservations about Michele because Rosalie shared the same concerns. If the relationship was going to grow and have a chance of succeeding, Bria needed to step back and let Rosalie and Michele find their way. It was the same approach Rosalie had taken when Bria and Luca made the decision to give in to their feelings, kiss their platonic relationship good-bye, and embark on a romance. Despite the unspoken agreement, both women knew that if Luca or Michele did something that warranted their intervention, they would not remain silent. They were best friends, closer than most sisters, and no man—or men—could come between them.

Not even Marco.

"Rosalie!" Marco squealed. "After the concert we're going to have a bocce tournament on the field near Hotel Positano. Would you be on my team?"

"You don't want your mamma on your team?" Bria asked.

"Not if I want to win," Marco replied.

Bria was so shocked by Marco's comment, it took her a moment to join in the laughter. She scooped Marco up in her arms and looked up at him. His smile beamed down at her, and it felt like the heavens had opened up and all the happiness, glory, and love it contained came pouring down on her. Until Marco put a stop to it.

"Mamma, put me down," Marco said. "You'll wrinkle my clothes."

He's worried about how he looks? Bria thought. *My little* bambino *is definitely growing up.*

"You look perfect as ever," Bria said, setting Marco on the ground.

"Michele, you can play with us, too." Marco attempted to tuck his shirt into his pants, which made him look more disheveled than ever.

"I love bocce," Michele replied, raising his beer bottle. "Giovanni, why don't you join us? Unless you need to go and find your date."

Bria's and Rosalie's eyebrows raised at the same time. Giovanni had come to the concert alone, having brought Marco to give Bria some time to be alone with Luca. Michele's comment was deliberately rude. Bria waited for Rosalie to admonish Michele in some way, but she didn't need to because as always Giovanni was able to handle the situation.

"The woman I wanted to bring wasn't available," Vanni replied. "I'd love to play later on, *grazie,* and by *play*, I mean win."

"*Attento,* Michele, you should watch who you challenge," Rosalie said. "After me, Vanni's the best bocce player in the village."

Michele attempted to smile at Rosalie, but Bria didn't think he quite achieved success. He then looked over at Giovanni. "Challenge accepted."

The piazza filled up quickly. Nunzi and a few other members of the police force casually milled around the perimeter of the plaza keeping their eyes on the tourists who were going to dinner or strolling down to the beach to enjoy the colors and sounds that were so unique to Positano. The piazza was more crowded than usual, however, because the locals who often stayed inside at this time of night knew that very shortly one of the most celebrated singers in the world would offer a private one-of-a-kind experience and they had come to bear witness.

Fifetta and Franco arrived with Lorenza and Fabrice all looking as if they shopped in the same section at the same store. Fifetta and Lorenza were both wearing yellow dresses with a green leaf pattern and Franco and Fabrice were wearing yellow short-sleeved polo shirts with khakis. On another group such a coincidence could lead to an argument, but the foursome embraced the fluke as a lucky accident.

"Bria, Bria!" Fabrice cried. "Don't we look like recording artists from the seventies?"

"You do!" Bria laughed. "You should call yourselves The Yellownotes!"

"I always wanted to be a lead singer of a band," Lorenza said.

"Not so fast, *amore mio*," Franco cautioned. "I used to be known as the poor man's Andrea Bocelli."

"Remember how beautifully your papa sang at Bria's wedding," Fifetta added. Then she saw Luca and immediately added, "Which was so long ago, who can remember?"

Bria instinctively clutched Luca's hand. She knew as everyone else did that Fifetta did not mean to bring up Bria's wedding to Carlo as a way to make Luca feel uncomfortable. Bria was a widow; it was a fact that couldn't be avoided, and it would come up in conversation from time to time. Luca also had past relationships that may at some point be revealed. But Bria still felt it necessary to make sure Luca understood another fact, that she and the rest of her family were ready for her to move on. So did Fifetta.

"*Perdonami*," Fifetta said, grabbing Luca's free hand and looking up into his eyes.

"There is nothing to forgive," Luca replied, not breaking Fifetta's gaze. He kissed her on both cheeks and they hugged. Luca pulled out of the embrace and looked at Franco. "Perhaps you could sing backup for Carlotta."

"Absolutely not!" Mimi was waving a finger high in the air as she walked over to join the group, followed by Enrico, Annamaria, and Paolo. "I came to hear that over-the-hill monster screech through every song and make a fool of herself. I will not permit a distraction."

"*Mamma mia!* I thought I was the village vixen, but Mimi might be competition."

All heads turned to face Valentina Travanti, local tour guide, Italian-American transplant from Oregon, and the sexiest widow since Anna Magnani strutted around in a black lace slip dress grieving for her philandering husband and cavorting with Burt Lancaster, who sported a rose tattoo on his chest.

Wearing a wraparound lilac linen dress with a plunging neckline and thigh-high slit, Valentina once again maintained her position as the most provocative dresser in Positano. On another woman such an outfit might appear cartoonish, but it was an expression of Valentina's personality, for which she made no apologies. Neither did Mimi.

"I'm sure I'm not the only one here who hopes the diva crashes and burns tonight," Mimi spat.

"Mimi! Basta!" Annamaria yelled. In a much softer voice she added, "Ludovica would not want you to carry on like this."

"Carlotta deliberately robbed my sister of the only opportunity she ever had to be more than just a wife and a mother," Mimi hissed. "I can never forgive that."

"I have to disagree with you, Mimi," Nunzi said as she passed by and caught the tail end of Mimi's rant. "Women must make their own opportunities."

"The woman in blue is right and I'll prove it," Valentina said. "Giovanni, I see that you, like me, don't have a date."

"I'm Vanni's date for the night," Marco said.

Valentina threw her head back, her long blond hair bouncing behind her, and laughed. "Then Vanni is the luckiest man in the piazza."

"You'd make Bravo feel lucky, too, if you came over with Genie for a visit," Marco said. "He misses her."

"It's a date," Valentina said. "Maybe if Vanni joins us, we could turn it into a party."

"That sounds like fun," Marco squealed. "Don't you think so, Vanni?"

Bria's worst fears were about to be realized. She wasn't going to deny Bravo the joy of romping with Genie, another Segugio Italiano dog, but was very worried that Giovanni would succumb to Valentina's advances and begin a relationship with her. There was no denying that the two would make a physically arresting couple, with Vanni's blond man bun and bodybuilder frame, and Valentina's obvious assets, but Bria was protective of Vanni and despite having had not-so-platonic feelings for him when they first met, she now looked at him as a younger brother and she knew that he could do better in a mate.

She didn't want to be obvious in her attempt to throw cold water on any potential hot date they may share, but she desperately wanted to change the subject. As he had done in the past, it was Fabrice to the rescue.

"Armando Puccia!" Fabrice shouted. "Over here!"

"Fabrice Belragasso!" Armando opened his arms wide and accepted Fabrice's embrace.

"Mando, Mando, Mando!" Fabrice pulled away to look at the man, then to Ombra, then back to Armando. "I can't believe you're finally settling down."

"No one's more surprised than I am," Armando replied.

Fabrice took hold of Ombra's hand, that appeared limp and tiny next to his, and he kissed it. "*Mille complimenti.* You must be a very special woman to capture this one's heart."

Ombra nervously pulled her hand away from Fabrice's, her eyes darting around the piazza. "You're very kind."

Bria was still curious about the dynamic between Ombra and Armando, but she was more interested in the relationship between Armando and Fabrice. "How do you know Armando?"

"We went to college together," Fabrice replied. "We don't travel in the same circles these days, him being a billionaire's son and me being a lowly pilot, but we still have many friends in common."

"*Ignoralo!*" Armando cried. "A friend from college is a friend for life."

"Only because they know all your secrets."

Armando's sly smile reappeared and he laughed along with Fabrice. He was still laughing when he noticed Valentina and began to scrutinize the woman from head to toe. He wasn't doing anything any other man had done in her presence; however, most men didn't do it with their fiancée standing by their side. Bria and Rosalie caught eyes and they couldn't believe that Armando was being so disrespectful.

"I love your outfit, Ombra." Bria was grateful for Rosalie's attempt to shift the focus of the conversation, but she questioned the subject matter. Ombra was wearing a long-sleeved gray swing dress that hung on her thin frame and fell to just below her knees. The outfit made no effort to enhance Ombra's natural beauty, but instead worked against it by making her face appear washed out by the drab color of the dress.

"*Grazie.*" Ombra ran her hands over her dress's fabric. "It was my mother's."

"It does look like a hand-me-down," Valentina said.

"Vintage clothes are the best!" Bria exclaimed. "Rosalie and I will have to take you to Vintage Positano, *è il nostro favorito,* a consignment shop that we adore. It has the most fabulous clothes and accessories."

"It's like taking a trip back in time," Rosalie added.

As exciting as the women made a shopping spree sound, Ombra wasn't interested in a new wardrobe. Her eyes were darting around the piazza in search of something—or someone—else.

"You seem nervous, Ombra," Luca asked. "Is everything all right?"

"Yes, *certo*," she replied. "Well, I am worried about my mother."

"Oh no! Is she sick?" Fifetta asked.

"Does she have jet lag?" Franco questioned.

"A case of laryngitis perhaps?" Mimi added.

"No, she's fine and her voice is as beautiful as ever," Ombra confirmed.

"She isn't scheduled to take the stage for another fifteen minutes," Luca said.

"I know," Ombra replied, her eyes continuing to dart about. "But so much can happen in those fifteen minutes."

"Like what?" Bria asked.

Bria's harmless question brought fear to Ombra's eyes.

"Opera is steeped in tradition, almost every story is about a myth or an omen," Ombra began. "If my mother saw a white dove or, *Dio non voglia,* a black crow, she could be on a ferry right now back to Naples."

"Wouldn't that be a pity," Mimi murmured as she sipped on a sixteen-ounce frozen limoncello. Flanking her on both sides, Enrico and Annamaria locked eyes, both looking concerned that Mimi would cause a spectacle before the show even started.

"I can't imagine she would do that," Bria said. "Carlotta chose this spot deliberately so she could sing in the piazza where she sang as a poor girl as a way to give back to the village."

Ombra laughed so heartily, Bria thought she was going to topple over. The young woman exuded more energy in that one response than she had since Bria met her. Whatever Bria had said had caused Ombra to transform.

"The only reason my mother wants to sing here is to remind me of how precarious life can be." Ombra's eyes once again darted around the piazza and, despite the young woman's bolder, more sarcastic attitude, Bria thought Ombra still looked like a little girl making sure her mother didn't catch her doing something wrong. "One second you can have nothing, the next everything, which is what happened to her. But she also wants me to understand that the reverse can occur. One second you can be on the verge of a blissful future and the next it can all be taken away."

"I can't believe any mother would want to teach her daughter such a lesson days before her wedding," Bria replied.

The laughter had subsided and Ombra glared at Bria. "Mothers come in all shapes and sizes."

"I don't think you have anything to worry about," Enrico quickly added. "This is going to be a glorious night and a wonderful way to start off your wedding festivities."

Mimi slurped loudly. "You really are a hopeless romantic, aren't you?"

"Haven't you learned that all Italian men are?" Franco said.

"Some of us are realists," Armando added.

Ombra's scowl was hard to interpret, and Bria wasn't sure if she was going to cry or attack Armando. "Tonight is very important and I want everything to go smoothly so we can put this all behind us and head back to Lake Como for the wedding."

"Put what behind you, *caro?*" Fifetta asked.

"If you haven't noticed, my mother's anxieties and insecurities are contagious. I need her to get through this concert so we can move forward." Ombra saw something in the distance that made her eyes widen.

Bria and several others turned around and saw that Fiorello had arrived. His transformation was even more prominent than Ombra's, and he looked like a movie star making his first long-awaited appearance on-screen. His hair was slicked back, which brought out the highlights of his face. High cheekbones, strong Roman nose, full lips, made all the more dramatic by the white jacket and red scarf that he wore around his neck. His appearance wasn't the only thing to change—his stance was more confident, and as he walked toward the group Bria swore he moved with a hint of a strut. If this was how the accompanist made an entrance, Carlotta would have a tough act to follow.

"*Santo Cielo!*" Nunzi exclaimed. "The piano player cleans up pretty well."

"*Dio mio,* Nunzi!" Rosalie cried. "Have you been taking lessons from that cat of yours on how to sneak up on people?"

"Primavera *is* an honorary member of the police force," Luca replied.

"He's taught me everything I know," Nunzi said.

Bria looked at Rosalie and willed her to keep her mouth shut. She wasn't successful. "That must be one stupid cat."

"*Uffa!*" Bria cried as Fiorello walked toward them. "Fio, you look like a young Marcello Mastroianni."

Fiorello didn't blush but accepted the compliment. "*Grazie*, Carlotta chose my outfit."

"She has excellent taste," Fifetta said. "I'm Bria's mother; We're so excited you're here."

"We can't wait to hear Carlotta sing," Franco added.

"Will this be your first time hearing Signora perform?" Fio asked.

Franco shook his head. "I had the pleasure of seeing her play Ilia in *Idomeneo* many years ago."

"One of Signora's favorite roles." Fio held a white-gloved hand to his heart. "I don't think I'll spoil things by telling you that she may sing an aria from that opera this evening."

"*Che meraviglia!*" Franco clasped his hands together. "It'll be like reliving my youth."

A waiter stopped in front of Fiorello holding a tray of limoncello champagne cocktails. Fio waved a hand in front of him declining the drink, but Armando, Lorenza, Annamaria, and Rosalie eagerly accepted. The waiter held the tray with one flute remaining in front of Ombra.

"*No grazie,*" she replied. "I need to keep my wits about me tonight."

Armando raised his glass in Fio's direction. "I see you decided to wear your formal gloves for tonight's masquerade."

Fio held his hands up, palms inward, then turned them around to examine the backs of his hands. "Signora felt they should match my jacket."

"And Signora is always right," Armando said, raising his flute.

"Armando, there's Donna Rosa, the American who owns her own villa and winery," Ombra said. "Papa wants you to set up a meeting with her."

"I'm half American," Valentina replied, extending her hand toward Armando. "Why don't I join you to prevent anything from getting lost in translation?"

Armando smiled and took Valentina's hand. "A billionaire son's work is never done."

Bria watched Ombra and was surprised to find that she wasn't very upset by Armando's blatant display of disrespect. If Luca did something like that, Bria wouldn't be able to control her emotions. Before she could dwell on it any further, there was a sudden commotion near the performing area and Bria thought that Carlotta had made her entrance, but it was another diva. Or was that two? Dante entered with Imperia on his arm. Although Imperia failed to convince Dante to cancel the event, the two still looked like the best of friends.

Probably knowing that he wasn't going to be able to upstage either Imperia or Carlotta, Dante wore a simple navy blue linen suit and white shirt. He still hadn't shaved his moustache, but since he had opted not to wear any other accessories, his overall look was less ostentatious than usual.

Imperia had also decided that less was more and wore a green silk pantsuit with an emerald necklace that only on Imperia could be called subtle. The only other color was her trademark red lipstick. She nodded over at Bria and Luca and allowed Dante to lead her to one of the seats close to the piano.

"We should all take a seat," Fabrice said. "The show is about to start."

Fabrice, Fifetta, and Franco moved in one direction toward where Lorenza was saving them seats as Bria, Luca, Rosalie, Michele, Marco, and Giovanni found seats on the opposite side of the piazza. When every chair was filled, Dante gazed out at the audience and lifted his arm. He held up his palm and suddenly there was quiet. Bria wasn't sure what had just happened, but quickly realized the fountain had stopped gushing water. She was sure Dante had signaled someone on the maintenance team to shut off the water, and she had to give him credit, it was an impressive feat. The only problem was that the Sirens looked even more sinister without water pouring out of their mouths.

"*Benvenuti.* Tonight we have a wonderful surprise for all of you, the people and guests of Positano," Dante began. "Tomorrow is *La Festa Della Mamma*, the day all mothers are honored, but tonight one mother, one legend, is going to sing for her daughter in celebration of her upcoming marriage," Dante announced. "I present to you, the one and only, Carlotta Incantaro."

Some members of the crowd oohed and ahhed at the mention of Carlotta's name, others merely applauded politely, the rest waited. And waited some more. After about thirty seconds Dante said her name one more time, but Carlotta still didn't appear.

Bria's heart sank and she grabbed Luca's hand. He looked at her and Bria knew they were thinking the same thing. History was repeating itself in the village and Carlotta Incantaro wasn't going to sing tonight because Carlotta Incantaro was most likely dead.

Chapter 6

The five minutes it took for Carlotta to make her way to the piano felt like a lifetime. It was worth the wait.

Standing next to the white baby grand piano, dressed in an off-the-shoulder, long-sleeved, red silk gown, Carlotta hardly looked dead, but she definitely looked nervous. Bria was intrigued because it was the first time she noticed a resemblance between the glamorous Carlotta and her dowdier daughter. It was because of their eyes. Not the shade—the mother's were green, while the daughter's were brown. It was how they viewed the world. Like the salamanders that slithered on the streets all throughout Positano, their eyes darted about to and fro constantly in motion surveying the area—searching for food or a quick exit—and always trying to avoid an altercation with an enemy. In this case, the enemy was Carlotta's audience.

For all of Carlotta's fame and accolades, she still doubted her talent. Carlotta stood before an eager crowd, who was clapping and cheering, and yet she looked like a woman who didn't truly believe she belonged. The diva was difficult and rude, but she was also fragile and scared. Witnessing the woman's truth, Bria was moved to clap as loud as she could in order to give the opera diva the strength she needed to overcome her fears and give herself over to the music. First, she needed to give herself over to her pianist.

Carlotta turned her head to face Fiorello and her beauty was heightened, her profile resembling a Roman empress greeting an arena. There were lines on her face and some sagging, but it only enhanced her look. Her beauty had been hard-earned.

Her blond hair was pulled back into a chignon, her aquiline nose, strong and slightly upturned, her neck and earlobes free of adornment so she looked even more vulnerable. Bria could see the love in Carlotta's eyes as she looked at Fiorello, a combination of friend, mother, and confidante. The connection was deep and the love sincere.

Slowly, Fiorello removed the white gloves from his hands and placed them on the seat next to him. With a bit of a flourish, he tossed one end of the red scarf he was wearing over his shoulder and then placed his fingers over the keys. Carlotta's body visibly shivered despite the warmth of the evening and she faced the audience. She closed her eyes, which must have been Fiorello's cue because at that moment he pressed his fingers onto the keys.

It was as if the sound of the music was like oxygen, an elixir, a life force that Carlotta couldn't live without. She took a deep breath and then produced a sound that made some in the audience whimper. Whatever fears or insecurities Carlotta may have had disappeared and all that remained was a woman who possessed an almost preternatural gift that she needed to share in order to survive.

The first few notes of "Casta Diva," a soft, lyrical aria from Vincenzo Bellini's opera *Norma*, sung by the title character, a Celtic priestess, transfixed the crowd. A hush fell over the normally bustling piazza as Carlotta's voice, clear and powerful, descended upon the audience like the majestic sunset that simultaneously lowered itself onto the horizon. Bria looked around and saw that everyone was staring at Carlotta, some with their mouths open in wonder and gratitude. Sitting in between Marco and Luca she glanced at them both and was thrilled to see that they were just as entranced by the beauty of Carlotta's singing as she was.

The flexibility of Carlotta's voice was a marvel. It quivered when she sang the lyric "Scatter on the earth the peace thou make reign in the sky" and roared when she declared "my voice will thunder." But when she sang "I'll protect you against the entire world" the mixture of conviction, dread, and unconditional love that surrounded each note brought tears to Bria's eyes. It's what she felt when she thought of Marco and how she would protect him no matter the cost.

There was a moment of silence when Carlotta finished her aria that was shattered by the rapturous and almost unanimous applause. Everyone was standing, although Bria noticed Imperia was slow to rise, and the only reason Mimi stood up was because Enrico and Annamaria, sitting on either side of her, each took an arm and yanked her to her feet. Imperia and Mimi held their hands together but refused to clap with the rest of the crowd.

Carlotta was visibly taken aback by the outpouring of love, and tears fell from her eyes. She slowly dipped into a curtsy, and held her hand over her heart, causing the roar from the audience to grow. She stood up and waited until her subjects quieted so she could speak.

"*Grazie, grazie mille.*" Carlotta peered out into the piazza. "It's good to be home."

For the next forty-five minutes, Fiorello played the piano with a panache that would fill Liberace with envy while Carlotta sang one aria after another in French, German, and her native Italian, lulling the listeners into a state of sheer bliss. By the time she sang her signature piece, The Queen of the Night's aria "Der Hölle Rache kocht in meinem Herzen" from *The Magic Flute,* with its rapid sequence of unbelievably high notes intertwined with extended, colorful lyrical swirls, the crowd had grown, and it was as if everyone in the entire village of Positano had crammed into the piazza. The earth-shattering applause when she finished was proof that Carlotta's comeback had been a triumph.

After four curtain calls, Dante figured it was safe to interrupt the lovefest and join Carlotta on the makeshift stage. "*Grazie* to the people of Positano, locals and visitors alike, for being the best audience an artist could hope for." Dante paused for the applause he knew would come and like the skilled orator he was, spoke before the sound completely disappeared. "We offer our humble thanks to you, Carlotta Incantaro, for sharing the miraculous blessing God has bestowed upon you. Your voice is a miracle."

Typically, Bria felt Dante's word choices were hyperbolic and the vocabulary of a not-so-subtle sycophant. After listening to Carlotta sing she agreed with every word he said.

She glanced over to see how Mimi interpreted Dante's speech and was surprised to see that her seat was empty. Bria glanced around the piazza, but Mimi was nowhere to be found. She must have left at some point during the last half of the concert, but Bria couldn't be sure because she was focused solely on Carlotta's performance and not the reactions of some less-than-enthusiastic members of the audience. When she looked to where Ombra and Armando were sitting she noticed that Armando was sitting alone. He didn't appear concerned about Ombra's absence because he had company. Impulsively, Bria grabbed Luca's hand and rushed closer to the groom-to-be in order to eavesdrop on his conversation. They stood in the aisle slightly behind them with their backs turned, but thanks to the less-than-subtle tones of their voices, they could hear every word they said.

"If Carlotta sings half as beautifully at your wedding as she did tonight," Valentina gushed, "it will be an event that will be talked about for decades."

"That's my mother-in-law's hope," Armando replied. "That

her daughter's wedding be a once-in-a-lifetime memory starring the mother of the bride."

"I'm sure it'll be a must-see event," Valentina said.

"Which is why I will personally send you an invitation." Armando took Valentina's hand, raised it to his lips, and kissed it. "Give me your address."

Bria gripped Luca's hand with such strength she threatened to crush his bones. When Luca whispered in her ear, she wanted to hurt the rest of his body.

"What do you mean it's none of our business?" Bria whispered.

"Just what I said," Luca whispered back.

"Did you hear him?"

"Every word."

"Did you see what he did?"

"Everyone did. I don't think he was trying to be discreet."

"That is one thing my fiancé is not."

Bria and Luca jumped a bit when they heard Ombra's voice next to them. *When did she get back?* Bria asked herself. Whenever it was, it was long enough to overhear Bria and Luca gossiping.

"It seems like he's met his match in that one," Ombra continued, indicating Valentina with a tilt of her head.

"I've been dying to get to Lake Como ever since I came back to Italy, now I have the perfect excuse," Valentina cried. "And the perfect reason to wear my favorite little black dress."

"Just how little is it?" Ombra asked.

Bria wanted to dig a hole and bury herself in it. Valentina, on the other hand, relished the attention.

"Short enough to cause a stir, but long enough to guarantee you won't be jilted at the altar." Valentina began to walk away and then turned her head toward Armando. "*Cin cin!*"

Armando laughed devilishly. "*Cin cin,* Valentina!"

Bria let out a sigh of relief when Valentina left but held her breath once again when she saw Imperia approach. Her mother-in-law looked as if she was headed into a business meeting where the number one item on the agenda was to fire half the staff.

"Ombra, *cara,* I thought your mother was exposing a piece of herself when she sang about hell's vengeance boiling in her heart," Imperia hissed. "I always thought it was so appropriate that Carlotta's rise to stardom began by playing opera's most terrible mother."

Ombra's eyelids lowered and her lips elongated. "It's a role my mother was born to play."

"Speak of the she-devil," Imperia purred. "Carlotta! Over here!"

Surrounded by Dante, Fifetta, Franco, Lorenza, and Fabrice, who were undoubtedly fawning over the diva like the true fans they were, Carlotta's complexion turned gray once she saw who was calling out to her. She smiled and nodded, and if it weren't for Dante, who grabbed her arm and began leading her over toward Imperia, she would have remained within the confines of friends and not into the waiting arms of the enemy.

"Imperia," Dante said, "wasn't Carlotta divine, *semplicemente divino!*"

"Yes, she was." Imperia nodded her head and bent as if she was meeting royalty. "Divinely inspiring and a reminder of how unflattering the wrong shade of red can be."

Luca laughed out loud but quickly turned his outburst into a cough when Bria pressed her foot on his toes. With no one to stop him, Dante's nervous giggle rang throughout the piazza. Carlotta, unlike the men around her, didn't make a sound.

Eyes glaring, lips tightly pursed, nostrils flaring, Carlotta was using all the power she possessed to control her body. Bria thought the woman resembled an animal in the plains facing off an adversary. But was Carlotta predator or prey?

"How long has it been since we were last in each other's

company?" Imperia didn't wait for Carlotta to reply. "Ah yes, when my Guillermo was still alive and you were trying to seduce him."

A flurry of words and sounds came out of Dante's mouth, nothing comprehensible or cohesive, in an attempt to defuse the bomb that Imperia tossed into the air. Bria could see Carlotta's restraint loosen, and she was poised to strike. Bria needed to act quickly before the women's claws were put to use.

"From what I heard this evening, Carlotta could seduce anyone with a single note," Bria said. "Signora Incantaro, you were spellbinding."

Carlotta's fierce expression softened and she nodded at Bria. "*Grazie*, Bria, and may I offer you an apology?"

"You're going to apologize to *her?*" Imperia asked.

"My behavior has been less than courteous since I've returned," Carlotta confessed. "Now that the concert is over I can relax and be myself."

"Is that supposed to be reassuring?" Imperia asked.

"Imperia, *amore mio,*" Dante said. "Remember that Carlotta is a guest in Positano and we, as elite members of our community, treat all our guests warmly."

"*Giusto*," Luca quickly added. "I know your stay with us will be short, but if there's anything you need while you're here, please let me know."

"Luca's the chief of police," Bria interjected. "I'm not sure if the two of you have officially met."

Carlotta's laugh was almost as melodious as her singing. "Why in the world would I need the help of the chief of police?"

"Someone may try and steal that exquisite ring you're wearing and sell it on the black market," Imperia remarked.

The same look that was etched into Carlotta's face when she first took the stage reappeared. She looked frightened, as if Imperia had the power of prophecy or was a sorceress who could manipulate future events. She brought her hand to her chest and Bria saw the ring Imperia referenced in its full glory. A ruby in the center of a diamond cluster. Strong, powerful, and captivating, just like the woman who wore it. Although she looked like none of those things at the moment.

"Fret not, Lottie," Imperia said. "If such a travesty befalls you, Luca and his team will find the culprit in less time than one of your lengthy arias. *Buonasera.*"

Once again it was Fiorello to the rescue. He joined the group as Imperia left, and swooped in, grabbing Carlotta by the shoulders and kissing her on each cheek. He held her hands and looked directly into her eyes. "You were magnificent, signora."

Carlotta stared at Fio for a few seconds. "*Grazie,* Fio, *grazie* for playing for me one last time."

Bria was confused. "Isn't Fio going to play for you at the wedding?"

"*Certo,*" Carlotta replied. "But that will be a private affair, this was a public concert for the people."

"And the people were enraptured," Dante declared.

"That was my hope," Carlotta said. "Now if you'll please excuse me, I think I will join my daughter and soon to be son-in-law for one celebratory drink before heading back to the B and B."

They all exchanged good-byes and after some small talk, Fiorello announced he was retiring as well, followed quickly by Dante. Bria got a text from Giovanni saying that Marco was getting sleepy, so they went back to Enrico's where Marco was spending the night to be with Bravo. She looked around and was surprised to see that the piazza had thinned out and only a handful of people were still standing around.

"Looks like the evening has come to an end," Luca said.

"Michele and I are going to head over to L'alternativa," Rosalie announced. "Would you like to join us?"

"A drink on the beach sounds lovely, but I'm exhausted from the day," Bria lied. "I think I'm going to call it an early night."

"Mm-hmm," Rosalie replied. "Is that what the kids are calling it these days?"

The women laughed as the men awkwardly stood alongside them.

"*Ciao, fratello,*" Rosalie said.

"*Buona notte.*" Michele turned and Rosalie followed him down the stairs of the piazza toward Spiaggia Grande Beach.

Luca was about to take Bria's hand until he saw her family approach them. Out of the corner of her eye, Bria saw Luca's hand fall to his side and his fingers nervously tap against his leg. Luca was an old-fashioned gentleman.

"I don't know the last time I had such an enjoyable evening in the company of a woman," Franco gushed.

"Papa!" Lorenza cried. "Don't say that in front of Mamma."

"*Va tutto bene,*" Fifetta assured. "He'll just have to make his own meals for the rest of the week."

"Like you'd ever let Papa starve!" Bria exclaimed.

"We're going back to the yacht," Lorenza announced. "Do you want to join us for a drink on the deck?"

"The yacht?" Bria asked.

"Sweet Imperia invited all of us to stay on her yacht," Fabrice announced. "Didn't you know that, Bria Bria?"

"No," Bria replied. "Bria Bria did not know that."

"But you'll come join us, won't you?" Fabrice said.

"*Per favore vieni,*" Lorenza pleaded. "Fabrice thinks everyone is sweet, but I'm still kind of scared of Imperia."

"Imperia may not always be sweet, but she's nothing to be scared of," Fifetta said. "She's family."

"Who happens to have several bottles of very expensive champagne chilling and waiting just for us," Franco said.

"We were going to take a walk and then go home," Luca said. "I have to get up early for work tomorrow."

"The chief of police never sleeps," Fabrice said.

Lorenza leaned into Bria and whispered, "Even when he's lying in bed."

Bria playfully slapped her sister's arm. "Enjoy sweet Imperia's sweet champagne."

Watching her family leave the piazza, Bria noticed Annamaria, Paolo, and Enrico were also taking Viale Pasitea back home. But there was something wrong. "Where's Mimi?"

Luca looked around and shook his head. "She must have gone home early."

"I noticed during the concert she wasn't sitting in her chair, but I thought she'd come back," Bria said.

"She made it very clear that the only reason she attended was to witness Carlotta's failure," Luca said. "Once she saw that her performance was going to be triumphant, she probably decided to leave."

"I guess that's true."

"No more talk about Mimi or Carlotta or anyone else," Luca said. "Let's enjoy us."

Luca took Bria's hand and they started to stroll in the opposite direction as lazily as the soft music that drifted into the piazza from one of the local bars. The breeze felt as if it had been dripped in citrus as it carried the scent of the orange trees. It was a perfect evening that Bria thought could turn into an even more perfect morning.

Since Marco was going to spend the night at Enrico's, Bria was ready to ask Luca to spend the night. Just as she was about to pop the question, Nunzi popped over with a statement that would derail any hopes Bria had for a quiet evening alone with her boyfriend.

"Chief, we need to get over to Villa Magia," Nunzi declared. "Someone's jewelry has been stolen and the manager is demanding you show up personally."

"Ombra's staying there," Bria said. "Is it hers?"

"The manager wouldn't say," Nunzi replied.

"Sorry, Bria," Luca said. "Let me take you home and then I'll go over to Magia."

"No, go do your job," Bria replied. "I'll take the long way home and unwind."

Luca smiled and glanced at Nunzi, who didn't pick up on Luca's social cue and kept staring at Luca waiting for him to leave. Bria shook her head, then grabbed the sides of Luca's face and kissed him on his lips. Luca appeared shocked, while Nunzi raised an eyebrow so high that it almost reached her bangs.

"I'll see you in the morning," Luca said before departing with Nunzi.

Not wanting to go home, Bria started to walk toward the beach. She heard the cadenced splashing of the waves in the distance and felt like one of those unlucky sailors being lured by the hypnotic call of the sirens. The lights of L'alternativa and the string of bars came into focus, and as much as she loved Rosalie, she was too tired to make small talk with Michele.

A sudden burst of wind flew past Bria sending a chill throughout her body. She had forgotten how quickly the temperature could drop at night. She pulled her pashmina tighter around her shoulders and glanced at her watch. She was surprised to see how late it had gotten; she must have been contemplating life longer than she thought.

Instead of taking the longer route, she retraced her steps back to Piazza dei Mulini, which was the quickest way to Bella Bella. When she entered the empty piazza she marveled at how quiet it was when a few hours ago it was filled with the sounds of Carlotta's magnificent voice and thunderous applause. The Sirens in the fountain were still silent, but their wide-open stone mouths no longer looked like they were screaming, they were rejoicing.

And why wouldn't they? The body sprawled out on the cobblestoned ground was proof that the mythical creatures had claimed yet another victim.

Bria didn't have to take another step to know that Carlotta would not have to worry about singing at her daughter's wedding because there would be no wedding. Ombra couldn't get married when her fiancé was lying face down in the middle of the piazza. A billionaire's son could buy a lot of things, but not even Armando Puccia could buy a life after death.

Chapter 7

Positano was rarely silent. No matter what time of day or night, the village made its voice heard. The breeze, the waves, the birds never stopped creating sounds that were as much a part of Positano as the winding, curved Viale Pasitea or the golden domed Santa Maria Assunta. The village laughed and cried, yelled and screamed, shouted with joy, and sighed with ecstasy. But every once in a while, there was a moment when it held its breath and made no sound. Because even in paradise, death had to be honored.

As Bria stood watching Armando's back, motionless and stiff, one arm tucked underneath his body, the other splayed out trying to grab something or someone, she couldn't help but stare in wonder. She wasn't questioning death itself because she knew, like every other human being on the planet, that death was inevitable and a part of the cycle of life. Some thought it was the end of existence, others believed death was merely the moment a physical body transitioned to another plane, a gateway to the next phase of life. Bria was questioning why she had been chosen—yet again—to bear witness to death's aftermath.

The piazza was eerily empty. It was only one a.m. and there was no one in sight. Positano wasn't a party town like Ibiza or a city that was alive twenty-four hours a day, like New York City or Berlin, but it also wasn't a sleepy hollow that closed up soon after the sun set. Despite the evidence that lay at Bria's feet, Positano was a very safe village where couples, families, and single tourists could stroll down the streets at any hour of the night or early morning without any fear. Still, Armando was lying on his side, his face pressed to the ground at the foot of the fountain, his body unmoving.

Kneeling down, she held her breath and placed two fingers on Armando's wrist. She waited for over a minute until there was no doubt her instincts were confirmed. Armando was dead.

She turned away and sent a text to Luca telling him what happened and where to meet her. Next, Bria typed a similar text to Rosalie and told her to bring Michele with her. If he was going to be a boyfriend to her best friend he was going to have to get used to seeing unusual texts. Like being summoned to a deserted piazza to stand over a corpse in the middle of the night.

Moments later, Bria received a text from Luca saying that he and Nunzi were on their way. Less than a minute after that Rosalie arrived. Alone.

"Where's Michele?" Bria asked.

"He had an emergency at the garage and went straight home," Rosalie replied. "I had a drink with Annamaria and was on my way back to the marina when I got your text."

"*Grazie Dio* you didn't get the text when you were still with Annamaria, otherwise the whole village would know by now that Armando was lying dead in the piazza."

"He was kind of a jerk, but I can't believe someone hated him enough to kill him." Rosalie shook her head and looked away from the body. "And right before he was going to get married; talk about terrible luck."

"Maybe not."

"What do you mean? He's dead."

"You saw how Armando was flirting with Valentina right in front of Ombra."

"You think Ombra will be happy that her fiancé is dead?"

"Not happy, no, but relieved maybe," Bria replied. "I was having a hard time believing they'd live happily ever after."

"Not everyone is destined for that."

Before Bria could respond or delve deeper into Rosalie's cryptic comment, Luca and Nunzi entered the piazza. Bria could see the concern on Luca's face and knew that he was struggling between acting as her boyfriend and the chief of police. Should he comfort his girlfriend or tend to his duties as an officer of Positano? He did both.

He stood in front of Bria blocking her vision of Armando's dead body and gently held her hand. "Are you all right?"

"Yes, *grazie*," Bria whispered. "Don't worry about me, just find out why Armando is lying dead in the piazza."

"He isn't," Nunzi replied.

"What are you talking about?" Rosalie cried. "You're kneeling over his dead body."

"Is he alive?" Luca asked.

"No." Nunzi grabbed Armando's shoulder and rolled it so his body was flat on the ground. She gave the group a few seconds for the truth to set in. "This isn't Armando, it's Fiorello."

"What?!"

Looking at Fiorello's dead body, Bria was confused. "*Santo Cielo!* How could I make such a mistake?"

"It's dark and you were in shock stumbling upon a dead body," Luca said. "Both men are similar height and build, it's easy to confuse the two of them."

"Not when one of them is wearing gloves," Bria replied. "Look at Fiorello's hands."

Nunzi took out what looked like a black marker from her pocket and pressed the top of it. A bright light emitted that revealed the marker was a flashlight. It also revealed that Bria was half-correct. Fiorello was wearing only one of his white gloves.

"I missed a telltale sign that the body was the piano player and not the groom." Bria shook her head.

"Because the hand with the glove was underneath his body," Nunzi explained. "You only saw his right hand, which didn't have a glove on it."

"Why would he still be wearing his gloves?" Rosalie asked. "I thought he only wore them because Carlotta was paranoid about him getting sick and wouldn't be able to play for her. The concert was over, the glove wearing should be, too."

"He still has to play at the wedding in Lake Como, well, *had to*," Bria pointed out. "He probably didn't want to risk the chance of catching the flu or a virus, so he kept wearing them."

"Fiorello tricked you," Luca declared. "Not once, but twice."

"What do you mean?" Bria asked.

"He isn't wearing the same jacket he wore during the concert," Luca explained.

"That's right!" Bria exclaimed. "He wore a white jacket when he was playing the piano! This one is blue."

"At some point after the concert he changed jackets," Luca said.

"Wasn't Armando wearing a blue jacket?" Nunzi asked.

"I don't remember, but why would they switch jackets?" Bria asked.

"Why would Fiorello change his jacket, but keep one glove on?" Rosalie questioned. "It isn't like he could put a glove on after he died."

"Somebody else could've put it on him," Nunzie suggested.

"Why would someone find a dead body, put a glove on that dead body's hand, and then leave the dead body without alerting the police?" Luca asked.

"Because maybe the person who did all that was also the person responsible for making the body dead in the first place," Bria surmised.

"Let me guess," Nunzi said. "You think Fiorello was murdered."

Bria deliberately ignored Luca's steely gaze. "It's a possibility."

"Among many," Luca replied.

"Such as?" Rosalie asked.

"He could have had a heart attack or a stroke," Luca suggested.

"He could have fallen from the top of the stairs," Nunzi added.

They all turned around to look at the stairs that led from the road into the piazza, and even in the darkness the three steps hardly looked fatal.

"It's a steeper drop from the dock onto my boat," Rosalie said. "If Fiorello tripped coming down the stairs I think he would have survived."

"Have you ever fallen and hit your head on cobblestone?" Nunzi asked. "Don't answer that—of course you have, which explains so much."

"Nunzi's right," Luca quickly added before Rosalie could respond. "If Fiorello fell and hit his head he could have died instantly from blunt trauma."

"Then where's the blood?" Bria asked.

"Not every fall ends with the victim lying in a pool of blood," Luca explained. "Like I always say, we'll need to wait for the results of the autopsy."

"We could find out if he fell right now," Bria declared.

"How?" Luca asked.

Bria walked over to Nunzi and held out her hand thrusting it toward the flashlight that was still lit, but now pointing toward the ground. "May I?" Nunzi gave Bria the flashlight and she shined the light over Fiorello's legs. "If Fiorello fell, it's very likely that he would have fallen on his knees, but his pants aren't torn or dirtied."

"That's an indication that he *didn't* fall," Luca said. "How can we find out if he did, in fact, fall to the ground?"

"The first thing you instinctively do when you trip is put your hands out to break your fall," Bria shared. "If Fiorello did that he should have scuffed up the palms of his hands."

"Or in this case, his hand and his glove," Rosalie said.

Nunzi knelt down, pulled latex gloves out of another pocket, and put them on her hands. She picked up Fiorello's right hand and slowly removed the glove. She held up his hand as Bria shined the light onto them and it was clearly visible that there wasn't a mark on his palm.

"Move your fingers away from his wrist," Bria directed.

When Nunzi did as Bria asked, they could all see several scratches on Fiorello's wrist. Not needing any further instruction, Nunzi laid Fiorello's right hand onto the ground and held up his left hand. Upon inspection, it looked identical to its companion. A smooth palm with scratch marks on the wrist.

"Looks like he scratched himself on the same place on both hands," Rosalie said.

"Is there anything on the inside of the glove that could have caused irritation?" Luca asked.

Nunzi ran her finger along the lining of the glove and shook her head. "No, it's smooth."

"Fio must have gotten into a fight with someone," Bria corrected.

"A minute ago you said he fell, and now you think Fiorello got into a fight," Luca said.

"I've seen enough of Marco's bruises and cuts from falling to know that the scratches on Fiorello's wrists were man-made," Bria shared. "He either scratched himself on both wrists in the same exact place, which I admit is possible if he was having some kind of allergic reaction, or he got into a fight with someone."

"Is that your professional opinion?" Nunzi asked.

Bria wasn't sure if Nunzi was gently ribbing her or being snarky. She decided not to analyze the subtext of the comment but focus on answering the question as honestly as possible. "We all know I'm no professional, but we also know I'm rarely wrong," Bria replied. "It's possible that Fio fell on both wrists, but the cuts are too symmetrical. It looks like someone grabbed his wrists during a tussle and scratched him with their fingernails."

"Maybe Fiorello's body contains more clues," Luca suggested. "Check his wallet and cell phone."

Nunzi looked in the pockets of Fiorello's jacket and pants and came up empty. "He doesn't have anything on him."

"Maybe he was mugged," Bria suggested. "That would explain how he got into a fight or was . . ."

"Was what?" Luca asked. "Finish your sentence."

"You know," Bria hedged.

"She was going to say murdered, *fratello*," Rosalie interjected. "You really need to pay attention."

"It is a distinct possibility given the clues," Bria declared.

"Why does your mind always go to the worst possible scenario?" Luca asked.

"In the past, haven't my wild imaginings proven correct?"

"That isn't the point," Luca said.

"I think it is, Chief," Nunzi added. "Bria's got a kind of sixth sense when it comes to murder."

"When you asked for my *professional* opinion, you weren't being sarcastic?" Bria asked.

"Not at all," Nunzi replied. "I think you have incredible insight when it comes to homicide."

"*Grazie,*" Bria said. "If I may make a suggestion, your delivery could use a bit of tweaking so your intent isn't lost."

Nunzi nodded. "Not the first time I've been given that critique."

"It isn't going to be the last time you'll hear me say this,"

Luca started,. "Let's keep our opinions to ourselves until we hear from the medical examiner and have all the facts concerning Fiorello's death."

The only fact Carlotta cared about was that Fiorello was dead.

After Nunzi left with the paramedics to take Fiorello's body to the morgue in Amalfi, Rosalie went back home to her boat in the marina and Bria and Luca went back to Bella Bella. They had hoped Carlotta would still be out with Ombra and Armando celebrating the success of the concert and they wouldn't have to break the news to the opera singer until the morning. Their plans were foiled when they came home and saw Carlotta sitting in the dark.

Silhouetted by the moonlight pouring into the main living room, Carlotta sat on the couch, holding a tumbler filled most likely with gin and ice, and was staring, eyes open, into space. Whatever she was looking at it couldn't be seen by anyone other than her, but it held her attention. Bria had to call her name twice to get Carlotta to acknowledge that she and her thoughts weren't the only ones in the room.

"*Perdonami.*" Carlotta's voice was no longer a booming instrument, but a husky whisper. "I was reliving my concert in my mind, an old habit from my years of trying to climb the ladder of success. Uncover what can be improved, focus on mistakes so they aren't repeated. I may have reached the pinnacle, but that lofty height still doesn't stop one from questioning one's talent."

"You should never question your talent or your ability," Bria said. "Your voice is an astonishment. A true gift from God."

Carlotta peered at Bria, lifting her chin. "You mean that, don't you?"

"*Certo*, every word."

"The world could use more honesty like yours," Carlotta replied.

"Which is why I'm here," Luca announced. "I have terrible news to share with you."

When Luca told her that Fiorello was dead, all the color drained from Carlotta's face. Her skin turned gray and then pure white. Her hand started to shake, and Luca took the glass from her hand before she dropped it and it shattered on the floor.

"What are you talking about?" Carlotta protested. "He played for me a few hours ago."

"We're not yet sure of the circumstances, but his body was found in the piazza an hour ago," Luca said. "I'm very sorry, but Fiorello is dead."

Carlotta couldn't press her hand over her mouth in time to quiet the shriek that escaped her lips. She sank into the couch and continued to sob and cry with such volume and intensity that Bria was grateful Marco was spending the night with Enrico so he didn't hear Carlotta's anguish. No one came out of their bedrooms so it appeared that the other guests were sleeping or still out. Bria winced and had to look away because Carlotta's reaction was so raw and unguarded that she felt like she was trespassing on the woman's soul. It filled Bria with pride to see Luca sit next to Carlotta and confront her pain.

"I want to see him." Carlotta's voice was thick with grief, but there was no mistaking that her words were a command and not a request.

"He's been taken to the morgue in Amalfi," Luca said. "You can see him tomorrow."

"He was my friend, he was the only person who truly understood me." The tears fell down Carlotta's face as she looked at Luca. "I must see him now."

Luca swallowed hard and sought out the one person who could help him make such a decision: Bria. She nodded her head twice and told him all he needed to know. It might be against police protocol, it might be interfering with how things typically ran, but Luca needed to honor Carlotta's request.

Luca stood and extended his hand to Carlotta. "Come with me."

Carlotta clutched Luca's hands tightly and bowed her head. She muttered *grazie* but it was hardly audible as she began to sob again. As Luca wrapped his arms around the woman, Bria's heart broke to witness Carlotta's pain, but it also swelled to see the man she loved be capable of exhibiting such tenderness and sympathy. She also felt a stirring in her gut that made her afraid.

After Luca and Carlotta left, she sat on the sofa and shivered. Her spine tingled and she felt ice-cold. She had been in situations like this before, where death intruded itself unexpectedly into her life, but this was different. Bria couldn't shake the feeling that Fiorello's death was only the beginning.

She opened the drawer of the side table and reached for the rosary beads she had placed there. Her first prayer was for Fiorello's soul, the next for the souls of everyone in Positano. She didn't comprehend it, but Bria knew with absolute certainty that lurking somewhere in the village that she called home was an unspeakable horror that was patiently waiting to strike again.

Chapter 8

An Italian mother is the heart and soul of the family. It isn't an overstatement or the subject of debate, but truth. And once a year the entire country officially honors her.

La Festa della Mamma, like the bulk of Mother's Day celebrations around the world, takes place on the second Sunday in May. In Italy, the custom began in 1952 and was officially established as a holiday in 1958. But those are formalities, because *la madre italiana* has been a revered figure since the beginning of time. Whether looked at through a social, biological, or religious lens, the significance of the mother, especially in Italy, cannot be overrated. No matter what kind of family it might be.

Fifetta's was the most conventional, consisting of a working father, stay-at-home mother, and three children, while Imperia was an anomaly in her time being not just a mother of only one child, but a businesswoman as well. Bria was a little bit of both. She was a single, working mother, but because she essentially worked from home, she had been able to create a traditional—although unconventional—family structure for Marco. Despite the differences, the three women were the undisputed centers of their families. And despite the early morning tragedy, it was still a day to be celebrated.

By the time Bria got up, showered, and dressed, her house was already full. She entered the main room on her way to the kitchen to make her morning coffee and was surprised to see her son sitting at the dining room table eating waffles topped with a generous helping of Nutella, and Bravo, who had his head in Marco's lap, ready to devour any crumbs. The moment they saw Bria, however, all thoughts of food were forgotten.

"*Buona festa della mamma!*"

Marco dropped his fork on his plate making a loud clank and jumped off his chair. He reached Bria a few seconds after Bravo. Like most mothers, Bria had enough room in her heart—and arms—for both of them.

"*I miei due piccoli cuccioli!*" Bria exclaimed, kneeling to embrace Marco and pet Bravo behind the ears.

"I'm not a puppy, Mamma," Marco protested.

"On *la festa della mamma,* whatever Mamma says, goes." Giovanni entered the dining room carrying a tray that was filled with all of Bria's favorites. A pot of Lavazza's Arabica Robusta, a cup of steamed milk, Giovanni's very own citrus croissants, and eggs *purgatorio*. "A feast fit for a queen."

"I guess if I'm a puppy," Marco said, "Mamma can be a queen."

"According to *La Vita Positano*, Signora Bartolucci has already been christened the Queen of Positano."

Bria recognized the voice, but when she looked up, she was still surprised to see Mimi. She wasn't at all surprised to see Enrico standing next to her.

"If Aldo Bombalino puts it in his paper," Enrico added, "it must be true."

Bria's instinct was to question Mimi about her whereabouts last night after she left the concert. For the moment, however, she was a mother and not an amateur detective. Interrogation would have to wait until after the presentation of gifts.

"These are for you." Enrico put a pink tinted glass vase on

the table that was filled with an assortment of flowers—petunias, roses, daisies, and daffodils—all in various shades of pink, Bria's favorite color. "Although they pale in comparison to the beauty you've brought to our little village."

"Enrico, *che dolce,*" Bria said. "It's the village, and everyone here who has brought beauty into my life."

"As *i bambini* like to say," Enrico said, "we can agree to disagree."

"I'm a kid and I don't disagree," Marco added. "Mamma has to be a queen because Bravo's the Prince of Positano."

"That makes perfect sense." Mimi laughed.

"What does that make you, Marco?" Giovanni asked.

Marco tilted his chin and furrowed his brow, an image that Bria wanted to bottle because it perfectly captured the transformation from little boy into young man. "I guess that makes me the prince's best friend."

Bravo barked twice, which either meant he completely agreed or he was hungry. To cover both bases, Marco gave him a belly rub and Giovanni served him a mixture of eggs, ground chicken, and some of the *purgatorio* sauce without the spices. Even though Bravo would never be a mother, he was being treated like royalty.

"I hope it's all right that we brought Bravo back," Enrico said.

"We figured that since the lady has already sung, it wouldn't matter if Bravo made her sneeze," Marco added.

Uffa! Bria silently shouted to herself. *I forgot about Carlotta!*

The events of the early morning rushed back to her with such speed and intensity, Bria had to clutch the back of the dining room chair. She glanced up to Carlotta's bedroom door and wondered if she was up, still grieving, and having to listen to their happy chatter. Life went on, of course, but still respect needed to be paid.

"I think it should be okay," Bria said. "But let's not make too much noise, Signora Incantaro had a long night."

"For some of us who actually had to listen to her sing, it was even longer," Mimi quipped.

"You didn't listen to the entire concert, Mimi," Bria said. "You left halfway through."

Bria had no reason to suspect the bookstore owner would want to kill Fiorello, but he had been Carlotta's close friend; perhaps he and Mimi got into an argument about the diva Mimi despised and it got physical. Mimi was a small woman, but Bria knew that size was not a good indication of someone's strength. Her mother, who was heavier than Mimi but the same height, was the strongest woman Bria knew.

"Her screeching gave me a splitting headache and I needed to leave," Mimi said. "I went straight home, took some aspirin, and went to bed."

"She even forgot she brought tomatoes in her purse," Enrico said.

"Looks like you have tomato stains on your finger," Marco said. "They do get kind of messy if you bite into them like an apple."

"Mimi, you're bleeding," Bria said.

Mimi sucked on her right forefinger. "Whoever said reading wasn't dangerous has never endured a paper cut."

"Come with me," Giovanni said. "I have Band-Aids in the kitchen."

"Don't you usually keep those in the bathroom?" Enrico asked.

"With Marco, we keep them in every room in the house," Giovanni replied. "If the patient will follow me, we'll take care of that cut."

Mimi followed Giovanni into the kitchen as Bria walked around the table and sat down in front of the food Vanni had prepared. "Marco, come sit, let's enjoy our breakfast and then head over to church."

"I need to give you your gift first." Marco ran out of the room, into his bedroom, and returned before Bria had a chance to take her first sip of coffee. He stood in front of Bria holding the poorly wrapped rectangular package and puffed up his chest. "I hope you like it, Mamma, I bought it all on my own."

It didn't matter what was being concealed by the lemon-themed wrapping paper. Bria knew that she would treasure it, like she did all Marco's gifts. When she tore away the paper, she was brought to tears and she knew she'd keep this gift forever.

"It's a paint-by-numbers of Positano," Marco said. "I want you to get back to your painting because whenever you talk about it your eyes light up and you get so happy."

How one honest comment could fill her with such regret amazed Bria. She knew that Marco had responded to the truth he saw in her eyes whenever she spoke about painting and her past as an art student. What he also understood, on some level, was the remorse she felt for abandoning her talent. Her son seemed to know his mother as well as Bria knew him.

"*Lo adoro*!" Bria put the gift on the table and embraced her son.

"I knew you'd love it," Marco said. "When you're done, we can hang it right next to the front door so everybody can see it."

"I was right," Enrico said. "You really do bring beauty to the village."

Bria waved a hand in front of her to dismiss Enrico's comment, and although she was conflicted, she couldn't wipe away the smile on her face. She glanced up at the second floor and knew there was a woman there who was grieving the loss of a man she considered a son, but she had learned these special moments couldn't be ignored.

"Enrico, we need to leave," Mimi announced as she came out of the kitchen with a fresh Band-Aid on her finger. "Annamaria just texted me. She and Paolo are already at the church."

"We'll see you all later." Enrico grabbed Mimi's elbow and

led her to the front door. Bravo got up from the floor to join them thinking he was still banned from Bella Bella. "No, Bravo, you stay with your mamma. The lady upstairs won't cause any more trouble. *Ciao.*"

Bria stared at the front door for a few moments, not even noticing the citrusy taste of the croissant she had bitten into; she was contemplating Enrico's odd comment about Carlotta. She didn't have much time to think about it because just as she swallowed, Ombra knocked on the door.

"*Scusi.*" Ombra stood at the door, not unafraid to enter but waiting for an invitation.

"Ombra, *buongiorno,*" Bria said. "*Prego*, come in."

Bria couldn't tell from Ombra's expression if she had already heard the news. She didn't look upset, but then again Ombra and Fio hadn't appeared to be very close. He had been her mother's friend, not hers.

Bria still hadn't shared the details of Fiorello's death with Giovanni, and while it was hard to believe that Annamaria was slipping as the village gossip and was in risk of losing her title as *La chiacchierona di Positano* since Annamaria didn't mention anything to Mimi about the latest death in her text, it was safe to assume that the information had not yet seeped out to the public. Carlotta more than likely told Ombra at some point during the night, which meant Ombra was coldhearted or as good an actress as her mother was a singer.

Not wanting to take the chance that Ombra had come to discuss Fiorello's death, Bria searched for a reason to get Marco to leave so he didn't overhear the conversation. One glance at Bravo and her problem was solved.

"I think Bravo needs to go for a walk before we all leave," Bria announced. "Marco, could you take him out *per favore?*"

"Come on, Bravo. You, too, Vanni," Marco announced. "Mamma wants to talk privately with *la signorina.*"

Vanni caught Bria's eye and she knew that he was asking if

everything was all right and if he needed to stay. Bria cherished their friendship and was so grateful that she'd listened to her mother instead of the townsfolk and had hired Giovanni to be her handyman. He had turned into a loyal employee and a trusted friend.

"*Grazie.*" Bria smiled and nodded at Giovanni. "Don't be too long."

After they left, Ombra walked farther into the house but she still appeared awkward. Maybe it was because Ombra was used to places like Villa Magia and Le Sirenuse, Bella Bella was Bria's pride and joy, but it definitely wasn't as luxurious as those hotels. Or it could be that Ombra felt awkward no matter where she was.

"Would you like some coffee?" Bria asked.

"No, *grazie,*" Ombra replied. "I came for my mother."

"It is important to be with your mother on *La Festa della Mamma.*"

"I came because Fiorello's dead," Ombra declared, her voice and her expression thick as concrete. "But you already know that since you're the one who found his body."

"I assume you spoke with Luca."

"Yes, he called me last night, well, early this morning to tell me the news," Ombra explained. "What was it like?"

"What was *what* like?"

"Seeing Fiorello in the piazza."

Ombra might not need any caffeine to get through their conversation, but Bria did. She poured herself another cup of coffee and filled it with milk. She took a long sip and faced Ombra, who was drumming her fingers against the side of her leg impatiently.

"It was a shock as you can imagine."

"I actually can't imagine what it's like to find a dead body."

"*È vero, mi dispiace,*" Bria apologized. "Before I saw Fio I did feel as if something was wrong."

"What do you mean? Did you see anything strange?"

"It was too quiet, there wasn't a sound in the piazza, not a bird, no wind, nothing."

"*La calma prima della tempesta*," Ombra muttered.

"Exactly. It was very calm and then I saw his body illuminated in the moonlight," Bria recalled.

"You make it sound peaceful," Ombra observed. "Almost beautiful."

Bria had never considered death to be beautiful, but she thought that in some ways it was. She didn't think Fiorello's death was shrouded in beauty, however. There were still too many unanswered questions and too many possibilities that his death was from unnatural causes.

"At first I didn't even think it was Fiorello," Bria shared. "I thought it was Armando."

"Why in the world would you think that? They're nothing alike."

"We think he might have been wearing Armando's jacket though we aren't sure why."

"*Sì, naturalmente!*" Ombra threw her head back and lifted her hands up to the sky. It was the most animated Bria had ever seen the woman. "That's why Luca asked me what Fiorello was wearing. It didn't make sense at the time, but now I understand. Armando spilled red wine all over Fiorello's jacket after the concert. Thank God my mother had already left to come back here or she would have been furious. I promised Fiorello I would clean the stain before she noticed, but it had gotten chilly and he couldn't risk catching a cold by walking around in a wet jacket or without one entirely because I knew my mother would kill him if got sick before the wedding, so I made Armando switch jackets with him. And yes, I am aware that I said my mother would have killed Fiorello, when he is actually dead. If you haven't noticed it by now, I did not inherit my mother's poise and elocution. I'm what my mother is fond of saying, an embarrassment."

Bria took another long sip of her coffee, not because she wanted to, but because she needed a moment to digest that caravan of information that Ombra had just parked in front of her. On the one hand, Ombra helped solve a mystery as to why Fiorello wasn't wearing his white jacket, but on the other hand, she created another mystery. If Carlotta and Ombra truly had such a dysfunctional relationship, why was the opera diva going to such an extent to make sure that her daughter's wedding was a memorable occasion?

"I'm sure your mother does not consider you an embarrassment," Bria said.

"I'm disappointed," Ombra replied. "Everyone said you paid attention to details."

"I do, and that's why I know that you're wrong," Bria said. "As a mother, I know that children can be challenging at times, they can make you want to rip out your hair, but no matter what they do, they're never embarrassing."

Ombra rolled her eyes and shrugged her shoulders. "Maybe one day I'll find out you're right. For now, could you please take me to my mother's room?"

"Of course, follow me."

When they got to Carlotta's door, Bria stopped and knocked quietly. After waiting a few seconds without a response, she knocked again, this time a bit louder. She was about to call out Carlotta's name when Ombra suddenly grabbed the doorknob, twisted it to the right, and pushed it open.

"Where is my mother?"

Bria couldn't answer Ombra's question because she didn't know.

"Mother, are you in here?" Ombra entered the room and walked to the bathroom, its door ajar, and pushed it open to reveal yet another empty space. "She isn't here. Didn't she come home last night?"

"I'm not sure," Bria answered. "Luca took her to the morgue

to see Fiorello's body after she insisted to see him, and I assumed he brought her back here or to stay with you."

"I'm sure she wanted to stay where she was comfortable, which would not be with me, but here in this little B and B."

Bria recognized the comment wasn't meant to be a compliment, but she didn't think it was the time to defend Bella Bella. What she needed to do was find Carlotta. Her heart started to race because the tingling sensation returned to her gut, a physical warning that danger was nearby. She closed her eyes and tried to listen to what the feeling was trying to tell her, but all she could hear was a cell phone ringing.

"It's coming from next door." Ombra held up her cell phone and Bria could see the word *Madre* indicating that Ombra was calling her mother. If she was doing that, why was the call coming from Fiorello's bedroom?

Bria followed Ombra as she followed the sound of the classical music, a melody Bria vaguely remembered, until they were standing outside Fiorello's bedroom. Once again, Ombra didn't knock or announce herself; she twisted the doorknob and pushed her way into the room. Bria let out a small cry when she saw Carlotta sleeping in Fiorello's bed, but Ombra merely scoffed and shook her head.

"That is just like my mother, always making everything about her."

Bria thought Ombra could be right, everything could be about Carlotta—including Fiorello's death. The white jacket she was clutching was definitely Fiorello's, and it was also definitely stained with red wine.

Chapter 9

Uffa! Bria silently shouted. *This doesn't look good.*

Even though Bria's inquisitive side was eager to get answers to explain what she was seeing, the more maternal, empathic side won out and Bria felt the unstoppable urge to protect Carlotta. Not wanting to disturb the grieving woman, Bria closed the bedroom door and led Ombra downstairs to the dining room. But by the time they got there, she realized how strange the situation was and how inept it would be to ignore it. Nosy Bria triumphed and she began asking questions.

"Do you have any explanation for what we just saw?" Bria asked.

"It's rather obvious, don't you think?" Ombra replied.

"Not to me."

"Have you ever seen *Madame Butterfly*?"

"Not since college, but I know the story."

"My mother had great success playing Cio-Cio-San, even though she was old enough to be the geisha's grandmother, and right before she kills herself at the end of the opera, she clutches her wayward husband's shirt in an attempt to bring him back," Ombra explained. "She's reenacting that scene upstairs."

Bria was taken aback by the coldness of Ombra's insight and

the bitterness in her voice. Now that the shock of seeing Carlotta in Fiorello's bed had started to wear off, Bria understood that the woman was holding one of the last garments Fiorello wore in an attempt to seek comfort. She was behind closed doors and hardly playacting; she was grieving. But maybe Bria was romanticizing what she saw because she didn't want to see the truth. After all, Ombra did know her mother better than Bria did.

Regardless of why Carlotta was in the fetal position clutching a dead man's clothing, there was still the question of how she orchestrated the scene.

"Ombra, you told me that Armando and Fiorello switched jackets after Armando spilled red wine on Fio," Bria said.

"That's right," Ombra replied. "You may not have had the chance to witness it, but my fiancé has a habit of getting sloppy after a few drinks."

"You also told me that you said you were going to try and get the stain out."

"*Anche corretto.*"

"I assume you brought the jacket back to Villa Magia to get someone in housekeeping to remove the stain."

"You're on a roll, Bria, that's true."

"Then how did it wind up in Carlotta's hands?"

Bria had seen that smile before. Ombra looked like many others she had questioned who had tried to maintain a friendly exterior while inside they were screaming their heads off. There were many different reasons why people responded to her with their lips pressed together and spread out into a facsimile of a smile while their eyes glared at her like deadly lasers. Some were offended by Bria's persistence, some were angry for allowing themselves to get tricked into saying more than they wanted, some were guilty. Bria found Ombra very hard to read and couldn't tell which emotion she was feeling.

"After the concert, Armando and I were on our way back to Villa Magia, when we ran into my mother," Ombra clarified.

"She saw the stained jacket and said she had a trick to getting stains out of clothing after years of wearing costumes. She said she was particularly adept at getting out red wine from white fabric thanks to playing Marie Antoinette in *The Ghosts of Versailles.* You know, because of the decapitation."

"*Grazie,* I made the connection," Bria replied. "That explains part of it."

"What else is there to explain?"

Bria couldn't explain it, but she didn't trust Ombra. She wasn't sure if the woman was complicated and hard to read or if she was a liar. Whatever the reason, Bria felt she should treat her with less empathy and compassion and be more straightforward and blunt. Even if Luca would be upset with her when he found out.

"The biggest question of all that needs explaining is why someone would want to kill Fiorello."

As expected, Ombra's expression barely changed. The fact that someone she knew may have been murdered barely registered.

"The police think someone tried to kill Fio?"

"I can't speak for the police, but personally I think Fio was murdered."

"*E' assurdo.*"

"Why is that absurd?"

"Because Fio has never done anything to anyone to make them want to kill him."

"I didn't realize you knew Fiorello so well."

"He was my mother's only accompanist when she was singing, and they've been inseparable since she decided to put on this concert," Ombra explained.

"How would you describe him?"

"Loyal, principled, talented."

"That describes Fiorello as your mother's pianist. What about as a person?"

Ombra paused and appeared almost startled at the question. "Whether you look at Fio as an accompanist or a person, I can't imagine any reason why someone would want to murder him."

"Neither can I from what I know of him at this point."

Suddenly Ombra smiled. "Now if it was Armando that you found dead in the piazza, I could think of a million justified reasons why someone would want to kill him."

If it weren't for the sound of Bravo's barking announcing his return, Bria would have pressed further to inquire why a woman would make such a comment about the man she was going to marry. She knew that not everyone married out of love or with the intent to stay married until the end of their life, but still, Ombra's comment was calculated and deliberate. There was much more to be revealed about her upcoming nuptials, and Bria wanted to continue that line of questioning, but at the moment there was a line of people—and one very excited canine—at her door.

"Did you have a good walk, *mio angelito*?" Bria bent over and rubbed the underside of Bravo's chin, her hair falling forward and tickling Bravo's long chestnut-brown ears.

Bravo barked twice, his tail wagging like a speedy pendulum, which Bria translated to mean he was answering in the affirmative. In case she misinterpreted Bravo's body language, Marco made sure to clarify.

"Sorry we took so long, Mamma, but look who we ran into."

Bria looked up and saw Giovanni and Luca standing behind Marco. Both men were smiling, and had she not known that they had spent most of their adult life disliking and mistrusting the other, she would have thought they were lifelong friends. She was delighted to witness the evolution of their relationship and proud that she was a large part of the reason they were able to stand side by side without name-calling or the potential of fisticuffs.

"*Ciao,* Luca." Bria stood up and started to lean into him to give him a kiss, but out of the corner of her eye she saw Ombra staring at her. Feeling as if she was in the presence of a hostile audience, Bria awkwardly stopped herself.

"*Ciao,*" Luca said.

"Is the chief of police here on business or is this a social call?" Ombra asked.

"Luca's dating Mamma, so it's a social call," Marco shared. "They do work on cases a lot so the lines get blurry."

Shaking his head and laughing, Giovanni reached forward and extended his hand. "I'm Giovanni Monteverdi, we haven't formally met yet."

"Ombra Incantaro, soon to be Ombra Puccia, but I'm sure you already know that."

"After last night, I think the entire village knows that," Vanni replied.

"*Grazie,* Bria," Ombra said. "I enjoyed our chat immensely, but it's time for me to get going. I have a lot of planning to do."

"I thought all of the wedding plans would've been taken care of already," Vanni stated.

"They are," Ombra replied. "Now I have to prepare for a funeral."

"A funeral?!" Vanni exclaimed.

"Who died now?" Marco asked.

Bria was about to say that she was going to explain everything later in private, but Ombra didn't give her the chance. "My mother's piano player."

"Fiorello?!" Vanni shouted.

"Oh no, I liked him," Marco said. "He was much nicer than that lady singer."

"Most people are much nicer than that lady singer," Ombra stated. "I should know, she's my mother."

Bria watched Marco's green eyes widen beneath raised eyebrows and her heart swooned. He had said something inappropriate and now he understood the implications of his words.

A small piece of his innocence had been chipped away, but it was replaced by acknowledgment of his actions.

"*Mi dispiace*," Marco said. "I didn't realize she was your mamma."

"That's quite all right; you were only stating a truth and you should never apologize for that." Ombra glanced once more at Carlotta's door and then turned back to the group. "When my mother tires of her self-exiled prison, please let me know, but I really better be going now."

"Don't leave on our account."

They all turned to the front door to see Nunzi in full police regalia standing in front of Matteo. She was holding her cap in front of her, and without it on top of her head, her new hairstyle actually complemented her outfit. It made her look even stronger than usual.

"*Buongiorno,* Nunzi!" Bria cried.

"You're definitely not making a social call dressed up like that," Ombra remarked.

"We need to examine Fiorello's room and his belongings," Nunzi announced. "I didn't think a search warrant was necessary, but I could go and get one."

"*Non essere ridicolo*," Luca scoffed. "Of course you can search Fio's room."

"No, she can't," Bria said.

"Why not?" Luca asked.

"As is often the case," Ombra interjected. "It's because of my mother."

"Why would Carlotta get in the way of our investigation?" Nunzi asked in a voice as strong as her new look.

"She isn't impeding your investigation or obstructing justice," Bria said. "She's just sleeping in Fio's bed."

"Is the bed in her room uncomfortable?" Nunzi asked.

"*Ovviamente no!*" Bria cried. "All the beds at Bella Bella are incredibly comfortable."

"Go online and check out our reviews if you don't believe us," Vanni added.

"Then why isn't Carlotta sleeping in her bed?" Nunzi asked.

"Because she wants to feel closer to Fio." When she spoke, Ombra finally sounded like a daughter who was trying to protect her mother and not condemn her. "His death has hit her very hard, as you can imagine, and if you could give her a bit more time alone in his room it would be greatly appreciated."

This time instead of answering immediately, Nunzi glanced over at Luca. Bria followed Nunzi's gaze and saw Luca close his eyes and nod his head almost imperceptibly. Although he wasn't in uniform and was wearing a light blue linen shirt, khakis, and brown loafers, he was still the chief.

"We can come back later this afternoon," Nunzi conceded. Right before she was about to follow Matteo out of the house, she turned around to look at Bria. "*Buona festa della mamma.*"

"*Grazie*, Nunzi," Bria said. "For everything."

"I'll come back later as well to move my mother out."

"You don't have to do that," Bria said. "I don't have another guest coming into that room until next week."

"But it isn't paid for." Bria noticed Ombra was nervously clicking her fingernails. "Fiorello always took care of those things for her."

"Don't worry about it," Bria said. "I'm not going to charge her to stay, and it goes without saying that I'm not going to charge anyone for Fio's room."

Ombra exhaled slowly, almost trying to hide her breath, and looked down at the floor. "That's very kind of you. Now if you'll excuse me, I've already taken up more than enough of your time. Enjoy the festival."

After Ombra left, Bria noticed that Marco was quietly sitting at the table, his head bowed, his lips moving, but making no sound. Her son was saying a prayer for Fiorello. It was yet another one of the many gifts he gave her on a daily basis.

Some gifts, however, were meant to be wrapped in pretty pink wrapping paper, like the one Luca was holding.

"*Buona festa della mamma,* Bria," Luca said, placing the small box in Bria's hands.

Blushing slightly, Bria smiled. "*Grazie*, you didn't have to get me anything."

Luca cackled. "That is such a lie."

Bria laughed just as loud because she knew it was true. She had been hoping Luca would give her a gift, but with all the commotion she hadn't had much time to think about it. Quickly, she unwrapped the present to reveal a gold necklace with a heart filled with a pink spinel and white opal, Bria and Marco's birthstones.

"Luca, this is beautiful," Bria gushed.

"There's room for more stones." Luca took the necklace from Bria and placed it around her neck. Standing behind her, he secured the clasp and leaned to the side so when he spoke, his lips brushed against her ear. "If you'd like to do that in the future."

Bria hoped by the way she smiled Luca would understand that she would love to add his birthstone to the heart, but in case there was doubt she turned around and kissed him softly on the lips.

"Is this a bad time?" Rosalie asked, entering the house.

Bria smiled at her best friend but was immediately concerned. She looked like her normal self, wearing a floral silk maxi vest in various shades of blue over a long sleeveless yellow dress, but despite the colorful outfit and acerbic comment, her demeanor seemed reserved, which was one word Bria had never used to describe her friend. Something was wrong, and sadly, Bria knew exactly what it was.

"I thought Michele was coming with you," Bria said.

"He isn't," Rosalie replied. "Paolo isn't feeling well and he thought he might have to take him to Naples to the emergency room."

Bria opened her mouth to speak and saw that Marco had done the same thing. Luckily, this time Marco thought about the ramifications of what he was about to say and realized it was better to keep quiet. Bria was certain he was going to say that Mimi had told them that Paolo was meeting them at the piazza, because it was what Bria was going to say. She would find a private moment before they arrived to share the news with Rosalie.

Until then Marco needed to share his gift.

With lightning speed, he ran out of the room and came back carrying a gift that was wrapped only slightly better than the one he had given to Bria. "This is for you, Rosalie."

Uncharacteristically, Rosalie remained silent. She didn't squeal, she didn't cry, she didn't even pick Marco up and twirl him around. She simply stood in place and stared at the gift as if it was an unearthed treasure of unknown identity.

"Why are you giving me a gift?" she asked.

"Because a *zia* is like a mamma, too," Marco replied.

Yet again, Bria's heart ached because she knew her friend was battling the longing to cry. And not just cry, but weep. Something was going on with Rosalie and it wasn't just boyfriend trouble; from the look on her face it appeared to be much deeper than that. But like a good aunt, Rosalie corralled her emotions and finally put on a huge smile for Marco's benefit. "*Grazie mille,* Marco, that's a beautiful thing to say."

"Open it up," Marco said. "I picked it out all by myself."

Instinctively, Bria clutched Luca's hand because she knew there was the very real chance that Marco had chosen something wildly inappropriate. When she saw Rosalie's expression as she held the picture frame, Bria knew her son had made a wise choice.

With tears filling her eyes, Rosalie turned the frame around so they could all see the photo. It was a Polaroid Bria had taken of Rosalie and Marco on her boat a few months ago. They were wearing matching ship captain's hats and the sea and sky behind them were in shades of blue almost as vibrant as their smiles. The photo had done what a photo should: it captured a joyful memory.

Knowing Rosalie was still trying to control her emotions so she could speak without bursting into tears, Bria—as best friends do—came to her rescue. "Marco! What a thoughtful gift! This is *bellissimo.*"

"It really is," Vanni added. "You both look so happy in the picture."

"It was a fun day," Marco said. "We had off from school because of a papal conference and it was so sunny, Rosalie said it was the perfect day for a boat ride."

"It was." Rosalie was finally able to speak. She picked Marco up, but instead of twirling him in a circle, she just held him tightly. "*Grazie.*"

"*Prego, Zia* Rosalie."

"Luca, would you mind helping me and Marco put the rest of his gifts into a bag before we leave?" Giovanni asked.

Although it was probably the first time Vanni had ever asked for Luca's help, Luca, understanding that the request was merely a ploy to give Bria and Rosalie some privacy, immediately acquiesced. "*Certo.*"

"I have to get ready to give my special gift, too," Marco added.

"What special gift?" Bria asked.

"It's a secret!"

As Luca followed Vanni and Marco into his bedroom, Bria didn't take her eyes off Rosalie. When she heard the door close behind the men, she took the frame Rosalie was holding and placed it on the dining room table. She then took her friend's hands and held them close to her chest so they were only inches apart.

"What's wrong?" Bria asked.

"I'd like to be a mother one day."

This was not the response Bria was expecting. It wasn't something they often talked about, but Bria did know that despite Rosalie's cavalier attitude toward life, she did want to have a family of her own someday. That day may have arrived.

"What's brought this on?"

"You know I've always admired how you took to being a mother and how your relationship with Marco only grew after Carlo's death," Rosalie said. "I want that kind of unconditional love in my life, but to do that I need to find the right man. I thought Michele could be that person, but lately, I'm having doubts."

"What has he done to you?"

"Nothing, really, other than some white lies, like with Paolo. Annamaria already sent me a photo of her and Paolo at the piazza asking when we're showing up."

Bria squeezed Rosalie's hands tighter and was glad that secret was out in the open. But there was more to it than just a few lies.

Rosalie inhaled and blew out a long breath. "I don't think Michele is a good enough man to be the father of my child."

Bria fought her own tears because she knew in her heart that her friend was right. She also knew that this wasn't the time to agree with her or share her thoughts about Michele's character. It was only time to give her friend a long hug.

When they got to Piazza Dei Mulini, it appeared as if Fiorello's death had never happened.

The piazza was crowded with families who had gathered for the day's celebration along with the usual tourists who were passing through on their way to the ferry, a café, or some other final destination. There were small tables and chairs on the perimeter of the piazza like there had been the night before, with vases of multicolored flowers on the tables, and in the center of the piazza the Sirens' Fountain created a constant rush of noise with the water rushing out of the sea nymphs' mouths. Overhead, a banner hung with the words *La Festa della Mamma* in light blue, a nod to the Blessed Mother, who was typically depicted wearing a cape of the same color. In the space where Carlotta had sung so rapturously the previous night was a trio of musicians who filled the air with music. The piazza was alive.

They greeted all their friends, waved to Dante and Valentina from a safe distance, and Marco, wearing a beaming smile, gave out his gifts. A small jar filled with all the ingredients necessary to make Nutella-flavored hot chocolate for Fifetta, a personalized book that turned the story of Pinocchio into a fairy tale between *Nonna* Imperia and her large-nosed grandson, Marco, and a very expensive 200 milliliter bottle of Bergamotto di Positano perfume for Lorenza that she had specially requested and, that despite its name, Bria had to order from London. Each woman was overjoyed by their gift and claimed it was the best they had ever received.

However, Fifetta, Bria, and even Rosalie were brought to unexpected tears when Giovanni presented Fifetta with a beautifully wrapped gift.

"Giovanni, *cos'è questo?*" Fifetta asked.

"A gift for you," he replied, his voice a gruff whisper. "If you didn't suggest that Bria should hire me, my life would be very different."

Fifetta swallowed hard and unopened the gift. "Oh, Giovanni, *quanto premuroso.*"

Bria silently agreed that writing out his grandmother's recipes along with some of his own and putting them into a journal was a very thoughtful gift.

"*Grazie mille,* Giovanni," Fifetta replied. "I'll make us a dinner from these recipes, just the two of us."

"I'd like that." Giovanni reached out to hold Fifetta's hand and looked her straight in the eye. "I want you to know that you've done more for me than my real mother ever did and I'm eternally grateful."

Although Fifetta couldn't comprehend a mother not giving up her life for her child, she knew that not every woman was fit for the role. "I'm sure she did her best, Giovanni."

"She did not, but that's in the past, and thanks to you and Bria, I have a future."

There was nothing else for Fifetta to say, and even if she wanted to, the tears falling from her eyes and gathering in her throat prevented her from speaking. Instead, she simply hugged Giovanni tightly to let him know that one mother did love him unconditionally.

Bria wiped her eyes and turned away and noticed Rosalie was doing the same. Everywhere she looked, women, young and old, were accepting gifts, hugging, and exchanging kisses. Despite the joyous occasion, Bria overheard people talking about the death that had taken place in the piazza only hours earlier.

The chatter was the usual gossip, speculation, and gory fascination that followed an unexpected death. What bothered Bria even more was that most of the people didn't even know Fiorello's last name, they only knew him as the piano player. He wasn't a friend, a relative, a colleague, or even an acquaintance, and still they all thought it was appropriate to speculate about his last moments on earth.

Bria bowed her head and said a quick prayer that Fio's soul would find peace and that the cause of his death would soon be uncovered. When Bria turned around, she saw that her son was no longer talking to Luca but was standing next to the piano behind Sister Benedicta with the rest of the children from his class.

"Thank you all for coming on this beautiful Sunday," Sister B started. "A special thanks to all the mothers for everything they do for their families. You are truly doing God's work."

Bria, like almost all the women in the piazza, nodded their heads and made the sign of the cross.

"As a special thank-you the children have prepared a song that they'd like to sing," Sister B announced. "One of our very own students will accompany them on the piano."

Bria and her entire family were shocked to see Marco walk over to the piano and hobble onto the seat. It was a jarring visual to see him sit at the piano, not only because it was exactly where Fiorello had been just last night, but because Marco didn't play the instrument.

"When did my grandson learn how to play the piano?" Fifetta asked.

"I have no idea," Bria replied.

"Maybe you should spend more time watching your son than galivanting throughout the village playing detective," Imperia quipped.

Before anyone could say another word, Marco began to do what no one thought he could: he played the piano. It was a simple Italian folk song—"*Un Cocomero Tondo Tondo*"—and told the story of a round watermelon. His playing was as expected, rudimentary and cautious, but it didn't prevent Bria, Fifetta, Franco, Lorenza, and even Imperia from starting to cry. When he kept hitting the same wrong note, they started to laugh. It didn't matter; to their ears Marco sounded like a prodigy. When the song ended, however, and the children returned to their families, Marco didn't share their opinion.

"I don't know why that one note sounded wrong," Marco said. "It was the right one, I know it was."

"*Amore mio,*" Bria said. "It doesn't matter, you sounded perfect."

"It does matter, and it wasn't perfect," Marco countered. "I wasn't making the mistake, the piano was."

"Marco, haven't we always told you that all that matters is that you try your best?" Franco said. "We don't care if you weren't perfect."

"But I was perfect," Marco insisted. "I hit all the right notes, didn't I, Sister B?"

Bria expected Sister B to reiterate her father's comment, but instead she agreed with Marco. "You did, I watched your hands the entire time and you hit all the right notes. Maybe the piano needs some tuning."

"That's impossible," Bria said. "Fiorello played an entire concert last night and didn't hit one bad note."

Luca shrugged his shoulders. "There's only one way to find out if there's an issue."

Leading the way to the white baby grand, Luca lifted its lid. It took him about ten seconds to see that Marco was right. "There's a string missing."

Everyone peered in to look at the soundboard, and one by one they saw the evidence to support Luca's claim. One of the wires had been pulled out of the piano.

"Did it break?" Rosalie asked.

"No," Luca replied. "It looks like someone removed the entire string."

"Why would anyone do that?" Fifetta asked.

Bria kept her mouth shut, but she locked eyes with Luca and knew that they were sharing the same thought. A piano wire was a perfect murder weapon.

Chapter 10

After Sister B led Marco, his grandparents, and most of the other families back to St. Cecilia's for cake and espresso, and the others had returned to their homes or their stores, the piazza resumed its primary role as a thoroughfare for passersby. It gave Bria, Luca, Nunzi, and Rosalie time to evaluate this clue.

Bria pointed to the piano wires and said, "I think we're looking at a murder weapon."

"You think someone killed Fio with this piano?" Rosalie asked. "Maybe they played some really bad music like that horrible song by Pupo, '*Gelato al Cioccolato*,' and made his ears bleed."

"I love that song!" Bria cried. "I used to sing it to Marco all the time."

"Bria isn't talking about the whole piano," Luca replied. "Just the wire."

"*Aspetta un secondo,*" Bria said. "You agree with me?"

"It's a real possibility based on the fact that the wire is missing, and not an imaginary scenario," Luca replied. "So, yes, I do agree with you."

"In all the cozy mysteries I read, this is what they call a turning point," Nunzi interjected.

"You read cozy mysteries?" Rosalie asked.

"All the time."

"I pictured you curling up with Primavera on your lap on a Saturday night reading hard-boiled, blood-and-gore novels like the ones Gianrico Carofiglio writes," Rosalie said.

"I used to, but they gave Primavera nightmares," Nunzi explained. "I switched to mysteries that are just as satisfying, but don't induce trauma, like J.D. Griffo's Ferrara Family mysteries set in the States. Alberta Scaglione is a widow who solves murders just like you, Bria, but she's sixty-five."

"Hearing more about your reading habits is fascinating, Nunzi, but could we return to the topic?" Luca asked.

"*Prego,* what did you mean that this is a turning point?" Bria asked.

"Luca, who represents the authority figure in a cozy mystery, has finally come around to accepting that you, Bria, the amateur sleuth, is an asset and not a liability to the investigation."

Bria whipped her head to face Luca. "You considered me a liability?"

"Never!" Luca shouted. "Nunzi, stop causing trouble."

"I'm only pointing out facts."

Luca waved a finger angrily at Nunzi and turned to face Bria and grinned. "You know I think you've been tremendously helpful to the police force, but you also know that I think you sometimes let your imagination take over."

"You do have a very big imagination, Bri," Rosalie pointed out. "That cannot be denied."

"Nunzi's right, though, this is a turning point because I agree with you," Luca stated. "The missing piano wire could have been used to kill Fiorello."

"Thank you for saying that," Bria said. "And just to be clear, I know you never considered me a liability."

"That was a poor word choice on my part," Nunzi corrected. "A nuisance maybe, but not really a liability."

"Nunzi!" Luca shouted. "Can we get back to the piano wire?"

"I think someone used the missing piano wire to strangle Fiorello," Bria declared.

"That can be an effective way to commit murder," Nunzi commented.

"Who do you think did it?" Rosalie asked.

"I'm not sure," Bria replied. "The piano was left in plain sight and wasn't being guarded; it could have been anyone who was at the concert."

"Or anyone who happened to be in Positano last night," Nunzi added.

"Which means the suspect list includes a whole lot of people." Rosalie suddenly pulled a shrimp out of her purse and started chomping on it.

"Where did you get shrimp?" Bria asked.

"They had a whole tray set up on the buffet table," Rosalie explained. "Which is why I brought my shrimp purse."

Luca threw up his hands. "You have a shrimp purse?"

"The purse I use when I know there's going to be shrimp," Rosalie replied. "I keep a plastic bag in there and stuff it with shrimp so I don't have to keep going back to the table."

"That's kind of brilliant," Nunzi said.

"I know," Rosalie replied. "Would you like one?"

Nunzi peered into Rosalie's bag and pulled out a shrimp. "No cocktail sauce."

"Don't get greedy, cop lady," Rosalie retorted. "Now back to the scene of the crime, so to speak. Luca, you really think someone could have used the piano wire to kill Fiorello?"

"I do. It's a simple and effective way to commit murder," he replied.

"That's only half-true," Nunzi said.

"Are you contradicting the chief of police?" Rosalie questioned.

"Only partially," Nunzi replied. "Have any of you ever tried to pull out a piano wire?"

Bria, Luca, and Rosalie all shook their heads.

"It's not an easy task," Nunzi shared.

"How hard can it be?" Bria asked.

"Try it," Nunzi challenged.

Bria started to put her hand into the belly of the piano when Nunzi grabbed her wrist. "Don't, you could hurt yourself."

"How am I going to know how difficult it is to pull out a piano wire if I don't try?" Bria asked.

"Do you trust me?" Nunzi replied.

Bria didn't have to think about it. "Of course I do."

"Then believe me when I tell you that it isn't easy," Nunzi said. "Unless you know what you're doing."

Without saying another word, Nunzi demonstrated that she was adept at the skill. She bent forward, her head all but disappearing within the insides of the piano, and less than a minute later she stood upright holding a long, thin wire in her hand. And a smirk on her lips.

"Obviously you've done this before," Bria commented. "Why is it so difficult?"

"The edges of the piano wire are sharp, and if you don't know what you're doing you can easily cut yourself," Nunzi explained.

"Since there wasn't any blood found on the body or nearby it's a good indication that whoever pulled out the piano wire knew what they were doing," Luca relayed.

"They could have cut themselves and were careful not to get the blood anywhere that could be seen," Bria suggested.

"I'll have the insides of the piano checked for blood," Nunzi announced. "If they did cut themselves on the wire, chances are there are remnants on the wood and brass. It'll be easy to check."

"*Dio mio!*" Bria cried. "I just thought of something."

"What?" Luca asked.

"Mimi had a Band-Aid on her finger," Bria shared. "She said it was from a paper cut."

"If Carlotta were the one you found dead in the piazza, I

might think Mimi had something to do with it because she hates the woman," Rosalie said. "But she never mentioned anything about Fiorello."

"There could be a secret we don't know about," Luca commented. "We really don't know anything about Fiorello."

"I've never heard Mimi talk so angrily about anyone before. Maybe her grudge against the woman extended to Fiorello," Bria shared. "I know it's a long shot, but it is a possibility."

"She did leave early from the concert last night," Nunzi said.

"I'll speak with her just to remove her from any potential suspect list," Luca said.

"You're going to want to check my hands, too."

They all whipped around to see Michele standing before them, looking tired and dirty, and holding up a grease-stained hand.

"I've got cuts all over my hands," he announced.

"You look terrible, Michele," Rosalie spat. "Where've you been all night?"

"Working on cars at my uncle's garage," he explained.

"Filling in because Paolo was sick?" Rosalie asked.

"He wasn't sick," Michele replied. "But you already know that."

"Yes, I do," Roslie said. "What I don't know is why you lied to me."

"Can we talk about that privately?" Michele asked.

"Maybe later," Rosalie replied. "We're in the middle of something."

"Whatever you're doing, Nunzi's right," Michele said. "The inside of a piano is like the inside of a car engine. Danger lurks in every nook and cranny."

"You can look anywhere and find danger," Luca replied. "If I ask Paolo, he'll corroborate your story that you were at the garage all night?"

"You'll have to ask him to find out," Michele replied.

Luca smiled, but there was no joy in his eyes, only suspicion. "I can guarantee that I'll do just that."

"Rosalie, seriously, could we go someplace to talk?" Michele asked again.

Bria gently grazed Rosalie's arm, and when Rosalie looked at her, Bria tilted her head in Michele's direction and widened her eyes. Rosalie understood the body language and sighed heavily. She turned to face Michele and turned her chin up. "Five minutes, and if you think you're getting any shrimp, think again, the purse is empty."

They all watched them leave, and while the air around them was filled with their unspoken comments, they all remained silent regarding Rosalie's personal life.

"I'll have forensics check to see if they can find any blood inside the piano," Nunzi announced. "But I don't think the wire is the murder weapon."

"Why not?" Bria asked.

"If you're going to kill someone with a piano wire, that means you're going to strangle them," Nunzi explained. "I don't remember Fio having any marks around his neck."

"He wouldn't," Bria said.

"Why not?" Luca asked.

"Because he was wearing that scarf, the red one that matched Carlotta's dress," Bria explained.

"That's right," Luca agreed. "The scarf could have prevented indentations from appearing on his neck."

"Very possible," Nunzi said.

"Nunzi, go talk to forensics and call the medical examiner to find out if she can confirm or deny our theory about strangulation," Luca ordered.

Nunzi touched her forefinger to her forehead and waved good-bye. The minute she was gone, Bria turned to Luca to tell him what she didn't want to be overheard. It was another theory she had about why Fiorello was killed.

"If someone tried to strangle Fio with the piano wire," Bria started, "they may not have meant to kill him."

"What do you mean?" Luca replied.

"In order to kill someone with a piano wire, you have to be behind them and throw the piano wire over their head."

"If you do that, your only intention can be to kill."

"Correct, but if they were behind Fio and Fio was wearing Armando's jacket, which he was, maybe the killer really wanted to murder Armando instead."

"You think that Fio was killed by accident?" Luca asked. "That he was wearing the wrong jacket at the wrong time."

"I didn't think much about it because the explanation as to why they switched jackets was logical, but Ombra said something that's stuck with me."

"What did she say?"

"She said that if I had found Armando dead, she could think of a million reasons why someone would want to kill him."

"She said that about her fiancé?"

"I was surprised, too," Bria said. "Maybe we're looking at this from the wrong angle. Instead of asking who would want to kill Fiorello, we should be looking for the person who'd want to kill Armando."

"According to his wife-to-be that list is really long."

Bria smiled slyly. "I think I have an idea where we can start."

Chapter 11

Positano was like the story of *Riccioli D'oro e i Tre Orsi*, Italy's version of Goldilocks and the Three Bears; it wasn't too big, it wasn't too small, it was just the right size. The seaside village was the perfect place to be whether you were looking for the perfect restaurant, the perfect gift shop, or you were searching for the perfect way to find out more information about a recent death. Especially if that death may have been a murder.

Bria's day started innocently enough and she went about her morning routine. Drinking coffee on her balcony, the warmth of the cup pressed against her chest working like the best alarm clock in the world, as she inhaled the ripe, earthy smells that drenched the air, remnants of an early morning rain shower. Rosso had company serenading her as the blue jays and gulls joined the robin and their collective chirps and cries created a natural symphony that was both calming and exciting.

Bria finished her coffee, took Bravo for a quick walk, savored her breakfast—a black olive, mozzarella, and mushroom frittata—showered, dressed, and along with Bravo walked Marco to school. It would be her first stop but not her last because she needed to see someone whom she suspected could give her some insight into Armando, whom Bria suspected may have been the real target. If, of course, a murder had truly taken place in the real world and not just in Bria's mind.

As was custom when they got to St. Cecilia's, Bravo walked right up to Sister B, or more specifically her left hand, to accept the treat she always had for him. She bent down like she did every time they met and whispered something in his ear. Bria was certain it was a prayer.

"That was such a wonderful surprise yesterday to see Marco playing the piano," Bria said. "*Grazie.*"

"Marco really has talent," Sister B replied. "Despite the musical malfunction."

Bria had learned that Sister Benedicta, while youthful and reserved, was far from the typical nun. She had grown up in a blue-collar neighborhood, the only girl among four brothers, in a family of mechanics. Sister B loved cars, fast driving, and a bit of adventure. She had also helped Bria solve some previous murders, but Bria never knew if the nun had shared clues deliberately or not. Just like she didn't know if Sister B was mentioning the missing piano wire as a way to veer the conversation away from pleasantries and toward private investigation.

"That was unfortunate," Bria replied. "But it didn't take away from the enjoyment."

"Not at all," Sister B agreed. "Everyone was delighted by Marco's playing."

"Except Marco," Marco pouted.

"Marco!" Bria chided. "You know I wouldn't lie to you; you played beautifully."

Marco tilted his head and pursed his lips. Bria had seen this stance so many times on her sister, her mother, her brother, and now here was proof that it ran in the family. "You would definitely lie to me, that's what mammas do."

Bria opened her mouth to rebut but caught Sister B desperately trying to hold in her laughter, and realized there was nothing she could say to argue against Marco's statement. He was right. She, like most mothers, would tell a white lie in order to boost her child's self-confidence and wash away self-doubt. It didn't matter that in this instance Bria was telling the truth; Marco's playing really was impressive despite the fact that the piano hadn't played along.

"Since when did you get so smart?" Bria teased.

"I think it was in first grade," Marco replied. "Isn't that right, Sister B?"

The nun's smile didn't completely fade, but Bria could tell that she was about to lean into her more prim countenance. "Humor is important, Marco, but remember that Jesus led by example to teach us humility."

The respect Marco—and all of the students at St. Cecilia's for that matter—had for Sister Benedicta was evident in how he looked at her. Not ashamed, not embarrassed, but thankful. "You're right, Sister B," Marco said. "Thank you for reminding me of that."

"Have you and Luca figured out how the missing piano wire went missing in the first place?"

Sister Benedicta's question reminded Bria, yet again, of the sister's two sides, and Bria wondered if she knew something or had an inkling as to how the piano had been tampered with. History had taught Bria that the nun wouldn't announce her thoughts directly. Bria would have to maneuver them out into the open.

"Not yet," Bria replied. "I did want to ask you if the school had the piano tuned after Carlotta's concert."

"Not to my knowledge," Sister B replied. "If the piano was good enough for an opera singer, it was good enough for our chorus."

"I thought maybe someone had to change the height of the piano bench or somehow raise the pedals so Marco could reach," Bria suggested.

"I'm sure you've noticed how much your son has grown," Sister B said. "The bench didn't need to be adjusted, but I wanted Marco to concentrate on the notes and the rhythm, so we didn't even tackle the pedals."

"*Va bene,*" Bria said. "For the moment, the missing piano wire will have to be a mystery."

The morning bell rang, causing Bravo to bark good-bye and Marco to run toward the rest of his classmates. "*Buona giornata,*" Bria said.

"*Addio.*" Sister Benedicta turned to follow Marco into the school but quickly turned back around. "There was one thing that was unusual."

Bria turned around so quickly that she startled Bravo who let out a high-pitched yelp. "What was that?"

"When we arrived in the piazza yesterday morning, the piano lid was up and I distinctively remember seeing Fiorello close the lid after the concert," Sister B remembered.

"Are you sure?" Bria asked. "It wouldn't be so odd to leave the piano lid up."

"I'm certain," Sister B replied. "Watching him close the lid was almost like watching Father Vincenzo's hands during the preparation of the altar. His movements were lyrical and filled with great love. He was gentle with the piano and he made quite an impression with me."

He did indeed. Bria had not been in Fiorello's company for very long, but except for the few moments she had noticed he was anxious about Carlotta, he was a soothing presence. If he was murdered, he didn't deserve that fate. Thanks to Sister B's comment, Bria was even more convinced he didn't die a natural death.

"*Grazie,* Sister," Bria said.

As Bria walked with Bravo a few feet in front of her, she pondered what Sister B had just shared. On the surface the comment was innocuous, but Bria understood that it had more serious implications. Since Fiorello had put the lid down on the piano after the concert, that meant someone had intentionally lifted it back up to pull out the piano wire and then forgot to close the lid to leave it the way they found it.

But why? If the wire had been removed prior to Carlotta's concert to sabotage her performance that would make sense, but Bria couldn't imagine anyone cruel enough to want to interfere with a children's recital. And if the wire had been removed before Carlotta sang, Fiorello would have known immediately what had happened. The only real answer was that someone waited until after Carlotta's concert to use the piano wire as a way to make decidedly unbeautiful music.

Lost in thought, Bria hadn't realized that she had aimlessly followed Bravo on a circuitous route back home and they had somehow wandered onto Via del Brigantino. Bria inhaled deeply and understood why Bravo had ventured into this part of town. The smells coming from La Brezza were mouthwatering. Fresh brewed coffee combined with rich chocolate and swirling in the mix, the unmistakable whiff of fennel. And right in front of her eyes was the unmistakable combination of a man and the other woman. Or at least a man and another woman besides the woman he should be with.

"*Uffa,*" Bria muttered to herself. "Does that woman have no shame?"

The woman in question was Valentina, who was exactly the woman Bria had planned on trying to see to hopefully learn more about Armando and if the man had done anything to acquire a deadly enemy. Valentina was street smart and understood men better than any woman she knew. Seeing them together, however, was not the plan. Bria had a natural inquisitiveness that made her a good interrogator, but that was when the questioning was one-on-one. It was much harder trying to get two people to share secrets with her and harder still if they shared secrets between themselves.

Bria turned and started walking in the opposite direction confident that Bravo would follow. Her faithful dog turned out to be very faithful, just not to Bria.

Barking wildly, Bravo sprinted toward the outdoor café and practically skidded to a stop when he got to where Valentina and Armando were sitting. He wasn't interested in the couple, but the other Segugio Italiano lounging at Valentina's feet. Genie raised her head and an eyebrow and appeared only slightly bemused that she had a visitor. Armando seemed even less excited.

"I didn't realize I had agreed to meet at a kennel," he scoffed.

Ignoring Armando's jeer, Valentina petted Bravo under his neck and gave him a warm kiss on the top of his head. "*Ciao, bello,*" Valentina cooed. "*Dov'è tua madre?*"

For an instant, Bria thought of hiding. It wouldn't be very good dog parenting to abandon Bravo, but he knew the layout of the village almost as well as the original architects and he could find his way back home without her. The only reason she didn't hide was because she was standing out in the open and there wasn't a tree, a car, or even a crowd that could serve as camouflage. Caught, the only thing she could do was join the group.

"*Ciao!*" Bria cried too enthusiastically. "What a lovely surprise."

"Bria," Valentina purred. "I could feel you lurking nearby."

"*Buongiorno,* Bria," Armando said. "Care to join us for a Finocchietto?"

"I'd love to!" Bria pulled an empty chair over to their table and squeezed in between them opposite where Bravo was now sprawled on the ground with his paw resting on top of Genie's. The dog hadn't pushed Bravo away, but she also wasn't showing any signs of enjoying his company, either. Valentina had taught Genie how to play hard to get very well. "But it's a bit early in the morning for me to drink anything other than coffee."

"You sound like Ombra," Armando sneered.

"The woman you're going to marry?" Bria asked not so innocently.

"If you haven't noticed, she can be a bit *una puritana,*" Armando shared.

"I don't consider not liking to drink before ten a.m. as the mark of a prude," Bria said, adding a chuckle so her comment didn't sound so judgmental. "Only on rare instances do I add some anisette to my coffee, though I do recall having a celebratory glass of limoncello with Giovanni when we realized Bella Bella had become a success."

"Is that the only thing you've shared with Vanni?" Valentina asked.

Bria smiled and hoped that Luca would understand that sometimes you had to act like a Roman. "We have swapped recipes and, of course, there's the occasional midnight snack."

"I take it back," Armando sneered. "You don't sound anything at all like Ombra."

"Speaking of Ombra," Bria said. "Where is she?"

"She's either with her mother or she ran off with her wedding planner." Armando took a long sip of his drink, and the fragrant smell of licorice filled the air. "Sometimes I think she's more interested in flowers than getting married."

"Every bride wants her wedding to be beautiful," Bria replied.

"The only thing Ombra wants is what her mother wants," Armando said. "Carlotta is calling all the shots even though my father's paying for the whole thing."

"Based on how she looked and performed last night, Carlotta has amazing style," Valentina shared. "I think it's a wise choice to let her spend your father's money to create a once-in-a-lifetime event."

Armando laughed and shrugged his shoulders. "I just didn't realize I was marrying two women." Armando took another sip, just as long, but slower. "Once we're married though, everything will change."

"What do you mean by that?" Bria asked.

His smile was almost sickening. "Rich boys always get what they want."

Armando downed his Finocchietto, placed it on the table, and smiled at both women. "*Addio,* Bria. Tina, it has been a pleasure. I'll take care of the bill on my way out. *Cin cin, bellas.*"

Bria watched him leave and when she turned around, she saw that Valentina was watching her. "Ask me?"

"Ask me what?" Bria replied.

"*Non fare til timida,*" Valentina said. "You're dying to know what we were talking about. It's written all over your face."

Bria waved her hand in front of her face. "I don't care at all what you two were talking about . . . here . . . in a public space."

"Bria Bartolucci! You are the worst liar who ever lived."

"I am not!" Bria examined Valentina from head to toe. "I absolutely hate your outfit."

Valentina looked down at her white sleeveless, wide lapeled blouse tied at her waist and her khaki pants cropped at the ankle that had a navy blue stripe down the side. "You do not; in fact, I bet you want to know where I got it."

Shaking her head and sighing heavily, Bria replied, "I do! It's really cute, all your clothes are."

"Some of us were born to lie, others were born to be nosy," Valentina said. "Go ahead, ask me."

"Aren't you going to tell me where you bought your outfit? I seriously want to know."

"Amina Rubinacci, the most delicious little boutique in Capri."

"*Grazie.*" Before Bria could formulate a question that had more to do with the real reason she wanted to speak with Valentina, the waiter appeared holding a piece of paper and wearing a sheepish expression.

"*Mi scusi,* signora," the waiter said. "Your companion neglected to pay the bill."

"That can't be right," Valentina protested. "He just said he'd take care of it."

"*Questo è vero, ma* he said he forgot his wallet at the hotel and said that the beautiful lady would pick up the tab."

Valentina's perfectly styled eyebrows rose and she looked at Bria. "He must have been talking about you."

"Me?!" Bria cried. "Valentina, when it comes to beauty you are in a class by yourself. Your only rival is Fabrice and according to my sister, he's no lady."

Chuckling, Valentina shrugged. "I have to agree with you, and it isn't vanity talking, just sheer fact." Valentina looked at the bill, pulled out some money from her pants pocket, and handed it to the waiter. "*Grazie.* Keep the change."

After the waiter left, Valentina's smiling demeanor changed. "He's a scam artist."

"The waiter?"

"No, Armando."

"Because he left you with the bill?"

"One of the reasons."

"I can't tell you how many times I've had to pay for Imperia's coffee. The rich don't often carry wallets," Bria shared. "They're used to people paying for them, getting things for free, or adding the charge to their monthly bill."

"True, but there's something about Armando that makes me think he's shady."

"Like the fact that he's having a pre-afternoon cocktail with a beautiful woman who just happens to *not* be his fiancée?" Bria suggested.

"Pre-afternoon cocktail?" Valentina pondered. "You should market that phrase, I think it would be a big hit especially in America, like a pre-owned car."

"Do you think it would be a big hit if Ombra found out you were spending time with Armando?"

Valentina leaned forward and rested her chin in the palm of her hands. "You seem awfully interested in Ombra."

"You seem awfully interested in Armando."

"Bria, I've told you this before, stop trying to hold people to your moral compass," Valentina said. "It isn't fair and, quite frankly, it's boring. No matter how beautiful you are—and yes, Bria, you are a very beautiful woman and you already know that so don't try and act embarrassed by the comment—no woman can afford to be boring. You don't want to wind up like Ombra and sit all alone in your little B and B waiting for Luca to return."

"I usually have guests at Bella Bella and I wouldn't describe it as little."

"Bria, I'm being serious!"

Reluctantly, Bria had to admit that there was a kernel of truth to what Valentina said. Not the part about Bella Bella, but that both partners needed to bring excitement, enthusiasm, and passion to their relationship for it to succeed. However, she didn't agree that Ombra was boring. On the contrary, Bria thought the woman to be very intriguing.

"I think you underestimate Ombra," Bria said.

"Honestly, I haven't given her much thought," Valentina replied. "I flirt with a very guilt-free conscience. I was walking Genie and saw Mando drinking by himself. He looked lonely so I said *ciao,* one thing led to another and soon he wasn't so alone."

"He calls you Tina and you call him Mando. Just how close have you two gotten?"

Valentina grinned. "There's the nosy Bria everybody talks about."

Bria rolled her eyes and tried to regain control of the conversation. "Why was Armando by himself?"

"I'm not sure, but he didn't look happy about it," Valentina replied.

"You didn't ask him why?"

"No, I did not."

"How could you not ask?"

"Because unlike you I'm not nosy. Some people mind their own business."

"I don't push myself into other people's business!"

"Haven't I already proven that you're a very bad liar? You love to get into people's business and find things out."

"Well, yes, that's true, but a man has been murdered not too far from here."

"Hold on a second," Valentina said. "Fiorello was murdered?"

Bria watched Valentina's face and zeroed in on her eyes. The woman was a self-described liar, but Bria felt she was reacting truthfully. She was surprised to hear that Fiorello had met with foul play.

"I thought he had a heart attack or a stroke," Valentina said.

"The medical examiner hasn't filed her full report yet, but we, I mean, I believe his death wasn't entirely natural."

"And you think Mando had something to do with it?"

"I didn't say that."

"You don't have to say anything, Bria, it's all in your eyes," Valentina said. "You have accusatory eyes. Has anyone ever told you that before?"

Startled, Bria had to think. "I don't believe so."

"Well, it's true; accusations are flaring out of your eyes like invisible lasers," Valentina said. "For what it's worth, however, I agree."

Bria was still thrown by Valentina's comment about her eyes that she wasn't sure what she was referring to. "You agree with what?"

"That Armando could have had something to do with Fiorello's murder."

"It hasn't yet been ruled a murder."

"If you say it was murder, I'm sure the medical examiner will back you up."

"We'll see what she has to say about it, but why do you think Armando is capable of something so horrible?"

"He's sexy, confident, rich, but he's got a darkness attached to him," Valentina shared. "I don't feel completely safe around him."

"You think he would hurt you?"

Valentina looked off into the distance behind Bria and remained silent for a few seconds. "Yes, I do. I've known men like him before and they can't be trusted. It's like they have a devil on their shoulder whispering in their ear to do certain things and they can only ignore them for so long until they follow their command."

"Valentina, that's frightening."

"I know, which is why I'm sharing it with you." Valentina placed her hand on top of Bria's and looked right into her eyes. "Be careful around him, Bria. You can be a very shrewd woman when you need to be, but your downfall is that at your core you're also a very good person."

"You consider being good a downfall?"

"You look for the light in people's eyes and sometimes all that's there is shadow." Valentina suddenly pulled her hand away, grabbed Genie's leash, and stood up. Genie followed suit, but added a stretch, a wiggle, and a slightly perturbed look when Bravo whimpered. "*Cin cin, Bria.*"

For several minutes, Bria didn't move after Valentina left. Her words had been too shocking. Bria didn't think Valentina had any proof to back up her claim, but Bria also knew Valentina was a woman who spoke the truth, which is why she sought her out.

Bria's cell phone pinged and alerted her to a group text from Fabrice. He and Lorenza were having an impromptu housewarming party at their condo in Rome later that night and invited Bria and Luca, Rosalie and Michele, and, a bit surprisingly—or was that fortuitously?—Armando and Ombra.

Despite Valentina's warning, Bria wasn't going to be able to avoid being in Armando's presence. Or the devil that refused to leave his side.

Chapter 12

The drive to Rome was not nearly as exhilarating a trip when riding as a passenger. Usually Bria drove herself in her 1970 Fiat Dino convertible, originally owned by her late father-in-law, Guillermo, inherited by his son, Carlo, and then willed to Bria. Of course, she loved the fact that it was a family heirloom, but more than that, it offered her freedom.

Growing up and all through college, Bria thought she'd graduate and explore the world. She got married and became a mother instead. Despite Carlo's immense wealth, which would have allowed them to travel anywhere around the globe, she and Carlo embraced domesticity and their inner homebody. When Marco was born the rest of the world ceased to matter because everything they needed and everything that was important could be carried in their arms.

For almost the past decade Bria's thirst for travel and adventure lay dormant. Recently, however, those desires had been awakened, and Bria relished the occasional joy ride to Rome or Naples. International travel and longer out-of-town jaunts had been put on hold as she got Bella Bella up and running, but now that the day-to-day operations for the bed-andbreakfast were largely under control thanks to Bria's hard work and determination and in large part due to Giovanni's extraordinary help, she'd have to give more thought to taking an actual vacation. For the moment she needed to forget how giddy she felt while maneuvering through the streets of Positano or handling the curves of Via E45 in her Fiat and get used to the much smoother and less exciting ride of Luca's Alfa Romeo Tonale.

Despite its sexy name, the Tonale was still a 4x4, more commonly known as an SUV and the epitome of American suburban life. It was safe, reliable, well-crafted, and the kind of car Bria probably would have bought if she didn't have the Fiat. It was also a much more realistic car than a mid-century convertible. The Tonale required little maintenance and it sat four comfortably, which was the only reason she was sitting in the passenger seat with Rosalie and Michele in the back while Luca drove. There was no way four people could ever fit in her Fiat two-seater.

Bria looked over at Luca and was once again taken by his beauty. He wasn't as stunningly gorgeous as Fabrice or as sexy as Giovanni, but Luca's long, straight Roman nose, olive complexion, cleft chin, and brown eyes gave him a classically handsome look. He possessed a masculinity that was by no means macho, but rather, grounded in confidence.

He wore a short-sleeved brown dress shirt, snug, but not obvious, and Bria admired the well-toned arm that gripped the steering wheel as he drove. She swooned a bit when she saw the gold bracelet dangling from his wrist, the one his father found and gave to his mother because he couldn't afford to buy an engagement ring. The fact that Luca had kept it, redesigned it by adding an emerald, and wore it frequently was another element of proof that he honored family. In Bria's mind—and more importantly—her heart there was nothing sexier than a family man.

Luca turned to Bria with a nervous look, the tiny crow's feet around his eyes not detracting, but enhancing, his good looks. "Are you sure they're going to like our gift?"

"Not at all," Bria replied. "But with only a few hours' notice, they can't expect much more than a model airplane kit and a bottle of homemade limoncello."

"I think they'll like the model plane more than the limoncello," Rosalie commented from the back seat. "Vanni let me try some and you still haven't figured out the secret ingredient."

"I know, we've tried so many variations and it still isn't quite right," Bria confirmed. "Is it drinkable?"

"They won't spit it out, but don't let them serve it tonight," Rosalie replied. "Tell them it's only good for special occasions."

"Isn't tonight a special occasion?" Michele asked.

Rosalie shook her head. "No, tonight's just for family and friends."

"Not quite," Bria interjected. "Fabrice also invited Armando and Ombra."

"Armando's his friend," Rosalie said.

"He can't be that good a friend, I've never heard Fabrice mention Armando's name before," Bria said.

"Maybe he wants to cheer the guy up," Michele suggested.

"Why does a man who's about to get married need cheering up?" Rosalie asked.

"Because he's about to get married less than a week after a family friend died under mysterious circumstances," Michele said. "Money can buy most everything, but not even a billionaire's son can bring Fio back from the dead."

The other bad thing about a luxury SUV was that the noise level was nonexistent. Even though they were driving at almost 130 kilometers and the air conditioning was on, when no one was speaking, an awkward silence hung in the air over their heads like a thick beam of steel that threatened to crush them. Michele didn't say anything that the other three passengers didn't already know. However, there was something about Michele's comment that was odd. Bria didn't think that he had been in Fiorello's or Armando's company other than meeting them briefly at the concert and, if she was being completely honest, she didn't think Michele was empathetic enough to consider how Fiorello's death would affect Armando. She was dying to sneak a glance at Luca to see if he was feeling the same way, but she didn't want to make an awkward situation more awkward. She would leave that to Rosalie.

"Right now everybody promise me something," Rosalie declared. "No one can mention anything about Fiorello, death, or murder all night long!"

In unison, Bria, Luca, and Michele replied, "I promise!"

Within fifty seconds of entering Fabrice and Lorenza's condo, Bria proved herself to be a liar. "How *is* Carlotta coping with Fiorello's death?"

It wasn't entirely her fault, however, because the first thing that Armando said when Bria greeted them was that he hadn't been sure they were going to make the party because Ombra wanted to stay home with her grief-stricken mother. Although his tone was far from sympathetic, Bria noticed the troubled look on Ombra's face and realized she was desperate for some compassion. If she wasn't going to get it from her fiancé, she might as well get it from the woman who wanted to learn all about her fiancé's past. Although Bria broke the promise she made in the car, Ombra seemed to welcome the question.

"Now that the shock is wearing off, the fact that Fiorello is truly gone is settling in." Ombra's voice was quiet and slightly shaky, nothing like the strong, acerbic tone she had used previously. Bria looked the women straight in the eye searching for a dent in her armor, an emotional Achilles heel, a clue to reveal Ombra's true motive or something that would explain why her attitude toward her mother changed quicker than she and Rosalie used to change outfits back in college.

Then again, Bria realized, a daughter having a perplexing relationship with her mother was hardly unique or suspicious. Bria's bond with her mother was exceptional. They bickered about silly, mundane things, but Bria had respected and trusted her mother implicitly from the time she was a young girl. Lorenza's relationship with Fifetta was more typical and consisted of loud arguments, constant disagreements, and an endless series of apologies. They loved each other unconditionally, but the demonstration of that love was often flawed.

Maybe that was the reality of Ombra's connection to Carlotta. Undying love desperately trying to breathe underneath a suffocating history of dysfunction. Either that or Ombra was a damn good liar.

"Fiorello and Carlotta were friends and friends aren't supposed to die and be taken away from us so suddenly," Bria shared.

Rosalie dipped a shrimp into cocktail sauce. "Is that the kind of party talk they teach at Grim Reaper school?"

"Fio wasn't Carlotta's friend," Armando said. "He was her employee, he worked for her, nothing more."

Ombra peered down at the floor, and although she addressed Armando she didn't look at him. "That isn't true and you know it."

"*Dio mio!* You can rewrite history all you want, but your mother treated Fio like a servant, not a companion." Armando's voice was not nearly as soft as Ombra's. "You weren't much nicer to him, either, but if it makes you feel better let's all raise a glass to Fiorello."

Slowly, one by one, everyone in the room followed Armando's example and raised their glasses. "To Fiorello!" Armando shouted. "May he tinkle the ivories whether he's floating on a cloud or if flames are licking at his heels."

"If one more person mentions death, dead, or dying, I will personally kill you myself!" Lorenza cried. "And as the sister to the chief of police's girlfriend I'll get away with it, too."

"That really isn't how law enforcement works, Renza," Bria shared.

"Is this my condo, Bria?" Renza asked.

"Yes, well, yours and Fabrice's."

"Then what I say goes!"

"Agree with her, Bria Bria," Fabrice said. "It makes life so much sweeter."

Once the conversation shifted from the corpse Bria found in the piazza to the condo Lorenza and Fabrice shared in one of the nicest sections of Rome, the evening started to resemble an actual dinner party and not an old episode of *The Law According to Lidia Poët*. Less crime talk, more coffee talk, but still a bit of tension in the air.

Bria hadn't been to the condo since Lorenza officially moved in, but she had visited several times during the past two years Fabrice had been living there. Fabrice didn't come from a wealthy family, but when his grandmother died while he was in high school, she left each of her grandchildren some money. Fabrice's sister, Ivetta, spent hers on a lavish wedding, which turned out to be a foolish decision since she got divorced two years later, while his cousins used their inheritance to open up a restaurant. Fabrice proved that he was as financially savvy as he was handsome. Against his father's advice, he invested most of the money into a fledgling company that created something called artificial intelligence. He quadrupled his investment in a few short years and if he didn't love being a pilot so much, he could probably live comfortably off his stock dividends.

Like most bachelors, Fabrice spent his money on a few frivolous items, such as alligator shoes that he never wore because they pinched his toes, a vintage Patek Philippe rose-gold Nautilus watch that Lorenza loved so much she made him buy her the women's version, and a Ducati Desmosedici RR motorbike that Lorenza hated so much she made him sell. She told him that she didn't want to be his widow before she became his wife.

Hands down the best financial investment Fabrice made with his money was buying the condo in the coveted Parioli section of Rome. Nestled in an elegant neighborhood near Villa

Borghese, one of Rome's largest parks, the condo was actually a town house and encompassed two floors over a private garage, a rarity in the city. It was filled with so many luxury details—like granite countertops in the kitchen, heated floors, a balcony with its own retractable awning—that Bria had lost count. Fabrice had hired an interior designer to decorate the condo in a mid-century modern meets Italian baroque style that, despite the obvious contradictions, worked. However, as Bria looked around, she saw concrete evidence that Lorenza had made Fabrice's bachelor pad their starter home.

Gone were the metallic blinds in the living room and in their place were olive-green velvet drapes that puddled on the floor and were the perfect color complement to the new navy blue velvet chesterfield couch. Bria recognized the end table as her grand-mère Chantal's vanity. The mirrored top with its gold boxed border and gold pedestal worked as perfectly in Lorenza's living room as it had in their grand-mère's bedroom.

Some bamboo wallpaper on one wall, family photos strewn about the rooms, and a large photograph that looked like something captured with a telescope pointing at the night sky but was actually a blow up of both their irises, filled up Fabrice and Lorenza's home. It was modern and stylish yet homey and comfortable at the same time, just like the two of them.

"Lorenza, I love what you've done to the place," Bria said. "*Squisita.*"

"*Grazie,* Bria," Lorenza replied. "I know it's an oversight, but how come you haven't said anything about my dress? I bought it just for tonight!"

Twirling in a circle, her Aperol spritz, dangerously close to spilling, Lorenza presented herself to the group making it no secret that she was waiting for applause and acclaim. She didn't have to wait long because the purple silk dress with long sheer organza sleeves and plunging neckline was indeed a crowd pleaser. For most of the crowd anyway.

As Bria told her sister how beautiful she looked, she noticed

Ombra self-consciously pulling at her own dress and smoothing wrinkles around her stomach. Her short-sleeved maroon A-line dress came down to just below her knees and could only be described as matronly. Ombra could be preparing for married life, Bria thought, but when you're marrying a man who could have a side hustle as a model and had a wandering eye, dressing in a matronly style was dumber than Ivetta's decision to blow most of her inheritance to celebrate a marriage that didn't have the legs to make it to the third wedding anniversary.

Domestic bliss had obviously taken hold of Lorenza because she was even more thrilled about Bria and Luca's housewarming gift than Fabrice. "How thoughtful!" Lorenza cried. "I can't wait until Fabrice is done putting the model together; we can put it on top of the étagère."

"You're not going to help me build it?" Fabrice asked.

Lorenza smiled at Fabrice and turned to the group. "Isn't he even prettier when he's silly?"

"*Scusi,* what's an étagère?" Michele asked.

"That thing over there." Armando pointed to the gold and glass tiered structure in the dining room. "It's a fancy bookshelf to hold overpriced knickknacks."

"I can confirm Bria didn't spend a lot of money on the model airplane," Luca joked.

"*Non preoccuparti,*" Lorenza said. "My sister will make it up for my birthday."

Armando raised his glass in Michele's direction. "Don't feel bad for not knowing what it was, rich people have their own vocabulary."

Bria and Rosalie immediately locked eyes. They were thinking the same thing. Defuse the situation before it got worse. Rosalie placed a hand on Michele's clenched fist but glared directly at Armando. "Are there dialects for rich people who've worked for their money and another for those who've been handed their fortunes on a silver platter?"

That type of antagonistic comment was not exactly what Bria was thinking. However, it did do the trick.

"Touché." Armando nodded his head in Rosalie's direction and then turned to Michele. "*Le mie scuse*, my reputation of being a jerk was not founded on false truths."

"I've read all about your past," Michele replied. "Especially the years you spent trying to play soccer."

The smile faded from Armando's face and he made no attempt to disguise the snarl that replaced it. "I did more than try, *mio amico,* I played successfully for five years."

The smile seemed to jump to Michele's face because he was grinning like a fox let loose in a free-range chicken coop. "Until you were barred from ever playing again."

"I was *disqualified!*" Armando yelled. "I wasn't barred!

"I've always said you got a bad rap, Mando." Fabrice didn't move from the deep green leather club chair he was sitting in, but he made sure that his voice, which normally resembled sweet honey, sounded like thunder. "I saw that game and you most certainly didn't hit that player; you bumped into each other."

"I saw it, too," Luca said. "Della Notto got a concussion and broke his wrist, but it was clearly an accident."

Bria watched Armando survey the room, his eyes moving from Fabrice to Luca to Michele, his fingers tightly wrapped around his glass. Next to him, Ombra continued to stare at the floor as if she was afraid to look at Armando because she knew what he was capable of. Bria remembered something her father said once while they watched a soccer game: If a man is capable of violence on the field, he's capable of violence at home. *Or in a piazza,* Bria thought.

"*Scusi,* I must have heard wrong," Michele said. "I'm just a mechanic and I'm not going to question the chief of police or a *capitano del Cielo.*"

"That was all a long time ago," Fabrice said. "Look at you now, Mando, second in command at Puccia Ventures."

"Your father must be very proud to have you working in the family business," Bria said.

"Then you don't know Papa very well," Armando scoffed. "Now he was the most violent player you could ever face on the field, and if you showed any sign of weakness, you'd become his target. Trust me, he wouldn't let up until he crushed you and you were begging for mercy."

"The rules were very different when your father played," Luca said. "There are guidelines in place to protect the players."

"Tell that to my father," Armando scoffed. "The world according to Pietro Puccia hasn't changed. He was ruthless as a soccer player, he's ruthless as a businessman, and he's even worse as a father."

The only sound that could be heard was of the twenty-year-old scotch being gulped down Armando's throat followed by the clink of his glass on the end table. Luckily, he was sitting on the other end of the couch, away from Grand-mère Chantal's end table; otherwise, he would've cracked the mirrored surface. However, he did place his drink down on the rosewood side table and not on the coaster. It was more than Lorenza could take.

"Basta!" Lorenza shouted. "I can handle snide remarks, arguments, and even the threat of physical violence in my home, but I draw the line at not using coasters!"

Lorenza picked up Armando's glass and placed it on the mustard-colored resin tile. "Glasses go on coasters, *capisci*?"

"*Capisco,*" Armando replied sheepishly.

"*Bene!*" Lorenza cried. "Now let's eat."

Had Bria not known her sister so well she would have believed she cooked the entire meal herself. But the last time Lorenza cooked anything was when their parents went away to Sicily for a week to attend their *grande zia* Mathilda's funeral and she nearly burned the house down trying to make fried meatballs to impress Salvatore Fortunato, who lived down the block. Turned out that Salvatore was a vegetarian, so they almost lost their house for no reason at all. Whether it was homemade or catered, the dinner was scrumptious.

Fresh arugula salad with chunks of mozzarella and tomato in a balsamic glaze, burrata wrapped in prosciutto, chicken parmigiana with rigatoni, steamed spinach, and stuffed mushrooms. By the time the main course was served, the argument earlier in the evening was ancient history. The conversation consisted of nothing but friendly chatter and making plans.

"There's a charity soccer game in Amalfi this week," Armando said. "But none of these guys can go with me."

"I'll go with you," Ombra said.

"You don't like soccer." Armando waved a forkful of chicken in Ombra's direction. "And you ask too many questions during the game."

Bria heard Ombra mumble something, but she couldn't quite make out what it was. She could see the hurt in the woman's eyes and wanted to say something to ease her pain but couldn't think of anything with Armando sitting at the table. Instead, she tried to make light of the situation.

"Luca, didn't I hear you and Marco talking about a charity game?" Bria asked.

"Yes, I thought I could get off work, but we're a bit short-staffed."

"Maybe I can take Marco?" Armando suggested.

Bria forced herself to maintain her expression and not give way to the concern she was feeling. She didn't know Armando very well and the little she knew about him made her question his chaperoning skills. She wasn't sure she wanted to let her son be in his company, but she couldn't admit that to his face at her sister's dinner party.

"Let me know when," Bria said, shoving some spinach in her mouth. "It's nearing the end of the school year and he has to study for final exams."

"Make sure he studies hard," Michele said. "Not everyone inherits a lot of money when they get older."

Before Armando could respond, Rosalie did. "Some of us inherit rocks."

"Rosalie, what are you talking about?" Fabrice asked. "Did someone die and leave you a pile of rocks?"

"Yes, Fabrice, that's exactly what happened!" Rosalie cried. "*Zio* Nazario died and left Luca a ski chalet and left me a bunch of rocks."

"When are we going skiing, Luca?" Fabrice asked.

"The deed hasn't even transferred over to me yet," Luca said. "Plus, it's May."

"The weather is fickle these days," Fabrice said. "You never know when there will be snow. We'll talk about it on Tuesday."

"What's happening on Tuesday?" Lorenza asked.

Fabrice's million-watt smile added another million to it. "Nothing."

"Then tell me," Lorenza demanded.

"Renza," Bria chided. "The secret to a successful relationship is to allow your partner to have a few secrets."

"Did he really leave you rocks?" Ombra asked. "That sounds like a cruel joke."

"They're not rocks," Luca corrected. "They're possibly fossils, from the Pompeii of the North."

"Really?" Ombra said.

"Don't act like you know what Luca's talking about," Armando said.

"If they're from that area, they could be historical and worth something," Ombra explained. "Believe me, there's a market for everything."

"Maybe your uncle left you a fortune," Michele suggested.

"He left me rocks!" Rosalie shouted. "What don't you people understand?"

While the rest of the group laughed, Ombra jumped up, covered her mouth with her hand, and ran to the bathroom.

"I think Ombra just remembered she's lactose intolerant." Armando laughed.

Lorenza rose and locked eyes with Bria. "Would you come with me to check on dessert?"

Bria wanted to finish her meal, but when Lorenza's eyes bugged out and she tilted her head a few times toward the bathroom, she knew she couldn't argue.

"*Certo,*" Bria said.

When they were outside the bathroom door and not visible by the rest of the party, Lorenza pressed her head against the door and then pushed Bria's head so she was in the same position. Without words and through a series of facial expressions, Bria asked Lorenza why they were outside the bathroom door and not in the kitchen. Lorenza told Bria to listen, and when she did, she heard the unmistakable sounds of vomiting.

Lorenza pulled Bria away from the door and whispered in Bria's ear. "Do you know what this means?"

"You went a little heavy on the cheese."

"No, didn't you notice Ombra wasn't drinking alcohol, but cranberry and club soda, and she was fidgeting with her dress so it wouldn't cling to her stomach."

Slowly, the truth started to creep into Bria's mind. "Yes, I did notice that, but I didn't connect them."

"So much for being a super sleuth!"

"*Dammi una pausa!* I have never called myself a super sleuth!"

"Because you're not!"

"How dare you say that!"

"*È vero!* I'm the one who put together these clues. Now that she's throwing up in my very expensive Ceramica Cielo toilet bowl it all adds to one thing."

"Ombra's pregnant," Bria whispered.

"But I'm the one who figured it out!"

"I bet you haven't figured out the final piece of this little puzzle."

Lorenza glowered at her sister. "What final piece?"

"Ombra might be pregnant," Bria said, "but she hasn't told Armando yet."

Chapter 13

Bria woke up with a headache. She lay in bed and looked at the ceiling. The cool breeze wafting in from the open window felt like a tornado and Rosso's chirping that was usually soothing and welcomed, sounded like a jackhammer. The day was not getting off to a good start.

She still hadn't come up with one good reason why anyone would want to kill Fiorello, and now she had discovered that Ombra was possibly pregnant and most likely concealing it from her fiancé. She also didn't know if the pregnancy had anything to do with Fiorello's murder. Or was that Armando's attempted murder if the killer had been trying to kill Armando and accidentally killed Fiorello instead? It was no wonder why Bria's head hurt.

There was no way she was going to solve both problems at the same time, which meant Bria needed to focus. She would deal with Ombra later; for now she needed to concentrate on why Fio had been killed and who had committed the murder. But first she had to get out of bed.

All the while making breakfast, taking reservations, washing bed linens, and paying bills online, Bria never once stopped thinking about Fiorello. Even though she didn't have definitive proof, she was convinced Fio didn't die of natural causes.

Looks could always be deceiving, but he had appeared to be in the picture of good health. Until, of course, he was found lying motionless in the piazza wearing another man's jacket, one glove, and sporting odd scratches on his wrists. The evidence was hardly conclusive, but Bria was convinced he had died from unnatural causes.

But if he was murdered, who did the deed? Fiorello was Carlotta's friend and confidant and seemed to be nothing more than an acquaintance to Ombra and Armando, which meant that on the surface none of them had a motive to kill. While a handful of people in the village hated Carlotta, no one had expressed a bad word—or a good one, for that matter—about Fiorello before his arrival. Come to think of it, few people had much to say about Fiorello after he died, either. It was like he was an invisible man.

There was also the possibility that Fiorello had not been the intended target and he was mistakenly killed because he was wearing Armando's jacket and someone wanted to end Armando's life. That was the much more plausible scenario. From everything Bria knew, had heard, and had witnessed firsthand, Armando was a first-class *sobbalzo*.

He had a violent and notorious past when he was a soccer player and must have acquired more than one enemy, he had a contemptuous relationship with his father, and he treated Ombra dismissively, as if she were a low-level employee instead of his fiancée. Even though it was dark in the piazza the night Fiorello was killed, was it plausible to think that Armando's fiancée, father, or even his future mother-in-law—who clearly tried to control Ombra's life—would mistake Fio for Armando and kill the wrong man? To commit a crime of passion, one must be in a passionate state, so it's feasible to think that whoever killed Fio was in such an emotional frenzy they simply assumed they were killing the right man.

Or was Lorenza actually right? Did Bria really consider herself to be a super sleuth? And more to the point, did Bria enjoy being considered a super sleuth even when there was no crime to sleuth?

It was true that Bria had solved some murders in the past. Aldo Bombalino, in fact, had put Bria on the front page of his newspaper a few times making her a bit of a celebrity in the village. Some even referred to her as *La Regina di Positano.* Had all the praise and accolades gone to her head? Did she really think she was some kind of queen? She was a mother, an entrepreneur, and now a girlfriend. Wasn't that enough? Did she need to add *super sleuth* to the list of adjectives that could be used to describe her?

After she finished making the bed in one of the guest rooms she sat down and looked out the window. She could just make out the sea behind a cluster of leaves from a low-hanging branch. Maybe after all the years of being nothing more than a wife and a mother, Bria was making up for lost time and making things up to make her life more exciting. Maybe she needed to stop talking to herself and go to the one person who would tell her the truth.

"Rosalie! Am I *pazza*?"

A seagull flew by and let out a loud cry. Bria ignored the gull and leaned back against the railing of the boat, waiting for her friend to answer.

"I need a little more context before I answer that question."

"Last night Lorenza accused me of being vain and thinking I'm a super sleuth."

"You are."

"That's not the point! But *grazie.*"

"*Prego.*"

"Am I letting my imagination go wild in thinking that Fiorello was murdered just because I want to solve another mystery?"

Sprawled out in one of the deck chairs, Rosalie took a long sip of espresso and closed her eyes. She was either attempting to go back to sleep or contemplating Bria's question. Despite the early hour and the fact that she had arrived unannounced, Bria didn't have time for Rosalie to search for the right answer. She had come to her best friend because she wanted to hear the unvarnished truth, not have her evade the question.

"Answer me!" Bria cried.

Rosalie didn't respond, but a seagull let out an obnoxious cry and swooped perilously close to Bria's head.

"*Uffa!*"

Swiping at the now-empty air, Bria screamed at the attacking seagull, lost her balance, and lunged forward. She tried to grab onto the railing but instead grabbed onto Rosalie's leg. Startled, Rosalie flung her hands into the air, managing to keep hold of the espresso cup, but its contents escaped, showering them both. Luckily, the espresso had cooled so they were stained, not scalded.

Sitting on the deck, Bria looked up at Rosalie and wasn't sure if she wanted to laugh or cry. It was times like these when a best friend proved their mettle.

"I think we need some fresh air to clear our minds."

Fifteen minutes later, *La Vie en Rosalie* was cruising east on the Tyrhhenian Sea. Rosalie was at the wheel and Bria was sitting next to her. Words, for the moment, were unnecessary, as both women sensed they each craved silence. Despite Bria's insistence for an answer to her question, it was sometimes essential to savor your surroundings, especially when they were as breathtaking as the view from the boat.

With the sun rising behind her, warmth glowing on her back and neck, Bria looked at Positano's unusual landscape. What a marvel. A jagged, forbidding landscape had somehow been turned into a cluster of inviting, sun-drenched homes and businesses. Bella Bella was now part of that landscape and it was the place Bria called home. But it was merely a setting; Bria turned to her left to face Rosalie and saw where her real home lay.

"Our lives are changing, aren't they?"

Rosalie didn't answer right away, she kept her focus straight ahead on the crystal-blue sea and the mass of land in the distance, the island of Capri. "Yes, but in different ways."

"What do you mean?"

"Your life is moving forward and I'm retreating."

"That isn't true." The second the words came out of Bria's mouth she knew they were false. Here she was, barging into her best friend's life, demanding honesty, and all she had to offer was thoughtlessness. "*Scusi*, you're right."

"Why do I keep making the same mistakes over and over again?"

Rosalie didn't need to be specific; Bria knew that she was talking about Michele. He was sexy and mysterious and exactly the type of man Rosalie typically fell for, but he wasn't the type of man that Rosalie needed in her life. She needed someone who was more like Luca—grounded, emotionally available, and respectful. As open-minded as Bria had tried to be about Michele, she knew that he was none of those things. It appeared that Rosalie had finally come to the same realization.

"I don't think you've made a mistake," Bria said. "You went into this relationship with your eyes open, you've seen the kind of man Michele is, and you know that he isn't worthy of your love. I consider that to be tremendous growth and hardly a mistake."

"After we came home from the party last night, Michele wanted to stay, but I told him I had to get up early this morning for a job," Rosalie confessed. "I think he knew I was lying, but he didn't challenge me."

"Maybe Michele has come to the same conclusion," Bria suggested.

"I think we both wanted this relationship to change our lives," Rosalie said. "Guess we both failed."

"Basta!" Bria got up and stood next to Rosalie. "You listen to me, Rosalie Serafina Augustina Vivaldi! You are not a loser! You are the most courageous, smart, exuberant woman I know, and just because you started dating a man who *you* have determined is not worthy of dating does not mean you failed. It means that you're taking control of your life and not taking the back seat. I will not allow you to second-guess yourself over some mechanic, no matter how sexy he looks in his dirty jeans and his unwashed hair!"

Fighting back tears, Rosalie couldn't contain her emotions and she wrapped her arms around Bria. "*Grazie, mia amica.*"

"*Ti amo tanto,*" Bria whispered, her voice gruff with her own tears.

"*Anche io,*" Rosalie replied, sounding the same.

After a few moments, Bria pulled away and started to wipe away her tears. "But seriously, how does Michele look so good when he hardly washes his hair? I skip a day and I look like *un mostro!*"

"It's because he's a man!" Rosalie spat. "They can be unshaven, unkempt, and unwashed, and they still look good! We women have to primp, diet, plaster our faces in make-up, dye our hair, straighten our hair, exercise so we don't jiggle and flounce, and still have to worry about how we look. It isn't fair! And worse, we women have allowed it to happen since time began. It doesn't make sense!"

Bria was listening to Rosalie's tirade, but she was more interested in what she saw in the water up ahead. She picked up the binoculars from the steering wheel console and held them up to her face so she could see better. "*Uffa!* You know what else doesn't make sense?"

"What?"

"Why is Carlotta in that little boat with that strange man?"

"Isn't she supposed to be grieving her piano player's murder?"

"You really do think Fio was murdered too?"

"Of course I do!" Rosalie cried. "I also wish I knew why Carlotta is in a boat with a very handsome man."

"The strange man is very handsome?"

Bria handed the binoculars to Rosalie. "Judge for yourself."

"*Mucca sacra!* That is a very distinguished and well-preserved older gentleman."

"I swear to God, the mother is as baffling as the daughter," Bria exclaimed. "I thought I understood Carlotta, but obviously I don't, and as for Ombra, she's a complete riddle to me. *Oh Dio mio!* I almost forgot to tell you, Ombra's pregnant, but Armando doesn't know yet."

"Bria Nicolette Faustina D'Abruzzo Bartolucci Vivaldi!"

"I'm not a Vivaldi!"

"Give it time," Rosalie quipped. "You're just now getting around to telling me about Ombra being pregnant."

"I couldn't tell you on the drive home; Luca and Michele were in the car, and I wasn't the one who figured it out actually. Lorenza was."

"Maybe super sleuthing is in your family DNA."

"No, my sister is usually oblivious to anything other than what she sees in the mirror," Bria said. "She was just annoyed because Ombra drank club soda and threw up in her fancy new toilet."

"She threw up? That dinner was delicious."

"It's because she's pregnant."

"If I ever get pregnant, Bria, I'm telling you right now, I will never throw up a good meal."

"Morning sickness doesn't discriminate by menu," Bria shared. "If it's gonna come up, it's gonna come up whether it's fast food or catered by Le Sirenuse. Now could we stop talking about grotesque bodily functions and focus on the opera diva in the boat up ahead?"

"*Bene.* You're the one who brought up barfing."

Bria looked through the binoculars and just ahead of the boat containing Carlotta and the man, was a cave. It wasn't an ordinary cave, but one that emitted an eerie blue glow. Bria looked at her watch and saw that it was ninety minutes since they left the marina. Had they really been traveling for that long? Knowing how quickly time flew when she and Rosalie started chatting, Bria realized they could be at the shores of Egypt instead of Capri.

"They're headed to the Blue Grotto."

"They don't open up until nine a.m."

"It's nine-fifteen!"

"*Seriamente?*" Rosalie questioned. "I really need to pay attention more when I'm at the wheel."

"Pay attention to what's in front of us," Bria advised. "Can you steer us into the grotto?"

"No, my boat's too big and they only allow canoes."

"We have to get closer to Carlotta and her mystery man to find out what's going on."

"Give me those!" Rosalie grabbed the binoculars from Bria and put them up to her face. "It is him!"

"You know the man Carlotta's with?"

"No, I know the man steering the boat next to her," Rosalie said. "Biaggi owes me a favor."

"Who's Biaggi?"

"One of the skippers who steers the canoes. I once helped him smuggle contraband to Malta. I bet he can get us into the grotto."

"What kind of contraband?"

"I can tell you, but then I'd have to kill you and you'll never find out who Carlotta's with."

Rosalie took a deep breath and Bria knew that her friend was going to show off her vocal skills by shouting the man's name. She would, no doubt, attract his attention, but she'd also attract Carlotta's attention, which would ruin any chance of

Bria finding out why she was in a canoe with a man without Carlotta knowing it. There had to be another way.

"Don't!" Bria clasped her hand over Rosalie's mouth just as Rosalie was about to shout Biaggi's name. "Carlotta will hear you."

"*Scusi,* I didn't think of that."

"Do you have Biaggi's phone number?"

"Brilliant idea! You throw the anchor over and I'll call him on his cell."

Bria ran toward the stern of the boat, opened the hatch that concealed the anchor, lifted it, and threw it over the side. By the time she returned to the bow, Rosalie had set their plan in motion. "*Grazie,* Biaggi, *grazie mille!*" Rosalie pressed a button on the phone and ended the call. "Get ready to jump overboard because he's coming to pick us up."

"What do you mean 'jump overboard'?"

"The canoe doesn't have a motor: we have to swim out to him and meet him halfway if we have any chance of getting close to Carlotta and her dreamy companion."

"I don't know if I would say he's dreamy."

"You can say he's dreamy, I won't tell Luca."

"Okay, *bene,* he really is dreamy, but Rosa, I didn't dress for swimming. Do you have an extra suit I can wear?"

"We don't have time for a costume change! He's getting really close to the entrance of the grotto," Rosalie said. "Jump and swim as fast as you can to Biaggi."

"The one waving in our direction?"

"That's him. He isn't as dreamy as Carlotta's fella, but beggars can't be choosers," Rosalie said. "Now jump."

Bria opened her mouth to protest, but didn't get a word out because Rosalie pushed her into the water. Just as Bria popped back up and broke the surface, Rosalie dove in. Although she didn't have a swimmer's body, Rosalie was a trained lifeguard and had spent years perfecting and honing her technique. Bria was a natural athlete, but had not inherited her mother's champion swimming talent, nor had she worked on improving her own skills like Rosalie had. By the time she made it to the side of the boat, Rosalie was already sitting inside, patting her face with a towel and chatting with the two other passengers. Biaggi, though wiry and short, was able to lift Bria into the boat with only one hand.

"*Benvenuta,* Bria," Biaggi said. "*Uffa!* You weigh more than you look."

Bria wasn't sure if she was more upset that someone had accused her of being overweight or that someone had stolen her signature catchphrase. She was about to dispute Biaggi's comment when she heard Carlotta's melodic, but loud, laughter fill the air like a spray of water from a dolphin's snout. Personal defense would have to wait; Bria needed to find out what Carlotta was up to.

"*Grazie,* Biaggi," Bria said. "But could you manage to get us closer to that boat over there?"

"Lucky for you, I'm stronger than I look," Biaggi replied, dipping an oar into the water. "Hold on."

Biaggi wasn't lying. Somehow the small-framed man maneuvered the canoe so quickly and expertly that when they entered the grotto, they were only one boat behind Carlotta's. Bria couldn't hear anything they said, but she could clearly see them.

As instructed, Bria, Rosalie, as well as Pablo and Riccardo, the Brazilian honeymooners whose tour they hijacked, lay back in the canoe so they could see the full effects of the grotto. Early morning wasn't the best time of day to visit the tourist site because the sun's position between noon and two p.m. was when the blue light inside the grotto was illuminated to showcase its shimmering beauty the best. Even still, Bria found herself distracted from her mission by the glistening blue waters and the iridescence of the cave itself. It was as if the rest of the world ceased to exist and they had magically ventured into a

Monet painting without the water lilies. The air was crisp, the sounds were distorted, and everything was saturated with a soft blue light. Lying back, Bria felt her eyes closing and her thoughts wandering to Luca and how she wished he was next to her. Those thoughts were ripped away when Rosalie elbowed her in the ribs.

"Pay attention."

"To what?"

"To that!"

Rosalie pointed at the canoe in front of them and Bria saw the man hand Carlotta a thick, white envelope. Carlotta clutched it greedily, but before the man let go of it, he leaned over, whispered something in her ear, and kissed her cheek. Even though their lips didn't meet, the kiss was not platonic. The man's lips pressed into Carlotta's flesh and lingered there for a few moments. The only reason he broke their embrace was because a wave suddenly rippled through the cave, causing the canoe to lift, drop, and tilt.

Just as Bria's canoe rose and rocked to the side, she saw something fly out of the envelope. Whatever it was caused the man to laugh hysterically, but Bria couldn't see the source of the laughter because she was thrown back in the canoe, her head hitting the gunwale on the starboard side. She shook her head and inched up in the canoe just in time to see Carlotta's boat exit the cave into the sea.

Bria sat up rubbing the back of her head and noticed something floating in the water. The rest of the sea was devoid of any pollution so Bria was certain whatever was floating had come from the envelope the man had passed to Carlotta. She leaned over the canoe and scooped it up in her hand. When she saw what it was, she realized Carlotta's mystery man wasn't just handsome, he was also rich.

Only a wealthy man could afford to laugh about losing a 500 euro note before the day had even begun.

Chapter 14

On the boat ride back to the marina, Bria and Rosalie spent the entire time trying to figure out why Carlotta had been riding in a canoe through the Blue Grotto with a handsome, wealthy stranger acting as if she didn't have a care in the world, when the last time Bria saw her the opera singer was literally prostrate with grief. What had happened to make Carlotta change so drastically? Could it have something to do with Fiorello's death? Whatever the cause, Bria was determined not to let her imagination take over; she was going to uncover facts.

By the time Rosalie anchored her boat in the dock, their hair and clothes had dried from their impromptu dip in the Tyrrhenian, but both women looked like they had had a rough morning. Even being a bit disheveled, however, couldn't dampen their spirits. On the contrary, the morning swim reenergized them both as women and friends.

"This morning proves it," Bria said.

"Proves what?"

"That I can't live without you."

Tears welled up in Rosalie's eyes, but because she never hid her emotions from Bria she didn't turn away. Her voice was gruff, but she managed to speak. "Neither can I."

"Even when I don't realize how much I need you, somehow I'm drawn to you," Bria said.

"We have Alphonso Del Trente to thank for that."

"*Uffa!* I haven't thought of him for decades!"

"Since we were kids when we both had a crush on him, but he was more interested in playing soccer with the boys," Rosalie remembered. "We realized we liked each other much more than we liked Alphonso."

"We were very smart little ladies, weren't we?"

"And wise," Rosalie added. "I heard that Alphonso just got out of jail after serving time for tax evasion and consumer fraud."

"Alphonso went to jail?

"For seven years, but he got out early for good behavior, so he can't be all bad."

"How did you find out about this? I lost track of him decades ago."

"Annamaria told me."

"Annamaria Antonelli knows that our school girl crush grew up to be a criminal?"

"They prefer being called an ex-con."

"*Abbastanza!* How does Annamaria know?"

"Alphonso is Annamaria's second cousin's first husband. He divorced Liliana when he got carted off to prison, but since his release he's gotten remarried to a lovely dietician named Donata."

"Sounds like he's had quite a life," Bria said. "I'm glad he's happy."

"Gives us all hope that we'll find that perfect someone someday."

Bria gripped Rosalie's shoulders and looked her in the eye. "Yes, we will." She hugged her friend tightly and then pulled away. "I need to go freshen up and then pay your brother a visit. He's the perfect someone to help me uncover the truth about Carlotta's early morning rendezvous."

Surprisingly, Bria did not get as warm a reception at the police station as she normally did.

Even before she was the chief of police's girlfriend, because of her relationship with Rosalie and, most important, her involvement in recent police investigations, the force had adopted her as a civilian liaison of sorts. She had no official rank, but she was acknowledged as a member of their team. The way Nunzi was eyeing her, it appeared that Bria's membership had been revoked.

"What are you doing here?" Nunzi must have recognized that she had barked her question, because she rephrased it, ran a finger through her bangs, and softened her tone. "I mean, *ciao,* Bria, what can I do for you?"

"*Ciao,* Nunzi, is Luca in?"

"No, he's out working on a case."

Nunzi dropped her head and started to shuffle some papers on her desk. Matteo walked over to them and plopped a file on top of her papers, startling both women. "Nunz, when the chief is out of his top-secret meeting in there, give that to him, he's expecting it."

"I thought you said Luca wasn't in?" Bria asked.

Nunzi still didn't look up from her papers. "He is, but he isn't."

"Annunziata," Bria said, in a tone that was usually reserved to chastise Marco. "What's going on?"

"*Niente,*" Nunzi replied.

"It's obviously something and if you won't tell me what's so top secret, I'll just ask Luca."

"Bria, please don't go in there!"

In retrospect, Nunzi's plea shouldn't have been ignored, but Bria had no idea of knowing that when she gripped the doorknob, twisted it to the right, and pushed her way into Luca's office. When she saw who was inside, she wished she had heeded Nunzi's advice because instinctively Bria knew it was only going to lead to heartache. She felt as if she had been punched in the stomach because she couldn't comprehend why Luca would be in a top secret meeting with Imperia and the man who had been riding in a canoe with Carlotta and handing her an envelope filled with money. All she knew was that the reason for this closed-door meeting had something to do with her. She knew that just by looking into Luca's eyes.

"Bria," Luca said. "What are you doing here?"

"Clearly, I'm interrupting."

"*Senza senso.*" Imperia remained composed, her face not giving away her emotions. But Bria noticed that her manicured nails, polished fire-engine red, were tap dancing against her thigh like Ombra had been doing when she was nervous. "We were just leaving."

Bria turned to the silver-haired gentleman sitting in the brown leather club chair across from Luca's desk and didn't think he looked at all like a man who was preparing to leave. He was leaning back, legs crossed, hands resting on the arms of the chair, smiling at Bria—no, more like surveying her. She wondered if he had caught a glimpse of her at the Blue Grotto, but she didn't think that was possible. It was quickly apparent that he wasn't examining her because he remembered her, he was staring at her because he wanted to get to know her much better. The man made her skin crawl, but she needed to find out who he was.

"*Ciao*, I'm Bria Bartolucci. I don't think I caught your name."

"Unless you're psychic you wouldn't have because I didn't mention it." The man's stare turned into a broad self-satisfied smile. "Because you're so beautiful I won't hold it against you."

The man stood up, and although he was only a few inches

taller than Bria, five foot nine at the most, he was powerfully built. He extended his hand, and when Bria took it in hers, she was surprised by how smooth it was. She had expected it to be rough and callused, the result of years of manual labor. It was the first of many surprises.

"Allow me to introduce myself formally," the man said. "I'm Pietro Puccia."

Time stood still for a few seconds as Bria digested this unexpected nugget of information. The man who had been going for a joyride with Carlotta, the man having a secret meeting with her boyfriend and mother-in-law, was the father of the man Carlotta's daughter was going to marry. Despite her ability to conjure up wild ideas, Bria was not so gullible to think that every coincidence had a deeper meaning or that it was a clue to a larger conspiracy theory. This coincidence, however, was too odd and too specific.

"Pietro!" Bria cried. "I've heard so much about you."

Pietro placed his left hand over their handshake and smiled mischievously. "I hope it wasn't all good."

"Not all of it. I can ensure you." Bria placed her left hand on top of Pietro's and as inconspicuously as possible extricated herself from Pietro's grip. She didn't like the feel of the man's skin on hers. And she didn't like the way Luca's eyes were staring at her. It was a strange mixture of fear and, what was it, pity?

"I thought you were in Lake Como preparing for the wedding," Bria said as casually as possible.

"I was," Pietro replied. "But you can't keep a good billionaire pinned down to one place for too long."

"Especially when that billionaire isn't all good."

Bria put on a show of laughing heartily at her own joke, and as she had expected Luca and Imperia didn't join in, they merely smiled politely. Pietro, on the other hand, was laughing louder than Bria. She realized it was because they all knew what

Bria had said was the truth. Pietro might not be a bad man, but he most certainly wasn't a good one.

"When Pietro heard about Fiorello, he wanted to come and personally extend his condolences to the family," Luca said.

"Fiorello's family is here?" Bria asked.

"No, I mean Carlotta and Ombra," Luca corrected.

"And of course to see Armando," Bria added.

Pietro's smile and any hint of laughter disappeared. "Why would I come see Armando?"

Startled, Bria wasn't sure how to respond, except to state the obvious. "He's your son."

"A son should go to see his father, not the other way around," Pietro declared. "*Prego Dio* that Ombra will be able to turn my son into the kind of man a father can be proud of and not the embarrassment that he is. I don't know if Armando is worthy of such a good girl like Ombra, but if her *innocenza* can't transform my son, nothing can."

Bria was speechless and couldn't find the words to respond. She desperately wanted to turn and see how Luca and Imperia were reacting to Pietro's words, but there was something so captivating about the man that she couldn't look away. Bria inhaled deeply in an attempt to regain her composure and break the hold Pietro had on her. She needed to be back in control if she wanted to get some answers.

"Have you seen Carlotta yet?" Bria asked.

"No, I needed to finish up some business with Imperia first," Pietro replied.

Bria turned to face Imperia, and before she could ask her what kind of business she had with the billionaire that she hadn't previously mentioned, Imperia announced "Bartolucci Enterprises and Puccia Ventures are partnering on a new endeavor."

"*Giusto!*" Pietro cried. "What was the name of it again? Sometimes my mind doesn't work as well as my body."

Bria noticed that Imperia looked as surprised by this announcement as she did. "Bartolucci Enterprises is partnering with Puccia Ventures to establish a scholarship in Carlo's name."

Stunned, Bria looked around the room and couldn't believe what she was hearing. She thought it was a lovely idea, but for some reason she felt it wasn't the truth. "Why didn't you say something to me before, Imperia?"

"If you remember, I told Sister Benedicta that I wanted her help with getting Mother Superior on board with an idea that I had," Imperia explained. "This is the idea. To offer educational scholarships to children in southern Italy."

"I think Carlo would absolutely love having his name attached to such a worthwhile endeavor." Bria reached out to hold Imperia's hand. "*Grazie.*"

Imperia's only response was a nod of her head and a quick smile.

"When Imperia suggested our companies join forces on this mission, I immediately agreed," Pietro stated. "Imperia, let me take you to lunch and we can talk more about this exciting new chapter in both our lives."

"I would love that."

Despite her positive response, Imperia didn't look happy to take Pietro's arm and leave Luca's office. Luca didn't look very happy to be left alone with Bria, either. When the door closed after Imperia and Pietro left, Luca looked like he was locked in a room with no exit.

"For the record, I didn't believe that was the real reason they were in your office," Bria stated. "Do you mind telling me the truth?"

There was that look in Luca's eyes again. "Remember what you said last night to Lorenza at the party?"

"I said a lot of things to my sister; you'll need to be more specific."

"That the secret to a successful relationship is to allow your partner to have a few secrets of their own."

Bria thought back to the previous night and realized she had, indeed, spoken those words to Lorenza. "Using my own words against me, are you?"

"I know that I share a lot of police details with you, but there are certain aspects of my job that I can't discuss with anyone, including the woman I'm in love with."

Bria's eyes searched left, then right. "That woman is me, *corretto*?"

Luca didn't answer verbally; he grabbed the sides of Bria's neck and kissed her deeply. It was the kind of kiss that would have led to many others had they been in a bedroom, a shower, or even a restaurant, instead of an office. It was also the kind of kiss that made Bria forget why she had come to Luca's office in the first place.

"I think you'll be much more interested in the results of the medical examiner's preliminary report," Luca said. "Which I can share with you."

"What does it say?"

"I'm not releasing the information to the public, but Fiorello did die from strangulation and not from a heart attack or blunt trauma from the fall."

"*Dio mio,* he was murdered."

"Yes, he was," Luca confirmed. "She thinks that the scratches on his wrists came from an altercation he had with someone either during the strangulation or right before, as they were fresh wounds."

"That must have been some fight."

"Fio put up a struggle, but piano wire is sharp and very hard to pull off your neck," Luca said. "There were faint scars around his neck and a definite bluish tint to the skin in the back where the wires would have crossed. Carlotta—the examiner, not the opera singer—wanted me to thank you for tipping her off about the possibility that he was strangled with piano wire, otherwise it could have gone unnoticed."

"Carlotta!" Bria exclaimed. "That reminds me of why I came here in the first place."

"You have news about Carlotta?"

"And Pietro."

"*Per favore,* speak in full sentences."

"Rosalie and I saw Carlotta and Pietro this morning on a canoe at the Blue Grotto."

"What were you and my sister doing at the Blue Grotto?"

Bria waved a hand in front of her face. "That doesn't matter. What matters is that we saw Pietro give Carlotta an envelope filled with money."

"Are you sure?"

"One of the bills flew out of the envelope and fell into the water. I picked it up with my own hands." Bria reached into the pocket of her jeans and pulled out the 500 euro note she rescued from the sea and handed it to Luca. "Is that enough proof for you?"

Luca took the money and stared at it for a moment. Bria could tell that his mind was racing, trying to come up with an answer to explain how Pietro's money had wound up in Bria's hands. And why he'd be giving money to Carlotta in the first place.

"Didn't you say that Pietro was paying for the wedding?" Luca asked.

"That's what I was told."

"Maybe Pietro was reimbursing Carlotta for something she had paid for, or he gave her money so she could buy something."

Bria tilted her head, letting her expression speak for itself.

"I know," Luca replied. "That's a stupid idea and doesn't make any sense."

"I do love when you see things my way."

"If it was a simple reimbursement or wedding payment, why make the exchange on a canoe at the Blue Grotto?"

"So what could it mean?"

"I have no idea," Luca admitted. "On the surface it's weird that they'd play tourists when so much is going on."

"Like weddings and a funeral."

"Billionaires are eccentric and Carlotta—the opera singer, not the medical examiner—is an artist," Luca said. "They probably thought it was perfectly normal."

"But you don't, do you?"

"Not at all," Luca said. "Guess I'm going to have to bring the elder Signor Puccia back for more questioning."

"Carlotta, too," Bria added. "If for no other reason than to tell her that Fiorello was definitely murdered."

"That news might push her into a tailspin."

"Or prompt her to book a tour of the Sistine Chapel," Bria quipped. "You can't predict how that one's going to react."

There was a knock on the door and Luca looked relieved to be able to tell whoever was on the other side to enter. Nunzi, however, didn't appear to share Luca's relief. "*Scusi,* Chief, do you have a minute?"

Bria looked at Nunzi and wasn't sure if she should still be annoyed with her for lying to her earlier. She shrugged her shoulders and realized the woman had only been doing her job. Still, she thought she'd have some fun. "Should I leave? I wouldn't want to interrupt another top-secret meeting."

A shadow brushed across Nunzi's eyes and she involuntarily looked down at the floor. She caught herself and repositioned her gaze toward Luca and Bria. "No, this is about the piano."

"What about the piano?" Luca asked.

"We've had it dusted for fingerprints and searched for blood, but came up empty on both counts," Nunzi conveyed. "I've arranged for it to be transported back to Paris, but the company wants to be reimbursed for the missing piano wire, and I keep telling them that the person who ordered the piano—Fiorello—is dead."

"Do they expect to get money from a dead man?" Bria asked.

"No, they expect to get money from the man whom they say ordered the piano," Nunzi replied.

"Which is Fiorello," Luca said. "Who's dead."

"Half-right," Nunzi replied. "Fiorello's dead, but allegedly the man who ordered the piano is Giacomo Lancia."

Luca shook his head. "I've never heard of him."

Bria raised her hand excitedly. "I have."

Luca and Nunzi both looked at Bria. "You have?"

"That's the fake name Fio gave when he booked rooms at Bella Bella," Bria explained. "He probably gave the same name to the piano company so they wouldn't know that it was going to be used in Carlotta's concert."

"Smart thinking, but the piano company knew exactly who was going to use the piano," Nunzi stated. "In fact, the piano was Carlotta's favorite, one that she's been using for decades."

"Then there was no need for Fio to use a fake name," Luca said.

"That we know of," Nunzi added.

"We clearly don't know a lot about Fio or Giacomo," Luca said.

"No, we don't," Bria agreed. "I think it's time we found out exactly who Fiorello Sanzari really was."

Chapter 15

Bria had learned that the best way to uncover a fact was to go to the source. In this instance, however, she wanted to find out information about Fiorello, which meant that her source was dead, and therefore, would not be cooperative. The second-best option would be to go to the source's last known residence, which in this case would be Bella Bella. Unfortunately, this created a secondary problem because Carlotta also currently resided at the B and B.

Although Bria didn't suspect Carlotta of murdering Fio, Bria had no choice but to put Carlotta on the murder victim suspect list since Carlotta was closely linked to the murder victim. Which meant it would be awkward to inspect the murder victim's residence while the murder victim's suspect was on the premises. It would only compromise her investigation and make the murder victim's suspect *suspect* that she was on the aforementioned murder victim suspect list. As her father, Franco, would joke when she was a young girl and faced a problem, *When faced with a dilemma, you have to make dilemmonade.*

The phone picked up on the second ring and Bria didn't wait for a greeting before speaking. "Vanni, I need you to make sure Carlotta is not at Bella Bella."

"*Ciao* to you, too, Signora Bartolucci," Vanni replied. "If it wouldn't be too much trouble, may I ask why?"

"*Scusa!* I'll explain everything when I get home, but I can't do it if Carlotta's there."

"She isn't."

"Are you sure?"

"I've been here all day cooking, cleaning, helping Marco with his homework, and pruning the garden so it doesn't resemble a forest, while you've been God knows where, and you're questioning me?"

Bria could tell from the singsong lilt in Giovanni's voice that he wasn't angry, but he also wasn't happy with her suggestion that his reply wasn't based in truth. She trusted Giovanni implicitly and needed to make sure he understood that. He was too important to her and she didn't want him to think that she was starting to take him for granted.

"My apologies, Vanni, *sinceramente*, I wasn't doubting you,. But this is important, Carlotta can't be there."

"Don't worry; even if she does show up, Bravo's here,. She'll run out clutching her throat like Mimi in the final act of *La Bohème* claiming she can't breathe because she's allergic to dogs."

"*Grazie*, Vanni," Bria said. "*Grazie* . . . for everything."

"*Non dirlo neanche,*" Vanni replied.

"It is worth mentioning because I couldn't do any of this without you."

"*Grazie,* and maybe after you find out who killed Fiorello, we can talk about giving me a raise."

"*Addio,* Vanni!"

When Bria, Luca, and Nunzi got to Bella Bella they saw that Giovanni was true to his word and Carlotta was nowhere in sight. Bravo, however, was there and in one of his needy moods. He craved attention, belly rubs, and treats, and he wasn't going to allow any of them to get away with not supplying one or all of the above. He was probably upset because of Genie's aloofness, but it was a nice distraction, and for a few minutes they all forgot about murder, death, and the search for clues until a sudden gust of wind blew open the screen door.

"*Uffa!*" Bria cried. "Was that Carlotta?"

"It was just the wind," Luca replied.

"With her lung power she could've burst open the door with one exhale," Nunzi added. "May I suggest we get back to business."

Bria nuzzled her face into the folds of Bravo's neck. "*Ti amo tanto*, Bravo. But Mamma needs to search a dead man's room." She got up and turned to Luca and Nunzi, both wearing bemused expressions, and cried, "*Andiamo!*"

Dutifully, the chief of police and his trusted ally followed the village amateur sleuth up the stairs to Fiorello's room. When they entered there was an eerie calm, which made sense because although he had been a calming presence in life, now that they knew he had been murdered the tranquility was laced with unease. At any moment something could happen that would completely change things, and they needed to control the situation as best they could, which was why Bria had insisted Carlotta not be present even though not everyone supported that decision.

"I still think Carlotta should be here." Nunzi stood in the corner near the door and put on the same latex gloves Luca and Bria were wearing. "From what we know, she was the closest to Fio."

"Which is exactly why she shouldn't be here," Bria said.

"Oftentimes a person is murdered by the one they're closest to," Luca added.

"Whether or not Carlotta is involved in Fio's murder, it's undeniable that she had a close relationship with him," Bria said. "She's distraught over his death. If she finds out that he had a secret life as this Giacomo Lancia, who knows how she'll react."

"I didn't think about that," Nunzi replied, raising her chin in thought. "The diva has a predisposition for the dramatic."

"*Santa madre di Dio!*" Luca exclaimed. "Look at what I found!"

Bria smiled. "Speaking of dramatic."

"What's Fio's wallet doing shoved into the corner of the closet?"

"Maybe someone took his money and threw it there," Bria said. "But I've never had a theft since we opened."

"Only a dead body," Nunzi corrected, remembering a past incident.

"I found that dead body before we opened, so technically, Bella Bella has a clean record," Bria stated.

"Fair," Nunzi replied. "Chief, can you tell if anything was taken from Fio's wallet?"

"Everything looks to be intact," Luca replied. "Money, driver's license, credit cards."

"Are they in his name or Giacomo's?" Bria asked.

Luca inspected the contents of Fio's wallet and when he was done, he shrugged his shoulders, "They're all in Fiorello's real name."

"That's odd," Bria said. "If he ordered the piano under Giacomo's name, he must have known he was going to have to use a credit card with the same name to pay for it."

"Not necessarily," Luca replied. "I'm sure the piano company wouldn't care whose name was on the card as long as the payment went through."

While they were talking, Nunzi had taken a small suitcase from the closet, placed it on the bed, and opened it up. "There are some clothes in here, his toiletry bag which I'll have forensics inspect, a book about Puccini. . . . Oh, how interesting, his suitcase also has a false bottom."

"Just like Imperia!" Bria cried, remembering Imperia's story of when she was a Miss Italia contestant.

"Imperia has secret compartments in her luggage?" Luca asked.

"I'll explain it later, but you should know by now that my mother-in-law has a lot of secrets."

"So does Fiorello," Nunzi interjected. "Perhaps he was going to pay for the piano by check." Nunzi held up a checkbook. "I found this in a hidden pocket of his suitcase."

"A checkbook?" Bria questioned. "That's a bit old school, isn't it?"

"May I remind you that you have a Polaroid camera," Luca said.

Bria waved a hand in front of her face. "A Polaroid camera is vintage, a checkbook is something an old lady clings onto."

"I have a checkbook," Nunzi declared.

Bria's mouth opened but nothing came out. She opened it again and this time she made a little sound that resembled the squeak of a door. On the third attempt, she reclaimed her vocabulary. "Do you carry it around with you in a special secret compartment of your suitcase when you travel?"

"No," Nunzi replied. "I keep it next to Primavera's cat food and my needlepoint."

Luca was genuinely surprised. "You needlepoint?"

"Yes," Nunzi replied. "I may or may not be working on a gift for your fifth anniversary as chief of police."

Bria tried unsuccessfully to stifle a chuckle. "I cannot wait to see that hanging in your office."

"I'm working on another one for you, Bria, that'll look perfect in the front entrance at Bella Bella," Nunzi added. "It's taking me more time than I had anticipated to perfect Vanni's upper torso."

"You're making me a needlepoint of Vanni?" Bria asked. "Bare-chested?"

"Trust me, your guests will love it," Nunzi said.

"Could we get back to Fio's checkbook?" Luca asked. "Has he been writing checks to anyone?"

"Except for a few random ones, all the checks are made out to a Regina Pomotori," Nunzi shared.

"She could be a girlfriend or a relative that he's supporting back home," Bria said.

"Our background check on Fio only revealed a short list of very distant relatives whom we haven't been able to locate yet and no significant others," Luca conveyed. "No one on the list was named Regina or had the last name of Pomotori."

"Maybe we should do a check on Eighty-Eight Keys, Inc.," Nunzi suggested.

Bria furrowed her brow. "Why?"

"Because that's how all the checks are made out."

"They're not made out in his name or Giacomo's?" Luca asked.

"No, they're all made out through this company."

"Probably a loan-out corporation for tax reasons," Luca surmised. "The name is obviously a reference to him being a pianist."

"And his connection to Giacomo." Nunzi turned her cell phone around so Bria and Luca could see the screen. "According to this search, Giacomo Lancia is the owner of Eighty-Eight Keys, Inc., a corporation with an address in Foggia."

"Was Fiorello from Foggia?" Luca asked.

"Honestly, I'm not sure where he was from," Bria said.

"For a dead man he sure is full of secrets," Nunzi mused.

"I don't understand why Fio would use a fake name," Bria said.

"I don't understand why he'd write a check to Mimi," Nunzi countered.

"He wrote a check to Mimi!" Bria cried.

"Not to her exactly, but to her bookstore."

* * *

Bria loved to spend time browsing the aisles of *A Word from Positano* searching for a new book for Marco so he could explore the world outside his home or stumbling upon an exciting new read for herself. A book that would inspire her, challenge her, make her forget all about her own life and step, albeit briefly, into someone else's world. Standing in front of the counter waiting for Mimi to finish up a transaction, she was hoping Mimi would be able to share information that would allow her to step into a world Fio seemed to want to keep hidden from prying eyes.

"*Ciao,* Mimi."

"Bria, what a lovely surprise," Mimi replied. "Have you come to buy a book or to investigate Fiorello's murder?"

Luca said he wasn't going to share that news with the public, Bria thought. *One guess how Mimi found out.*

"Did Annamaria tell you that?"

"Who else?" Mimi replied. "She said he'd been strangled, and if you ask me, that witch, Carlotta, did it! Have you seen her hands? They're like bear paws!"

Once again Bria was stunned by the animosity Mimi showed toward Carlotta, although she did make a mental note to check out Carlotta's hands the next time she saw her, as she didn't remember them being disproportionately large.

"That's confidential police information and no one's supposed to know."

"You know."

"I have a connection to the police," Bria hemmed.

"Enrico and I couldn't be happier!" Mimi beamed. "In fact, the entire village is overjoyed that you and Luca are finally a couple. I assume the reception will be held at Mondo dei Sogni since your parents own the place."

"*Aspetta un secondo*!" Bria held up both hands in front of Mimi's face. "Luca and I are not getting married."

"Yet."

"Mimi! We've only been dating a few months."

"Seven to be exact."

"*Dio mio!* Are you keeping count?"

"Enrico is," Mimi replied. "He's better with numbers than I am."

If Bria didn't love Mimi and Enrico so much, as well as the rest of her friends in Positano, she would have been seriously angry. But she understood that they were happy for her and Luca. It did make her wonder if Luca had marriage on his mind, but she didn't have time to contemplate her future; she needed to focus on the present. Or at least the very recent past.

"Did Fiorello buy books from you and pay with a check?"

"Fifetta did teach you well," Mimi remarked. "You really do know how to change the subject."

"*Grazie,*" Bria replied, but then realized Mimi had changed the subject and avoided answering her question. "So did Fiorello come here and buy a book?"

"As a matter of fact, he did," Mimi confirmed. "And yes, he paid by check."

"Isn't that odd to pay with a check these days?"

"It is—most everyone uses a credit or debit card—but that day our machine was down for a few hours and we could only process cash transactions."

"I'm guessing that Fio didn't have enough cash on him to cover the purchase?"

"*Corretta,*" Mimi replied. "You really are so smart, Bria; no wonder Luca fell in love with you."

"*Grazie,*" Bria said, blushing slightly. "Didn't you question why the check was in a different name?"

"You knew that, too! I don't know why Luca doesn't get you fitted for a policeman's uniform. Or a policewoman's. Do they say policeperson these days?"

"I'm not sure." Bria also wasn't sure if Mimi was being her usual chatty self or if she was deliberately trying to confuse Bria to get her off track and stop asking questions about Fiorello. "When you noticed his name wasn't on the check did you ask him about it?"

"Of course I did, but he said it was his company, and he is a piano player so Eighty-Eight Keys made sense," Mimi explained. "Plus, I knew the check would clear in a day and he wasn't scheduled to leave until the day after, so I figured I'd be able to find him if the check bounced."

Disappointed in the results of her questioning, Bria realized she hadn't learned anything valuable. Until she remembered she didn't know why Fio was buying books in the first place.

"Do you remember the books Fio bought?"

"*Certo,* it was a very odd combination."

"What do you mean?"

"He bought three books," Mimi disclosed. "A biography of Puccini."

"Yes, we found that in his room."

"One about the history of Claterna."

"The Pompeii of the North?"

"*Molto bene!* Hardly anyone knows about Claterna anymore."

"Luca and Rosalie's uncle died recently and they had to drive up there for the reading of the will."

"Poor Rosalie still hasn't recovered from being bequeathed a bag of rocks!" Mimi was laughing so hard at her own joke that Bria couldn't help but join in. It took her a moment to remember that Mimi said Fiorello bought three books and Mimi had only told her about two.

"What was the third book he bought?"

"It was a book about pregnancy," Mimi said in a bit of a whisper. "He said he was buying the books for a friend, but I could tell by the way he was beaming that Fio was very happy to become a father."

"Could you be more specific? Did he say he was buying all of the books for a friend or just the pregnancy book?"

Mimi leaned her head back, presumably pondering the question. "I'm stumped. You could be a prosecutor, too, Bria; you're very good at cross-examination."

"I'm only asking some questions."

"The hallmark of a good prosecutor is that they always ask the right questions, which is exactly what you do."

"So you can't be sure which books Fio was buying for a friend?"

"Not completely sure, but I've seen many fathers come in here and buy books about pregnancy and childcare and they always have this look on their faces, a mixture of pride and fear, and that's just how Fiorello looked, the poor soul."

"*Grazie mille*, Mimi, you've been very helpful."

"*Grazie,* Bria." Mimi suddenly grabbed Bria's hand and her expression turned deadly serious. "Now you have to do me a favor."

"*Ovviamente,* what is it?"

"Promise me you'll make that evil Carlotta pay for what she did to that poor man and his unborn child."

On the way back to Bella Bella, Bria was so deep in thought that she didn't notice anything around her. Not the young delivery guy on the Vespa who was paying more attention to the group of girls on the other side of the street than the road and had to swerve at the last second to avoid colliding into Bria; not the trio of seagulls that kept dive-bombing the remnants of a discarded pizza pie from the top of a garbage can; not even the vendor at one of the souvenir shops who asked Bria if she'd like to try their new Orangecello ice pops. Nothing else mattered except for the possibility that Fiorello had possibly been expecting a child.

Bria hadn't known Fio very long but the only time she ever noticed him beaming with pride was when he spoke about Carlotta. He truly revered her talent and was honored to work with her. Carlotta was long past her reproductive years, but her daughter was about to become a mother. Or at least that was Bria's assumption.

The more plausible explanation was that Fio was telling the truth to Mimi and was buying the books for a friend—Ombra. He didn't appear particularly close to her, but if the child Ombra was carrying was going to make Carlotta a grandmother, then it made sense that he would be delighted to help. It also made sense for Carlotta to ask Fio to buy pregnancy books in order to keep Ombra's condition a secret from the baby's father and the baby's father's father.

If Ombra really was pregnant, she wouldn't want Armando to know about it because he was a playboy, and while getting married was life changing, it was a sacrament that could be broken; fatherhood stayed with you for life and it wasn't something you could opt out of. If Armando found out about the pregnancy before the wedding, he might freak out and call the wedding off, which was not something a pregnant fiancée would like to see happen.

Worse than that would be Pietro's reaction. In the brief conversation Bria had with him, he made it clear that he expected Ombra to reform his son. What would the billionaire do if he found out that the good girl who was going to marry his son had forgotten to keep her legs crossed until the honeymoon? Poor Ombra should be bursting with joy in the run-up to her wedding day, but instead she was praying that no one would find out about her dirty little secret.

Bria stopped in her tracks just in time to avoid crashing into a speeding teenager on a motorized scooter. Another possibility popped into her head. Mimi was right and Fiorello was going to have a baby, but with this Regina person he was writing checks to and not with Ombra. This scenario caused an even bigger problem: they had no idea who Regina was.

Bria practically ran the rest of the way home to get help from the one person who seemed to be the master of online sleuthing.

"Vanni!" Bria cried as she entered Bella Bella. "I need you to go online and find out what you can about Regina Pomotori."

"Who's that?"

Once again Bria stopped in her tracks because Vanni hadn't replied to her; Carlotta had.

Instead of being greeted by Vanni, Bria had been greeted by Carlotta. And instead of Carlotta being in the fetal position clutching one of Fiorello's garments or clutching her throat claiming she couldn't breathe in a house that housed a dog, the opera singer was kneeling next to Bravo, clipping a leash to his collar and rubbing his neck affectionately. It took a moment for Bria to comprehend what she had walked in on. Either Carlotta was a glutton for punishment or a liar.

"I thought you said you were allergic to dogs."

"I lied."

At least some mysteries were quickly solved.

"Why would you lie about such a thing?"

"*Sono così dispiaciuto!*" Carlotta stood up, the leash hanging in her hand as Bravo lay resigned at her feet unaccustomed to the restraint. "When I'm getting ready to sing, I develop a split personality and turn into this other person who must have complete control of everything and everyone around me in order to be as perfect as I can be the night of a performance."

"A diva?" Bria suggested.

"*Esattamente!*" Carlotta cried, causing Bravo to stir a bit. "This time was worse because I haven't sung in public in years."

"Despite your lies, Carlotta, your concert was truly magical," Bria admitted. "The quality of your voice, the power, the ability to convey such a range of emotions only through sounds was astonishing."

Carlotta sighed and bowed her head, processing Bria's compliment. "You are a very kind woman, Bria." She stopped to compose herself. "You remind me of Fio in that way."

"Fio was very kind." Bria took a deep breath and decided to take a risk. "Did you also know he was about to become a father?"

Shock immediately registered on Carlotta's face, though the rest of her body remained motionless. "*Che cosa?* How do you know about this?"

"Fio bought a book from the local bookstore about pregnancy."

"It must have been for someone else; Fio never mentioned to me that he was going to become a father."

"I think it was for him and his girlfriend."

"No!" Carlotta shouted. "I would know if he had a girlfriend."

"It seems that he did."

"Who?"

For some reason Bria thought that Carlotta seemed nervous. Then it dawned on her that just because Carlotta couldn't be carrying his child didn't mean that she couldn't be in love with him. Bria realized a little bit too late that when you took a risk, you could wind up breaking someone's heart.

"Who is this woman?" Carlotta asked. "This supposed girlfriend?"

"It's just an assumption, but I think it's someone named Regina," Bria replied. "Maybe he was planning to bring her to the wedding."

Carlotta shook her head. "No, he was coming by himself."

"Probably because he was going to be working and playing the piano."

"*Aspetta!* Don't you think if he had a girlfriend he'd want to bring her so she could hear him play?"

Bria had to admit that Carlotta made a valid point. Still, Fiorello definitely had a connection to Regina, and for the moment, Bria could only imagine that it was personal. The only person who could confirm or deny that assumption was Regina.

"We're going to try and find this Regina."

"Why would you do that?"

"Don't you think the woman has a right to know that the father of the baby she's carrying is dead?"

"What if you're wrong, Bria?" Carlotta asked. "What if Regina has nothing to do with this? If you share this information with that woman, you could be playing with fire."

Bria shouldn't have been surprised by the ferocity in Carlotta's voice. She did have a flair for theatrics and she was overprotective of Fiorello, more so now that he couldn't protect himself. But there was something about her response that unsettled Bria, because she felt Carlotta knew more about Regina than she was admitting.

Before she could tap back into her prosecutorial skills and continue her cross-examination, Bravo objected with a series of loud, high-pitched barks. He wasn't upset about being tethered to a leash or acting as a guard dog, he was excited. When Bria turned around, she understood why.

"Genie!"

Valentina stood in the doorway holding Genie on a leash. In comparison to Bravo's barking and animated prancing, Genie looked like a statue. She really had mastered the technique of playing hard to get, or she truly had no interest in Bravo whatsoever. Luckily, Bravo didn't let Genie's air of disinterest diminish his exhilaration at being in her presence.

"What a surprise?" Bria said.

"I was taking Genie for a walk and thought you and Bravo would like to join us," Valentina replied. "It's been a while since we had some girl talk, but I see you have company."

Bria was about to correct Valentina, since they had just seen each other the other day, but realized Valentina—like Sister Benedicta often did—was speaking in code. She needed to say something to Bria that she couldn't say in mixed company. Luckily, Carlotta understood that she was in the way.

"Why don't I take both dogs for a walk?" Carlotta suggested. "I could use the fresh air to clear my mind."

"*Grazie!*" Valentina handed Genie's leash to Carlotta. "They won't give you any trouble at all."

"I'm sure these little angels will be perfect," Carlotta said. "We'll go for a little walk and give you ladies some time to chat. *Ciao.*"

"*Addio,*" Valentina said, accompanied by an overenthusiastic wave.

After Carlotta left with the dogs, Valentina grabbed Bria by the shoulders. "I have to confess!"

"Don't you think Sister B is more qualified to hear a confession than I am?"

"Not one like this," Valentina said. "She doesn't have the, um, right qualifications to understand."

"What are you talking about? She's a nun, that's the perfect qualification."

Valentina let go of Bria and threw her hands in the air. "If I had to confess about lying, cheating, or stealing, maybe, but not this."

"*Dio mio*, Valentina, what did you do?"

"I slept with Armando."

Chapter 16

Involuntarily, Bria made the sign of the cross. Then she raised her arms up to the ceiling and shook her head in disbelief. Finally, she pointed a finger at Valentina.

"You said you didn't cheat!" Bria exclaimed.

"I didn't."

"Yes, you did! You slept with Armando."

"That isn't cheating."

"*Uffa!* How is that not cheating?"

"I'm single! He's the one who cheated; he's engaged."

"To another woman!"

"I am fully aware of that."

"Which doesn't make what you did last night right."

"I know that! I also know that what I did last night doesn't fall into the column of cheating."

"Then, *prego,* tell me, what column does it fall under?"

"I don't know." Valentina groaned and started pacing the floor. "Foolish mistake? Falling back into bad habits? Thirst for adventure?"

"If you want an adventure, you can go ziplining in Furore!" Bria cried. "Valentina, this is more than a foolish mistake and you know it, or else you wouldn't be here confessing."

"Now don't you see why I had to come to you and not Sister

Benedicta?" Valentina asked. "If I told her, she'd have me saying twelve Hail Marys and a few dozen Our Fathers."

"I think you'd find Sister B to be much more helpful than that. She isn't a nun cloistered in a convent, she's very in touch with the real world, but that's beside the point," Bria said. "Why are you really here?"

"I told you, because I need to confess what I've done."

"Then you need to add lying to your sins." Bria scolded. "You're cavalier, you're the sexy tour guide, the woman who doesn't believe in living by society's rules. That woman wouldn't feel any guilt or regret for sleeping with a man who was about to walk down the aisle and share vows with another woman. What's this really about?"

"*Madonna mia,* Bria, you really are insightful."

"You're also a bit on the obvious side, so don't give me too much credit," Bria replied.

"You're right, this is not really about me sleeping with Armando."

"Then what's it about? Did Armando threaten you? Did he hurt you?"

"No, nothing like that; our rendezvous was mutually consensual."

"Are you sure? You said Armando was capable of violence."

"I'm completely certain; he didn't coerce me in any way even though I still think he's a violent man."

"Valentina, if you think that, why did you sleep with him?"

"I told you I like a bit of adventure."

"*Dio mio!* If this isn't about cheating or committing adultery, you need to spell it out because I don't know what you're trying to confess."

"It's about Fiorello's murder and the person who I think did it."

Suddenly, Bria's thoughts shifted and she no longer wanted

to shake some sense into Valentina, she wanted to drag information out of her. "Let's sit down and have some coffee."

Bria walked over to the dining room table, picked up the coffeepot, and filled two cups while Valentina continued to pace the floor. She sat at the table and took a sip to give herself a moment to calm down, and then filled another cup. "Now, come sit down and confess all your sins to the other Sister B."

Valentina sat down across from Bria and took a long sip of coffee as if she was hoping the caffeine would work as fuel to give her the courage to tell her story. Bria watched the woman nervously drum her fingers on the table and realized she had never seen this side of Valentina before. Whatever happened with Armando, whatever led her to connect her dalliance with murder, had greatly affected her.

Physically, she was the same. Her long blond hair fell loose around her face and grazed her shoulders, her lightly tanned skin made make-up unnecessary and was enough to highlight her sharp cheekbones, aquiline nose, and full strawberry-hued lips, and her off-the-shoulder linen blouse was the exact same light blue as her eyes. Bria understood completely why a man would be attracted to Valentina: she looked as if she'd stepped out of a fashion magazine or a daydream. Bria didn't understand why underneath all that physical perfection there was anxiety and a little bit of fear.

"Why don't you tell me how you wound up in bed with Armando?" Bria said. "Unless the two of you found other accommodations."

Finally, Valentina smiled. "You really do know me very well, don't you?"

"Like I've said, you leave little to the imagination," Bria replied.

"Every woman knows her strength and I know mine, which is why when I saw Armando I knew I could have him within sixty seconds."

"How exactly did you know that?"

"I was having a drink at Hotel Marincanto in La Sponda. Do you know it?"

"Very well," Bria replied. "Imperia took me and Marco there for her birthday last year; it's exquisite."

"I go there every so often because the views are magnificent and the guests are of a more elevated caliber than the tourists who frequent the cafés on the beach," Valentina said.

"You went looking for company."

"Precisely," Valentina confirmed. "Who should I find sitting at the bar all by his lonesome, but Armando Puccia."

"He wasn't with Ombra?"

"He's rarely with Ombra, but you've already noticed that." Bria tilted her head and smiled. She raised her cup and pointed it at Valentina, urging her to continue. "He said that he had been having dinner with her and Carlotta and the ladies got into an argument, which he said was the norm for them, something about the flowers for the wedding. He said he couldn't stand watching Ombra cower in her mother's presence any longer and he left."

"To drown his sorrows in some drinks at Hotel Marincanto."

"That was the plan."

"Until you showed up."

"When I saw him, I told him that he owed me a drink for leaving me with the bill at La Brezza. The next thing I know we're at my place."

"Wasn't there a room available at Marincanto?"

"He suggested that, but I wasn't going to run the risk of having to foot the hotel bill."

"*Eccola!* There's my savvy Valentina," Bria cried. "There are other ways we pay for the things that we do than with money."

"Bria, let me make something very clear. I do not feel guilty for what I've done," Valentina started. "I didn't coerce Armando into doing anything he didn't want to do. He wasn't drunk, and when we got to my front door, I told him that he could leave and I wouldn't say another word about it."

"Clearly he didn't come to his senses and run back to his fiancée."

"No, he didn't, and it's no surprise. Ombra isn't in Armando's league. He's gorgeous, he's a billionaire's son, she's a shadow of a woman—which is ironic because that's what her name means in English. Did you know that? A shadow. They're mismatched. I don't know why they're getting married, but it's a mistake, and Armando knows it, too."

"Regardless of what you think Armando knows, he's still planning to marry this shadow woman," Bria said.

"Unless Ombra puts an end to it first."

"What's that supposed to mean?"

"I think Ombra may know about Armando's cheating," Valentina said. "I mean, he's hardly subtle about it and I know I wasn't the first. I may not even have been the first since they arrived in Positano."

"You think Ombra is going to cancel the wedding because she knows Armando hasn't been faithful?"

"I think Ombra knows her fiancé is a snake and she may have already tried to kill him, but killed Fiorello instead."

Bria took a long sip of coffee and contemplated Valentina's hypothesis. She was correct in that Armando and Ombra did not seem to have a solid relationship. Armando was dismissive and outright nasty to Ombra, and she was mousy and more preoccupied with her wedding than with being a wife. They weren't working together to become a couple; it was as if each had their own agenda. Could Ombra's endgame be murder?

"I'm not sure if that's possible," Bria said. "Surely, Ombra can tell the difference between her fiancé and her mother's piano player."

"I heard from Violetta who heard it from Paolo who said

that Annamaria told him that when you found Fiorello dead in the piazza he was wearing Armando's jacket instead of his own."

"That is true," Bria confirmed. "But Ombra's the one who told me that Armando accidentally spilled red wine on Fiorello's white jacket, which is why they switched in the first place. Ombra knew that Fiorello was wearing Armando's jacket, so she wouldn't have confused the two men."

"Did you see how the white jacket got stained?"

"No, but there's no reason to doubt Ombra."

"Are you sure about that?" Valentina asked.

Valentina was right. What if Ombra's explanation was really an alibi?

Bria was only accepting that what Ombra told her was the truth, when it could all be a lie. Fiorello and Armando could have indeed switched jackets for some reason that no one knew about, including Ombra, and when Ombra tried to kill Armando, it was only afterward that she realized she had killed Fiorello instead. When she noticed that the reason she had mistaken Fiorello's identity was because he was wearing Armando's jacket, she devised a plan to make it appear that she was aware of the switch beforehand. It did mean that she would have had to have found Fiorello's white jacket after killing him in order to douse it with red wine, but if she went to the trouble of pulling out a piano wire to strangle a man, doctoring a garment shouldn't be difficult. It was a stretch, but plausible, and a reason for Bria to question Ombra's motives. It also meant that Ombra might not just be a killer, but a cold-hearted murderess.

"I think you might be right about Ombra," Bria said.

"You think she killed Fiorello, too?!"

"I don't know about that. I mean that she can't be completely trusted."

"You can say what you want about women like me, but we

don't make any excuses or pretend we're one thing when we're the exact opposite," Valentina said. "It's women like Ombra, lurking in the shadows, who are the ones you need to be scared of, because they're the ones who have nothing to lose."

"Despite your protests, Valentina, I have to ask," Bria started. "Don't you have even one regret about what you did last night?"

"Oh, I do hope it was something decadent! The only things worth regretting are things that make the moral blush."

Carlotta burst into the room followed by Bravo and Genie. For the first time it appeared that Genie was demonstrating affection for her canine companion. By the way Bravo's tail was wagging, he was overjoyed. By the way Valentina scowled at Carlotta, it was clear that his elation wasn't infectious.

"I can ensure you that my calendar last night was filled with enough activity to mortify a heathen." Valentina slowly brought the cup up to her smiling lips. "I am, however, a girl who doesn't tell after she kisses."

"It sounds almost operatic," Carlotta gushed. "If I had the time, I would channel the hypnotic skill of the Queen of the Night to put you under my spell and compel you to do as I say and tell me every juicy detail, but I'm late for an appointment."

"Don't worry," Bria said. "If I know Valentina, she will have more nights that will be overflowing with regret."

Both Valentina and Carlotta were shocked by Bria's comment. And both women were also wildly amused.

"Sister B might not approve of such talk," Valentina howled. "But I certainly do."

"Bria, you're a woman after my own heart, full of surprises!" Carlotta grabbed her purse that had been hanging from a hook near the hall closet, flung it over her shoulder, and opened the front door. "*Bravo,* Bria, and *arrivederci!*"

At the sound of his name, Bravo raced after Carlotta, quickly followed by Genie, but the front door closed behind Carlotta before either dog could get outside. Which was fortunate because Bria's gut suddenly felt like it was on fire, an indication that something was wrong. Experience had taught Bria not to ignore her instinct, but to do so she needed to get rid of her guest.

"This has been an illuminating conversation, but I need to run some errands." Bria bent down and took the leash off of Bravo's collar. "Let's absolutely do this the next time you have something to confess."

Valentina took hold of Genie's leash and opened the front door. Before she left she turned around and her face was devoid of any smirk, snarl, or sarcastic look. "*Grazie,* Bria, thank you for listening. *Cin cin.*"

Bria waited about ten seconds after Valentina and Genie left and then kissed Bravo on the head and ran out. She didn't know if her instincts would lead her in the right direction, but she didn't want to take the chance and miss an opportunity. Outside, she saw Valentina and Genie walking north on Viale Pasitea, which was a relief because Bria was headed south and she didn't want any further distractions.

If Carlotta had been with Pietro the other day at the Blue Grotto and Pietro was now in Positano it made sense that they may try and meet up again. If they did, they could, of course, meet anywhere. Had Bria not heard Pietro speak so disparagingly about his own son, she would have gone directly to Villa Magia where Armando and Ombra were staying. But Pietro made it clear that a son should follow his father and not the other way around. No, it made more sense that Pietro would be with the last person she saw him with—Imperia. Which was why Bria was speed walking to the marina.

En route, she didn't question her actions, she didn't try to rationalize her thought because if she did, she would have stopped and gone back home. Pietro could be anywhere and Carlotta could have an appointment with Donatella, the best manicurist in the village, but Bria knew there was some kind of connection between the future in-laws and she wanted to see if she was right.

Walking on the dock, Bria saw Mariana, Rosalie's deckhand, polishing the railing.

"*Ciao,* Mariana," Bia said. "How've you been?"

"*Bene, grazie,*" she replied, wiping her brow with the back of her hand. "Busier than usual, but that's a good thing."

"Yes, it is," Bria said. "Where's Rosalie?"

"She's out with that guy who's always around," Mariana replied. "They went for lunch somewhere, but she should be back soon; we have a night cruise booked."

Bria thought it was odd that Rosalie would be having lunch with Michele considering their last conversation, but perhaps she was trying to give him one more chance. She hoped that wasn't the case but knew Rosalie would share all the details with her later. For now, she needed to barge onto a yacht.

"*A dopo,* Mariana!"

"*Arrivederci!*"

Bria walked up the plank toward Imperia's yacht and when she was about 200 meters away, she banged her fist into her thigh. She wanted to pump it into the air, but that would be too ostentatious and might catch Carlotta's and Pietro's eyes. Bria slowed down her gait, and as she did on a daily basis thanked God that she was wearing her espadrilles because she didn't make any sound as she approached the unsuspecting couple.

They were facing each other, both at a slight outward angle, almost as if they didn't want to be seen as being together, just two people who happened to be in the same space. It meant that Bria was behind them and couldn't be seen. Bria, however, had a bird's-eye view, and when Pietro leaned into Carlotta, she saw him slip another white envelope into her open purse that was hanging from her shoulder. The diva gave the billionaire an air kiss as she snapped her purse shut, the envelope no longer in view. It was the perfect time for Bria to reveal herself.

"Carlotta, Pietro, what a nice surprise!" Bria shouted as she walked onto the deck of the yacht.

Pietro spun around and looked even more dashing in the late-afternoon sunlight than he had in the fluorescent lighting of Luca's office. The harsh light, not to mention that scowl she was wearing, transformed Carlotta's normally attractive features into a grotesque mask.

"Have you been following me, Bria?" Carlotta asked.

"Of course not," she replied. "Sheer coincidence."

"Sheer delight is more like it." Pietro took Bria's hand and kissed it. His lips lingered on Bria's flesh a second or two longer than necessary and it was clear where Armando got his philandering gene from. "Bria, the pleasure is all mine."

Bria saw that Carlotta was no longer staring at her but had now turned her gaze on Pietro and was grimacing at his actions. But she didn't know if Carlotta was disgusted or jealous. As Imperia entered from belowdecks, however, she looked afraid.

"Bria," Imperia said, as she joined the group. "Barging in again unexpectedly."

"I came to visit Rosalie, but she isn't around and as I started to leave, I saw your guests on the deck," Bria lied. "I thought I'd stop by and say *ciao.*" Bria smiled as broadly as she could and then added, "*Ciao!*"

Even though Bria knew that neither Imperia nor the others had any reason to suspect what she was saying wasn't the truth, she felt nervous. It didn't have anything to do with the strange connection between Carlotta and Pietro, but everything to do with Imperia's energy. Her mother-in-law looked the same—her hair was styled as always, a page boy with a bit of height, her deep red lipstick, and one of her perfectly tailored business suits, this one in royal blue. It was how she held herself: a bit too clenched, her hands were clasped in front of her, she was holding her breath, and avoiding eye contact.

Bria felt it had something to do with the earlier meeting in Luca's office, but then she caught Imperia staring at the ring on Carlotta's finger. A ring that could also be called a rock. It was a square cut black opal etched in diamonds. Simple, but stunning.

"Carlotta, that is quite a significant ring," Imperia said. "It may look better on Pietro's hand."

Again with a comment about Carlotta's jewelry looking better on a man? Bria thought. *Carlotta really does bring out Imperia's petty side.*

Flustered, Carlotta chuckled and waved her hand in front of Imperia, making the ring look even larger than it really was.

"No man would ever wear something like that," Pietro announced. "My son would, but he isn't what I consider to be a man."

"Don't be too harsh on the boy, Pietro," Carlotta said. "Look at the shoes he needs to fill."

"*Vero*," Imperia said. "You are a very hard act to follow."

Pietro smiled at the flattery but shook his head. "Sometimes I think my life would have been better if I had a good little girl like your Ombra."

"*Grazie,* Pietro." Carlotta actually bowed her head. "Very soon my sweet Ombra will be part of your family. And so will I."

"I only pray that the both of you will be able to hold up to your end of the bargain," Pietro said. "You know how much I loathe disappointment."

The smile never left Carlotta's face, but Bria could see the change in her eyes. She was panicked. Bria was surprised the woman didn't start screaming that the yacht was sinking and race for a life preserver. Instead, she reached out to grab Pietro's hand.

"As do I, Pietro," Carlotta said, in a tone that was serious and hushed.

"Which is why we're such a good team," Pietro declared.

"You and Imperia seem to be a good team, too," Bria said. "*Grazie* again for joining forces and helping so many needy children."

Pietro looked perplexed. "*Scusi?*"

Imperia placed a hand on Pietro's arm. "Bria is speaking about the scholarship our companies are creating. You remember we were ironing out the details in Luca's office."

Recognition overwhelmed Pietro's face. "Ah yes, *prego;* it is most important to do what we can for the children. Now, *le signore,* please excuse us. I promised Carlotta lunch at La Tagliata, and Antonietta, the owner, *madon,* she has quite a temper if you're late."

They exchanged their perfunctory good-byes and then Bria and Imperia watched Pietro and Carlotta walk down the plank toward the village in silence. The fire in Bria's belly had subsided, but only a little; she knew something was wrong. What was going on between Pietro and Carlotta? Was he paying her to get Ombra to marry Armando? Was he that desperate to tame his wild child? Pietro was wealthy and a traditionalist so it was possible, but why would Carlotta go along with it and basically sell her daughter off to the highest bidder? Yes, it would be prestigious to marry into the Puccia family, and Ombra, while in no means homely, wasn't the type of woman who would attract a very eligible bachelor, but wouldn't it be better to remain single than be forced into marriage for the wrong reasons?

Imperia cleared her throat and Bria was reminded she wasn't alone. She wasn't sure if her mother-in-law could provide insight into Carlotta and Pietro's relationship when there was the very real possibility that Imperia had her own relationship with Pietro that she wanted to keep secret. There was one question Imperia could answer though.

"Why do you keep telling Carlotta that her jewelry would look better on a man?" Bria asked.

A howl escaped from Imperia's mouth. "*Perdonami,* I know it's childish and I know Carlotta's grieving—or at least she claims she is—but I cannot resist having fun at her expense."

"You don't think Carlotta's grieving?"

"The woman is an actress, which by the very definition of the role means she's a liar, a charlatan. I don't believe anything she says."

Bria couldn't argue with that because Carlotta confirmed the accusation a few hours ago. She lied about being allergic to Bravo and blamed it on being a sensitive artist. Her whole heartbroken diva routine could be nothing more than an act as well. Convincing, but a lie.

"*Capisco,* but I really don't understand why you're focusing on her jewelry," Bria continued. "Are her pieces fake?"

"No, they're real," Imperia confirmed. "The supply is just dwindling."

"What do you mean?"

"I had a recent visit with Dr. Frangipani to get an undereye treatment and he told me that Carlotta sold him a ring she no longer had a need for and asked him if he could sell a few other pieces on the black market."

"Isn't a doctor bound to patient confidentiality?"

Another howl escaped from Imperia's lips and filled the air. "I love Dr. Frangi, but his lips are looser than some of the sagging breasts he nips and tucks."

"But why is she selling her jewelry?"

"Bria, open your eyes. The bitch is broke," Imperia spat. "The once-famous opera star doesn't have any money."

Chapter 17

Bria felt as if the yacht had suddenly pulled away from the marina and they were careening faster over the water than Valentina's *Merry Widow* speedboat could ever travel even with Valentina pushing down full throttle. It seemed that every time Bria had a conversation with someone, every time she opened a door, every time she thought a bit more about Fiorello's death, she uncovered something new.

Fiorello had been strangled, but it was possible that the intended murder victim was Armando. Armando and Ombra were engaged to be wed in less than a week, and yet Armando had just slept with Valentina. Ombra was pregnant, but keeping it a secret. Carlotta perpetuated a persona as a former opera diva turned jetsetter, when in reality she was bankrupt. Were none of these people being honest? Were they all lying?

As much as Bria wanted to leave the yacht and get back onto firm ground, the one person connected to all these people was Imperia. She navigated in their circles, she understood how they lived, and how their minds worked. Although Bria didn't have any real financial worries thanks to the money Carlo left her, as well as his share of the Bartolucci empire, she and Carlo had never socialized with the social elite. They were homebodies who spent most of their time with Bria's family and their friends from college, upper middle-class people who had worked hard for their money, and no matter how much they saved they'd never be able to afford a yacht. Bria couldn't leave, she needed to question Imperia further.

"*Oh, testa mia.*" With one hand Bria held onto the railing, with the other she held her forehead. "Imperia, could I please have a glass of water. I'm feeling lightheaded."

"Sit down." Imperia pulled on a string near the railing and a bell rang. Bria never knew such a thing existed before. Secrets were literally everywhere. "I've told you before to wear a wide-brimmed hat. It cools the scalp and keeps the sun away from your eyes, especially the corners where you already have enough lines for a woman twice your age."

Bria's tactic worked. Imperia felt like she was in control, which was the best way for Bria to get information from her mother-in-law without having her suspect anything.

One of Imperia's employees, a young man with an impossibly square jaw, materialized from somewhere with a glass of water on a tray. Bria had no idea how the pull of a string and the ringing of a bell had translated into the appearance of a glass of water, but Imperia's yacht was chock-full of tricks Bria didn't know about. She simply accepted the glass with a smile and drank.

A few seconds later, with Imperia sitting across from her, Bria acted as if she had regained her strength and resumed their conversation. "Is Carlotta having a hard time making ends meet or is she penniless?"

"I would say the pendulum is swinging closer to her going back to her roots to hold an outdoor concert for the coins people would throw at her feet so she could afford a night in a fleabag hotel," Imperia replied.

"But she had such a celebrated career."

"She did and her success was warranted," Imperia confirmed. "I don't like Carlotta, but her talent is undeniable."

"Then how did she go broke?"

"She's an artist, not a financier," Imperia barked. "I learned early on that the only person you should trust with your own money is yourself. Never let someone else handle the money that is rightfully yours."

"I let you handle the money that's meant for me and Marco."

"*A volte, Bria!*" Imperia cried. "I'm family, that's different. I'm not going to steal from people I love."

Now Bria really did feel lightheaded. She had never heard Imperia use the word *love* in a sentence in which she was referenced. Although she wanted to thank Imperia for making such a comment, she knew that any acknowledgment would threaten to derail their conversation. Bria filed away the information and was grateful for the strides she'd made in her relationship with Imperia, but for the moment she'd let the remark slide.

"Is that what Carlotta did?" Bria asked. "Give strangers control of her money?"

"They mismanaged her funds, embezzled some, and gave her bad advice," Imperia explained. "I didn't know the extent of her financial woes until she came to town and then things started to click."

"What things?"

"The truth about the wedding, for starters," Imperia replied. "It's a sham, a business transaction."

"I didn't think Armando and Ombra were head over heels in love, but I didn't think it was an arranged marriage."

"That's because you've been very lucky, Bria. You've had one great love and it looks like you're headed for another, but not all women experience that; some need to look at marriage like brokering a deal as opposed to sharing a life with a soulmate."

Imperia had done it again. She had spoken about Bria as if she genuinely cared for her. Bria had known that was true, but Imperia's sentiments and feelings were usually kept hidden.

Imperia didn't allow her emotions to be exposed or her vulnerability to be visible; she only wanted the world to see her as formidable and, as her name implied, imperious. Perhaps in the same way that Bria felt like she was emerging from a cocoon, so was Imperia. Perhaps they were more similar than either one had thought.

"We are the lucky ones," Bria said. "Your marriage to Guillermo and mine to Carlo were based on mutual love and respect. I suspect that we could have lived in poverty and still had wonderful lives."

Imperia's laughter rang out so loudly some of the nearby seagulls joined in. "Let's not get carried away, Bria, I'm sure I could do without many of my luxuries, but living in poverty, *no, grazie*!"

"Is it truly Carlotta's fate?" Bria replied.

"It would be if weren't for Pietro."

Slowly the pieces of the puzzle started to form into place. "Pietro is the one who arranged this marriage."

"According to Dante."

"How's Dante involved?"

"As I'm sure you can tell by the absence of lines on Dante's forehead and the addition of a too-thin moustache on his upper lip, he's a frequent visitor to Dr. Frangi," Imperia began. "Pietro has also been known to partake in a little rejuvenation now and then and the two men met while having a treatment at Dr. Frangi's clinic in Milan. Dr. Frangi was talking about how Carlotta was trying to sell some jewelry and it soon turned out that the only commodity Pietro was interested in buying was her daughter."

"*Uffa,* Imperia! You make it sound so crass. Like a quid pro quo."

"That's exactly what it was, *qualcosa per qualcosa*," Imperia confirmed. "Carlotta had something to offer and Pietro had something to buy. I'm sure you noticed the envelope Pietro tried to discretely hand over to Carlotta."

"I did while I was walking toward the yacht," Bria confessed. "But how did you see it? You were below-decks."

"When will you understand that I did not reach this position in life without having eyes in the back of my head?" Imperia shook her head, but she was smiling. She was thoroughly enjoying this gossiping session with Bria, and although it was illuminating things Bria had already suspected, it was still creating more questions.

"I can understand Pietro wanting his gigolo of a son to find a nice girl to settle down with and I can understand Carlotta wanting to marry into a rich family," Bria said. "What I don't understand is why Armando would go along with it. Why would such an eligible bachelor agree to settle down with a woman who is clearly not his type?"

"Because Armando isn't so eligible."

"He's good-looking, seemingly healthy, and incredibly wealthy."

"*Due su tre non sono male.*"

"What do you mean only two out of three?" Bria asked. "Is Armando sick?"

"No, he's as broke as Carlotta!" Imperia cried. "Pietro won't give Armando his inheritance until he marries a woman Pietro approves of. Until then Pietro holds all the purse strings."

"*Oh Dio mio!*" Bria gasped. "Armando is marrying Ombra so he can get his hands on his inheritance."

"*Easattamente!* Armando gets his money, Ombra marries up, and Carlotta gets to live in the style she's accustomed to. Everybody wins."

As disturbing as this scenario was, it helped Bria understand why Carlotta had been so nervous. She hadn't been anxious about her singing, she'd been worried that Armando might back out of the wedding. If Valentina was right and Armando hasn't been entirely quiet about his philandering, Carlotta might be aware that he's been stepping out on Ombra. She probably thinks at some point Armando would come to the decision that marrying Ombra wouldn't be worth it just to have access to his money.

But that must mean that Carlotta doesn't know about the pregnancy, either. If she did, she wouldn't have a care in the world because she'd know that Armando would have no choice but to marry Ombra. If Pietro found out that Armando dumped Ombra while she was pregnant with his child, he would disown his son. Ombra was the only thing keeping him linked to his father's bank account.

"Everybody does win," Bria said. "The only thing that would make things better for Carlotta is if Ombra were pregnant."

Imperia started to choke on the exceptionally smooth gin she was drinking. "That would be the worst thing that could happen, the absolute worst."

"Why? Doesn't Pietro want to have a grandchild?"

"What man wouldn't want to see his legacy continue? But it isn't going to happen."

"How can you be so certain?"

"Trust me. I know that Armando and Ombra are never going to have a child together."

Bria stared at Imperia for a few seconds hoping she would elaborate, but she remained silent, and Bria knew that nothing she could say would make Imperia speak any further on the matter. It did give Bria quite a bit to think about; maybe she and Lorenza were wrong and Ombra wasn't pregnant. She could just be lactose intolerant after all, or she could have had a stomach flu. Bria thought it might help if she changed the subject.

"I couldn't tell you how surprised I was to see both you and Pietro in Luca's office this morning."

In response, Imperia pulled on a different cord near the railing and another bell rang in a slightly lower ringtone. Imperia stood up from the table and peered down at Bria. "I have a conference call with Athens and if you keep those people waiting for more than thirty seconds, they just haul themselves back to the beach. I think you know your way out."

Imperia almost bumped into the same square-jawed waiter, who had returned to take away Bria's glass of water, when she spun around to walk toward the stairway to the upper decks. Bria watched her mother-in-law with an odd mixture of awe and confusion. She felt like they had gotten so much closer and then Imperia just pulled back. Bria knew that Imperia was hiding something from her, but she had no idea what it was. She'd worry about that later; for now, she wanted to find out more about Armando.

Bria had another two hours before she needed to be home for dinner because Marco had choir practice after school and Giovanni was picking him up after going to Sorrento to run some errands. With some free time she thought she'd pay Ombra a visit at Villa Magia and see if she could find out if Ombra really was pregnant or if Bria had once again jumped to a conclusion without first confirming it was a fact.

While walking to the hotel, Bria realized she knew someone else who could give her information on Armando's past and why he wasn't suitable husband or father material. Someone who always jumped at the chance to help Bria. Someone who loved to chat no matter what time of day.

"Bria Bria," Fabrice said. "I'm so sorry I can't talk."

Except for today.

Bria was thrown by Fabrice's response because he had never once not taken her call, and she had called him once while he was in the middle of an emergency landing in Cairo. "I won't keep you long, Fabrice, but I've heard some rumors about Armando and I was hoping you'd be able to give me some details about his past."

"Armando and I aren't really that close," Fabrice said. "But if I think of anything I'll call you. *Ciao!*"

Bria thought that she must be losing her touch, and then another, much worse, thought popped into her head. What if Fabrice and Lorenza were having problems in their relationship? If they were, Fabrice would assume that Lorenza had filled Bria in on their problems and he would feel awkward having a conversation with Bria. That had to be it. But no! That would be terrible.

Had Bria not seen Ombra and Sister Benedicta kneeling together in the garden of Villa Magia, she would have called Lorenza immediately to find out if she and Fabrice had had a lover's quarrel, or worse, if they had separated. But the image of the two women kneeling side by side was too strange to ignore. Bria waited until they stood up to join them.

"Sister B, you are the last person I expected to find here," Bria said. "Why aren't you at St. Cecilia's?"

"Bria, how nice to see you," Sister Benedicta replied. "Sister Caterina is teaching a few of my classes today. Mother Superior thought it a good opportunity to give her some practice in the classroom."

"And you decided to pop out and spend some time with Ombra?"

"I called Sister Benedicta and asked her to come pray with me," Ombra interrupted.

"That's lovely," Bria replied. "Were you praying for Fio?"

"No," Ombra replied. "I found out this morning that an old girlfriend from school died very suddenly."

"*Mi dispiace tanto*," Bria said. "That's terrible news on top of everything else."

"Which is why I agreed to come right away," Sister B said.

"Usually, my mother and I pray together," Ombra said. "But she's been preoccupied lately and very busy with the wedding coming up so soon."

"There's been a lot happening," Bria said. "My apologies again. I didn't mean to disturb you."

"Bria," Sister B called out. "I almost forgot to tell you that Paolo told me he has a 1962 Fulvia Berlina in his garage. Don't tell Mother Superior, but I'm going to say a prayer that we'll get to drive it. I think it has a quicker engine than your Fiat."

Bria wasn't sure why Sister B was bringing up a vintage car when she was supposed to be praying with Ombra, but she did know how much the nun loved cars. "I'm sure I could convince Paolo to let us take the car out for a spin."

"*Grazie mille*!" Sister B exclaimed.

It took Bria almost three blocks to realize that Sister Benedicta had done it again. She had given Bria a message in code. There was no Fulvia Berlina in 1962 because the car wasn't made until 1963. And the car's full name was *Lancia* Fulvia Berlina. The first name was the same last name as Fiorello's made-up name, Giacomo Lancia.

Ombra wasn't praying for a childhood friend. Thanks to Sister B, Bria knew that Ombra was praying for Fio.

Chapter 18

Gradually, the light disappeared and in its place was a gray shroud. A thick veil of not quite darkness, but an entrance to it. The beginning of gloom and heartache and the danger Bria had felt when she had first discovered Fiorello's body. She didn't understand the feeling; it was unlike anything she had ever experienced before, but it wouldn't go away.

Even when she had learned that Carlo had died and her world had changed in one horrible instant, she was overcome with inconsolable grief but not fear. She was never afraid because she was surrounded by friends and family, she had Marco, and although she didn't know it at the time, she had her own indefatigable strength. She conquered the darkest period of her life with the power and goodness of her soul. Oddly, she wasn't sure if that was going to be enough to fight whatever was lurking in the shadows.

It didn't help that all the potential suspects seemed to have split personalities, one day acting one way and the next day the complete opposite. She didn't know who Carlotta, Ombra, Armando, or Pietro were, and although she didn't want to admit it to herself, she didn't really like any of them. Armando was a philandering playboy, Pietro was a terrible father, Carlotta was a narcissistic diva, and Ombra was a deceitful liar. None of them seemed to have morals or strong ethics, which made them all capable of murder. But why?

Fiorello seemed harmless and, except to Carlotta, inconsequential to all their lives, but he was also hiding something. He had an alter ego in Giacomo Lancia and he was writing checks to a woman named Regina Pomotori, who may or may not be his pregnant girlfriend. Bria wished she could forget it all and just focus on the start of the tourist season and put all of her energy into making Bella Bella an even more enticing and comforting place for travelers to call their home away from home. But she couldn't. The fire in her belly wouldn't go out, and now that she felt the slow creep of fear travel up her spine, she had to see this through. She had to figure out who killed Fiorello and why. Not just for her sake and Fiorello's, but the entire village of Positano as well.

First, she needed to call her boyfriend and fill him in on the latest small clue she believed she had uncovered. In order to do that he needed to answer his cell phone. Even when he was working, Luca always took Bria's call if only to say that he was in the middle of something and would call her right back. He was either uncharacteristically busy or, worse, he was ignoring her.

Bria wasn't as explosive as her sister, but she had been known to throw a fit—or a shoe—when she lost control of her temper. There was no way she was going to toss an espadrille over the side of Viale Pasitea to let off some steam because she was frustrated, but she also wasn't going to let Luca off the hook. She took out her phone and dialed his number.

"Police station."

"You're not Luca," Bria said.

"No, this is Nunzi."

"Where's Luca?"

"Who's this?"

"*Uffa!*" Bria exclaimed. "You know it's me, Nunzi. Why isn't Luca answering his phones?"

"I'm answering his phone because the chief's busy."

"He's never busy."

"Would you like me to tell him that?"

"You know what I mean! He's never too busy to take my calls."

"Today he is."

Something wasn't right. "Nunzi, what's going on? You've all been acting strangely since I caught Imperia and Pietro in Luca's office."

"They weren't actually caught, they were in a meeting."

"Nunzi, I know something's up and I want to know what it is."

Just when the silence began to get awkward, Nunzi finally spoke. "It's police business."

Bria understood the drill; she wasn't part of the police department no matter how many times she solved their cases for them. However, she was hardly a newcomer who couldn't be trusted, and the relationships Bria had with Luca, Nunzi, and a few of the other members of the force transcended the traditional dealings the police had with citizens.

"We're also friends," Bria said.

There was another, even longer pause. "Let me see if I can get Luca."

As Bria waited, she noticed the sky had only gotten darker. Rain in Positano wasn't rare, but it also wasn't common. The rainy season—if it could even be called that—was from November to April, and even then, except for a few circumstances throughout the decades, a rain shower would be sudden and strong and then give way to sunshine. Hardly ever did rainstorms stay for an extended period of time. Perhaps the Sirens who guarded the seaside village wouldn't allow it because they wanted to be the ones to destroy curious sailors and not Mother

Nature. Or perhaps even the rain knew that a place as beautiful as Positano didn't deserve to be disrupted. But maybe it did need to be cleansed.

"Bria, *scusi,*" Luca said, sounding sincerely contrite. "I was on a call with Dante and you know how he likes to hear himself talk."

"What did Dante want?"

"Pietro's been bothering him about an update on the investigation so Dante bothered me."

"Why does Pietro care about who killed Fiorello?" Bria asked. "He doesn't even care about his own son."

"He wants this murder solved so his son, his fiancée, and Carlotta can leave Positano and head to Lake Como."

"What did you tell Dante?" Bria asked, ignoring Luca's explanation.

"Dante? Oh right. I told him the truth, that we've confirmed the cause of death and are speaking to people of interest and gathering clues and that they should all be able to leave here soon."

Despite her uneasiness, Bria decided not to pursue the real reason behind Dante's call and share the information with Luca, which was the real reason for her call in the first place.

"I think Ombra is closer to Fiorello than we originally thought."

"Why would you think that?" Luca asked.

"I went to talk to her to ask some more questions about Armando's past and I saw her praying with Sister Benedicta in the garden at Villa Magia."

"An Italian woman praying is hardly unusual."

"No, it isn't, but Ombra lied to me about what she was praying about."

"How do you know she was lying?"

"Because Sister B told me that Paolo has a 1962 Fulvia Berlina in his garage."

Luca gasped. "He does?!"

"No because one doesn't exist! The car didn't debut until 1963."

"*Certo!* That's right."

"Sister B was giving me a clue."

"How do you know that's what she was doing?"

"Because she's done it before," Bria said. "She's sly that one, she's like one of the nuns in *The Sound of Music*."

"I love that movie!" Luca gushed. "Has Marco seen it yet? We should all watch it together. I think there's a sing-a-long version. I know all the words to the songs, do you?"

Bria dropped her phone to her side and looked up at the dark sky. She shook her head and then smiled. This must be what it's like for Luca most of the time, listening to her and Rosalie.

She put the phone back up to her ear to continue the conversation and quickened her pace. It looked like it was about to downpour and she wanted to get home before she got drenched. "I do know all the words, but could we please focus on Sister B right now."

"*Scusi*. Tell me more about this clue in Paolo's garage."

"There isn't a Fulvia Berlina in Paolo's garage!"

"Then why did Sister B mention it?"

"Because of the manufacturer."

"It was made by Lancia."

"Finally! Does that name sound familiar?"

Luca gasped again. "That's the last name of Fiorello's alter ego, Giacomo Lancia."

"Sister B was trying to tell me without Ombra knowing that Ombra was praying for Fiorello and not some old girlfriend."

"*Santo cielo!*" Luca cried. "She really is a sly one. That's a great clue, but why wouldn't Ombra want you to know that she was praying for Fiorello?"

"That I can't figure out," Bria replied. "Maybe she was closer to him than we thought."

"Or maybe she's closer to the killer than we suspected."

"You think the only reason she was praying for Fio was because she knows who killed him?"

"It's possible," Luca said. "The way he was murdered indicates that it was premeditated and not an act of random violence by a stranger."

"It was personal."

"Yes, I'm convinced of that," Luca said. "Since Fio had no ties to Positano that makes the suspect list very short."

"Carlotta, Armando, Pietro . . ."

"And Ombra."

"Or someone we don't know," Bria added. "There's the possibility that he's connected to someone living or visiting here. When we first met Michele, we didn't know Paolo was his uncle."

"True," Luca replied. "We also wouldn't have known that Carlotta started her career singing in Piazza dei Mulini if Dante hadn't told us."

"That leaves us back to square one," Bria said. "Who killed Fio?"

"I don't know, Bria, but if I don't get going Nunzi's going to kill me. I'm late for a department meeting."

"*Anch'io*. If I don't start to run, I'm going to get caught in this rainstorm."

"*Stai attento,* it looks ominous out there."

The moment Bria got to Bella Bella and closed the door behind her, it started to rain. And not just a steady plummet, a torrential downpour. She called out, but no one answered. She did, however, hear a whimper.

"Bravo! *Tesoro mio, vieni dalla mamma.*"

Slowly, Bravo emerged from Bria's bedroom, his lean body close to the ground, head down, his big brown eyes searching out the familiar face. The moment he saw Bria he quickened his pace but still lay low. When Bria scooped him up in her arms, he whimpered slightly but affectionately licked her cheek.

"It's only the rain, *mio angelo;* it can't hurt you now that Mamma's here."

She bounced Bravo up and down like she used to bounce Marco in her arms when he was being cranky and wouldn't fall asleep. Bria had not been like other girls who dreamt of being a wife and mother since they were given their first doll to play with, but she was ecstatic when she found out she was pregnant and took to motherhood like it was a role she was destined to play. Holding Bravo like a baby made her realize that Marco was growing up so fast, and before she knew it, he'd be off to college. She wanted Marco to explore the world, but she also wanted him to stay right by her side.

Bria swirled around and saw a note on the dining room table with her name written on it that said, *Had to help Rosalie. Be back soon. Giovanni.*

Bria looked at her watch and saw that she had another hour to pick up Marco. If the rainstorm was typical, it would be over by the time she had to leave for St. Cecelia's. In the meantime, she thought she'd take advantage of the quiet and make herself a nice iced cappuccino and get a snack for Bravo.

Carrying Bravo, she went into the kitchen and with one hand put coffee into the new Gaggia Carezza espresso machine she had recently bought on her last trip to Sorrento. While the cappuccino was brewing, she put Bravo—who was much calmer now that Bria was near—on the floor and steamed some milk and whipped it into a froth. When the machine stopped purring, she poured the cup into a glass filled with ice and topped it with the foamed milk. She sprinkled a bit of cinnamon on top and took a sip.

"*Delizioso.*" Bria sighed.

Bravo, on the road back to his old self, barked. "I didn't forget you, *ragazzo mio.*"

Bria pulled open the bottom cabinet and Bravo's tail instantly started wagging. He knew it meant he was about to get his favorite treat. Dolci Impronte's Batticuore strawberry-flavored cookies that Bria found on a trip to Venice and had a monthly order sent to the house. Bria grabbed a handful of cookies, closed the cabinet door with her foot, and went into the sitting area with Bravo right behind her. She grabbed a copy of *Bell'Italia* magazine from the cocktail table, the cover line promising an in-depth look at Sicily, and sat down on the couch. She placed the cookies at her feet and Bravo started crunching excitedly. Both content, they set in for a relaxing hour before they would have to go pick up Marco.

At least that was the plan.

"Bria! Are you home?"

Looking up from the couch, Bria saw her sister enter the house followed by Fabrice a few feet behind her. Despite being drenched from the rain, they both looked very serious and Bria tried to say *ciao*, but the word caught in her throat. Instinctively, she knew something was wrong.

"Lorenza? Fabrice? Go get some towels and dry yourselves off, you're soaked," Bria instructed.

Lorenza pointed at Fabrice. "You stay and talk to Bria, I'll get the towels."

Despite the order, Fabrice remained quiet.

"Go on, Fabrice!" Lorenza yelled while pulling out some towels from the linen closet near Bria's bedroom door. "Tell her everything!"

"Tell me what?"

Bria started to get up, but Lorenza waved her back down. "You need to be sitting down for this."

"*Smettila!* You're scaring me."

"Bria, no, there's nothing to be scared of," Fabrice said. "But Lorenza's right, you should sit down."

Fabrice took a towel from Lorenza and wiped his face and

hair quickly before sitting down on the edge of the sofa next to Bria as Lorenza sat on the side chair. Lorenza patted her ankle and Bravo, satisfied by his cookies, gladly sat next to her. Bria, however, knew whatever Fabrice needed to tell her was deadly serious, not because of his grave expression, but because he only called her Bria and not Bria Bria like he usually did.

"What's wrong?" Bria asked.

"Remember at our dinner party when everyone was leaving and I said I would see Luca at that thing on Tuesday?" Fabrice asked.

"I do," Bria replied. "I assumed it was about racquetball. Don't you play a weekly game?"

"Yes, but on Thursdays."

"Then what was happening on Tuesday?"

"I needed to testify with the police."

"Testify? About what?"

"I didn't want to say anything and I even kept it from Lorenza," Fabrice said.

"I had no idea until this morning," Lorenza confirmed. "Once I knew what was going on, I told him that he had to tell you at once or I would."

"What does Fabrice's testimony have to do with me?"

"It has to do with the company I used to work for as a pilot, before I got this job," Fabrice explained. "When I worked for La Russo Enterprises."

"I've never heard of them," Bria said. "Who are they?"

"The parent company of Pietro's conglomerate."

"*Scusi,* Fabrice, I don't mean to be dense," Bria said. "What does any of this have to do with me? Lorenza, why must I know this?"

"Fabrice, tell her the rest," Lorenza demanded.

Fabrice inhaled and blew out a long breath. "La Russo Enterprises is the manufacturer of a computer chip that was in the plane that Carlo was flying when it crashed."

The glass Bria was holding in her hand started to shake, the ice cubes clinking against the sides. Fabrice took the glass from Bria and placed it on the cocktail table. "The police think that the chip could have caused a malfunction in the plane that led to the crash."

"The crash that killed Carlo?" Bria asked.

"Yes," Fabrice confirmed.

Images of Carlo's dead body lying on a slab of metal in the morgue invaded her mind's eye. She blinked to shut them out, but it was no use, they were too powerful. Next, came the sounds of the plane, whirring loudly, careening through the air, nose down flying directly into the mountains. Finally, the screams. The last sounds that she imagined escaped her husband's lips.

Involuntary tears filled Bria's eyes and she shook her head. She heard the start of a scream rise from her stomach and she clutched her hand to her mouth to silence it. She wasn't trying to stifle it to prevent Fabrice and Lorenza from feeling uncomfortable—they had seen her break down before. She wanted to smother the scream because she couldn't bear to relive the pain. Carlo was dead, she had grieved and mourned, and now she was ready to move on; she could not return to the scene of the crime. She needed to let her dead husband stay dead and not return to haunt her. But how could she avoid it now? After what she had just learned.

"I can't believe this," Bria said. "I didn't even know there was an investigation."

"It's been done very quietly because the company involved is quite high-profile," Fabrice explained. "Both the Swiss and the Italian police wanted to make sure news didn't leak out, otherwise they would have been interrupted or shut down."

"Why didn't anyone tell me?" Bria asked, her voice sounding like a wounded child's.

"Luca asked us not to say anything until he had answers," Fabrice said. "He didn't want to upset you for no reason."

"I told Fabrice that you had every right to know no matter how upset you would get," Lorenza said.

"Lorenza, did you work for that company, too?" Bria asked.

"La Russo?" Lorenza replied. "No, never."

"Then why did you have to testify?"

"I didn't, only Fabrice did."

"But Fabrice said, 'Luca asked us' not to say anything to you," Bria said. "If you didn't testify along with Fabrice, who did?"

"Imperia and Pietro," Fabrice confirmed.

"*Dio mio!*" Bria cried. "That's why they were in Luca's office."

Abruptly, Bria rose from the couch and started to pace the floor. She knew the scholarship wasn't the real reason they had met, and Imperia mentioned it only to divert the conversation. Bria had racked her brain trying to come up a real reason Imperia and Pietro would be meeting with Luca and couldn't think of anything except the far-fetched thought that Imperia was there to tell Luca he needed to sign a prenuptial agreement with Bria if he harbored any thoughts of marrying her. That didn't account for Pietro's presence, but it meant that Luca was in on the deception from the start.

Bria clenched her teeth so the thoughts in her head didn't rip through her mouth. *How could he lie to me!*

"I am so sorry, Bria, *molto dispiaciuto.*" Fabrice stood up and tried to grab Bria's hands to make her stand still, but he couldn't catch her. She continued to pace the floor, walking into the dining room area, the fear that she previously felt in her stomach now full-fledged rage.

"No one thought that I should know!? Not Imperia, not Luca!" Bria screamed. "How *dare* they keep this from me!"

"That's why I made Fabrice come right here to tell you," Lorenza said. "Carlo was your husband and you have every right to know the truth about how he died."

The sisters—like most sisters—may have had their differences over the decades, but they always had each other's back. It was more than she could say about Luca.

"Does Luca know that you've told me?"

"No," Lorenza said. "I told Fabrice not to say anything to anyone in case they tried to convince him to remain quiet."

"*Grazie*, at least someone's on my side."

"Bria, please understand we're all on your side," Fabrice said. "Especially Luca. He loves you and he simply didn't want you to relive that horrible night if he could prevent it. He was protecting you."

That word again, *protect!* Ever since she was a little girl that's all Bria had ever heard from her family, at school, in books, on TV; girls needed to be protected. When was the world going to comprehend the truth?

"It's time Luca understands that I don't need *anyone's* protection."

This time when Bria entered the police station, she slammed the door shut behind her, and ignored Nunzi, Matteo, and the rest of the police officers who told her she couldn't go into Luca's office. No one was going to stop her from confronting Luca, no matter who was on the other side of the door. When she entered, she realized the only thing she was interrupting Luca from was his own bad conscience. She could see from the pained expression on his face that he knew exactly why she was standing in the middle of his office, breathing heavily, with both fists clenched.

"*Per favore,*" Luca said. "Let me explain."

"Explain how you colluded with Imperia, Fabrice, and Pietro behind my back?!"

"I wasn't colluding."

"How about lying? You lied right to my face, Luca! I asked you why they were here and you told me it was nothing!"

"I didn't want to upset you for no reason. This investigation does not have a lot of internal support; we're being forced to conduct it and there's a very good chance it could lead nowhere."

"It could also lead to the reason my husband was killed!"

"Yes, that is possible, and if that turns out to be the case, of course I would tell you. I wouldn't let anyone else do it."

"Why, so you could be my hero?"

"What?"

"So you could be the one to swoop in and be there for me when I break down from the news."

"No, because I want to be the one person in your life who is the bearer of all news, both good and bad!"

"Yet you still kept this from me! And *Dio mio,* you forced everyone else to keep quiet, too!"

"Obviously I didn't do a very good job because Fabrice must have been the one to open his big mouth and tell you. *Dannazione!* This is exactly what I didn't want to happen!"

"He only told me because Lorenza forced him to! At least my sister doesn't treat me like a child."

"I wasn't treating you like a child! I was treating you like the woman I love!"

"You don't know the meaning of love! Carlo would *never* have treated me like this!"

"*So che!* Because Carlo was a saint! No man can *ever* be as perfect as Carlo!"

"That's right! He would have never lied to me and kept something this important from me! He would have never done that to me!"

"Well, guess what, Bria? I'm not Carlo!"

"I am perfectly aware that you are *nothing* like my Carlo."

"Go on, keep comparing me to your first husband, and you and I will never have the relationship that I know we can."

"*Sei pazzo*?! After this betrayal we don't have a relationship! And we never will!"

They both turned to look at Nunzi when she closed the office door. Her face was pale and she looked terrified.

"Nunzi, what is it?" Bria asked.

"Marco's been kidnapped."

Chapter 19

Bria couldn't breathe.

The room began to tilt, and the floor felt like mud; she was swaying and sinking, and she felt her lungs tighten. The world around her had changed in an instant and she was fighting to stay conscious. All she wanted to do was forget the words she had just heard and retreat into sleep.

Bria was vaguely aware that people around her were talking, and she felt a hand on her elbow and another at her wrist. She was only upright because she had help. She was being protected, which is exactly what she didn't want.

She heard a voice from somewhere next to her or coming from inside her own brain, she couldn't tell, but it was loud and forceful. *Fight! Marco needs you!* Her son's face appeared before her, but he didn't look the way he did this morning; he looked frightened, terrified, and he was screaming. Bria tried, but she couldn't hear his words, she only saw his mouth open wide over and over again, fear clinging to his face like sweat. What was he saying?

"Mamma! Help me! Help me, Mamma!"

Bria tried to reply, but the words rumbled in her throat and hurled themselves out of her body in a guttural cry. "Noooo!!!"

"Bria, listen to me. We're going to find him, I promise."

She stared into Luca's face, into his eyes, and saw that their beauty was shadowed by fear. She knew he loved Marco deeply and he was also suffering. But he had betrayed her; she didn't want to share this pain with him.

Strength began to return to her body, and she pulled her arms away from both Luca and Nunzi, who were holding her. She gulped the air—she needed fuel to move forward—and took several deep breaths. Tears spilled down her cheeks, but she didn't waste the time wiping them away; she needed to find her son.

She grabbed Nunzi's arm and looked her in the eye. Once again Bria had control of herself. She wasn't going to give it up again until her son was back in her arms.

"Tell me everything you know, Nunzi."

"Sister Benedicta called the police station and reported that Marco was missing," Nunzi explained.

"Why didn't she call me first?" Bria asked.

"She said she tried several times, but you didn't pick up."

Bria reached for the phone in the back pocket of her jeans and was shocked to see that Sister B had called her three times and she had texts and voice messages from Giovanni. She closed her eyes and cursed herself. She hadn't heard the phone because she'd been arguing with Luca. Because of him she had lost precious time searching for her son. But something wasn't right; Nunzi wasn't giving her the full story.

"First, you said he was kidnapped," Bria said. "Now, he's missing. They're not the same thing."

"Sister B said that Sister Caterina was watching the students after school as their parents and guardians came to pick them up, but because of the rain some waited inside and some waited underneath the awning on the other side of the playground, which is where Marco was," Nunzi said. "Caterina saw that a man picked up Marco whom she didn't recognize, but Marco didn't put up a fuss, so she thought it was all right."

"Maybe it was Giovanni or Enrico!" Bria cried.

"Sister Caterina has lived here for years; she knows most everyone in the village and she didn't recognize him."

"Then why did she let him take my son?!"

"She thought Marco knew the man."

"Can she describe him?" Luca asked.

"Dark hair, Italian," Nunzi said. "Nothing outstanding."

"Why did Sister B call?" Bria asked. "If Caterina didn't question the man, what changed?"

"A little while later, Giovanni came to pick up Marco, and Sister Caterina realized what had happened," Nunzi explained. "They tried to call Marco on his cell phone, but he didn't pick up. That's when Sister B called you and then the police."

A new wave of fear bombarded Bria's body and she shut her eyes and clenched her fists. She wasn't going to let it weaken her. She screamed in frustration and thrashed her arms into the air.

"We have to talk to Sister Caterina," Bria declared. "Now!"

They took their Vespas to St. Cecilia's, Bria making a point of sitting behind Nunzi on her bike instead of riding with Luca. The roads were still slick from the sudden rain shower so they had to drive more cautiously, making the short ride feel like an eternity. On the way Bria recited the Hail Mary several times interspersed with short prayers begging God to keep her son safe and unharmed. She wanted to scream out loud like the mythological gods who founded Positano centuries ago and make the world kneel at the sound and remove all obstacles to reveal a path that led to her son. But she knew that screaming wasn't going to find her son; she needed to remain calm and focused. Once Marco was safely back home, she would scream until she collapsed.

When they pulled into St. Cecilia's, Giovanni, Sister B, and Sister Caterina were standing at the gate. Behind them was a smattering of children playing in the schoolyard who were still waiting for their parents to pick them up. Nunzi hadn't come to a full stop and Bria was already off the bike.

"Sister Caterina," Bria said. "Are you sure that you have no idea who this man is?"

The sister looked like a shorter, rounder version of Sister B, right down to the tearstained cheeks. "I'm so sorry, I thought he was a relative," Sister Caterina said. "Marco seemed to know him, so I didn't question it when they left together."

"It's my fault." Giovanni looked pale and his voice was thick. "There was traffic on the way back from Sorrento and then I was on the phone with Rosalie. She was complaining that she couldn't find her rocks and was wondering if I moved them when I was helping Mariana on the boat." Giovanni seemed to become aware that he was rambling and abruptly stopped and shook his head. "I lost track of time. Had I been here on time . . ."

"Vanni, no!" Bria hugged her friend and then pulled back and grabbed his hands. "This is not your fault, *capisco*? Someone took Marco; whoever did this, it's their fault, no one else's."

"Did anyone else see this man?" Luca asked.

Caterina looked around the schoolyard. "I'm not sure, but I don't see why they wouldn't have; he wasn't trying to hide."

"He just came up and said hello to Marco?" Luca asked.

"Yes," Sister Caterina replied. "As if he was expected; there wasn't anything unusual about it."

Bria looked around and shouted when she saw a familiar face. "Tomaso!"

A young boy, roughly Marco's age, but taller and larger, turned around when he heard his name. "*Ciao,* Signora Bartolucci."

"*Per favore,* I need to speak with you."

Bria walked over to Tomaso who was standing with his

mother. Bria recognized the woman but realized they had never had a conversation before. Normally, she would have introduced herself and exchanged pleasantries, but she didn't have the time. She needed to find out if Tomaso witnessed anything that could help them find out where Marco had been taken.

"Tomaso, did you see the man Marco left with?" Bria asked.

The boy didn't speak because he was too frightened, looking at the group standing behind Bria: two police officers, two nuns, and a man who looked like he could break Tomaso in two. His mother looked at Bria, and without Bria having to say a word the woman knew she was in anguish because something had happened to her son. She put her hand on Tomaso's shoulder and said, "*Va bene,* Tomaso, tell them everything you know."

"He seemed nice, the guy," Tomaso said. "He wasn't weird or *strano*."

"Did you hear his name?" Bria asked.

"No, Marco just said he was going to take him to the game."

"What game?"

"The charity soccer game in Amalfi," Tomaso replied.

A huge wave of relief washed over Bria followed immediately by a torrent of rage. She knew exactly who took her son. Unfortunately, it was a man that she did not trust.

"It was Armando."

"Armando?" Luca asked. "Are you sure?"

"He talked about the game at Fabrice and Lorenza's dinner party," Bria said. "He even mentioned taking Marco, but I didn't think he was serious and he never mentioned it again."

"He isn't picking up his cell phone," Nunzi said.

"You have his cell phone number?" Bria asked.

"Of course," Nunzi replied. "He's a person of interest in Fiorello's murder."

"*Dio mi perdoni,*" Sister Caterina gasped. "I had no idea he was such an evil man."

Luca put his hand on the nun's shoulder. It didn't stop her from crying, but her body didn't shake as hard. "We don't know that Armando has done anything criminal, and I do not believe that he would hurt Marco."

"But we need to get to him," Bria said. "Now!"

"Yes," Luca agreed. "Let's go back to the station and take the car to Amalfi."

"I've already called Silvio; he was there on patrol duty for the climate change protest," Nunzi conveyed. "He's on his way to the soccer field and said he'd call once he spotted Marco."

"Tell him not to approach them, just watch from a safe distance," Luca instructed.

"Why don't you have him arrest Armando?" Giovanni asked.

"We don't know Armando's state of mind," Luca replied. "If he feels like he's cornered, he may lash out."

Bria was on the back of Nunzi's Vespa by the time she approached. "Enough talking! We have to go!"

No one responded verbally, but they all took action. Nunzi and Luca jumped on their Vespas, and before Luca could start the ignition, Giovanni sat on the seat with him. "I don't like this position, either," Vanni said. "But I'm going with you."

"No, you're not," Luca said.

"Luca!" Bria cried. "This isn't the time to be petty!"

"I'm not being petty, I'm thinking about Marco!" Luca replied. "When he sees the police, he's going to be scared. It'll be worse if he has to drive home in a cop car. Giovanni can take your car to meet us there and then drive Marco home. It'll make him feel safer."

Bria swallowed hard. She felt like an idiot for accusing Luca of holding onto past grudges against Vanni and she wasn't able to see her current anger toward Luca. He was thinking about the well-being of her son and there wasn't anything else she could ask for.

"*Bene*," Bria said. "*Grazie.*"

* * *

By the time they got to the police station and transferred into Luca's Fiat Panda, his official patrol car, Bria had called Marco seven times. She had just gotten him a refurbished Nokia cell phone in bright orange so it would be harder for him to lose. It didn't have smart phone capabilities and it had an antiquated texting system, but she thought it was important for Marco to know that he was still attached to his mother while he began to embrace his own freedom. It also gave Bria a sense of relief to know that she'd always be connected to her son. But in order to do that Marco had to pick up the phone when it rang.

"Why isn't he answering?"

Bria was sitting in the passenger seat next to Luca and Nunzi was in the back. They had been silent since they had gotten into the car, no one knowing the appropriate thing to say. The fallout from Bria and Luca's fight hung in the air like the thick clouds that continued to loiter the sky. Without any confirmation that Marco and Armando were at the soccer field or any news on his condition, the only conversation would be speculative. When a child was in danger it was much too easy for the mind to jump to the worst-case scenario. Which was where Bria was headed.

"There's always a lot of screaming and cheering at a game," Luca said. "He might not even hear the phone."

"The battery could have died," Nunzi said. "Or he could be out of range."

All logical reasons, and yet Bria couldn't help but worry there was another more nefarious reason. "What if Armando took the phone away from Marco so he couldn't call me?"

Luca turned to face Bria and the pain in their eyes was identical. He placed his hand on hers and after a moment's hesitation, squeezed it tight. "Bria, I promised you, we're going to find him safe and sound."

Despite the anger she'd felt toward Luca only a short time ago, she believed him. She wasn't sure if she believed him because he was worthy of her trust or because she was desperate. She felt her head nodding in agreement and she was about to squeeze his hand back when she suddenly pulled it away. She couldn't forget what he had done to her. There was nothing she could do about it now—she needed to corral all her strength until she saw Marco's smile again—but she wasn't going to forgive Luca's betrayal. The pain was still too raw.

"Silvio can see them!" Nunzi passed her phone to Bria. "Look, he took a photo of them."

"Marco!" Although Bria shouted her son's name, it sounded more like a howl, an anguished lament filled with deep pain, but also a hint of hope. "We're almost there, *amore mio*."

"Tell Silvio not to let them out of his sight," Luca ordered. "If they start to leave, he needs to intervene and get Marco out of there."

"Done," Nunzi confirmed.

Luca pressed his foot down on the gas pedal. "Hold on."

Twenty minutes later they pulled into the small parking lot next to the soccer field. Giovanni had already arrived and had parked a few cars away. He came running over with Silvio.

"The game started late because of the rain and ended only a few minutes ago," Silvio said. "But they haven't moved."

Bria reached out to grab Vanni's arm. "You didn't go over to Marco?"

"No, of course not," he replied. "Luca said not to approach them and the first face he should see should be yours."

People were starting to walk to their cars, while a few others were hanging around the stand, raucously talking about the game and trying to get an autograph from a player. Marco and Armando were sitting on a bench, their backs to them, and they could hear Marco laughing. The boy seemed fine, but until they separated him from Armando, they couldn't be sure that he wasn't in harm's way.

Bria knew that she should wait until she was next to her son to call out, otherwise she'd be giving Armando the opportunity to grab Marco and run off into the park, but seeing them together reminded her of when Carlo used to take Marco to the park when he was just a toddler. She didn't trust Armando—she believed he had the potential to be a very dangerous man—and although she didn't understand it, she knew in her heart that he wasn't going to hurt Marco.

"Marco!" Bria cried out.

Instantly, Marco and Armando turned around. Marco's eyes lit up with delight while Armando's face turned pale.

"Mamma!" Marco yelled. "We just saw the best game ever!"

Bria ran toward Marco and when she got next to him, she fell to her knees and hugged him tightly. Her heart was beating wildly against Marco's chest and her lips were moving quickly saying a prayer of thanks and tickling his ears. For the first time that she could remember, Marco resisted Bria's hug and pulled away. He looked up and saw Luca, Nunzi, Vanni, and a police officer standing behind them. Bria thought that his face aged right in front of her eyes.

"Mamma, what's wrong?"

He didn't fully know what was happening, but he understood the seriousness of the situation. Bria could see that Marco was confused and her instinct—like all mothers—was to lie and say everything was fine. But how could she lie to her own son just to protect him when she was furious with Luca for doing the same thing to her? She deserved the truth and so did Marco.

"Why do you look so scared?" Marco asked.

"I didn't know where you were," Bria admitted. "I thought something bad might have happened to you."

"We all did," Luca added. "But you were just having a good time at the game."

"We did have a great time," Armando said. "Didn't we?"

Marco turned to face Armando but didn't let go of Bria's arm. His brow was furrowed like he was trying to solve a puzzle or a math problem. "You lied to me."

Armando smiled his dazzling billionaire son smile that Bria had seen before. It must have gotten him out of hundreds of scuffles and incidents that would have led a poorer man to jail, but Bria knew it wasn't going to work here. Her son was too smart to be fooled.

"You told me that Mamma said it was okay for you to take me to the soccer game."

Bria made sure her son heard the truth, so she spoke first unwilling to give didn't Armando the chance to speak first and have an opportunity to distort the facts. "He did ask me if he could take you to the game and I said that it should be okay, but he never mentioned it again, so I didn't know if he was serious about his offer or even when the game was going to be played."

Marco turned back to face Armando. "That sounds like lying to me."

To his credit, Armando didn't try to dissolve the truth with another smile. He didn't look away but faced Marco and nodded. "You're right. I should have properly asked for permission."

"That's why you said we should turn off our phones," Marco said. "It wasn't so we could concentrate on the game, it was so Mamma wouldn't know where I was."

Bria didn't know what was happening, but she could swear that it looked like Armando was going to cry.

"No, I . . ." Armando started. "I just wanted the two of us to enjoy the game."

This wasn't how the scenario was supposed to have played out. Bria was sincerely grateful that Marco was unhurt physically, though she knew that he was emotionally wounded, but seeing Armando contrite and ashamed didn't make sense. The man was a bully, he was loud, condescending, crass; he was not a man who looked like all he wanted was forgiveness.

"I'm sorry, Marco," Armando said. "But thank you very much for a really nice afternoon."

Marco stared at him and looked like he just noticed a bad odor descend onto him. He turned to face Bria and said, "I want to go home."

"*Certo*," Bria replied. "Vanni will take you home in my car."

Marco gripped Bria's arm tighter. "Aren't you coming, too?"

"I need to stay here and talk to Armando for a bit." Bria noticed a look of concern etch onto Marco's face. "Don't worry, I'll be fine."

"Luca, you'll stay with Mamma and make sure she's okay, right?"

"Of course I will," Luca replied. "*Prometto*."

Marco threw his arms around Bria and she held him tightly. She fought back the tears until she heard her son whisper "*Ti amo*" in her ear. She didn't trust herself to speak because she knew she would simply sob, so she squeezed Marco tighter.

After Vanni and Marco left, Bria stood up, turned away from everyone, and wiped her tears. Armando didn't move, not even when Luca approached him. "We'll be right over there so don't try and run off." Armando didn't respond; he simply lowered his eyes and shook his head. Luca, Nunzi, and Silvio walked a few feet away, out of hearing distance, but close enough to intervene if there was reason.

Bria sat down next to Armando and was perplexed. The cocky rich boy was nowhere to be found; in his place was a lost soul.

"*Mi dispiace molto*, Bria."

"I don't want an apology, I want an explanation," she replied. "What is this all about?"

"A woman like you wouldn't understand."

"Don't assume you know anything about me or any woman,

for that matter," Bria hissed. "Explain your actions and I'll be the one to decide if I understand them or not."

Armando looked off into the distance and shrugged his shoulders. "I wanted to know what it was like to be a father spending an afternoon with his son."

"Marco is not your son."

"I know that," Armando replied. "Just like I know I'm never going to be a father."

"How can you say that? You're . . ." Bria cut herself off abruptly. She was going to say "You're about to become a father" when she realized that if Armando was being sincere, and he most certainly appeared to be, he truly didn't know Ombra was pregnant. She took a deep breath and ended her sentence differently. "You're a young man, about to get married. Ombra will probably get pregnant on the honeymoon."

"That's impossible."

Bria stared at Armando, who continued to gaze at something Bria could not see. "What aren't you telling me, Armando?"

"We'll never have children because I had a vasectomy years ago when I was in college."

Bria thought a vasectomy was an extreme form of birth control for a young man, but perhaps Pietro forced him into it knowing his son was not just an heir, but a rapscallion. "Those things can be reversed."

"I didn't have a vasectomy because I didn't want to accidentally father a child," Armando explained. "I had one to prevent that possibility from ever happening for the sake of the child."

"Any child would be lucky to have you and Ombra for parents."

Armando smiled weakly. "I told you that you wouldn't understand." He turned away from Bria and looked straight ahead, his hands flat on the bench tucked under the backs of his thighs. "You're a good woman from a good family; you have no idea what it's like in my world."

"Are you forgetting that my mother-in-law is a billionaire as well? I know all too well how people in your world behave."

"When I was in college, I slept with any girl I wanted to," Armando started. "Some of them were more willing than others, but that didn't stop me. Sometimes I used protection, sometimes I didn't. If a girl got pregnant, I made them get an abortion, paid for by Pietro Industries, of course. If the girl didn't want to terminate her pregnancy, I forced them into it. Until Gina."

"Who was Gina?"

"My girlfriend in senior year of college," Armando replied. "I loved her, but she came from a very modest family and my father was not happy with my choice. When Gina told me she was pregnant, I ignored the fact that she was smiling and I told her I'd pay for the abortion. She adamantly refused and said that she was having her baby with or without my help. She quit school and went back home, and I'm ashamed to admit that I never went to find her nor did I tell anyone that I was about to become a father."

"You've never seen your child?"

Armando bowed his head. "Several months later I saw Gina in the park; she was waiting for me because she knew it was the way to my dorm. She told me that she had lost the baby."

Bria made the sign of the cross. "I'm so sorry."

"I wasn't at the time. I was relieved," Armando said. "Imagine that? Relieved because my firstborn child was never born."

Bria opened her mouth to speak but quickly shut it. There was nothing she could say that wouldn't sound phony, contrite, or judgmental. She waited for Armando to continue his story.

"Gina said that she wanted me to know that there were complications," Armando said. "Of course I blurted out that I would pay for all her medical expenses. She slapped me in the face for that remark."

"Gina sounds like my kind of girl," Bria said.

"You two share many of the same qualities, the main one being kindness," Armando said. "Gina told me that our baby had Trisomy 18, more commonly known as Edwards Syndrome, a very genteel name for a horrible disease."

"I've never heard of it."

"It's very rare and most babies die in the womb or within days after childbirth," Armando explained.

"*Dio mio!*" Bria gasped. "That's horrible."

"Some children live a few months, but none reach their first birthday," Armando said.

"Miscarriages are unfortunately common with the first pregnancy," Bria said. "I know many women who've miscarried the first time who went on to have many children."

"Not if the father of the child has the gene that carries this congenital disease, like I do," Armando said.

This was what Imperia was trying to tell Bria and perhaps why Pietro thought his son his defected. Bria was beginning to understand why Armando was so desperate to spend some time alone with Marco.

"I'm the one who passed this gene onto my child and I'll pass it on to any child I ever have, which is why I decided to have a vasectomy and never risk becoming a father again," Armando confessed. "My father is a terrible man, so part of me was relieved that I would remove any chance of turning into him and repeating his mistakes. I never thought I'd regret not being able to be a father until this whole marriage thing with Ombra. I don't love her—she knows that, and I know you do, too—but despite that fact I started to fantasize what it would be like to be the head of a little family, have my own child. When I saw how Marco looks at you, with such trust and unconditional love, I wanted to know what that was like, if only for one afternoon."

"You were wrong about me," Bria said. "I do understand your actions. And I forgive you."

A choked sob escaped Armando's throat. "I don't deserve anyone's forgiveness."

"You have to start by forgiving yourself," Bria said. "You made a mistake. Marco will recover and so will you. What you've been through is terrible, it's life changing, but remember you're young and wealthy, you could adopt a child."

Abruptly, Armando started to laugh. "My father would never allow me to adopt a child; the Puccia bloodline must remain pure or end with me."

"There's no way that Ombra could carry your child without them inheriting this disease?"

"Doctors to the super rich never like to deliver bad news," Armando said. "They've implied that there's a *possibility* the gene wouldn't get passed to my child, but I'm not willing to take that risk."

"Does Ombra know?"

"I haven't found the courage to tell her yet."

"Don't you think she has a right to know?"

"I'm not sure if you've noticed, but this wedding is the most important thing in our parents' lives," Armando said. "I'll tell Ombra after the wedding. If she wants to divorce me, she'll get a nice fat settlement and I can go back to being the obnoxious oh-so-eligible rich bachelor I was before. No one will suffer."

Ombra was lying to Armando and Armando was lying to Ombra, but the only one who was going to suffer was Ombra's unborn child, whose mere existence would be proof that their marriage was broken before it began. Now that Bria knew the truth, she had an incredibly hard decision to make. Should she keep quiet or should she expose the engaged couple's lies before it was too late?

Chapter 20

Even though Bria was exhausted she couldn't sleep. It had been one of the worst days of her life and the residual emotions clung to her like barbed wire piercing her skin and refusing to let go. She had lost Luca and she had almost lost her son. Life couldn't get much worse. Unless, of course, she was Ombra.

That poor woman was harboring a lie that was going to blow up in her face. Without a doubt she was carrying another man's child that she thought she'd be able to pass off as Armando's. But since Armando was harboring the secret that he could never father a child, Ombra's plan was going to backfire the moment the bump in her belly was too big to ignore.

Their whole sham of a marriage was going to implode once the truth was learned. Bria knew that she wasn't entirely justified in her thinking, but she felt it was further proof of the destruction that was caused when a man kept a secret under the guise of trying to protect a woman.

Clearly Armando was a coward. Part of the reason he kept his vasectomy hidden and never revealed that he carried a cruel congenital disease was because he was afraid that he would be perceived as less of a man by society, his new wife, and mostly, his father. How could he exist if he was no longer seen as the playboy, but as the diseased loser who couldn't produce an heir? Such a fall from grace would be devastating. But what if the coward could transform himself into the hero? Perhaps then his reputation would be salvaged and he would earn the respect he craved. Protect Ombra from the horror of carrying his child and Armando would protect himself from the public's and possibly his father's disapproval.

When would men understand that women didn't need protection? It was something that had always infuriated Bria because she was one of those girls who didn't grow up believing the fairy tales she was told or the storybooks she read; she didn't need help navigating life, she was her own charming prince.

"Mamma, why does Talia marry the king?" Bria had asked her mother as a child. She had just finished reading Giambattista Basile's story *Sun, Moon, and Talia,* the first known European version of *Sleeping Beauty.* "He let her sleep for so many years without helping her?"

"*È una ragazza sciocca,*" Fifetta had replied.

"I would never be that silly, Mamma. I'd tell the king to go away and leave me alone."

"That's because you're strong, *mi amore,*" Fifetta had replied. "One day you'll want your prince to stay, but only if he's worthy of your love. Now come *mangia la tua pasta.*"

Was any man worthy of a woman's love? Maybe deep down Armando thought Ombra would thank him for sparing her from tragedy. It was absurd, but some men could twist their rationalizations to justify any action. Like Luca.

I thought Luca was worthy of my love, Bria thought, *but now I'm not so sure.*

The only man worthy of her love was standing in her doorway in his pajamas, with tousled hair and sleep still clinging to his eyes.

"'*Giorno,* Mamma," Marco said. "You couldn't sleep, either?"

"'*Giorno,* Marcito," Bria replied. "Come, sit by Mamma."

Marco didn't run toward Bria's bed, but he also didn't walk slowly; he was as eager for company as Bria was to hold her son. Under the covers, Marco snuggled close to Bria and she put her arm around his slender frame. She kissed the top of his head and breathed in his familiar scent of apples and sweat, a mixture of his shampoo and his natural odor. She listened as his breathing slowed down and assumed he had woken from a nightmare and sought comfort from the one place he knew he would find it, in his mother's arms.

"We had a bit of an adventure yesterday, didn't we?" Bria said.

"I thought it was an adventure," Marco replied. "But it turned out bad."

"It wasn't so terrible; you did see a terrific soccer match."

"But I made you worry—you were scared because you didn't know where I was."

"That's true, I was very scared."

Marco wiggled himself free of Bria's embrace and sat up on his knees in bed facing Bria. "*Mi spiace, Mamma.* I didn't mean to make you worry."

"I know you didn't, you should forget all about it."

"No, I shouldn't. I need to remember so I don't make the same mistake again."

"And what mistake is that?"

"I should never go with anyone unless I tell you first," Marco said. "Or Rosalie, because I trust her like I trust you."

"Yes, you can trust *Zia* Rosalie completely."

"Or I can tell Vanni or Luca," Marco said. "I can trust the both of them, too."

Bria made sure that she didn't change her expression; she kept smiling, watching her son begin to navigate his own life. She did agree with him that he could trust Vanni and Luca—they both loved Marco and would never do anything that would put him in danger. Just because she wasn't sure that she could trust Luca didn't mean her son shouldn't put his faith in him.

"I hope you know that Armando didn't mean to hurt you or

cause any trouble by taking you to the game." Bria controlled her voice to sound as nonchalant as possible. She didn't want to make a big deal out of what she was saying, but she needed Marco to understand that Armando's motives were, in an odd way, pure. "He got so excited about spending time with you watching a sport you both love that he made a mistake."

Marco leaned back and into Bria's side. "I get it. He was wrong, he should've told you we were going, but we all make mistakes."

"Yes, we do." Bria kissed the side of Marco's head and sat up in the bed. "What do you say we go make ourselves some pancakes for breakfast."

Before Marco could agree, the third member of their little family bounded into the bedroom. Bravo stood in the doorway, his tongue dangling out of his mouth almost as long as his drooping ears, his tail wagging like a windshield wiper in a rainstorm. His mere presence, as always, made both Bria's and Marco's eyes light up.

"Bravo must have heard you say *breakfast*," Marco said.

In confirmation, Bravo barked, pranced toward the bed, grabbed the sheet in his mouth, and pulled it off them. Squeals of giggles filled the air as Bria and Marco jumped off the bed and showered Bravo with kisses and hugs. They only stopped when they heard Giovanni shouting from the kitchen.

"Pancakes are ready! *Vieni a mangiare!*"

"Pancakes!" Bria cried.

"How did Vanni know we wanted pancakes?"

"He must be psychic."

"Maybe Vanni's like Eusapia Palladino!" Marco cried.

"Who's Eusapia Palladino?"

"A famous psychic from a long time ago; she could read minds and held seances to talk to ghosts."

"How did you hear about this?"

"Rosalie told me."

"*Uffa!* Don't listen to what she says. You can't trust her when she starts talking crazy."

"But, Mamma, you just said I could trust *Zia* Rosalie."

"With your life, yes, with facts, no." Bria gave Marco's bum a little slap. "Now let's go before Bravo eats all our pancakes!"

After devouring breakfast Marco took Bravo for a walk to visit Enrico. There was a part of Bria that wanted to join them, but she felt that it was important to let Marco reclaim his independence and not be afraid after yesterday's incident. She did text Enrico and asked him to text her the moment Marco arrived and when he left. True to form, Enrico followed her orders without question. Traits like that were why Bria knew he was the perfect partner for Mimi, who was much bossier and liked to remain in control.

Bria showered and got dressed, pairing her khaki shorts with a long-sleeved, blue-and-green floral chiffon top that tied at the waist. She found the vintage piece the last time she and Rosalie went to the consignment shop in the village. Green clip-on earrings that resembled exclamation points, a green headband to keep her hair from falling into her face, and her dependable espadrilles completed her outfit. She reached for the necklace Luca had given her for *La Festa della Mamma*, but on second thought decided against wearing it, telling herself it wouldn't go with her outfit and not that she didn't want to be reminded of Luca all day long. She needed a respite from her emotions, which meant she needed a day of fun with her best friend.

She sat at the dining room table and was about to pour herself a second cup of coffee and scroll leisurely through the online version of *La Repubblica*, one of Italy's most popular daily newspapers, when Marco returned.

"That was a quick visit," Bria said.

Marco didn't look up but crouched down to grab some treats

from the bottom shelf of the cabinet to give to Bravo. "Enrico wasn't in the mood to talk."

Bria let out a laugh. "When is Enrico ever *not* in the mood to talk?"

"When he's fighting with Mimi."

"Enrico and Mimi were fighting?"

"Don't say anything, Mamma. Enrico asked me not to tell you."

"Then why are you telling me?"

Marco sat across from Bria and grabbed a banana from the bowl in the center of the table. "Because it wasn't their regular fighting, you know, like when *Nonna* Fifetta and *Zia* Lorenza yell at each other. They sounded really angry."

"Do you know what they were fighting about?"

"It had to do with that lady who sings."

"Mimi doesn't like Carlotta."

"And Mimi doesn't like that Enrico disagrees with her."

"What do you mean?"

"Enrico said that Mimi doesn't know Carlotta like he does."

"What else did he say?"

"Nothing; they stopped talking when they saw me and Bravo. Then Mimi left for the bookstore and Enrico said that I shouldn't say anything to you about their arguing."

That was interesting news. More interesting because Enrico wanted the news to remain buried. Could Enrico also have a connection to Carlotta? He had lived in Positano his entire life, he could have known the singer when she was a young woman. Why wouldn't he have said something about it when Carlotta first arrived?

Bria knew she had to delve further into this potential relationship and question Enrico to get to the truth, but for the moment the only thing that mattered was seeing Rosalie.

When Bria walked down the marina toward Rosalie's boat, she knew her instinct had been correct. Well, half-correct. Bria thought she needed to have some fun with Rosalie, but it looked like Rosalie was the one who needed her best friend.

Bria saw Rosalie sitting on the deck of the boat and Michele walking down the dock toward her. His head was down and his hands were shoved into the pockets of his jeans. Bria couldn't tell if he looked contrite or shifty; whichever it was it meant he wasn't leaving Rosalie's on good terms.

"*Ciao,* Michele." Bria's greeting caught Michele off guard, and when he saw Bria he practically stumbled to a stop. "You're in a hurry this morning."

Michele smiled and ran a hand through his long, black hair, tucking it behind his ear. "Yes, I need to go out of town for a few days."

"By yourself?"

Bria knew that her question sounded accusatory, but she couldn't help it, that's what she was being.

"Yes, I'm going to visit my *zia* Teresina," Michele shared. "She hasn't been feeling well lately, so I'm going to help her around the house."

Bria wanted to believe that Michele was telling the truth, but she didn't. "*È molto carino.*"

"I . . . um . . . owe her a lot and I need to make up for the way I've treated her in the past," Michele admitted. "This trip will be good for the both of us and maybe I can repay her for all she's done for me."

Bria thought he sounded sincere, but still there was something about his eyes, the way they couldn't maintain contact with hers and how they danced around, that led her to believe that he was lying.

"I'm sure Teresina will love having you," Bria said. "How long will you be away?"

"I'm not sure, depends on how quickly she gets back on her feet."

Michele looked like he wanted to say more, but he remained quiet. She wished she could help him, but there was a larger part of her that wished he would never return and stay out of her friend's life forever.

"*Grazie,* Bria."

"For what?"

Michele shrugged his shoulders and shook his head. "Nothing. Everything." He smiled again and raised his hand. "*Ciao.*"

Bria watched him leave and resigned herself to admitting that she couldn't figure him out. The mystery of Michele would remain unsolved for another day because Bria was ready to begin a new chapter in her friendship with Rosalie. When she stepped onto *La Vie en Rosalie,* it appeared that the boat's namesake didn't share her enthusiasm.

Rosalie was wearing a multicolored caftan, sitting on the floor, looking off into the distance. A silver espresso pot and cup at her feet. Mingling with the fresh sea air was the unmistakable aroma of coffee beans and licorice. Bria stood in front of Rosalie, put her hands on her hips, and looked down. "Are you having sambuca with your espresso or espresso with your sambuca?"

Rosalie looked up and squinted. "Why is there a *gigantessa* on my boat?"

"Get up." Bria held out her hand and didn't move until Rosalie took it. Bria yanked her friend up from her seated position and, like Michele on the marina, Rosalie stumbled a bit before maintaining an upright stance. "Are you going to let some man make you cower in a dark corner of your boat and drown your sorrows in liquor?"

"Sambuca is a versatile spirit, it also goes well with orange juice." Rosalie pointed to a pitcher on the table. "Try some."

"Basta! I know you're upset about Michele, but you have to admit that his leaving is a good thing. Weren't you just saying that you didn't think he was the right man for you?"

"I might have *mused* that we were ill matched."

"Mused?!" Bria cried. "You don't muse! I don't even think you know the meaning of the word."

"I do, too."

"Then tell me, what does *muse* mean?"

"To contemplate, mull things over, weigh all sides of an argument."

"*Bene!* You know the meaning of the word, but when have you ever mulled anything over? You dive right in without thinking, you leap before you look, you start an adventure with no idea how you're going to finish it."

"Look where that's gotten me?!" Rosalie cried. "Alone on a boat wondering when my boyfriend is going to come back."

"You're not alone, Rosalie."

Rosalie paused and took a deep breath. "Yes, I am. You're my best friend in this whole universe and I know, God willing, you'll be at my deathbed, but you know it's true. I am alone."

Bria didn't dare look away, she needed to see the pain in her friend's eyes, and if it meant that Rosalie had to see the sorrow in hers, then so be it. Any relationship—platonic or romantic—couldn't survive if the uglier moments were washed away, covered and ignored. They needed to be exposed, not fixed, but acknowledged. Like any good friend, Bria knew that even the most dire of circumstances held room for hope.

"For now you're alone," Bria replied. "Who knows what tomorrow will bring?"

"The forecast calls for more rain."

"*Perfetto!* I have a brand-new umbrella in hot pink that's big enough to shield us both from the rain," Bria said. "Luca got it for me when he was in Naples."

At the sound of Luca's name, Bria's mood shifted and looked like a mirror image of Rosalie's dour attitude.

"Betcha a pitcher of orange juice and sambuca sounds pretty good right now, doesn't it?" Rosalie asked.

Bria rolled her eyes. "Pour me a glass."

"I have a better idea," Rosalie announced.

"I thought you said this concoction is delicious."

"It is, but I think what we need more than alcohol is company," Rosalie said. "Let me get dressed and then we'll visit Annamaria at her café."

"*Perfetto!*" Bria cried. "While I wait, I'll test out this drink and see if it's something Vanni might add to the menu."

"Who do you think told me about it in the first place?!"

Rosalie disappeared downstairs and Bria poured herself a small glass of the sambuca-spiked orange juice. She took a sip and once again was impressed with Giovanni's creativity. She raised her glass. "Here's to Vanni."

"Have you given up on Luca already?"

Bria whirled around and saw Imperia standing on the dock. Her jet-black hair was lifted slightly by the wind as were her yellow linen slacks and loose-fitting top in the same shade. She still looked commanding, but there was a softer aura to Imperia. Bria had noticed lately that her armor had cracked, but she expected it to be mended and back in place like it had in the past. Perhaps Imperia was also ready to start a new chapter in her life. One of the meddling mother-in-law.

"Imperia, I didn't see you standing there."

Imperia stepped down into the boat. "Because you were too busy raising a glass to your hunky handyman."

"He gave Rosalie a new recipe, orange juice and sambuca."

One finely tweaked eyebrow arched on Imperia's almost wrinkle-free face. "Let me be the judge."

Bria was about to pour Imperia her own glass when Imperia reached out and grabbed Bria's. Imperia took a generous sip, held the liquid in her mouth for a few moments, and then swallowed. Her expression meant that she was undeniably impressed.

"Your Giovanni isn't the only thing that's mouthwatering."

Bria gasped loudly. "Imperia!"

"*Che cosa?* I'm old, but I'm not blind."

"I think a blind woman would still know how handsome Vanni is," Bria joked.

"And it would take a stupid woman not to know that she

owes her daughter-in-law an apology," Imperia said. "I'm sorry for not telling you about the investigation."

"*Grazie,* Imperia, I appreciate you saying that."

"Even still, if I had to do it all over again, I would lie to you because that's what families do."

"They lie to each other?"

"In order to protect them, yes."

"I told Luca and I'm telling you, I don't need your protection."

"Of course you don't—you've proven that countless times over the years—but your family needs to protect you," Imperia said. "It's impulse, it's what you do without thinking when you love someone."

"I understand and I'm grateful to be surrounded by so many people who love me, but this is different."

"Why? Because it has to do with Carlo?"

"Partly, yes."

"Carlo is dead, he isn't coming back no matter what the investigation turns up."

"Imperia, I know that, but I deserve the right to know why my husband died."

"You also know that Luca would have told you if the investigation turned up any credible result," Imperia said. "He wanted to spare you the pain of living that horrific time in our lives—he had the power to do that—and he did what any man would do: he lied to the woman he loved to save her more anguish."

Bria wanted to run off the boat or better yet, dive into the water and submerge herself so she couldn't hear words anymore, so all she could see was the bright sun shining beneath the surface of the sea. She crossed her arms in front of her and tried to control her breathing. "I appreciate what you're trying to do, Imperia."

"I'm not *trying* to do anything, I'm *telling* you that you should forgive Luca."

"I . . . I don't know . . ."

"It's obvious how much you love him," Imperia said. "I see the way you serve him food, just like a wife serves her husband, the way you used to serve Carlo."

The restlessness began to subside and in its place was a growing fear. Imperia rarely spoke about Carlo in Bria's presence, although when she did it was always with the clear indication that Bria was Carlo's wife. That was changing and now Bria was Luca's girlfriend, which meant that there was a new man in Bria's life. She was not sure how Imperia was going to take that. Thus far, she hadn't said much, but now it felt like Imperia was going to tell her exactly how she felt about Bria's new relationship.

"I miss my son every hour of every day and I will until I die and see his beautiful face once more," Imperia confessed. "I know you carry that same pain, but I also know that there's love in your eyes when you look at Luca. Not the same love you shared with Carlo—you'll never have that again and you know that—but it's real, and Luca certainly loves you back. You cannot deny yourself this second chance to be happy, so stop wasting precious time and forgive the man."

Imperia raised the glass to her lips and finished the drink. She placed it on the table with a loud clink and started to leave. Just as she was about to step off the boat, she turned to face Bria. "I never imagined you were a foolish woman, Bria, Don't disappoint me now."

Stunned by Imperia's words and her vulnerability, Bria didn't hear Rosalie return.

"Are you ready for Annamaria to regale us with the village gossip?"

"You have no idea," Bria said. "Let's go."

Caffè Positano was pulsating with life. The tables outside were filled with tourists sipping iced cappuccinos and eating pastries filled with fruit, chocolate, or cream. There was music coming from the distance, the cries of gulls piercing the air, the smell of coffee and lemon, the noise of the Vespas, cars, and scooters. It's just what the ladies needed.

Bria and Rosalie found a table in the back courtyard, and while they waited for Annamaria to bring them their mochaccinos and tiramisu they chatted about what people were wearing and which woman was going to twist her ankle first because her heels were too high. When Annamaria came to join them, she brought more than just their order.

"Paolo!" Bria exclaimed. "How've you been?"

"*Bene,* he replied. "*Grazie.*"

Rosalie looked at the pastries on Annamaria's tray and her brow immediately furrowed. "That's not what we ordered."

"I know," Annamaria said. "Paolo brought back homemade *chiacchiere* and I thought it would be a special treat."

"You made *chiacchiere*?" Rosalie asked.

"No!" Paolo replied, laughing heartily. "Teresina did."

Slowly, Rosalie and Bria turned to face each other. "Teresina made *chiacchiere*?"

"Yes, she made a fresh batch when I saw her yesterday," Paolo said. "She wouldn't let me leave without bringing some home."

"How was she?" Bria asked.

"She was good," Paolo replied. "I don't know if the two of us will ever be close after everything that's happened, but it was nice to see her again."

"I made Paolo go visit," Annamaria said. "Family is family no matter what."

"How was she feeling?" Rosalie asked.

"Teresina's fine," Paolo replied. "Her arthritis bothers her a bit, but at our age you get used to it."

"Holy Mussolini!" Rosalie cried. "That *bastardo* lied to me!"

"Which *bastardo*?" Annamaria said. "There really are so many in this village."

"Michele," Rosalie said. "He told me he had to leave town for a while to help Teresina because she was sick."

Paolo looked stunned. "He told me that he was going to Foggia for a few days."

"Foggia?" Bria asked.

"Something about a lucrative new job offer," Paolo explained. "I don't want to lose him—he's the best mechanic around—but I also can't stop him from taking a better opportunity."

"No, you can't, Paolo," Annamaria said. "You did the right thing to give Michele the chance to work for someone else."

"I hate to say it, but I think his new boss might be dead," Bria said.

"What are you talking about?" Paolo asked.

"Fiorello's company, Eighty-Eight Keys, Inc., is also based in Foggia," Bria shared.

"You think Michele went to work for a dead man?" Rosalie asked. "Instead of staying with his live girlfriend."

"Bria's saying that she thinks Michele might be mixed up in Fiorello's murder," Paolo said. "Isn't that right, Bria?"

"Yes, that's exactly what I'm saying."

Chapter 21

Back at Bella Bella, Bria and Rosalie should have been celebrating and enjoying life with their boyfriends, but instead, they were wondering if they should keep them in their lives.

Luca played God by concealing important information from Bria and coercing others to remain silent, and Michele adopted a more blatant style and lied straight to Rosalie's face. It made the women want to scream. Or test out Vanni's latest recipe for Bella Bella's very own limoncello.

"What's in this one?" Rosalie asked.

"Raspberry and the slightest hint of mint." Vanni handed the drink to Rosalie and waited for her to take a sip. "What do you think?"

"You call that a hint?" Rosalie replied. "It tastes like you filled a pitcher with half limoncello and half mint, let it chill overnight, and then this morning you took out the limoncello to add more mint."

"Am I correct in that you're saying there's not enough mint?" Vanni asked.

"Maybe we should give up?" Bria said.

"On men?" Rosalie asked.

"No, trying to find our very own limoncello recipe that we can serve here at Bella Bella."

"Culinary art takes time," Vanni said. "It may take years, but we will find a recipe that's worthy of being called Bella Bella Limoncella."

"I do love that name," Bria said.

"And I do hate the taste of mint," Rosalie said. "Vanni, could you make me an espresso martini so I can wash this taste out of my mouth?"

"Coming right up!" Vanni turned on his heel, whipped the towel he was holding over his shoulder, and walked into the kitchen.

"Wait until you taste it," Bria said. "I bought a new machine, Gaggia Carezza."

"*Molto bello!*" Rosalie cried.

Bria made sure Vanni was in the kitchen and then leaned closer to Rosalie. "I had hoped Michele were more like Vanni."

"Bad boy looks, but reformed personality?"

"Exactly, but all his lies and now this connection to Foggia and Fiorello makes it quite clear that he hasn't changed his ways."

Vanni entered the main room carrying three martini glasses and a carafe filled with a brown liquid. "Signoras, your espresso martinis have arrived."

"I didn't order one," Bria said.

"My boyfriend just dumped me, I'm not drinking alone," Rosalie declared.

"We're all going to drink," Vanni said, pouring the drinks. "And we're all going to put our heads together to get some answers so Fiorello can finally rest in peace."

Vanni raised his glass and the women followed him. "*Salud!*"

"This is delicious, Vanni," Bria said.

"*Grazie.*"

"Do you have a plan as to how we're going to give Fiorello a slumber that's both eternal *and* peaceful?" Rosalie asked.

"Yes, I do," Vanni replied. "We'll call Luca."

"No!" Bria and Rosalie screamed at the same time.

"I'm not speaking to Luca at the moment," Bria declared.

"I don't want him hauling Michele into jail on trumped-up charges," Rosalie said.

Vanni turned to Bria and said, "You don't have to talk to him." He then turned to Rosalie and said, "You can't protect your boyfriend if he's a criminal." He then took out his phone and dialed Luca's number, put the call on speaker phone, and after a few rings Luca picked up. "Vanni? What's wrong? Is Bria all right? Is Marco at home?"

"Everyone is fine," Vanni replied. "Marco is in his bedroom doing some homework and Bria is right here with Rosalie, but neither one of them want to speak to you."

"*Salve* signore," Luca replied. "I'm glad everyone's all right, but if they are, why did you call, Vanni?"

"Because I have information about Michele."

"What kind of information?"

"The kind that could link him to Fiorello's murder," Vanni conveyed.

"*Allegedly* link him!" Rosalie shouted. "Allegedly!"

"I thought you weren't talking to me," Luca said.

"*Stai zitto!*" Rosalie cried. "Don't arrest him just because he dumped me."

"He dumped you?" Luca exclaimed. "*Ringrazio Dio!* My prayers have been answered."

"You should send someone to Foggia, which is where he told Paolo he was going," Vanni instructed.

"Where in Foggia?" Luca asked. "It's a rather large city."

"We don't know," Vanni admitted. "But Fiorello's company, Eighty-Eight Keys, is also located in Foggia, so maybe he's going to that address."

"That's a long shot, but it could turn something up," Luca said. "Matteo is in that area visiting family; I could ask him to check it out."

"*Grazie,*" Vanni replied. "Let us know what you find out and I'll try to get these two icebergs to thaw."

Vanni pressed a button on his phone and ended the call. When he looked up, he saw both women staring at him with enough fire in their eyes to defrost the entire Arctic Circle.

"*Prego!* I know what'll make you two feel better," Vanni announced. "Let's rummage through Fiorello's room and see if we can find more clues."

"We did that already," Bria said.

"But all you found was his wallet," Vanni said. "You could have missed something."

"You're right." Bria took a gulp of her martini and placed the glass on the table. "Let's go violate a dead man's room."

Halfway up the stairs, however, they were brought to a halt when they heard Carlotta singing. The rich, pulsing, staccato notes of The Queen of the Night's aria resonated through Bella Bella and once again made them all realize why Carlotta had such a popular and critically acclaimed career. It also made them realize they weren't alone in the house like they thought they were.

"Why didn't you tell us Carlotta was in the house?" Rosalie hissed.

"I thought she had gone to meet Ombra after she fixed the espresso machine," Vanni said.

"*Dio mio!*" Bria cried. "That machine is brand-new *and* expensive."

"I was going to send it back, but Carlotta played around with it for a few minutes and, well, you've tasted the results."

"That's one multitalented opera singer," Rosalie said.

As quickly as the singing started it stopped. They all stood still and held their breath half-expecting Carlotta to emerge from her bedroom, but the only thing they heard was the chirping from the sparrows outside trying to mimic the music. They paled in comparison to Carlotta's rendition.

"I have to see if she's in there," Bria whispered over her shoulder, not taking her eyes off of the door to Carlotta's room.

"Why?" Rosalie asked. "She's not going to approve of us going through her dead piano player's things."

"*Esatto*," Bria replied. "I'll keep her busy while you and Vanni search the room."

"Luca's right about you," Vanni said.

"What did that man say about me?"

"Luca said that you really have a detective's mind," Vanni shared. "You often think of things and uncover clues that the police miss."

"Yet I didn't uncover the fact that Luca is a no-good liar!" Bria said.

"I could've told you that," Rosalie quipped. "Now would you mind starting Operation Distract Carlotta?"

Bria stood in front of Carlotta's door as Rosalie and Vanni positioned themselves in front of Fiorello's door. Rosalie turned the doorknob and opened the door slightly, but waited for Bria to knock on Carlotta's door to make sure it was going to be safe for them to enter. Bria knocked, but there was no response.

"Carlotta." Bria knocked on the door again. "I didn't know that you were home."

When there was still no response, Bria knocked and called out her name again.

"How could she not be home?" Rosalie whispered. "We just heard her singing."

"That's her again!" Vanni cried.

Once again, The Queen of the Night aria filled the air. This time instead of knocking, Bria opened the door to confront Carlotta, which she wasn't able to do because the room was empty and Carlotta was nowhere to be found. Bria entered and peered into the bathroom to find that was also empty, even though Carlotta's voice still reverberated throughout the room.

There was a slight pause in the music and then Carlotta hit a series of high-pitched staccato notes. Bria turned to the right, toward where the sound was coming from, and realized Carlotta was hiding in the closet.

"Carlotta!" Bria cried. "What are you doing in the closet?"

She opened the door to find another empty space. Well, almost empty except for a suitcase and a cell phone that was ringing. Bria picked it up and saw that the cell phone case was an image of a keyboard.

"It's Fio's cell phone!" Bria cried.

"Answer it!" Rosalie commanded. "It could be a clue."

"Put it on speaker so we can all hear," Vanni added.

Bria did as she was told and Carlotta's voice disappeared only to be replaced by another woman's voice. This woman wasn't speaking, she was shouting. The sound wasn't nearly as pleasant as Carlotta's singing.

"When are you going to tell the husband?" the woman barked.

Bria looked at Rosalie who looked at Vanni who looked at Bria. None of them moved an inch. They were in shock and didn't know what to do.

"Answer me!" the woman shrieked. "You got me into this mess and I want you to get me out of it."

Bria mouthed the words *"What should we do?"* and Rosalie, very unhelpfully, shrugged her shoulders.

"Giacomo!" the woman screamed. "*Giuro su Dio,* if you don't answer me, I will go to Lake Como, attend that farce of a wedding, and tell him myself!"

Whoever the woman was on the other end of the phone thought she was speaking with Giacomo Lancia and not Fiorello Sanzari. While the women looked at each other still not knowing how to respond, Vanni grabbed the phone and held it under his chin. He swallowed hard, threw his shoulders back, and spoke in a voice that neither Bria nor Rosalie had ever heard before. It wasn't his own voice, but an imitation of Fio's.

"Basta! I told you that it's none of your business!" Vanni shouted.

Bria and Rosalie held their breath during the pause that followed Vanni's improvisation. They weren't sure if the woman on the other end of the line was convinced by Vanni's attempt or that she knew she was no longer talking to Giacomo. When she replied, screaming louder than before, they got their answer.

"It's none of my business?!" she howled. "Thanks to you I'm the girl's doctor! Her pregnancy is completely my business."

Doctor! Bria knew exactly who Vanni was speaking to; it was Regina Pomotori. Bria whispered into Vanni's ear, "Her name's Regina."

"Regina, you listen to me!" Vanni started.

"You listen to *me,* Giacomo!" Regina replied. "If you want me to keep my mouth shut and not tell the husband—who you failed to mention was a billionaire!—the next check better be double my fee, or I swear on my Hippocratic oath that I will kill you!"

"I don't think she understands how the Hippocratic oath works," Rosalie whispered.

Bria put a finger to her lips to get Rosalie to stop talking.

"Regina, *calmati,*" Vanni said.

"Don't tell me to calm down!" Regina shouted. "You know something, forget about the money. I've had it with this game and I want out! Tell Armando that he's about to marry a *puttana* who's carrying another man's baby, or I will!"

Luckily, Regina ended the conversation because Vanni's jaw dropped and he couldn't think of a single word to utter in response. Bria, on the other hand, had so many thoughts and words ricocheting throughout her brain, she didn't know where to begin. Rosalie was the only one who possessed the power of speech.

"Bravo, Vanni," she said. "I had no idea vocal impersonations were part of your skill set."

"*Grazie*, but until I heard the words coming out of my mouth, I didn't know it either."

"Well, you sounded just like Fio and you clearly fooled Regina," Rosalie said.

"Who actually thought I was Giacomo," Vanni said. "Which was a bit confusing."

"Not at all." Bria had finally corralled her thoughts and was able to start unraveling the clues gleaned from the unexpected conversation. "Regina Pomotori is the one Fio has been sending checks to from his Eighty-Eight Keys, Inc. account and Giacomo Lancia is the president of that company."

"But there is no Giacomo, right?" Vanni asked. "It's Fiorello's pseudonym."

"Fancy word," Rosalie said.

"*Grazie,*" Vanni replied.

"That's correct," Bria confirmed. "I couldn't understand why Fio used a fake name, but it could be because he was trying to hide Ombra's pregnancy."

"Do you think Regina is the person Michele left town to try and meet?" Rosalie suggested.

"It's possible," Bria replied. "Maybe he somehow found out about the pregnancy and Regina's connection and went to blackmail her."

"That sounds like something Michele would do," Vanni said.

"How I wish I could argue with that," Rosalie replied.

"Let's put Michele to the side for the moment and focus on Fiorello," Bria advised. "Fio must have found out that Ombra was pregnant and that the child wasn't Armando's, and for whatever reason—maybe loyalty to Carlotta—he decided to help Ombra keep the pregnancy a secret, which is why he enlisted a doctor no one knew about to be Ombra's obstetrician."

"In order to keep his name out of it, too, he paid Regina with checks signed by his corporation," Rosalie continued. "Which is under his fake name."

"Regina doesn't even know she's dealing with Fiorello," Vanni added. "She thinks she was hired by Giacomo."

"That's all correct," Bria said. "But we're ignoring one huge possibility."

"What's that?" Rosalie asked.

"That the reason Fiorello is helping Ombra is not out of loyalty to Carlotta," Bria replied. "But out of loyalty to Ombra."

"Why would he feel he has to be loyal to Ombra?" Vanni asked. "They didn't seem to be particularly fond of each other."

"Maybe that's what they wanted us to think," Bria said. "Fio may have helped Ombra because he's the father of her baby."

"*Dio mio!*" Rosalie cried. "Now that I think of it, Ombra and Fiorello are much more suited for each other than Ombra and Armando, except, you know, that Fiorello's now dead."

"If this is true," Bria said. "We may have found our killer."

"Who?" Vanni asked.

"Armando!" Bria replied. "He told me himself that he wouldn't even entertain the idea of adoption mainly because his father would never allow it. Can you imagine how Armando would react if he found out he was going to have to raise another man's child?"

"He'd want revenge," Rosalie asserted. "What better revenge than to kill the man who impregnated your fiancée."

"Armando does have a history of violence," Vanni said. "On and off the soccer field."

"That rage may have led him to kill a man right here in the piazza," Bria declared. "There's only one problem."

"What's that?" both Rosalie and Vanni asked.

"Armando had a vasectomy because he has a congenital disease that he will almost certainly pass on to any of his children," Bria explained.

"*È orribile!*" Vanni said.

"It is horrible and he appeared devastated by it," Bria said. "Which is why he wanted to spend some time alone with Marco so he could know what it's like to be a father."

"What are you getting at, Bria?" Rosalie asked.

"Armando doesn't really want to marry Ombra; he's being pushed into it by his father," Bria said. "If he found out she was pregnant with another man's child, that would give him the perfect excuse not to go through with the wedding."

"So, you don't think he killed Fio?" Vanni asked.

"I'm not sure," Bria replied.

"Then why do you look like you're frightened and about to shout Mussolini from the rooftops?" Rosalie asked.

"Because if he did kill Fio, it was because he couldn't control his rage and had to strike out against the man who betrayed him," Bria explained. "If that's the case, there's another person who betrayed him."

"Ombra," Rosalie said.

"The cheating fiancée," Vanni added.

Bria nodded her head. "Or the woman who's about to become Armando's next victim."

Chapter 22

"We need to warn Ombra," Rosalie said.

Bria scrunched up her face and tilted her head to the left. For good measure, she held up a hand to make sure her message was fully conveyed. "Not just yet."

"Why not?" Rosalie asked.

"We can't just tell Ombra that her fiancé killed the father of her child," Bria replied.

Rosalie threw up both hands. "I repeat, why not?"

"Because we don't know if Armando did kill Fiorello or if Fiorello is the father of Ombra's baby," Bria explained. "We need a few more answers and much more proof before we start hurling accusations and spreading theories."

Rosalie gasped, pressed her hand to her heart, and fell onto the bed. "I never thought I'd see this day, but it's finally arrived."

"What are you talking about?" Bria asked.

"You've turned into my brother."

"Ah!" Bria cried. "How dare you?"

"How dare I?" Rosalie asked. "How dare *you*?"

Bria looked confused. "How dare I *what*?"

"How dare you become methodical, put fact before instinct, suppress your imagination, and, worst of all, put a young girl's life in danger!"

"I'm not doing any of that!"

"You are," Vanni said. "A little bit."

"If you can't trust the trusty handyman," Rosalie said, "who can you trust?"

"I can't believe the two of you would turn on me like this," Bria said. "I am nothing like Luca Vivaldi."

"You may not have his five o'clock shadow or his hairy chest," Vanni started.

"Yet," Rosalie interjected.

"But you have acquired his sense of protocol and follow-by-the-rules mentality," Vanni finished.

"I can't believe you would say something like that to me, Vanni," Bria replied. "You of all people should know that I don't follow the rules."

"I'm not saying it's a completely bad thing," Vanni said.

"I am," Rosalie interrupted.

Vanni shook his head at Rosalie and smiled at Bria. "It's just an interesting metamorphosis to watch."

"I'm glad you two find me so entertaining," Bria replied.

"I am not entertained," Rosalie quipped. "I am unnerved and flummoxed!"

Bria gasped and Vanni laughed out loud. "You don't even know what those words mean," Vanni said.

It was Rosalie's turn to gasp. "Giovanni Giuseppe Marcello Monteverdi!"

"You know his full name?" Bria asked.

"*Certo*," Rosalie replied. "You're not the only one who notices details."

"Basta!" Bria cried. "I don't care if you think I'm just like Luca—which I am not!—but I still say that we can't warn Ombra until we know that she needs to be warned. In order to do that we need to do some more digging."

"What do you suggest?" Giovanni asked.

Bria held out her hand. "Give me Fiorello's phone." Vanni

gave it to Bria and she started to tap the screen. "Don't you think it's odd that there's no password?"

"If it was his secret phone maybe he didn't think a password was necessary," Vanni suggested.

"Another possibility is that Carlotta knew his password and unlocked it," Bria said.

"*Molto interessante*," Rosalie said. "I just thought of something."

"What?" Bria asked.

"Whether or not Carlotta unlocked the password, she still had access to the phone's history, voicemails, texts," Rosalie deduced. "She probably knows about Regina and the possibility of Fiorello being the father of Ombra's baby."

Bria scrolled through the phone, stopping to read some of the texts. "Fio texted with Regina several times and talked about the pregnancy. Listen to this. **'Regina, a friend is in trouble and she needs an obgyn who can be discreet.'"**

"How does Regina respond?" Rosalie asked.

"*Uffa!* I don't know if Regina is a good doctor, but she's definitely a shrewd businesswoman," Bria said. **"'Discretion costs. Payment first, appointment second.'"**

"She gets right to the point," Vanni said. "Are there any other texts?"

Bria continued to scroll down the messages. "There are a few random texts with unnamed numbers, but most all of them are with Regina . . . oh wait, a few of the most recent ones are from someone else."

"Another unnamed number?" Rosalie asked.

Bria shook her head. "No, it's an unknown number."

"Which means it's probably from a burner phone," Vanni said. "What do the texts say?"

"Most of them are very short. **'We need to talk. This has to end.'"**

"They're definitely from Armando," Rosalie said.

"Or Ombra," Vanni added.

"Or Carlotta." Bria held up the phone. "The texts could have come from any of them."

"When did Fio start receiving the texts?" Rosalie asked.

Bria scrolled through the texts. "It looks like they started the day Fiorello checked into Bella Bella."

"Does the person call him Fio or Giacomo?" Vanni asked.

"They don't use a name," Bria said. "*Dio mio!*"

"Why are you *Dio mio'ing*?" Rosalie asked.

"The last text he received was on Saturday night around midnight," Bria shared. "It says **'Meet me at Piazza die Mulini in thirty minutes.'"**

"*Dio mio* is right!" Rosalie exclaimed. "Fio was lured to his death."

"Whoever sent that text to him must be the killer," Vanni said.

"Which means this was definitely premeditated murder," Bria said. "Whether they thought he was Giacomo or Fiorello posing as Giacomo, they wanted to kill him."

"Don't you think it means something else, too?" Rosalie asked.

Bria rolled her eyes but couldn't disagree with her friend. "We have to warn Ombra."

On their way downstairs, they needed to heed another warning.

"Rosalie!" Marco ran out of his bedroom carrying his tablet and followed closely by Bravo. "You have to be careful!"

"Of what?"

"The *mazzamurello*!"

Marco held his tablet up to show Rosalie a picture of the mythical creature, but Rosalie already knew that the *mazzamurello* was a green gnome wearing a red hat, having read the story about the Italian version of the leprechaun countless times as a child. What Rosalie didn't know was why she needed to beware their presence.

"Why do I have to be careful of the *mazzamurello*?"

"Because I think they may have stolen your rocks."

"Now that's using your imagination to solve a problem," Vanni said.

"*Grazie,*" Marco replied. "I heard you say that you can't find your rocks, and since the *mazzamurello* are always stealing gold, I thought they might want some rocks, too."

"*Mio figlio* is so clever!" Bria exclaimed.

"*Grazie,* Marco," Rosalie said. "I'll keep my eyes out for the green thief, but if you see him first, don't let him get away."

"I won't," Marco said. "Bravo and I will make sure he doesn't escape."

"Vanni, do you mind staying here with Marco while Rosalie and I take care of that thing we were talking about?" Bria asked.

"Of course," Vanni replied.

"What thing?" Marco replied.

Rosalie scooped Marco up in her arms and held him high overhead. "Nothing for little boys to worry about."

Giggling, Marco replied. "I'm not little!"

"Tell me about it." Rosalie dropped Marco not so gently on the ground. "I think my lifting days are over."

"That's okay, Vanni can still lift me up," Marco said. "He's got big muscles. Go on and feel them; they're harder than your rocks."

Bria noticed Rosalie blush a bit and she couldn't blame her. There had been moments in the past when Bria imagined grabbing onto Vanni's muscles to confirm that they were as smooth and as hard as she hoped. She knew her friend was having the same not-so-platonic thoughts.

"We don't have time for any of that, we need to go," Bria declared. "*Arrivederci, ragazzi!*"

Although the setting sun was casting a magical glow over Positano, making the vertical city come alive in all its shimmering, pulsating splendor, the scene in the garden of Villa Magi was dour. With an almost unreal backdrop of undulating oranges, yellows, and reds behind them, Carlotta, Ombra, and Armando appeared as if they wandered into a Fellini film when they were really looking for an Ingmar Bergman set. Their faces indicated none of the joy of the former and all of the angst of the latter.

If it weren't so inappropriate—and too on the nose—Bria would have asked "Who died?" Instead, she took a more empathetic approach. "*Ciao a tutti!*"

They all replied, but none of them sounded as if they were particularly happy to see Bria or Rosalie. Bria assumed that it could have been because she was the link to Fiorello's death since he was staying at Bella Bella and Bria was the one who found him murdered in the piazza. She took a deep breath because if that was the case, they were only going to get surlier when she and Rosalie started asking questions about Fiorello's murder.

"We're sorry to interrupt," Bria said. "We were just taking a walk because the weather is so beautiful after all that rain, and when we saw you in the garden, we couldn't just walk by without saying hello."

"You'll have to forgive them," Armando said. "They're still grieving the piano player's demise."

"And you're not?" Bria asked.

Armando's black eyes practically pierced through Bria's flesh. "I hardly knew the guy, not that I wished him to drop dead in the piazza."

"He was actually murdered," Bria corrected.

"Which is better if you ask me," Armando said.

"How in the world is that better?" Rosalie asked.

"At least he died like a man," Armando explained. "Fighting for his life."

"Mando!" Ombra cried. "That's terrible."

"Don't act like Fio was your best friend," Armando snapped. "You're just upset because this has thrown a wrench into the wedding of the century. Find another piano player and get on with it."

"Fiorello cannot be replaced!" Carlotta cried.

Armando stood up so abruptly his chair teetered back and fell onto the ground. "Then let's call off the wedding."

"No!"

Both Carlotta and Ombra stood up at the same time. Bria wasn't sure if anyone else noticed Ombra place her hand on her stomach, a gesture pregnant women adopt early on in their pregnancy without even realizing it. Carlotta had clutched her throat, but Bria knew that was part of her dramatic oeuvre and not entirely because she was shocked by Armando's comment. Whether or not she was grieving, she was still a diva.

"The wedding will go on as planned despite this interruption," Carlotta said.

"Aren't you supposed to get married the day after tomorrow?" Bria asked.

"That was the original plan," Armando replied. "Now that the chief of police has ordered us not to leave this village. Who knows when we'll get to Lake Como?"

"Once we . . . I mean, once the police find out who killed Fiorello, all innocent parties will be allowed to leave," Bria said.

Carlotta waved her arms about her, making the long, flowing sleeves on her chartreuse linen top flutter about her like an anxious butterfly. "That's all right. Pietro booked the villa for two weeks. If it takes Luca a bit longer to find whoever did this horrible thing, the guests will be enjoying themselves in the lap of luxury and the wedding will be held a few days later."

"What if they don't find the murderer so quickly?" Armando asked.

"Luca can't keep us prisoners here forever," Carlotta said.

"It isn't like we're going to flee the country, we're only going to Lake Como."

"We haven't done anything wrong," Ombra insisted. "Now I don't want to hear anything more about cancelling the wedding, not after I finally picked the perfect flowers for the tables. The most delicate gray Japanese roses."

"Gray is an interesting color choice," Bria said. "Is it a play on your name?"

"Yes, it is," Ombra replied. "Shadows don't have any color."

"I chose the name because I wanted my daughter to always be with me," Carlotta said.

"Walking two steps behind you," Armando muttered.

"It's a beautiful name," Bria said. "The flowers will be beautiful, too."

"They better be or I'll kill that wedding planner!" Armando barked. "The amount of time Ombra is on the phone with him is unbelievable. If he wasn't gay, I'd think she was secretly planning to marry him instead of me."

A burst of nervous laughter filled the air. Ombra's pale complexion turned red and Bria thought it must be a day for blushing; first Rosalie and now Ombra.

"Don't be silly, Mando," Ombra said. "Flowers are very important to a wedding."

"My planner and I were joined at the hip when I was preparing my wedding," Carlotta said.

"I'd rather not compare my wedding to yours," Armando said. "Didn't your husband die before you reached your first anniversary?"

"You have nothing to worry about, Armando," Ombra said. "Giacomo and I are just friends."

Bria felt Rosalie press down on her foot. "Who is this Giacomo?"

"My wedding planner," Ombra said. "He's really wonderful and I don't think any of this would be happening without him.

He knows just how to plan things, he takes care of everything, and whenever I start to get nervous or fretful, he knows exactly the right thing to say to calm me down."

"See what I mean?" Armando shouted. "Giacomo this and Giacomo that."

"Does Giacomo have a last name?" Bria asked. "I might be needing a wedding planner in the near future."

"Giacomo Lancia," Ombra said. "I wouldn't be in this condition without him."

Chapter 23

Mussolini!!

Bria screamed the safe word that Rosalie had chosen for them while they were in college in case they were ever in a precarious situation, at the top of her lungs. But she shouted it silently because this situation—at least from Bria's point of view *was* precarious. She needed to take a pause; she needed to retreat to a safe corner to contemplate what Ombra had just said out loud and in front of her mother and her fiancé. Did she actually just admit to carrying Fiorello's baby? No, that was impossible. Why would she admit such a thing? Unfortunately, there were tons of reasons.

The utterance could simply have been a slip of the tongue, something that Ombra had been contemplating, but never meant to share. It could also be that Carlotta and Armando already knew about the pregnancy. By the way they had been acting it was plausible that they knew there was a bun in Ombra's oven even though that bun hadn't started to fill the air with its sweet, delicious scent.

Armando had not only been treating Ombra disrespectfully, but he had cheated on her. Those were the actions of a disgruntled partner, a frustrated man who felt trapped and betrayed. Bria had thought that if he knew of Ombra's pregnancy he would use it as an opportunity to call off the wedding, but what if Pietro didn't know about Armando's unfortunate condition? What if Pietro was unaware that Armando had had a vasectomy to prevent fathering a child who would be destined to have a brief, painful life? Armando could have kept that a secret from his father as easily as he had kept it from Ombra and Carlotta. It was odd that Imperia knew, but Bria realized that as a wealthy, formidable businesswoman, her mother-in-law considered secrets to be assets. She acquired them in the same way and for the same purpose that she acquired smaller companies—to be kept under her control and used when their impact would be most effective.

Knowing about Ombra's pregnancy also explained Carlotta's behavior. Even though she was grief-stricken over Fio's death, if she believed her daughter was pregnant by a man whose father thought Ombra was a good girl in the old-fashioned, antiquated sense of the word, she would be desperate to make sure the wedding happened as originally planned. If she waited much longer, Ombra's belly would be sure to make Pietro rethink his assumption of the kind of girl he thought his would-be daughter-in-law was. Once he learned the truth, it could easily lead to the end of Carlotta's hopes for the futures of both her and her daughter.

But what if the truth Bria believed to be the truth wasn't, in fact, the truth, after all? Although she had been trying very hard to push Luca's face, voice, and mere presence from her mind since she'd discovered he had lied to her about the investigation into the plane crash that killed Carlo, she had not been entirely successful. It was hard to block out the face of the man she loved. And admired. And respected. And as much as she loathed to admit it, the man whom she leaned on to be a pillar of rational thought amid the sea of wild imaginings that could sometimes be Bria's thought process. Because the truth of the matter was that Ombra might not be pregnant.

Bria tried to calm her mind and focus on the facts to see if they did add up to Ombra expecting to give birth roughly seven months after she said "I do" to Armando in a few days. She had avoided drinking alcohol at Lorenza and Fabrice's dinner party in Rome and threw up in their bathroom. Ombra was incredibly fond of flowing dresses that hung loosely on her body and didn't accentuate her waistline. Fiorello as Giacomo had hired Regina to be someone's obstetrician and Regina had told Giacomo that she no longer wanted to be that someone's obstetrician. Regina also told Giacomo that he had to tell the woman that her fiancé wasn't the father of the unborn child. There was no proof that the pregnant woman in question was Ombra other than the fact that the name of her wedding planner was also the name of Fiorello's secret alter ego.

Bria shook her head. *You're wrong, Luca!* she silently screamed. *Ombra is definitely pregnant and there's a very good chance that Fiorello is the father.* Which meant there was a very good chance that Ombra may have just inadvertently exposed herself. But if that was the case, why weren't Carlotta and Armando acting surprised or, at least, intrigued?

That's when Bria heard Luca's voice loud and clear in her mind: *Because Ombra said Giacomo put her in this condition, not Fiorello.*

"*Uffa!*" Bria exclaimed.

"*Dio vi benedica.*" Rosalie's attempt to cover up Bria's outburst by making it appear that she sneezed was mildly successful.

"Excuse me?" Ombra said.

"What?" Bria replied.

Ombra looked at Bria and was clearly confused. "You shouted something."

"*Per favore,*" Bria replied. "I sneezed. Sometimes all the beautiful flowers trigger my allergies."

"Can we please stop talking about flowers?" Armando said.

Bria smiled at Armando but continued her line of questioning. "*Prego,* but Ombra, what did you mean that this Giacomo person put you in this condition?"

"What do you mean?"

"You said that if it weren't for Giacomo you wouldn't be in this condition."

Ombra's expression went blank and she stared at Bria for several seconds before speaking. "I don't think I said that."

"I believe you did."

"What my daughter said was if it weren't for Giacomo she wouldn't be in this situation," Carlotta lied. "Isn't that correct, dear?"

"Yes," Ombra replied. "That's what I said."

"Then what *situation* would that be?" Bria asked.

"Of having everything ready several days before the wedding," Carlotta replied. "Ombra doesn't have to worry about a thing because everything has been taken care of thanks to Giacomo."

"Except that your accompanist is dead." Rosalie looked around at the shocked faces and looked equally as shocked by their surprised expressions. "*Mi dispiace,* but I'm not saying anything that we don't already know."

"The only thing we don't know is who would want to kill the guy." Armando looked up and waved his drink in front of the group of women. "Haven't you and your police boyfriend figured it out yet?"

"Luca and his team are still working on some clues." Bria noticed that Carlotta flinched a bit when she heard that news. Impulsively, she decided to see if she could make the opera singer squirm even more. "We're on our way to see him because we found Fiorello's cell phone."

"Really?!" Carlotta exclaimed. "Where did you find that?"

"In your room at Bella Bella," Bria replied.

The way Carlotta reacted proved that while she was a consummate singer of unparalleled talent, she wasn't nearly as good of an actress. "*È impossibile!*"

"It might be impossible," Rosalie said. "But thanks to you it's the truth."

"Thanks to me?" Carlotta replied.

"Fiorello's ringtone is your Queen of the Night aria from *The Magic Flute*," Bria explained.

Carlotta practically swooned. "The role that made me famous."

"Typecasting if you ask me," Armando muttered, and quickly took a sip of his drink.

"Why did you have Fio's phone?" Bria asked. "The police have been looking for it."

Carlotta looked like she was waiting for the orchestra to begin. She closed her eyes for a few seconds and opened them when she heard her cue. "Ombra gave it to me. Isn't that right, *cara*?"

A transformation took place in front of their eyes. A gray pall fell over Ombra's face as her spine lengthened and her shoulders rolled back. She wasn't standing, but she was at attention, ready to go to war. Bria didn't know if she was going to war for or against her mother.

"Yes, yes, how stupid of me to forget," Ombra said. "I did find it later on, after Fiorello was killed and I gave it to my mother."

"That is stupid!" Armando hissed. "Why wouldn't you give it to the police?"

"I didn't know that Fio had been murdered," Ombra replied. "I only found out later that he didn't die of natural causes like we all initially believed."

"The first thing you do after you find a dead man's cell phone is run straight to your mother," Armando commented. "You know, Carlotta, sometimes I think you've brainwashed your daughter not to do anything on her own without telling you first."

"That isn't true." Carlotta laughed.

"It's the absolute truth," Armando insisted. "Ombra's your little wind-up doll, like Olympia in *Les Contes d'Hoffmann*."

"Who's this Olympia and what's a Hoffmann?" Rosalie asked.

"Olympia is the character of a doll in a rare opera that I'm surprised you know about, Armando," Carlotta stated.

"I was shipped off to Ecole d'Humanité in Bern and learned a thing or two about the arts," Armando replied. "You're like Hoffmann; you've created Ombra to be your pet, to do your bidding."

Carlotta fluttered and shook her head. "It only seems that way because Ombra is so devoted to me."

It was Armando's turn to laugh. "Like you are to your daughter?"

"I see that you excelled in day drinking at Ecole as well." Carlotta turned her back on Armando to face Bria. "I think it's good that my voice led you to Fiorello's cell phone; now you can give it to your fiancé."

"What?!" Bria shouted. "No, I don't have a fiancé."

"You just said you might be needing a wedding planner," Carlotta replied.

Come on, Bria, don't lose focus! Bria silently cried.

"No, no, not for me," Bria stammered. "For Rosalie!"

Because they had been best friends for decades Rosalie and Bria understood each other implicitly. Rosalie understood that Bria needed a scapegoat and without hesitation she offered herself up as the sacrificial lamb.

"That is correct," Rosalie deadpanned. "It is I who may need wedding planner services very shortly."

"Who are you going to marry?" Armando asked.

Rosalie smiled broadly and turned to Bria. "*Amica,* why don't you make the announcement."

Bria clutched Rosalie's hand extra tight. "Michele, of course."

Armando laughed even louder than he did before. "This is turning out to be quite an entertaining afternoon. First Carlotta is hiding a cell phone and now Rosalie thinks she's going to get Michele to marry her. I always knew Positano was a romantic destination. I didn't know it held a comedy festival, too."

Despite Rosalie's misgivings about Michele and her decision to all but break things off with him, Bria knew that her friend still was holding out a little bit of hope that he might change. She knew her best friend as well as her best friend knew her. That's why she knew Rosalie was not going to let Armando's snide comment go unanswered.

"Why is the possibility of my becoming a wife so hilarious?" Rosalie asked.

"That's not the funny part," Armando replied. "You're successful, independent, funny, attractive, you'd make most any man very happy to be your husband."

"Any man except Michele," Rosalie said. "Why would you say that? You hardly know him."

"I know enough about him to know he isn't the marrying kind," Armando said. "Unless you have a secret compartment on that boat of yours filled with millions of euros."

"You think Michele is only after Rosalie's money?" Bria asked.

"That isn't what he's saying," Ombra said.

"Do not answer for me." Armando glared at Ombra while guzzling down the rest of his scotch. "You're not my wife—yet."

"I didn't mean to answer for you," Ombra said. "It's only that I spoke with Michele and he's ambitious, yes, but not a gold digger."

"When exactly did you speak with Michele?" Rosalie asked.

Before Ombra answered, she glanced at her mother, who was staring at her. It was almost as if Ombra was magnetically pulled toward Carlotta, like there was a psychic connection between the two. Immediately, Ombra lowered her eyes to break contact. "The day before the concert, I think. I can't really be sure."

"Do you remember what you talked about?" Bria asked.

"He was asking about Fiorello," Carlotta interjected. "Isn't that what you told me?"

"Well, yes, he did ask about Fiorello after," Ombra said.

"After *what*?" Rosalie asked.

"After he inquired about Claterna," Ombra replied.

"That's the historical site Luca was talking about," Bria said. "The Pompeii of the North."

"I was a Classics major at university and Michele was very interested in the area as an ancient archaeological site," Ombra explained.

"He was interested in those rocks," Armando said.

"The rocks my uncle left me?" Rosalie asked.

"Once he found out they were from that area he realized they were probably fossils and could net a huge profit on the black market," Armando said. "If you want to hold onto Michele's hand in marriage, Rosalie, you should give him one of those rocks as a wedding present."

Bria turned to face Rosalie. She knew what her friend was thinking because she was thinking the same thing. Michele didn't wait to receive a present from Rosalie; he took the rocks as a parting gift.

Abruptly, Armando rose. "Ladies, if you'll excuse me."

"Where are you going?" Ombra asked.

"Elsewhere," he replied. "I need some air."

"There's such a beautiful breeze coming in from the sea," Ombra replied.

Carlotta scowled at her daughter. "Ombra, you must remember that men need their private time." She smiled demurely at Armando. "Don't worry, Mando, she'll learn."

With a huff, Armando left the garden. Ombra mumbled something Bria couldn't decipher and quickly followed him. Carlotta looked at Bria and Rosalie with an air of resignation.

"My daughter doesn't possess the same qualities that we do," Carlotta declared.

"What qualities would those be?" Bria asked.

"Inner strength, ambivalence and, of course, self-respect."

Carlotta reminded Bria of Pietro; they both voiced harsh criticisms of their children. Bria couldn't help but feel as if Carlotta had also criticized her and Rosalie, even though she presented her statement as if it was a compliment.

"I do consider myself as having inner strength and a strong sense of self-respect," Bria said. "But not ambivalence."

"*Prego,* don't be insulted, I meant it as praise," Carlotta urged. "You must be ambivalent if you could end your relationship with Luca so quickly."

"I didn't *end* things," Bria said. "Not permanently."

"It doesn't matter. You've shown Luca that it's possible things will end," Carlotta replied. "A woman needs to use all of her powers, and the power of appearing indifferent and uninterested is one of the greatest a woman can use when it comes to ensnaring a lover. Unfortunately, my daughter never learned that subtle skill and it's only because of me that she's going to walk down the aisle in a few days. At least one woman in our family is looking out for our future."

Carlotta put on her oversized straw hat trimmed with a coral scarf and grabbed her bag from the table. "Thank you again for bringing Fiorello's cell phone to the police. Something else my daughter should have taken care of."

Bria watched Carlotta leave and when she was out of view, she turned to Rosalie. "I don't know which one I mistrust more—Carlotta, Ombra, or Armando."

"Don't forget Michele," Rosalie added. "He left me for a bunch of rocks and could be in cahoots with a dead man."

"He's definitely in cahoots with Fiorello," Bria said. "Well, *was* in cahoots."

"What makes you so sure?"

"Mimi told me that Fiorello bought three books from her and one was about Claterna," Bria explained. "Now that Michele has gone to Foggia, where Fiorello's company is, I think Fiorello bought that book for Michele."

"That does make sense," Rosalie said. "It seems like everyone was connected to Fiorello in some way."

"I don't know if Carlotta realizes that Armando isn't the father of Ombra's baby or that she suspects Fiorello could be her baby daddy," Bria said. "But I'm convinced she knows her daughter is pregnant and she's desperate for this marriage to take place before anyone else finds out."

"For that to happen, my brother has to let them leave the village," Rosalie said. "We both know the quickest way to do that."

"We do?"

"Yes! Bring Fio's cell phone to Luca and show him all the texts!" Rosalie cried. "If you don't, I will."

"*Bene!* I'll go on one condition."

"What's that?"

"Come with me," Bria stated. "I'm not ready to face your brother alone."

"Don't get excited, we're here on official police business," Rosalie said.

Luca was sitting behind his desk and Bria fought the urge to slap herself in the forehead when she felt her stomach flip because he looked so much sexier than he had the last time she saw him. The razor stubble, the tousled hair, the shirt unbuttoned at the neck so his tie hung loosely, and the sleeves rolled up to expose a hint of his firm forearms, created a look on Luca that Bria found hard to resist. Part of her wanted to push

Rosalie out of the room and lock the door behind her and part of her wanted to slap Luca across the face. She found him very attractive, but she was still very upset.

Bria could tell that Luca was having the same inner struggle. He was acting as if he was disinterested in Bria and Rosalie's sudden appearance in his office. He rummaged through some papers, but Bria could tell that he wasn't focusing on the words because she was watching his eyes. They weren't slowly moving right to left examining the text like they did when Luca was fully engrossed in material, and they also weren't quickly moving top to bottom like they did when he was skimming a report or an article in search of one specific phrase or fact. Luca's brown eyes weren't moving, but staring straight ahead just above the top of the page. He could have been gazing at the eyes of Giuseppe Thaon di Revel di Sant'Andrea, the first Commanding General of the Carabinieri, whose framed photograph hung on the far wall opposite Luca's desk, but Bria knew that he was trying hard not to gaze at her.

Luca held out for as long as he could but eventually looked up. When their eyes met, Bria almost crumbled to her knees. She saw only sadness and regret.

Quickly, he glanced away and directed his comment to Rosalie. "What kind of official business could two women who have no official connection to the police department want to conduct?"

"Actually, we come on two official pieces of business," Rosalie replied. "First, it looks like Michele took the rocks *Zio* Nazario left me and skipped town."

"He stole from you?"

"Yes, he did, *fratello*."

Bria felt another flip in her stomach when Luca rose showing his shirttail hadn't been properly tucked into his form-fitting navy blue pants.

"Nunzi!" Luca shouted. "Put out a search for Michele Vistigliano; he's stolen Rosalie's property."

Within seconds, Nunzi was standing at the door to Luca's office. "You want me to track down Michele because he stole your sister's heart?"

"He didn't steal my *heart,* Annunziada!" Rosalie cried. "He stole my *rocks*!"

"Aren't they the same things?" she deadpanned.

"Nunzi, this is serious, those rocks are priceless," Luca said.

All three women in the room responded at the same time. "They are?"

"Yes!" Luca cried. "They're fossils from an historical site. You can sell them for hundreds of thousands of dollars to a museum or a private collector."

"Why didn't you tell me this?" Rosalie asked.

Bria smirked and crossed her arms. "Because Luca likes to keep secrets." She knew she sounded catty, but she couldn't help herself. The way Luca looked at Bria, it appeared that he didn't mind her sarcastic tone of voice, he was just happy she was speaking in his presence.

"I wasn't keeping it a secret, I've been trying to hint at it," Luca said.

"Why didn't you just say it so I could understand what you were saying?" Rosalie asked. "Why must you always talk in this mysterious code?"

"Because he's a man, Rosalie," Bria hissed. "Men love to talk in code."

"Uncle Nazario's lawyer gave me a letter specifically telling me that I couldn't tell you about the rocks for at least a month because *Zio* wanted you to figure it out on your own," Luca explained. "You know how much he loved playing games with you."

Rosalie's face lit up at the memory. "He was a jokester, that one." Just as quickly, Rosalie shook the light from her face. "You still should've told me; it isn't like he was going to yell at you for telling his secret."

"*Dio mio!*" Luca cried. "I tried, but you were too busy feeling sorry for yourself and being jealous that I got a ski chalet and you got a bunch of rocks."

"I am not jealous!" Rosalie was about to continue her tirade, when she looked at Bria, who was giving her a look to get her to shut up. Everyone in the room knew that Rosalie had been jealous of Luca's inheritance. "Well, maybe just a little."

"Evidently, Michele was just as jealous," Nunzi said. "Rosalie, why don't you come out here and tell me where I can find Michele."

Rosalie didn't move. "He went to Foggia."

"*Grazie,*" Nunzi replied. "I could really use your help out here."

"You should also check with Dr. Frangipani," Bria said.

"The plastic surgeon?" Luca asked.

Bria nodded to Luca but turned to continue speaking to Nunzi. "He loves to buy things off the black market."

"*Grazie,*" Nunzi repeated. "Rosalie, come with me. I need you to fill out a report."

"I'm not done with my official business," Rosalie protested.

"I'm sure Bria can take care of it," Nunzi said.

Ignoring Nunzi, Rosalie pulled Fiorello's cell phone out of her pants pocket and tossed it on the pile of papers on Luca's desk. "We found this is in Carlotta's room at Bella Bella."

"What is it?" Luca asked.

"It's Fiorello's cell phone," she replied. "Scroll through and you'll find a few surprises."

Luca sighed heavily. "Could you please give Bria and me a moment?"

"Bria, is this what you would like also?" Rosalie asked.

Bria hesitated, but only because she wasn't sure she could trust herself to be alone with Luca. Then she remembered that she had inner strength. "Yes."

Rosalie nodded dramatically. "I will be right outside that door, and if I hear raised voices or the smashing of furniture, I will be back in here quicker than Marcell Jacobs running the hundred-yard dash with this one by my side." Rosalie tossed her head at Nunzi, who merely grunted in response. Slowly, Rosalie walked out of the room and just before she shut the door she added, "I'm right outside."

Alone, Bria and Luca just stared at each other. The tension was thick, and while neither of them wanted to start the conversation, they also didn't want to turn away from each other. They were trying their best to avoid a connection, but neither of them was successful.

"I'm sorry," Luca said.

"I know."

"I should have told you everything the moment I knew there would be an investigation."

"Yes, you should have."

"I hope you understand why I didn't."

Bria paused before replying. "Imperia did explain things to me and suggested I see things from your perspective."

"I'll have to thank her when I see her again."

"It's still a betrayal."

"I understand how you'd feel that way."

Bria took a moment and stared at Luca. "But you don't agree that you betrayed me?"

"*Betray* is a harsh word."

"But it fits the situation."

"Didn't you tell me that Carlo bought Bella Bella without consulting you first?"

"Are you seriously bringing up my dead husband when we're fighting?"

"We're not fighting."

"We are now!" Bria screamed.

Suddenly, the door opened and Rosalie was holding onto the doorknob. "I hear raised voices!"

Nunzi placed her hand on top of Rosalie's and pulled the door shut. "Leave them alone, Rosalie!"

"Carlo did what he did because he loved me!"

"Which is the same reason why I didn't tell you about the investigation!"

"Because you love me?" Bria asked. "That's your excuse?"

"Yes!" Luca cried. "You know I do."

"If that's how you show your love, Luca Vivaldi, I don't want any part of it!"

The next day, Bria was sitting at her dining room table. The aroma from her Lavazza coffee didn't have the same power it usually had. It didn't calm her nerves and give her the quiet strength she needed to start the day. She was agitated, frustrated, and distracted. So much so that she didn't hear her cell phone ringing until the fourth ring.

She picked up the phone and saw that Sister Benedicta was calling her. She had just dropped Marco off at school. There couldn't be another problem, could there? "*Ciao,* Sister, is Marco all right?"

"Yes, he's fine," Sister B replied. "But I need you to come to Imperia's yacht right now; there's something I must show you."

Before Bria could ask the sister why she wanted to meet her at the yacht and not at St. Cecilia's, Sister B added, "Hurry, Bria, it's an emergency."

What kind of an emergency could a nun have on a yacht? Bria asked herself.

The answer to that question would have to wait because the nun had hung up.

When she walked onto the deck of the yacht and saw Imperia standing next to Sister B, Bria's curiosity was fully piqued. "Why are we meeting here and not at St. Cecilia's?"

"You'll understand," Sister B replied.

"Follow me," Imperia instructed.

Following them downstairs into the lower deck of the yacht, Bria's curiosity started to turn toward anxiety. What exactly was going on? Sister B turned around and Bria knew she couldn't hide the concern from her face.

"There's nothing to worry about, Bria," Sister B conveyed. "Things are often like lyrics to a song or characters in a play; we don't know their purpose until the song is over or the curtain drops."

The sister's comments were not helping ease Bria's apprehension. On the contrary, her fears were only growing.

"It's like how Ombra sometimes reminds me of Pamina," Sister B said. "Not just the character, but how she exists within the entire play."

Bria tried to disentangle Sister B's words into something comprehensible, but didn't have the chance because Imperia announced their arrival. "Here we are."

Bria knew exactly where she was but had no idea why she had been led here. "You're having an emergency in the wine cellar?"

Imperia opened the door to reveal Rosalie, Nunzi, and Luca.

"We've looked everywhere, Rosalie," Luca said. "There aren't any rocks here."

"Only idiots," Bria commented.

Luca turned around and was shocked to see Bria standing at the door.

"What's going on?" Luca asked.

Like a well-orchestrated scene, Rosalie and Nunzi moved as one toward the front door as Sister B and Imperia backed out into the corridor.

"It's for your own good, *fratello*!"

"Everyone knows how smart you are, Bria," Imperia said. "Don't make fools out of us now."

Bria couldn't believe what they were doing; they were locking her and Luca in the wine cellar to get them to resolve their problem once and for all.

"Sister B!" Bria cried. "You lied to me!"

From behind the closed door, Sister B yelled back, "I'm only doing God's work."

Bria looked at Luca, who was smiling like a cat staring at a cornered mouse with three broken legs, and thought for the first time in her life that at the next opportunity she was going to strangle a Catholic nun.

Chapter 24

Bria had a flashback to her childhood.

She was seven years old and she had broken the statue of Baby Jesus that had been in her mother's family for three generations. They only saw it one month out of the year, from mid-December to January 6, Little Christmas, when Fifetta brought it out from its primary residence of an old shoebox housed at the top of her bedroom closet to bring it to its place of honor on the small table next to the Christmas tree. It was one of the final decorations Fifetta brought out every year, and each time she did it was like a ceremony, a ritual that captivated Bria and her siblings.

Fifetta told her children how her grandmother, Gigi, was given the Baby Jesus by her husband's friend, an artisan, when she married Lorenzo in Florence. Gigi had given it to her daughter, Chantal, on her wedding day, and in turn, Chantal had given it to Fifetta when she married Franco. The piece of art was part of the family tapestry and a treasured and protected item that held nostalgic and spiritual importance. Which was shattered when Bria decided to show Lorenza and Gabrielo how to lull a baby to sleep.

Bria had cradled the Baby Jesus in her arms and reached out to grab Gabi's bottle from him to feed Jesus, whom Bria deduced was hungry after spending so many months cooped up in a box in the closet. Gabi, however, claimed to be just as hungry and resisted. Bria had tried to reason with her younger brother but couldn't convince him that it would be an unselfish Christian act to give his bottle of milk to Jesus to drink. She even pointed out that Father Hippolito, their parish priest, would be so proud he'd probably dedicate an entire Mass to him. Still, Gabi clutched his bottle tighter than a martyr clutched a rosary. Like most big sisters, when Bria didn't get her way through verbal persuasion, she resorted to physical confrontation.

Bria had lunged forward, Gabrielo had lurched backward, and Baby Jesus had plummeted to the floor. They looked down in shock to see that Jesus's left foot and three fingers on his right hand had broken. Bria and Lorenza had gathered up the decapitated body parts just as Fifetta had walked into the living room to witness the carnage. It was one of the few moments when Fifetta yelled at her children. She didn't hit Bria—neither Fifetta nor Franco had ever struck their children out of anger or an attempt to discipline—but what she did was much more powerful; she expressed her disappointment in her eldest daughter, who, Fifetta said in a quiet, sad voice, should have known better.

That's how Bria felt stuck in a wine cellar on Imperia's yacht with the man she was in love with, who also happened to be the man she was very disappointed in. She should have known better. She shouldn't have blindly followed Sister B's odd instructions and she should have known better than to think that Luca could be completely honest with her.

She was paying for her stupidity and she knew that it was useless to bang on the door and demand to be released. Sister B, Imperia, and Rosalie—with whom Bria would definitely have some words to share when she was freed—were not going to open the door until they were convinced that Bria and Luca had reconciled. In order for that to happen, however, they needed to begin a conversation, and Bria was leaning into her stubborn side. At least Luca found the situation to be humorous.

"You weren't kidding about Sister B," Luca said. "She's not your average nun."

"Did you dream up this plan?" Bria asked.

"To lure you into a trap so I could be alone with you? I think you know me better than that."

"It isn't going to work, you know. This isn't going to solve anything."

"Not if you keep up that attitude."

"What attitude?"

"That one!" Luca shouted. "The close-minded attitude that refuses to hear reason."

"And you consider yourself to be the voice of reason?"

"In this situation, yes!"

"Basta! This is going to get us nowhere. If you *must* talk, talk about something else other than your lies. Let's talk about our case."

"*Our* case?"

"Yes! Our case! I have more clues and information about the suspects than the police do."

"You mean, you're withholding more information from the police."

"I was going to tell the police everything, but I was interrupted and brought to my mother-in-law's wine cellar! Now do you want to hear what I found out or not?"

Bria noticed that Luca's eyes were twinkling and the right side of his mouth was turned up slightly. He was trying not to smile. How could he want to smile at a time like this?

"Yes, I would love to hear what you found out," Luca said. "I'm all ears."

"Ombra is pregnant and most likely carrying Fiorello's baby."

"*Sul serio?*"

"We don't have confirmation, but Ombra is showing all of

the telltale signs of a woman in her second trimester," Bria replied. "She's throwing up, she's wearing loose clothing, she isn't drinking alcohol."

"Are you sure Fio is the father?"

"As sure as I can be without doing a DNA test."

"If she is pregnant and Fio is the father, why can't Armando raise the child as his own?" Luca queried. "He's so desperate to be a parent, he kidnapped Marco. Why would he kill Fio and risk spending the rest of his life in jail?"

"Because if Fio found out he was the father, he would not have kept his mouth shut, and if he told the world he and Ombra were having a baby, Armando would lose everything. Pietro only wants Armando to marry Ombra so he can become a respectable man. If the truth came out, there's a very good chance Pietro would disinherit Armando."

"This is all speculation," Luca said. "There's also a chance Armando is the father."

"No, there isn't," Bria said. "There are the calls made to Fio's cell phone."

"From Ombra?"

"No, Regina."

"Who's Regina?"

"Her obstetrician—at least we think so."

"What do you mean 'we'?"

"I was with Rosalie and Giovanni and we heard Carlotta singing. It turned out to be Fio's cell phone ring and Carlotta had his phone in her bedroom."

"*Dio mio!* I asked that woman point-blank if she knew where the phone was or if she had anything of Fio's, and she lied to me."

"I'm not sure if Carlotta knows about the pregnancy, but that would be a strong motive for her to keep the phone," Bria stated.

"Did you speak to this Regina?"

"No, Vanni did and he did a spot-on impersonation of Fiorello! We couldn't believe how perfectly he captured Fio's voice."

"Are you sure he fooled Regina?" Luca asked. "Maybe she was playing along."

"No! She said he had to tell the woman's husband about the baby or she would."

"*Mi dispiace,* how do you know that Fio is the father of Ombra's baby? Why can't it be Armando?"

"Because Armando had a vasectomy and can't have children."

"Why would he do such a thing? He's so young."

"He has a congenital disease that he will more than likely pass onto any child he fathers."

"Can't doctors do something about it?"

"It's a life-threatening disease, the child might not even be born, and if it is, its life expectancy is a few days."

Tears started to well in Luca's eyes. "That's heartbreaking."

"It is, and he only found out about it because he got a girl pregnant in college who refused to have an abortion like the others and her child died shortly after she gave birth."

"That must be why Ombra always seems to be so nervous," Luca said. "She's like a bird sometimes, eyes darting all over, her body shaking."

"I've noticed that, too, but it has nothing to do with Armando's condition because she doesn't know."

"How could she not know? She's marrying the man."

"Armando hasn't told her."

"He's keeping a secret like that from the woman he's going to marry."

"You should know how easy it is to keep secrets."

Bria knew her comment wasn't warranted the moment she said it, but once she said it she couldn't take it back so she allowed it to contaminate the air and poison their silence. Luca bowed his head and focused on the ground for a long while. When he finally looked Bria in the eye, his voice was quiet and strong.

"I know I've hurt you, but I also know that you understand why I didn't tell you about the investigation. Carlo's death hurt you deeply, the pain cut right into your soul, and I was not going to allow you to suffer that type of pain again if it wasn't necessary. My plan was to complete the investigation and then present you with the results once the case was closed. As I suspected, the computer chip had nothing to do with the plane crash; it was an unfortunate accident and the result of an unexpected and violent storm, nothing more."

Bria lowered her head but Luca didn't turn away. He was true to his word; he wanted to share everything with Bria—the joy and the pain. "I was not trying to keep Carlo's memory from you, I am not at all jealous of your feelings for him. I was protecting you, and if we can get beyond this, which is my hope, I will keep doing that until the day I die because I love you, Bria Bartolucci, and if you weren't so stubborn you would admit that you love me."

Bria felt the anger she had been holding onto slowly disengage from her veins and rise from her skin. It was like a veil was being lifted, not from Luca so his true self could be seen, but from her, so she could see into her mind, admit her motivation, and confront her fear. Hearing Luca speak, vulnerable and without a hint of guile, she had no choice but to concede that she had been wrong.

Luca's silence about the investigation was not proof that he was a liar like Armando, or a misogynistic control freak like Pietro, it was testament to how much he loved Bria. Even though Bria had claimed to be ready to move on and begin to explore what life would be like with Luca by her side, she had been afraid. Would people think she was moving on from Carlo too quickly? Shouldn't she discover what life was like alone without being part of a couple? Nothing mattered except for what lay in Bria's heart.

The first kiss was soft and tentative, an apology. Bria was unsure if Luca would respond to her, but the moment her lips touched his, she felt his warmth and his desire. They kissed as one, breathed as one, until suddenly they both pulled away.

"I'm sorry."

Neither knew who said it first, but it didn't matter, the words were accepted as truth. They were mature enough to know that there wasn't a magical potion that would prevent them from ever having another fight or misunderstanding, but they were also mature enough to know that their feelings for each other were absolute, they were pure and shouldn't be tainted with petty poison.

The next kiss was like a wave; it began calmly and then quickly exploded into passionate fury spreading out from their lips to their arms and legs. They became entangled, and soon they were partially undressed, and then they had an audience.

They only stopped kissing when they heard Sister B gasp. When they turned around, they saw that Rosalie was holding her hand over the nun's eyes while Imperia was holding her hand over Sister B's mouth. If Bria wasn't so utterly embarrassed to be caught half-naked in front of a nun, who also happened to be her son's teacher, she would have laughed out loud at the comical display. Instead she scrambled to get dressed.

"Looks like you took Sister Benedicta's words to heart and decided to do God's work," Imperia said.

"I guess this means the two of you have kissed and made up," Rosalie said.

Sister B tried to talk, but they only heard a muffled sound. Imperia removed her hand, but Rosalie kept the nun's eyes covered. "From what I saw they were doing more than just kissing."

Bria couldn't hold in her laughter any longer and she was quickly joined by Luca, Rosalie, and even Imperia.

"When you've finished God's work, you can let yourself out." Imperia tossed the key to the wine cellar and it landed with a loud clank next to Bria's feet. Louder still was the sound of the door closing shut when the women left.

Alone, Bria turned to face Luca who was smiling like a little boy. Mischief oozed out of every pore. She didn't know whether she wanted to slap him or kiss him harder than she had done before.

"You cannot be thinking what I think you're thinking," Bria said.

"If you think you know what I'm thinking then you should stop thinking and just kiss me," Luca replied. "You know you want to."

Bria was going to protest, but Luca was right. And so she did.

An hour later, Bria and Luca were strolling down Viale Pasitea holding hands and basking in the memory of their morning *faccia a faccia,* the Italian version of a tête-à-tête, when their reminiscence was interrupted by the sight of Ombra leaning over a garbage can and gripping the rim. She looked like she was once again in the throes of morning sickness. Bria thought it looked like a good time to swoop in and finally expose the little baby elephant in the room.

"Ombra, let me help you." Bria grabbed Ombra's arm and helped her stand up straight. "Are you all right?"

"Yes, *grazie*, I'm fine," he replied. "I'm not used to this heat. It isn't nearly as hot up north where I come from."

Despite the discomfort that was etched onto her face, Ombra allowed Bria to lead her to a bench and sit down. Luca came over with a bottle of water that he bought from a street vendor and handed it to Ombra. "Drink this, it's important to stay hydrated."

"Especially in your condition," Bria added.

The discomfort on Ombra's face turned to fear. "What do you mean?"

"Ombra, we know that you're pregnant," Bria said quietly.

Instead of fighting Bria's comment, arguing against the obvious truth, Ombra exhaled and seemed to be relieved that she no longer had to hide a secret, at least from two people.

"It'll be a surprise, but Armando is going to love this child," Ombra said. "I know he will."

"You haven't told your fiancé that you're pregnant?" Luca asked, already knowing the answer.

"We briefly discussed children and I know his father is expecting us to have a large family so Armando will be happy even though it's coming sooner than we both originally planned," Ombra said.

"The two of you discussed having a baby?" Bria asked.

"Not in so many words," Ombra hedged. "But why else do young couples get married? To have a family."

"Does your mother know about the pregnancy?" Bria asked.

At the mention of Carlotta, Ombra's expression changed; it was almost like she was a Pavlovian dog and a lab technician threw a kibble onto the floor. Ombra reacted almost involuntarily, instinctively. Her face became a mask, but her eyes looked terrified.

"No, she doesn't know," Ombra said. "I couldn't tell her, she wouldn't understand."

"I think she's going to find out very soon," Luca said. "Along with Armando and the rest of the world."

"That's why we need to leave tomorrow and get back to Lake Como to have this wedding," Ombra said. "I know that you said we need to stay here until you catch whoever killed Fio, but we consulted our lawyers and you can't keep us here unless you charge one of us with murder."

"That is true," Luca replied.

"Is that what you intend to do?" Ombra asked. "Charge us with murder?"

Bria watched Luca stare at Ombra and couldn't tell what he was going to say. She knew that he suspected Fiorello's killer was not a random stranger, but someone who knew him very well. Although they tried to find someone in Positano who had a connection to Fiorello, they couldn't. The closest they came was Mimi, Imperia, and Fifetta, all of whom had some kind of connection to Carlotta. Bria knew her mother was incapable of murder, and although in the past she had suspected Imperia could commit such a heinous act, she had since learned that her mother-in-law cherished life too much to take another or risk losing her own. The anger that Mimi still held for Carlotta could have erupted into violence, and if Carlotta had been the victim, Bria would have labeled Mimi as a prime suspect.

There was also Michele. It was too much of a coincidence that he ran off to Foggia, the same city where Fiorello's corporation was based. That link, however, was tenuous at best until they had more information. The unfortunate truth was that they still only had a handful of clues and speculation, but no proof as to who committed this calculated and horrific crime.

"No, Ombra, I don't intend to charge any of you with murder," Luca stated.

"*Bene,* it's ridiculous to think that any of us would've harmed Fio," Ombra replied. "He was our friend."

"Please understand that I'm not charging you because I don't suspect any of you," Luca corrected. "I'm not charging you because I don't have any proof."

"Well, that . . . that's just . . ." Ombra stuttered.

"I'll be very clear with you," Luca began. "I believe Fiorello was killed by someone he knew."

"We found a text on his cell phone from someone asking to meet him at the piazza a few minutes before his death," Bria said.

"Since Fiorello presumably complied with those instructions, it only makes sense that he knew his killer," Luca said. "That means our suspect list is very short."

"I'm sure he knew a lot more people than just my mother,

me, and Armando," Ombra said. "But I need to go; my mother is expecting me."

Ombra got up from the bench so abruptly she needed to turn back and grab her bag. At the same time Bria picked it up to give it to her. Once again Bria was reminded of the Baby Jesus falling to the ground, when a rolled-up jacket fell out of Ombra's bag. The white jacket unfurled on the ground exposing the large red wine stain.

"That's Fiorello's jacket!" Bria cried. "The one Armando spilled wine on."

"We were running tests on that," Luca said. "Why do you have it?"

"Matteo gave it to me." Ombra picked up the jacket and started to fold it. "He said the police had run all the necessary tests and didn't need it any longer. I forgot I still had it."

When Luca didn't argue any further, Bria assumed that information was correct. However, the way Ombra was holding the jacket and folding it like it was made of precious material, it was clear that she had known the whereabouts of the jacket. She was carrying it around with her for a reason.

"I should just throw it away."

Although she made a valiant attempt, when Ombra got to the garbage can, the jacket poised above it, she couldn't let it out of her hands. Quickly and furiously, she shoved it back into her bag. "I'll try to get the stain out of it and donate it to charity. Fio would like that."

"I think he would like that very much," Bria replied.

"Do you both promise not to tell anyone that I'm pregnant?" Ombra asked.

Bria nodded. "You have my word."

Ombra turned to face Luca. "What about you?"

"Unless I find that information necessary to disclose in order to move forward with the investigation, I will remain silent on the subject," Luca replied. "This is your story to tell."

"*Grazie.*"

When Ombra was out of earshot, Bria turned to Luca. "She was in love with him."

"Who?"

"Fiorello!"

"Well, that's good because she slept with him and is carrying his baby."

"What are you, twelve?" Bria asked. "A woman can have the baby of a man she doesn't love. In this case, however, Ombra was definitely in love with Fiorello. The way she was holding his jacket was like she was cradling his dead body."

"That doesn't make any sense."

"Why not?"

"Ombra obviously doesn't love Armando and he doesn't love her," Luca pointed out. "If Ombra loved Fiorello and was having his baby, why wouldn't she leave Armando and marry Fiorello?"

"Because Armando is rich and Ombra doesn't have any money."

"She doesn't?"

"No! She and Carlotta are broke."

"That's why Ombra's going to try and masquerade Fio's baby as Armando's," Luca said.

"Which Armando will never believe because he can't have children."

"But neither Carlotta nor Ombra know that."

"*Corretto*," Bria replied. "Which is incredibly helpful to the investigation."

"Into Fio's murder?" Luca asked. "How is that helpful?"

"Because they were worried that Fiorello was going to make it known that he was the father," Bria explained. "From what we know about Fiorello, he was a good person, and those texts and cell phone calls make it clear that he most likely knew the truth."

"If he loved Ombra like she loved him, it was only a matter of time before he came forward and did the right thing," Luca said.

"By doing that, Armando would have no choice but to call off the wedding and Carlotta and Ombra would not get the financial lifeline they so desperately need."

"Which means there's only one person who could have killed Fiorello," Bria said.

Unfortunately, Bria and Luca disagreed on who that person was. As Luca said "Ombra," Bria said "Carlotta."

They both looked at each other and despite the gravity of the situation—trying to determine who murdered an innocent man—they couldn't deny their competitive nature. Luca believing that the path to truth was only found by following unquestionable facts, while Bria had learned trusting her gut instinct almost always helped her solve a mystery. They spoke at the same time and proposed the same challenge.

"Prove it."

Chapter 25

Bria had a plan. She and Luca had agreed to spend the next twenty-four hours investigating on their own. At the end of that time, they would meet up and compare notes. Hopefully, one of them would come up with the smoking gun that would definitively prove that either Carlotta or Ombra killed Fiorello. Otherwise, Luca would not be able to keep mother, daughter, and fiancé in Positano any longer and they would be free to leave to get married in Lake Como. With immense wealth and resources at their disposal, they could flee the country, change their identities, and never be caught and prosecuted. Bria didn't know what Luca was going to do to prevent that from happening, but she was headed to the place some locals called the heart of the village—Caffè Positano.

When she arrived at the café, Bria saw that the heart was beating, but in a much different way than she imagined. Annamaria, Mimi, and Valentina were sitting at a table, hunched forward having an animated conversation. Although their eyes looked hungry, their espressos and *bomboloni* lay untouched on the table. They wanted gossip, not food.

"*Salve signore!*"

Upon hearing Bria's greeting, the women immediately stopped talking and turned around wearing expressions that reminded her of how Marco looked the last time she caught him eating *fragola* out of the tub with his fingers. Once they realized the voice belonged to Bria, they shifted gears and cried out in joy. According to Annamaria, Bria was exactly the person they wanted to see.

"*Prego.*" Bria made a calculated decision. She grabbed an empty chair from a nearby table and sat down in between Valentina and Annamaria and across from Mimi. "Why did you want to see me?"

"Because Mimi wants to know why Luca hasn't arrested Carlotta yet," Valentina said. "And you're the closest thing to Luca other than his tight-fitting police uniform."

"Tina!" Annamaria cackled and playfully slapped Valentina's arm. "No wonder they call you The Merry Widow!"

"I think Valentina christened herself The Merry Widow," Bria said.

"*Vero.*" Valentina shrugged her bare shoulders and tilted her head so her blond hair bounced freely in the air. "It's best to be honest with yourself. I know what people say behind my back. Not everybody's like you, Bria. At least you tell me to my face."

"Because Bria tells the truth," Mimi declared. "So tell us, Bria, when is Luca going to arrest Carlotta?"

"What makes you think he's going to arrest her?"

"Because she killed that poor man," Mimi replied.

"Do you have proof?"

"*Certo che no!*" Mimi cried. "That's not my job, that's yours."

"Mine?" Bria replied.

"Like Tina said, you know everything that goes on in Luca's mind," Mimi said.

"Even though the two of you had been fighting," Annamaria interjected.

"How do you know we were fighting?"

"The entire village knew you were fighting!" Annamaria

cried. "We took bets on how long it would take the two of you to reconcile."

"You took bets?!" Bria cried.

"Of course we did!" Annamaria exclaimed. "Rosalie won, by the way."

"Rosalie?!" Bria muttered a string of words that luckily couldn't be heard by anyone besides the three women at the table. "I am going to kill her!"

"You'll have to wait your turn," Valentina said. "I told her it wasn't fair for her to bet because she's too close to the both of you, she had an inside edge."

"She won fair and square," Annamaria said. "We're all so happy that the two of you have kissed and made up."

Valentina grinned and raised her espresso cup. "I heard you did more than just kiss."

"Tina!" Once again Annamaria slapped Valentina on the shoulder, this time less playfully. "Sister B told us that in confidence."

"*O mio Dio!*" Bria shook her head to try and fling the embarrassment she felt from her bones. "I think I'd rather get back to talking about Carlotta."

"You mean the murderer," Mimi seethed.

"Alleged murderer," Bria corrected.

"*Caro Dio in paradiso!*" Mimi threw her head back and her hands to the sky. "You sound just like Enrico."

"He doesn't believe Carlotta killed that piano player, either," Annamaria said.

Bria felt a familiar flame ignite in her stomach. She tried to ignore it but couldn't. She had learned to trust herself with this feeling as it typically meant that someone needed her help. Someone needed her to come to their aid because they didn't have anyone else. Especially when that someone was dead.

"His name was Fiorello Sanzari." Bria's voice was soft, but her tone was strong. The women knew what she meant. The dead man, the poor soul, the piano player all had a name even if they no longer had a life.

"*Perdonaci,*" Annamaria said. "Sometimes we get carried away, but we didn't mean to disrespect the man."

"I hardly knew him," Valentina added. "But he seemed very nice."

"He couldn't have been that nice if he was friends with Carlotta," Mimi spat. "Everything that woman touches gets poisoned. Take a look at her daughter."

Although Bria was searching for clues that would point the finger at Carlotta, she couldn't ignore Mimi's comment about Ombra. "What do you mean by that?"

"The woman is young, in the prime of her life, she's about to marry a very good-looking billionaire, and yet she mopes around like she has the weight of the world on her shoulders," Mimi said. "I've known women like her before, the self-described martyrs."

"Usually an old widow," Annamaria clarified. "Not merry like you, Valentina, but Mimi's right, Ombra does act sometimes as if she's a seventy-year-old woman who has nothing to look forward to except being reunited with her departed loved ones."

Bria stifled a gasp not because of the harshness of Annamaria's words, but their accuracy. If Ombra had truly loved Fiorello and thought there might be an opportunity to have a life with him and their child, she could be looking at her upcoming wedding as the beginning of a prison term. A lifelong sentence to live with a man she did not love and be forced to keep a terrible secret.

"It's no wonder Armando isn't excited about marrying Ombra," Valentina said knowingly. "I assume he's only going to go through with it because Pietro wants him to settle down."

"Men like him never settle down," Mimi said. "Ombra is going to get her heart broken, I guarantee that, the same way I guarantee Luca is going to find proof that Carlotta was the one who strangled Fiorello to death with that piano wire."

"That hasn't proven to be so easy," Bria said. "The missing piano wire hasn't been found and the forensics team tested the piano itself, but couldn't find any fingerprints or traces of blood. We know how Fiorello was killed, but not why or who did it."

"That man—*scusami*—Fiorello, must have known something about Carlotta that she didn't want the world to know," Mimi described. "She killed him before he could speak."

"What could he have possibly known?" Annamaria asked. "Carlotta's been a public figure for decades."

"Not since she retired," Bria corrected.

"Then she did something during the years she was out of public scrutiny that Fiorello knew about and threatened to expose," Mimi deduced. "Enrico refuses to believe me when I tell him that woman is trouble just because he remembers her differently."

"How exactly does Enrico remember Carlotta?" Bria said.

"He won't tell me the whole story, but yes, he remembers her when she was starting out," Mimi said. "When she was merely backstabbing people and not strangling them to death."

Bria had known that Enrico knew Carlotta decades ago when she was first starting her career, thanks to Marco. She hadn't had the chance to question Enrico further, but she couldn't pass up the opportunity to ask Mimi.

"Did Enrico have a relationship with Carlotta years ago?" Bria asked.

For the first time since Bria joined them, Mimi hesitated to speak. Enrico's softness for her nemesis was clearly a sore spot; it probably had been the cause of many arguments between the couple and not just the one Marco overheard.

"I don't know what the two of them shared all those years ago and I don't want to know," Mimi declared. "She was a hateful, vicious woman then and she has proven she hasn't changed. I don't know why she killed Fio, but I'm sure that she did."

Involuntarily, Bria's eyebrows arched and her eyes widened. "Fio?"

"You said we should refer to him by his name, didn't you?" Mimi asked.

"Yes, but I didn't know you knew him well enough to call him Fio," Bria replied.

"Fio, Fiorello, what does it matter?" Mimi asked. "I'm sure I picked it up hearing you or someone else saying it."

Bria thought that was logical. Rosalie had started to call Giovanni Vanni, and just in this conversation both Annamaria and Mimi referred to Valentina as Tina, which they hadn't done in her presence before despite the fact that it was Valentina's preference. Still, coming from Mimi it sounded odd, out of place for her to refer to Fiorello as Fio, and it sounded as if she didn't mean to say it and it was a slip of the tongue.

The next thing Mimi said was definitely not a slip, but a calculated remark. "Bria, I get the sense that you suspect me of somehow being involved with Fiorello's murder."

It was Bria's turn to hesitate. She paused, making sure not to give too much away with her eyes, and decided that she respected Mimi enough to be honest with her. Even if such disclosure could prove difficult to their friendship.

"I understand why you don't like Carlotta," Bria started.

"I hate the woman," Mimi corrected.

"That's what I don't fully understand," Bria admitted. "I know that she destroyed your sister's career, but that was a long time ago, and you said that she went on to marry and have a family."

"She did," Mimi admitted. "But I have never forgotten that her dreams were destroyed by that vicious snake!"

"A lifetime is a long time to hold a grudge," Bria stated.

"Not long enough as far as I'm concerned." Mimi stood up, grabbed her bag with her shop's logo on it, and roughly put her arm through the strap. "I know you think I'm biased, Bria, but if Luca doesn't arrest Carlotta, he's going to let a murderer go free. *Addio.*"

"*Ciao,* Mimi," Annamaria said.

"*Cin cin,*" Valentina chirped.

The three women sat in silence for a few moments after Mimi's departure. They occupied themselves by sipping their espresso and nibbling on their *bomboloni*. Bria knew the other two women were thinking the same thing she was: How could someone as even-keeled as Mimi still be so angry about something after decades?

"I think it's hilarious that Enrico and the rest of you people in this village think I'm the wild woman." Valentina laughed. "Mimi's got me beat by a mile."

"I've known her for years and I've never seen her this upset," Annamaria added. "Or speak about someone with such utter hatred."

"I haven't known her nearly as long, but the Mimi I know is kind, generous, and funny," Bria said. "Nothing like the woman who just stormed out of here."

"Everyone has different sides," Valentina said. "Furious Mimi has probably been there all along waiting for a chance to rear her ugly head."

"No, there's more to it." Bria stood up. "And I know who will have the answer."

Flowers by Enrico always smelled so intoxicating, Bria would sometimes visit her friend just to inhale the fragrant mixture of smells. The aromas from the petunias, roses, lavender and the rest of the flowers in his shop intertwined to create one delectable scent. But today she was here on a mission. She needed to find out if there was another reason why Mimi hated Carlotta so deeply and if that reason could have anything to do with Fiorello.

"Bria!" Enrico rolled a bouquet of white irises in pink tissue paper and tied the stems with twine. "What a pleasant surprise."

"*Ciao,* Enrico. Those flowers look beautiful."

"*Grazie.* They're for Dante's office, he has a weekly order."

"That's where I've seen them before."

"Do you need some flowers for Bella Bella? Or would you like a bouquet for Luca? I know men always say they don't like to receive flowers, but that's a lie, everyone appreciates flowers."

"That's actually a lovely idea and I will put an order in, but I didn't come for flowers, I came for answers."

"I see, so this isn't a personal visit."

"*Scusi*, but something has been bothering me about Mimi and I'm hoping you can help provide some clarity."

"This has to do with Carlotta, doesn't it?"

"Yes, and her hatred for the woman."

"Mimi sees Carlotta as a *rapinatore di sogni.*"

"A dream thief?"

"Yes, a stealer of dreams," Enrico said. "It's easy to understand why she'd despise the woman and be upset that she's come back into her life after all these years."

"Don't you think she's taking this grudge too far? I mean, that was forty years ago."

Enrico took some lilies and dropped them into a vase then added a bit too much greenery. He hesitated but finally spoke. "Dreams are hard to let go of."

"For the person who was betrayed, yes, but Carlotta didn't steal Mimi's dreams."

Enrico didn't answer, but started fussing with a bunch of roses, whose color was as bright as the lemons that could be found at every store and restaurant in the village. "Mimi thought Carlotta had come back to see me."

"You?"

"When we were much, much younger, I was in love with Carlotta," Enrico began. "We were kids; I was learning this business from my father and she was at the beginning of her career. I thought I had found the person I would spend the rest of my life with and for a time Carlotta felt the same way about me. Then she was discovered."

Bria had figured that Enrico and Carlotta had crossed paths decades earlier, but she had no idea they had been in love. She remembered when Enrico came to Bella Bella with flowers for Carlotta and how she practically recoiled in horror and acted as if she didn't recognize him. Carlotta had broken his heart a second time.

"I'm so sorry, Enrico." Bria reached out and took hold of his hands. "Have you been able to speak with her since she's returned?"

"Signora Incantaro made it very clear that she wanted nothing to do with me." Enrico lifted Bria's hands and kissed them. "I've pursued many women in my lifetime, Bria, but when you get to be my age you know when to stop trying."

"For what it's worth, I think Carlotta remembers everything and she was simply playing a game."

"That may be, but it was the wake-up call I needed."

"What do you mean?"

"I foolishly told Mimi about Carlotta when I found out she was coming back to Positano, never thinking that my lady friend—*scusi,* I can't bring myself to call Mimi my girlfriend—harbored such ill will toward Carlotta. I was as shocked as I know you were."

"Now I understand. Mimi hates Carlotta, that's true, but she despises her because she thought she was going to steal her boyfriend from her as easily as she destroyed her sister's career."

"No woman could take me away from Mimi. It's taken me a while to realize it, but she is the only woman for me."

"Have you told Mimi that?"

"Every day, but *mamma mia* she can be stubborn!"

"Because she's Italian!"

Enrico glanced up at the clock on the wall. "I'm sorry, Bria, but I need to deliver these to Dante. You know how he can get when he doesn't get his way."

"Why don't you let me deliver them to Dante? I'm heading that way anyway."

"*Grazie.* That'll give me more time to surprise Mimi with a homemade dinner."

"Just go easy on the garlic. Mimi isn't as bad as my sister, but too much upsets her stomach."

"You came here looking for answers and all you've done is help me."

"Remember what I've learned since I've come to live here, Enrico—it takes a village!"

"*Dio mio!* If it isn't Bria Bartolucci clutching a bouquet of irises on my doorstep," Dante crowed. "I am witnessing one of my dreams coming true."

"*Ciao,* Dante, I bring you flowers by Enrico from Flowers by Enrico," Bria replied. "May I come in?"

"*Certo, certo.*"

Dante stood out of the way to let Bria into his office and closed the door behind them.

"Sit down and make yourself comfortable," Dante said. "Would you like some wine, limoncello?"

"Some limoncello would be nice, *grazie.*"

Bria didn't want anything from Dante except answers, but she had learned that the way to get Dante to speak was to make him feel like he was in control. And, of course, to make him feel as if he had a chance at winning Bria's heart. Which he didn't, which made Bria feel bad. But deceiving him was necessary if she was going to get him to open up about the past and provide her with the missing link that she was currently missing.

Dante handed Bria a glass of limoncello and gracefully moved so that the only place Bria could sit was on the settee and not one of the armchairs. That meant Dante would be able to sit next to her, which is exactly what he did, smiling mischievously. Bria sat back and crossed her legs. She raised her glass, clinked it against Dante's, and took a sip.

Say what you wanted to about Dante, but no one could argue that he had the best taste in town. Whether it be clothes, food, or limoncello. The only misstep Bria felt he had taken recently was his pencil-thin moustache that he was still sporting. Oh well, everyone was allowed a slip once in a while.

"I feel as if I haven't seen you for ages," Dante cooed. "What's been taking up all your time and preventing you from visiting me?"

"Well, there was another murder in the village and I've been working with Luca to try and find out who the culprit is."

"Dreadful affair and after such a wonderful concert."

"Carlotta was superb."

"Yes, indeed she was. Everyone said so."

"Everyone except Mimi."

"That's understandable."

"Because of her sister."

"What sister?

"Mimi's sister."

"Mimi doesn't have a sister."

"What are you talking about? Of course she does. Ludovica."

"You mean her brother, Ludovico."

"No, Mimi has been telling everyone that Carlotta destroyed her sister, Ludovica's, chances of being an opera singer decades ago when they were just starting out in their careers."

Although Bria didn't think her comment was funny, Dante

did. He laughed uncontrollably. It took him about a minute to regain his composure so he could continue speaking.

"That Mimi, she is a vixen that one. Carlotta didn't destroy her sister or her brother's career."

"Then why does Mimi hate Carlotta so much?"

"Because Carlotta destroyed Mimi's career."

"What?!"

Dante downed his limoncello and got up to walk across the room. Bria didn't interrupt him and let Dante act as the master of his domain like he wanted to. He pulled open the bottom drawer of a filing cabinet and started to rummage through the files. He lifted some papers, peered at them, then put them back. He did this several more times until he found what he was looking for.

"Here it is!" Dante practically skipped over to Bria and dropped the paper onto the cocktail table. "I don't usually read this rag, but sometimes it comes in handy."

Bria stared down at the table at an almost fifty-year-old copy of *La Vita Positano*. It looked very similar to the current issue that had just come out except that the editor-in-chief's name wasn't Aldo Bombalino, but his uncle Tonio, who left him the newspaper when he died. Bria knew what she was looking at, but didn't know why.

"What has this got to do with Mimi or Carlotta?"

"Flip it over and you'll see that it has to do with both of them."

Bria did as she was told and she gasped out loud. Right there in faded black-and-white were side-by-side photos of Carlotta and Mimi as very young women, barely twenty, both wearing gowns, but only Carlotta was wearing a smile. The headline above their photos read *due cantanti, un solo dolore.* Bria knew she was looking at two singers, and even without reading any further she knew that Mimi was the one who had a broken heart.

"Mimi was the singer whose career Carlotta ruined?" Bria asked.

"Supposedly." Dante poured himself another glass of limoncello and sat next to Bria. "I was very young at the time so I don't really remember, nor can I judge the quality of Mimi's singing. However, being an opera diva is about much more than having one good audition. I strongly suspect that Mimi simply wasn't good enough and has blamed Carlotta all these years for having the career that she so desperately wanted as a young woman."

"I can't believe she made up such a lie."

"A lot of people make up lies," Dante said. "It's easier than confronting the truth."

Bria knew what Dante said was true and it actually explained why Enrico had been cagey with her earlier. He had to know the truth, but was keeping it secret to protect Mimi. Bria couldn't blame him because she knew that he was already on thin ice because he had been in love with Carlotta; if Enrico exposed Mimi's secret, his current love would dump him as well.

But this revelation still didn't help her get closer to Fiorello's murderer. Even if Carlotta was the one who destroyed Mimi's career and Mimi had plotted to kill Carlotta in revenge, she could never have mistaken Fiorello for Carlotta like someone may have mistaken him for Armando since he was wearing his blue sports jacket. Mimi's revenge couldn't have extended to Fiorello; she wouldn't have even known the man. It was possible that Mimi knew Carlotta was only pushing Ombra to marry Armando for his money and she set out to kill Armando and killed Fiorello by mistake. But that was a highly convoluted thought. Even if Mimi wanted to do that, there was no way she would be able to strangle a man; Fiorello was more than double her size. Bria didn't even think Mimi could get the piano wire around his throat unless she was standing on a ladder.

The fact that Mimi's sister Ludovica was a fabrication and Mimi was the one whose career Carlotta had thwarted was shocking, but it wasn't proof that Mimi or Carlotta killed Fiorello. Bria wanted to kick herself because she had deliberately gotten cozy with Dante and had no evidence to show for it. Until she remembered that Dante's tentacles stretched quite wide. If he couldn't give her information about Fiorello's murder maybe he could give her information about Michele's disappearance.

"Dante, I hear Dr. Frangipani dabbles in the black market."

Luckily, Dante was looking away from Bria when he spit out the limoncello he was drinking, so none of it landed on her.

"Where did you hear such slander?"

"It's all over the Amalfi Coast," Bria lied. "Some have even suggested he'll accept rare coins, paintings, and jewelry in exchange for medical procedures."

"Imperia told you, didn't she?" Dante walked over to the bar to refill his glass. "Sometimes that woman lives up to her reputation."

"Trust me, I'm not going to turn Dr. Frangi in. I would actually like to see if he's interested in some items I'm thinking of putting up for sale."

Dante whipped around to face Bria. She tried to read his expression, but his thin little moustache got in the way. "What do you want to sell?"

"Some historical pieces that have recently fallen into my lap." Bria stood up and walked toward Dante as provocatively as possible without looking provocative. "I know they have significant value and I was hoping Dr. Frangi could steer me to the highest bidder."

Bria placed a hand on Dante's shoulder and felt his body shudder. "I would be ever so grateful if you could make an introduction."

"*Certo,* Bria, *certo*. I can text him right now."

"*Meravigliosa!* Tell him I can be in Milan tomorrow."

"He isn't in Milan."

"Isn't that where his clinic is?"

"His main clinic, yes, but he opened up a new one recently."

"*Dio mio,* yes! You did mention that he had opened up a new clinic."

Dante beamed. "You remembered that?"

"Where's this new clinic?"

"Next to his daughter's practice."

"His daughter's a plastic surgeon, too?"

Dante started to blush. "No, Regina is an obstetrician."

Bria tried to contain the screams that were emanating within her skull. "What's his daughter's last name?"

"Pomotori," Dante replied. "Regina divorced many years ago but kept her name. I told her she should use her maiden name and benefit from her father's success, but she's one of those *independent* women and didn't want to be accused of nepotism."

"Does this new clinic happen to be in Foggia?"

"How do you know these things, Bria?! Are you psychic? I myself have been plagued with clairvoyant tendencies since I was a young child, which I believe is why we're drawn to each other."

"*Grazie,* Dante, you've been such a tremendous help."

Bria was so excited she grabbed Dante by the shoulders and kissed him on both cheeks. He fell back onto the settee, his mouth agape, as he watched Bria leave. "Tell Dr. Frangi I'll see him and his daughter tomorrow at noon."

Chapter 26

No matter how many times she got behind the wheel of her Fiat, it always made Bria smile. Rosalie not so much. That was usually because whenever they went on an impromptu road trip out of the village, Bria knew where they were going and why, but Rosalie was typically left in the dark. This time, however, Rosalie knew where they were going and why and she still wasn't happy.

When Bria called her last night to tell her to be ready by eight a.m. to drive the three hours to Foggia, Rosalie immediately knew it was to search for Michele. Thus far the police had been unable to track him down through his connection to Fiorello and his corporation, Eighty-Eight Keys. But as was often the case, Bria had better information than the police.

Thanks to her encounter with Dante she knew that Dr. Frangipani had opened an office in Foggia next to his daughter's OB/GYN clinic and that his daughter happened to be the obstetrician Fiorello had hired as Giacomo to be Ombra's doctor. Bria didn't know how all the pieces fit together, but there were too many coincidences to ignore. If they couldn't find Michele, Dr. Frangi might be able to give them clues as to where to find him. And hopefully, Regina could confirm that Fiorello was indeed the father of Ombra's baby, which would give Carlotta and possibly Armando motive to kill him. This was all very serious business and Bria understood that, yet she still couldn't stop smiling as she drove.

The gray clouds and rain were a distant memory and the sky had restored itself to its typical beauty. Soft blue without a cloud to be seen and bright sunshine that caressed the skin. The top of Bria's bright yellow 1970 Fiat Dino convertible was down and she was wearing her black-and-white oval La Giardiniera sunglasses that she only wore while driving. She had tucked her hair back in a white kerchief and felt like a movie star playing hooky from having to be confined to a day on a film set.

Sitting next to her, Rosalie looked like the disgruntled continuity girl forced to sit in a chair and keep her eyes focused on the script while all around her was excitement. She was wearing a green linen sleeveless jumpsuit with matching sunglasses and instead of letting her curly hair blow in the wind like she normally did, she had wrapped a white-and-green plaid silk scarf around her head that made her look like a cross between Norma Desmond and Rhoda Morgenstern. The only other accessory she wore was her scowl.

"I cannot believe I got all dressed up just to see Michele," Rosalie barked. "Who I never want to see again."

"First, *amore mia,* you are not all dressed up."

"You don't like my outfit?"

"It's perfectly fine, but you're not even wearing jewelry, or a belt, or an ankle bracelet; for you, you're practically naked."

"I didn't want to look too good and let Michele think I was taking him back."

"You've achieved your goal."

"*Grazie.* And second?"

"We don't know if we're going to see Michele. I imagine he's long gone by now."

"Then why are we going?"

"To talk to Dr. Frangi and see if Michele actually connected with him to sell your rocks."

"I cannot believe my rocks are fossils. You realize this whole thing is Luca's fault."

"How is it his fault?"

"If he had only told me the rocks were worth a lot of money, I would've put them in my safe, I wouldn't have left them lying around my boat for anyone to steal."

"No one else would have taken them and you know that."

"I swear right in front of you that I am done with the bad boys! I want a nice guy who isn't going to steal from me."

"Once we find Michele and get your rocks back, we'll start looking for him."

"Don't we also have to find out who killed Fiorello?"

"Well, yes, of course, and I'm hoping Dr. Frangi's daughter can help us with that."

"I can't believe we're going to meet the mysterious Regina!" Rosalie shouted. "Do you think she knows Fiorello is dead?"

"Even if she did hear that he was killed, she knows him as Giacomo."

"That's right, fake name and all that."

"Regina probably thinks Giacomo just ran out on her."

"When we meet her let me do the talking," Rosalie declared. "She and I obviously have a lot in common, like our choice in men."

Bria had decided to take Via Alfonso Gatto, which was a slightly longer ride than Via E842, but more scenic. Foggia was a city in Puglia northeast of Positano, landlocked, but closer to the Adriatic Sea. It was located in an area that Bria rarely traveled to, so it was nice to see the sights instead of just a highway.

For most of the ride the women enjoyed the view, but of course when Bria and Rosalie were together they couldn't remain quiet for very long. After about twenty minutes they started to chat and during the next three hours made many decisions. They decided they were going to keep Mimi's secret that she was actually Ludovica and once an aspiring opera singer because it wouldn't help the investigation to reveal that truth and the reveal would only embarrass their friend. They weighed the pros and cons of Nunzi's new hairstyle, which Rosalie reluctantly admitted was starting to grow on her, and decided to support Nunzi's make-over. The only time they debated a topic was when Rosalie asked if Bria was going to change her last name when she married Luca.

At first, Bria balked and said she wasn't ready to contemplate marriage, but Rosalie wouldn't take no for an answer. And although Bria loved how her name sounded, she admitted that if she were to ever marry Luca she would become Bria Vivaldi. Despite looking like a glamorous film star, Bria was a traditional girl at heart.

"For a moment I thought it might be fun to change my name to Rosalie Vivaldi-Vistigliano, but that's a mouthful and I don't think there are enough boxes on the forms I have to fill out to renew my boating license to fit all those letters plus a hyphen."

Bria reached over and grabbed Rosalie's hand, who happily accepted it. They both savored the connection for a few moments without acknowledging it. "I'm sorry Michele didn't turn out to be the man you hoped he would."

"Me too. But I'm proud that I didn't make excuses or ignore his faults and my concerns. I looked it in the eye and said, 'Not for me.' "

"*Brava!*"

Bria saw the look of concern that still lingered in Rosalie's eyes. "Are you worried you might change your mind if you see him again?"

"Not at all. I am worried that I might punch him in the face and get arrested. Which reminds me, did you bring bail money?"

"Rosalie Vivaldi! Do I look like an amateur?"

"Actually, you do."

"Check my purse and make sure I have enough cash; if not we'll stop at an ATM. If there's one thing I've learned on these excursions of ours, it's always better to be safe than sorry."

As they drove into Foggia, Bria couldn't really understand why Dr. Frangipani would want to open up a clinic here. The city was nice, but not one of Italy's crown jewels, like Milan, Venice, or Florence. It wasn't a tourist destination, it didn't have a particularly wealthy population, and after being decimated in World War II, the architecture of the new buildings looked sturdy but hardly had any visual appeal or character.

The city itself didn't hold much historical significance, and the major artistic export was Umberto Giordano, a film composer who wrote a song that was included on the soundtrack for *To Rome with Love.* Foggia did have a quirky landmark, a customs office in the Palazzo Dogana built exclusively for sheep. The Royal Customs of Sheep Trading was active until the nineteenth century and today the building houses exhibits and galleries.

As they drove down Viale Manfredi, however, Bria's opinion changed and she realized that Foggia was the perfect location for a plastic surgeon's clinic, especially if they catered to an elite clientele. Dr. Frangi's patients could come here and not be seen unlike when they were in Milan. Getting a nip and tuck when you traveled within a certain higher echelon of society was commonplace, but not everyone wanted the world to know they were going under the knife. Choosing to have a procedure in Foggia was a great option for those who wanted to go unnoticed.

They turned onto Via Montegrappa and saw a string of residential buildings, not town houses, but apartment buildings, a few with storefronts. There was a café, a stationery store, and at the corner was a nondescript building with a small parking lot attached. If Bria hadn't been driving slowly, she would have passed right by, especially because the names Frangipani and Pomotori were nowhere to be seen. The sign on the building said Foggia OB/GYN and Plastic Surgery Clinics.

"Dr. Frangi must be extremely good," Bria said, pulling into a spot in the parking lot.

"Why do you say that?" Rosalie asked.

"There is no way Dante would be caught dead in a place like this if Dr. Frangi couldn't work miracles."

Bria and Rosalie got out of the car and then manually put the top back up. It wasn't that Bria thought someone was going to try and steal her car or its contents, it was just that she didn't trust that someone wouldn't. It was that kind of neighborhood.

Rosalie hooked her arm through Bria's as they walked to the front door. "Let's say that you're here for a plastic surgery consultation and I need a pelvic exam."

"*Uffa!* I know I haven't gotten a lot of rest lately and I've been under some stress, but do I look like I need a plastic surgeon?"

"Of course not, but I just ended yet another relationship. I don't need a man telling me my boobs could use a lift."

The inside of the clinic didn't look much better than the outside. A row of folding chairs lined both sides of the wall in the windowless reception area. A long, oval fluorescent bulb hung from the ceiling, a water cooler occupied a space in the corner, and on the small desk on the far side of the room was a sign-in sheet attached to a clipboard. Bria picked up the pen that was attached to the clipboard with an elaborate mechanism made up of rubber bands and chain links and tried to write her name, but the pen was out of ink. Had she not driven three hours to meet two people who could offer clues and help solve a murder and/or find a felon, she would have turned around and gone home. Instead, she yelled.

"*Ciao!* Is anybody home?"

"Why does everyone think I'm the loud one?" Rosalie mused out loud.

"*Aspetta! Sto arrivando!*" a man called out from somewhere within the clinic.

"*Grazie!* It's Bria Bartolucci, Dante La Costa's friend from Positano."

"Ah yes! *Un momento!* I'll be right out."

After a few moments, Edoardo Frangipani entered the room. The first thing Bria noticed was his moustache. It was identical to the one Dante was sporting, but on his face it actually worked.

From what Bria had found online about the doctor, she knew Frangipani was in his mid-sixties; however, his skin was as smooth as a forty-year-old's. He had the faintest of lines on his forehead, a few crow's feet around his eyes, and slight vertical lines on the sides of his mouth. Unless the doctor was preternaturally endowed with skin that didn't age, he did amazing work. No wonder Dante and Imperia revered him like a god.

He had a full head of hair, but it was rather thin and slicked back to the right. His black eyes shone like onyx and his jawline was strong. Combined with his moustache, his features gave him the air of a 1930s film star like Errol Flynn. Bria understood why he had such a loyal following.

"Dr. Frangipani, how nice to meet you."

"The pleasure is all mine, and please call me Edoardo."

"*Buongiorno,* Edoardo," Bria said.

"It was nice to get Dante's call to make an appointment for you, but I must say I expected to hear from you years ago."

"Why is that?" Bria asked.

"Every time I meet Imperia she says that she wants me to work on her daughter-in-law before permanent damage sets in."

"There's no one quite as thoughtful as Imperia," Rosalie commented.

"This is my friend Rosalie Vivaldi," Bria said.

"*Ciao,*" Edoardo said, extending his hand to shake Rosalie's. "You have beautiful bone structure."

"I know, *grazie.* I'm not here for your services," Rosalie said. "But as Imperia said, Bria is in need of some emergency care."

"Nonsense! Imperia was just being . . . Imperia." Edoardo lifted Bria's chin with his index finger and inspected her face. "Dante didn't lie. You have amazing cheekbones and your neck, it's like a swan's."

"*Grazie,*" Bria said, wrapping her hand around Frangipani's fingers and bringing them away from her face. "Dante has raved about you for years."

"He's one of my most loyal patients."

"You've worked wonders on him," Bria gushed. "He doesn't look a day over forty!"

"You're too kind," Edoardo replied. "Why don't we go back into my office and you can tell me what you'd like done. Should we start with the nose?"

"We aren't here to discuss any procedure."

"Dante said I needed to squeeze you in today, that it was a matter of life or death."

"Dante does have a tendency to exaggerate," Rosalie joked.

"We're here because we think you can help us find someone," Bria said. "Michele Vistigliano."

Dr. Frangipani aged about five years right in front of their eyes.

"I have no idea who that is," Edoardo protested.

"We aren't here to cause any trouble, but he stole something from me and we know he was coming here to try and sell it to you," Rosalie explained.

"We want to get back Rosalie's stolen property," Bria explained.

"And find Michele so I can kill him," Rosalie added.

"She's kidding."

"Not entirely."

Edoardo banged on the desk. "I knew I never should have trusted him!"

"Don't blame yourself, Michele is a con man," Rosalie said.

"Not Michele, Giacomo!"

"You know Giacomo Lancia?" Bria asked.

"He's the one who introduced me to Michele and the one who sold me some of Carlotta's jewelry, which turned out to be worth half the price I paid for them," Edoardo said. "Imagine my surprise when I tried to sell diamond earrings on the black market only to find out they're Lucite! I have a reputation to uphold!"

"*Scusi, per favore,* where is Michele now?" Bria asked.

"I don't know. I met him two days ago, we made our transaction, and then he left," Edoardo explained. "I told him I would contact him when I found a buyer."

"So you still have my rocks?!" Rosalie cried.

"I think you're referring to the fossils," Edoardo corrected.

"Where are they?" Rosalie demanded.

"You must believe me, I had no idea they were stolen," Edoardo said. "He told me his *zio* Nazario left them to him in his will."

"*Zio* Nazario is my *zio* and he left them to me!" Rosalie cried. "First Michele steals my rocks, then he steals my story."

"Dr. Frangipani," Bria started.

"Edoardo please, we're friends."

"*Scusi,* Edoardo, the rocks are fossils that belong to Rosalie. I know you're innocent and you do not want us to call the chief of police to help us retrieve the items in question."

"Oh no! You cannot involve the police!"

"We don't want to, either," Bria said.

"Even though the chief of police is my brother."

"And my boyfriend."

Edoardo screamed and almost fell to the floor. Bria understood completely why Dante admired the doctor, they were like twins separated at birth. "I am innocent. You understand that, don't you?"

"We'll keep your name out of this completely," Bria said. "We just need the rocks."

"She means fossils," Rosalie corrected.

"Regina!" Edoardo shouted. "Bring me the black box in the closet of the breast augmentation room."

Bria and Rosalie locked eyes, and it wasn't because they had just found out there was a breast augmentation room, but because they were about to meet Regina Pomotori.

"Dante told me that Regina is your daughter who runs the OB/GYN clinic," Bria said.

The mention of his daughter's name brought Edoardo out of his state of shock. "Yes, I'm so proud of all the hard work she's done and how selflessly she serves this community."

"By 'community' are you including the black market?" Rosalie asked.

Luckily, her question was drowned out by the noise Regina made as she walked down the hallway in her wooden clogs and by her shouting.

"Papa! You had to put the box on the top shelf?! I almost killed myself trying to get it down, and it weighs a ton. What the hell is in here?"

"Rocks," Rosalie said.

"Seriously?" Regina replied. "I thought that was code for something like diamonds or a stuffed ocelot. We sold one of those once to a Hindi prince."

"Dr. Frangi . . . I mean, Edoardo, would you mind terribly helping Rosalie carry the box out to my car." Bria took the key out of her purse and shoved it into Edoardo's hand. "It's the yellow convertible parked right in the lot."

"*Certo.*"

Edoardo took one side of the box from Regina and Rosalie took the other. The box was heavy, but Rosalie could have carried it on her own, she was used to lugging things on and off her boat. However, Bria wanted to be alone with Regina. She waited until they were at the door and then said, "I'll be right out, I have a few questions for Dr. Pomotori."

"Do you need to be examined?" Regina asked.

After the door closed, Bria turned to Regina and couldn't believe she was staring at the voice from the other side of Fiorello's cell phone. She didn't look like a blackmailer, she didn't look like she would take advantage of a pregnant woman in trouble, but she was. Bria felt no pity for the woman; she was educated, she was successful, she didn't need to steal from others, she was a doctor who had taken an oath to help people. But like father, like daughter.

"I've driven a long way and I don't have a lot of time," Bria started. "I know Giacomo Lancia hired you to be Ombra Incantaro's obstetrician."

All the color faded from Regina's face. "I have no idea what you're talking about."

"I have proof. You've been calling and texting Giacomo demanding more money or you're going to tell Armando who the real father of Ombra's baby is."

"I don't have to stand for this."

"You can either tell me or I press one button on my phone and my boyfriend will send the local authorities here, and since my boyfriend is the chief of police in Positano he has the power to do that."

Regina glared at her and finally resembled the blackmailer Bria had heard screeching on the other end of the phone. "What do you want to know?"

"Who's the real father of Ombra's baby?"

"Some musician named Fiorello Sanzari."

"Why were you threatening to tell Armando the truth?"

"Because he deserves to know everything."

"What else is there besides the fact that his fiancée is pregnant with another man's baby?"

"The fact that Ombra never intends to marry Armando."

"What are you talking about? They're supposed to get married in two days."

"That's what she wants everyone to think, but it's a lie. Ombra and Fiorello are going to run away together and get married so they can live happily ever after. Her wedding to Armando is never going to happen."

Back home after she had dinner with Marco and heard all about his day, she put him to bed and left him and Bravo to their dreams. She poured herself a glass of merlot and sat on her balcony to gaze at the stars. Tomorrow she was going to meet with Luca and they were going to reveal to each other who they believed killed Fiorello. Bria knew what she was going to say, but she still didn't have the definitive proof she wanted, just tons of circumstantial evidence. She thought it was enough to convince Luca she was right, but she wasn't certain.

Before she was about to go to bed, she noticed her pants lying on the floor. She picked them up, folded them, and as she was putting them in her drawer, she accidentally knocked over her purse.

"*Uffa!* Will this day never end!"

As she picked up her purse something else fell out—the old newspaper that Dante had showed her with the photo of Carlotta and Mimi. She looked at the photo again and Dante was right, the print had faded and it was very difficult to read. She took out her phone and turned on the magnifying glass app Vanni downloaded for her. Blown up, the text was much easier to see. She started to read the article and then had to search within the paper because it was continued on the inside.

By the time she finished, she knew exactly who had murdered Fiorello. If what Bria believed happened to the poor man was true, it was utterly horrifying.

Chapter 27

By the time Bria got to Piazza dei Mulini, Luca was already waiting for her. The terrible thoughts that clung to her loosened their grip slightly so she could take in the sight. Even though it was only a few minutes after seven a.m., he was impeccably dressed and looked more handsome than Bria had ever seen. It could be due to the fact that the early morning sun was casting a golden glow around his tanned face or that despite the serious reason for their meeting he was grinning like a man who knew that no matter what happened in the next hour, he'd be spending the night with the woman he loved. Or it could simply be because Bria had silenced her fears and realized—thanks to her family and friends—that Luca wasn't perfect, but he was the perfect man for her.

As she walked across the piazza, her heels clicked against the stone. She had deliberately chosen not to wear her favored espadrilles, but instead put on a pair of navy blue slingbacks with a thin two-inch heel. She wore a pale pink sleeveless dress, that was anchored by a thin navy blue lasso belt, with a ruffle at her knee that bounced with each step she took. She glanced at the Sirens in the fountain, once again using rushing water as a substitute for a deadly song, and instinctively knew that they would be pleased with her. She wasn't sure if she should be happy about that, but she needed all the support she could get.

"'*Giorno*." Bria kissed Luca on the lips softly.

"'*Giorno, donna* sexy." Luca's breath was hot on Bria's ear and she felt a shiver stroll down her spine. "You look beautiful for a woman who's about to end someone's freedom."

"I'm only going to present the facts, you're the one who's going to make the arrest."

"That'll actually be handled by Nunzi."

Luca tilted his head toward the right, and when Bria looked in that direction she saw Nunzi sitting at a café table in plain clothes like an undercover detective. Bria was mortified when she realized Nunzi had witnessed her brazen strut across the piazza and her sultry kiss. From the other side of the piazza, Nunzi raised her espresso cup and smiled devilishly at Bria. Bria waved back and then slapped Luca on his arm.

"You could've told me we had an audience."

Luca gazed over Bria's shoulder. "Don't look now, but our audience is getting bigger."

Bria turned around and saw that the prime suspects had entered the arena. Carlotta was leading the group, followed closely by Armando, and trailing behind was Ombra. Bria wondered if they knew the real reason they had been summoned by Luca. He had told them that they had found new evidence in their investigation into Fiorello's murder that he wanted to share with them before they left town.

At first Armando and Ombra balked, but Carlotta convinced them that they owed it to Luca to agree to his request. She argued that if he had found the missing clue that would point him toward the culprit, he could arrest Fiorello's killer and they could go off to Lake Como for the wedding without a dark cloud hovering over their heads. Bria wasn't sure if Carlotta was courageous or a fool.

"*Mattina,*" Carlotta announced, almost cheerfully, as she entered the piazza.

Bria thought the diva had also dressed to impress, and not for what she thought would be a long day of traveling. A beige linen top and pants with a black long-sleeved sheer maxi-length coat that billowed in the soft breeze. She was wearing black-and-white costume jewelry around her wrist, neck, and dangling from her ears. Nothing expensive, but also nothing subtle.

"Isn't it a glorious morning?" Carlotta asked. "With each breath I can smell the sea. It's invigorating, filled with life."

"Which is ironic, Mamma, because we're here to talk about death," Ombra said. "Unless you've conveniently pushed that from your mind."

Carlotta shot a look at Ombra that made the young woman cower and Bria wince. Bria couldn't imagine ever looking at Marco with such derision in public or private. Chastising your child was sometimes necessary if they did something wrong or disappointed you with their choices, but it was a parent's responsibility to teach their child to become better, not to push them down and make them feel worthless or fill them with shame. Bria had witnessed this type of interaction between Carlotta and Ombra before, but there was something different about the exchange.

"Signore, *per favore*." Armando rolled his eyes as he sat in one of the chairs in the piazza. "Could you please keep the bickering to a minimum? We have a long trip ahead of us."

"*Prego,*" Carlotta replied. "You're right as usual, Armando, we do have a long day of travel. Luca, why don't you begin and tell us why you've brought us here? We're dying of curiosity."

"I'm sure you are," Luca replied. "Fiorello was very special to you."

"That he was," Carlotta demurred. "He was more than a piano player, he was a confidant, a friend."

"And the father of Ombra's unborn child."

Everyone turned to look at Bria, including Luca and an equally shocked Nunzi, who had surreptitiously moved her chair closer to the group and had been eavesdropping on the conversation. Luca's mouth was open and his eyes were wide. Bria knew that he'd be surprised by her sudden announcement, but he looked so comical, that if she didn't continue her questioning, she risked the possibility of laughing out loud.

"I applaud your reactions," Bria started. "The only one who has a legitimate reason to be surprised is Armando."

Proving Bria's point, Armando tried to stand up from his chair but couldn't find the strength in his legs. He looked at Ombra with such an expression that if Bria didn't know him better, she would have thought the woman had just broken his heart. Instead, she knew that the playboy wasn't used to being duped.

"You're pregnant?" Armando asked.

Ombra looked as if she was standing before a firing squad. Her pallor was grayer than usual and her breathing had become rapid. Instinctively, she clutched her stomach giving Armando his answer before she spoke.

"Yes." The word was a whisper, and when Ombra opened her mouth to continue, no more words came out.

"With Fio's baby?" Armando's face was etched with hurt and confusion. "How?"

"I would think that a man like you would know all about *gli uccelli e le api,*" Luca replied.

"I know how babies are made," Armando scoffed. "But how . . . you barely said two words to Fio."

"Mando, *per favore*, Bria doesn't know what she's talking about." Carlotta nervously raised one arm toward him and one toward Ombra, her sleeves looking like two waves of darkness. "Ombra is pregnant with your child."

Armando shook his head slowly. "That's impossible."

"We're all adults here," Carlotta said. "I know my daughter isn't an innocent and you are a passionate man."

"I said it's impossible!" Armando bellowed so loudly that a few birds that had been searching for scraps of food in the piazza flew away abruptly. "Ombra cannot be having my child."

"Why?" Ombra asked. "Is that such a horrifying concept?"

"Yes!" Armando stood up so quickly that his chair fell backward behind him.

Ombra didn't lower her head, but she began to cry. Slowly, tears ran down her face, and it was so painful and raw that Bria had to force herself to not look away. "Do you hate me that much?"

"You really are a naïve little girl, aren't you?" Armando said. "No wonder my father thinks that you can save me."

"Maybe I can," Ombra replied. "Me and our baby."

"It isn't my baby!" Armando cried. "I had a vasectomy years ago."

"What?!" The complexion drained from Carlotta's face as Armando's words and their implications resonated and punched a hole in her story. "Pietro would never allow that."

"My father may think he's omniscient, but he doesn't know everything about me," Armando spat.

"I know you said you didn't want children," Ombra said. "But men say that when they're scared."

"I'm not scared, Ombra, I'm terrified!" Armando shouted.

"Of what?" Ombra asked.

Armando clenched his fists and pressed them against his forehead. He let out a guttural groan and finally shared with Ombra the truth. "I carry a gene in my blood that will kill any child that I father! It's happened once and I had a vasectomy because I vowed that it would never happen again. I don't know if the baby you're carrying is Fiorello's or not, but I am certain it isn't mine."

"It's the reason Armando took Marco to the soccer game," Bria shared. "He wanted to experience what it would be like to be a father."

"*Fantastico!*" Carlotta shouted, a smile irrationally forming on her lips. "Now you'll get to experience that every day of your life."

"Every day of my life I'll be reminded that my wife slept with another man while she was engaged to be married to me," Armando said. "If you think I'm going to live with that for the rest of my life, you're as crazy as those women in your operas!"

"I promise you, Armando, I'll never tell anyone, especially not your father," Ombra said. "No one will ever know this child isn't yours."

"I'll know!" Armando shouted. "And if you think my father won't find out, you're just as crazy as your mother."

"Pietro will be delighted to be a grandfather," Carlotta said. "He told me that's his dream."

"His dream is for his son to become a man and bring him a grandson," Armando said. "I can never do that, I can never fulfill my father's dream."

"I can," Ombra said. "You just have to be the man Pietro wants you to be and keep quiet about the truth."

"That's exactly the kind of son Pietro wants! The kind who doesn't know his fiancée was having a secret fling with the hired help right under his own nose!" Armando cried. "How long were you sleeping with Fiorello?"

Ombra began to tremble and shake her head. "It doesn't matter, I was never going to be with him, no matter how much I . . ."

"No matter how much you loved him?" Armando asked. "Is that what you were going to say?"

"My feelings for him don't matter," Ombra said. "All that matters is that you and I are going to get married. I signed the prenuptial agreement like you wanted."

"Which requires that I pay you quite a lot of money no matter when we get divorced," Luca said.

"It's hardly a lot of money," Carlotta said.

"I think five million euros is a nice payday," Armando said.

"That's because you're a billionaire's son," Carlotta hissed. "You don't know the meaning of money!"

"You don't know what it's like to constantly worry if you're going to be able to pay your bills or feed yourself!" Ombra shrieked. "Or how you're going to raise a child on your own!"

"I've always known you were after my money; your doting mother-in-law routine is about as subtle as your Queen of the Night performance," Armando sneered. "But you, Ombra, really? All you wanted was my money?"

"Don't act so innocent, Mando," Ombra bit back. "All you wanted was a girl who could help you win your father's approval."

Armando closed his eyes and shook his head. "How did I not know about this?" he asked. "How could I not see what was right in front of my eyes?"

"You did see it," Bria said.

"What are you talking about?" Armando asked.

"You knew Ombra was in a relationship with another man, you questioned her about it, and even remarked about it in front of me," Bria explained. "You just didn't know that Giacomo Lancia, Ombra's wedding planner, was actually Fiorello."

"What?" Armando cried.

"Fiorello had a fake name," Bria explained. "I'm not entirely sure why, but it definitely helped keep his relationship with Ombra a secret."

"I can't believe this, Ombra," Armando said. "I can't believe you were going to let me marry you even though you're carrying another man's baby."

"She wasn't," Bria said.

"Shut up Bria!" Ombra yelled.

"At least not according to Regina," Bria added."

"Who the hell is Regina?" Armando asked.

"Ombra's obstetrician," Bria clarified. "Fiorello handpicked Regina Pomotori, who happens to be Dr. Frangipani's daughter, for Ombra because he knew Regina would keep quiet. But at some point Regina developed a conscience and told Fiorello—or Giacomo, which is what she thought his name was—that if he didn't tell Ombra's fiancé that Ombra was pregnant with another man's child, she would. I met with Regina the other day, who is unaware that Fiorello is dead, by the way, and she told me about their plan."

"What plan?" Armando asked.

"The plan for Ombra and Fiorello to run away together and get married before she could marry you," Bria replied.

Armando spun around to face Ombra. "You were planning to leave me standing at the altar? In front of my father and the rest of my family?"

Either Ombra couldn't find the right words or couldn't remember how to speak because she remained silent and stared at the ground. Carlotta sighed heavily and closed her eyes. She shook her head slowly from side to side and smiled weakly as she placed her hand on her daughter's shoulder.

"You don't seem very surprised by this, Carlotta," Luca said.

"I think this is all very entertaining, but I'm still waiting for the revelation of fact," she replied. "Where's this evidence that you found that will reveal Fiorello's killer?"

The moment had come and Bria still didn't feel prepared. A shiver of pure fear run down her spine. "You mean killers."

"Killers?" Luca shouted, then lowered his voice. "Bria what are you talking about?"

"If you give me a moment, I'll explain," Bria started. "But I warn you that you're going to find it hard to accept."

"I find this whole charade unacceptable," Carlotta barked.

"I think this farce needs to come to an end right now. We have to get to Naples to catch our train."

"You're not going anywhere until Bria finishes," Luca ordered.

"Sister Benedicta told me that Ombra reminded her of Pamina," Bria started. "I didn't know who that was, so I looked it up, and it's the name of the Queen of the Night's daughter in the opera, *The Magic Flute*. I always loved that aria because when I've heard it in the past I simply focused on how glorious it sounds and not its intent. But when you listen to the words, the song becomes something much more harrowing: it's a call to murder."

"I demand that this nonsense end now!" Carlotta cried.

"How does the song begin?" Bria asked. "'The vengeance of Hell boils in my heart.' Is that how you felt, Carlotta, when you found out Ombra was pregnant with Fiorello's child?"

Carlotta turned so quickly to look at Ombra, Bria thought her head might snap off. The look she gave her daughter was vicious and grotesque. "I was furious as any mother would be who doesn't want to see her daughter destroy her future."

"So you decided to destroy Fiorello's," Bria said.

"We should go, this is ridiculous," Ombra said.

"No one's going anywhere!" Armando shouted. "Let Bria finish."

"What's the next line of the aria, Carlotta?" Bria asked rhetorically. "'If Sarastro does not through you feel the pain of death, then you will be my daughter nevermore, disowned, abandoned, destroyed forever.' Replace Sarastro with Fiorello and the song becomes foreshadowing. You both knew the kind of man Fiorello was and that he would never abandon his child. Based on what Regina told me, both your instincts were right on target. Fiorello wanted a life with Ombra and their child and neither of you were going to let that happen."

"Oh my God." Armando slumped back down in his chair. "You don't mean . . . ?"

Bria couldn't look Armando in the eye and had to glance away. "Carlotta forced Ombra to help kill the father of her child to prevent him from ever revealing the truth."

"I cannot believe this!" Armando jumped up and started to walk around Ombra and Carlotta. "Ombra, how could you do such a thing?"

"I . . . I didn't," Ombra stammered. "Mamma, tell them, tell them the truth."

"Keep your mouth shut and don't say another word," Carlotta seethed. "They have no proof of this."

"Nunzi," Luca said. "Are you ready?"

Nunzi nodded and pulled out a cell phone from her shoulder bag. She pressed a button and suddenly it was as if a piano concerto was taking place in the piazza. Romantic, delicate music filled the air and it could be traced to Ombra's purse. Ombra started to sway and Armando and Luca rushed to her side to prevent her from falling to the ground. As they did, Bria took the purse from her and pulled out her cell phone.

"Nunzi is holding Fiorello's cell phone and she dialed the number of a burner phone that clearly belongs to Ombra," Bria announced. "It's the same phone she used to text Fiorello to ask him to meet her at the piazza the night he was killed. You lured him to his death."

"Let go of me!" Ombra broke free of Armando and Luca's hold and shook herself. "Tell them the rest Bria. Tell them what really happened!"

"Ombra!" Carlotta slapped Ombra across the face, and seconds later, Nunzi grabbed both of her arms and held them behind her back.

"Go on then!" Ombra exclaimed. "Tell them!"

Bria took out the newspaper Dante gave her from her bag and held it up for all to see. "This is an issue of *La Vita Posi-*

tano from when Carlotta was first starting out, singing right here in Piazza dei Mulini," Bria said. "The article talks about the up-and-coming coloratura, how her voice can be delicate and fierce at the same time, and how she is also quite handy fixing things."

"My mother has so many skills that she doesn't like to talk about," Ombra said.

"Bria, keep reading," Luca said.

"During a concert, a piano wire broke. Carlotta removed it and replaced it with a new one within minutes," Bria explained. "She was the one who removed the wire from the piano and then waited in the darkness for Fiorello to arrive for his secret meeting with Ombra. And then she did the unthinkable."

"I did what any mother would do!" Carlotta cried.

"You can't actually believe that," Bria said.

"I was protecting my child!"

Bria knew that she would do almost anything to save Marco, except force him to commit murder. She swallowed hard to prevent the shriek of horror that was building up in her throat escape and be unleashed into the air. She couldn't believe what she was about to say was true. "Carlotta then watched as Ombra did what she had been instructed to do: hold onto Fiorello's hands and never let go, no matter how hard Fiorello struggled, no matter how hard he fought to live, no matter how desperately he wanted to see his child be born into this world, Ombra could not let go while Carlotta strangled him."

"Oh dear God!" Mando shouted.

Bria looked around and she saw the faces staring back at her, professionals who fought evil every day, all of them as shocked and horrified as Mando was. "Like Pamina in the opera, Ombra had a job to do; she had to prevent Fiorello from fighting back and getting loose. That's why Fio had scratch marks on his wrist. They were from Ombra's nails."

"This can't be true," Armando muttered and sat down in his chair. "You *both* killed him?"

"I didn't do anything," Ombra said. "She's the one who strangled him."

"Ombra!" Carlotta lunged toward Ombra, but Nunzi tightened her grip. "Your hands are as blood-soaked as mine!"

Armando reeled back and almost tumbled over in his chair before steadying himself. "I thought I was a horrible person. I thought I didn't deserve someone as good as you, Ombra, but you . . . you two are pure evil."

"You have no right to judge us from your ivory tower, from your life of privilege!" Carlotta struggled to break free from Nunzi, but the policewoman's hold was too tight. "You have no idea what it's like to have nothing! To have to beg and plead just to have enough to survive!"

"For all your efforts, Carlotta, you're only going to spend the rest of your life in jail," Bria said.

"Right next to your daughter," Luca added.

"You killed a man to give your child a better life and all you did was make him an orphan," Bria said. "Neither of you have any idea what it means to be a mother."

Bria felt bile collect in her throat and tears well in her eyes. She turned away and breathed in deeply. Carlotta was right; she could smell the sea, but she could also smell the terror and fear that Fiorello must have felt in his last moments when the realization hit him that the woman he loved, the woman he thought he was going to marry, the woman he thought was going to bring his child into the world was the same woman who was killing him.

She shook her head and wiped away her tears. When she turned around she saw that Nunzi was leading Carlotta off in handcuffs and Matteo had arrived and was doing the same to Ombra. Several other cops were walking with them and someone was helping a visibly distraught Armando get to a chair.

It was almost too much for Bria to bear. A mother forcing her child to join her in extinguishing a man's life. Not just any man, but someone they cared about, someone they loved, someone who did not deserve such an ending.

She felt Luca's arms around her and she held on tight. Slowly, she felt the ugliness and the terror loosen its grip and she opened her eyes to the light, the beautiful view—and understood that even in an idyllic coastal village like Positano, there was darkness. But thankfully, there was also light.

She only needed to turn around and look up into Luca's eyes to be reminded of that. He kissed her softly, first on her forehead and then on her lips. They stood in silence, staring at each other, as the world around them faded away. Until the only thing that remained was love.

Epilogue

A week later the village was still more than a little obsessed with the sordid tale about the opera singer, her daughter, the billionaire fiancé, and the ill-fated piano player. Four individuals, whose lives intersected and culminated in a ghastly, tragic event. One dead, two imprisoned, and one traumatized.

Logically, Bria understood how Fio lost his life. Emotionally, however, she still couldn't believe Carlotta had been that desperate to kill her friend, and Ombra had been that brainwashed to follow her mother's inconceivably horrendous orders. She looked at the jagged Lattari Mountains that made up the craggy surface of Positano, and was grateful the events were behind her. It was time for her to focus on her own life.

Bria entered Bella Bella just in time to hear her mother scream at Lorenza. "You did what?!"

"We got married." Lorenza held up her hand with a shiny gold wedding band around her ring finger to prove that she was telling the truth. "Aren't you happy for us?"

Bria, Fifetta, and even Franco all responded at the same time and with the same one-word answer. "No!"

"What do you mean you aren't happy for us?" Lorenza asked. "Is it because you don't think I'm good enough for Fabrice?"

"Renza, *bambina*," Fabrice cooed. "I'm the one that's not good enough for you."

"Basta!" Bria cried. "You're both perfect for each other and we love you, but how could you get married without us?"

"It's all my fault," Fabrice said. "I got too excited and caught up in the moment."

"I think I need to sit down." Fifetta started to swoon and Bria and Franco grabbed her from either side and sat her down at the table. "Lorenza, tell me the truth and do not lie to your mamma! When is your due date?"

"I'm not having a baby!" Lorenza cried. "Have you all lost your minds?!"

"I meant that I got too excited when we had a layover in Las Vegas," Fabrice explained.

"We were in front of the Bellagio Hotel and the fountains were dancing to 'That's Amore' by Dean Martin," Lorenza explained. "Fabrice dropped to one knee and proposed."

"Then we went to one of those chapels and got married," Fabrice finished. "Please allow me to introduce my wife, Lorenza Belragasso."

"Of course we're going to have a real wedding at *Mondo dei Sogni,* that you and Papa will throw for us, and the entire family will attend," Lorenza said. "The wedding in Vegas wasn't a real wedding."

"It wasn't?" Fabrice asked.

"Legally yes!" Lorenza cried. "But not an Italian wedding."

"*Ringrazio Dio!*" Fifetta hugged Lorenza tightly. "It'll be the most beautiful wedding we ever held."

"How could it not be?" Franco asked. "We'll have the most beautiful groom in all of Italy."

"*Grazie,* Papa!" Fabrice and Franco hugged like the family they already were.

Bria placed her hands on Lorenza's shoulders and gazed into her sister's brown eyes. There wasn't a big gap in their ages, but for some reason Bria had always felt like another mother to Lorenza or an aunt. It didn't diminish the love they shared, it only meant that Bria felt even more protective of her than a big sister normally would.

"I am so happy for you." Bria hugged her sister and whispered in her ear. "Remember to treat Fabrice with the respect that he deserves. It isn't easy to find a good man in this world."

Lorenza pulled away from her sister and cocked an eyebrow. "Really? This from the woman who found two. First Carlo and now Luca."

"I didn't say it was impossible, I just said it wasn't easy!" The two women laughed so hard they didn't hear the next wave of guests enter the room.

Luca and Nunzi were quickly followed by Rosalie and Giovanni. The foursome looked like they had been caught cheating and had been sent to the principal's office. Bria knew that Luca had the day off so she was surprised to see that both he and Nunzi were wearing their uniforms.

"I thought you were off today?" Bria asked.

"I was," Luca replied. "Then Nunzi called me to tell me that they found Michele in Treviglio."

"Dr. Frangi cooperated and tipped us off," Nunzi explained.

"What's going to happen to him?" Bria asked.

"Rosalie has decided not to press charges," Giovanni shared.

"*Zio* Nazario always told us that you don't kick a man when he's down, and Michele is as far down as a man can get," Rosalie said. "There was no need for me to make things worse for him and I really do hope he can turn his life around now."

"You're a better man than me, Vivaldi," Nunzi said. "I would've thrown the book at him."

"No, you wouldn't!" Rosalie cried. "You want everyone to think you're this hardened cop with a hard-to-pull-off hairstyle, but you're a softie like the rest of us. Don't think I didn't see you pay Michele's taxi driver before they left."

"Where did he go?" Bria asked.

"He said he's going to Frosinone and stay with Teresina for a while until he figures out what he wants to do next with his life," Rosalie said.

"What about you, Rosalie?" Fifetta asked. "Is it the best thing for you?"

"Yes, Mamma D'Abruzzo, it is for the best." Bria watched Rosalie's eyes dart in Giovanni's direction. "I need to focus on me and all the good things that are right before me."

"*Bene*," Fifetta said. "There are so many good things right here."

"Yes, there are."

Once again Rosalie looked at Vanni, who didn't turn away, but held her gaze. Bria's jaw dropped. She couldn't believe that her best friend and her employee were falling for each other. How could she not have seen it before? They were perfect for each other. Bria was so excited she felt like she was going to burst, but then she caught sight of Luca and his eyes were begging her not to make a big deal out of the situation. He was right. If Rosalie and Vanni were getting close and exploring a relationship, they didn't need Bria exposing them in front of a crowd. She would wait until everyone left and then corner Rosalie until she confessed everything. It's what a best friend would do.

The surprises continued when Marco walked into the house followed by a very unlikely group: Bravo, Genie, Valentina, and Imperia. All smiling.

"What in the world is going on?" Bria asked.

"We're just two merry widows out for a walk with our dogs," Valentina announced.

"And me!" Marco squealed.

Imperia picked Marco up in her arms and brought him over to Bria. "Sometimes, Bria, you have to grab life. Otherwise, it may pass you by." Bria reached out to take Marco from her mother-in-law, but at the last moment, Imperia put Marco into Luca's waiting arms. "Now that's a good fit."

Bria stared at Imperia like she had never seen her before, and yet with that one gesture she finally knew for certain everything she needed to know about the complicated woman. Despite her haughtiness, her airs, her occasional insults, Imperia was her family. They may not be bound by blood, but they were bound by love and mutual respect and nothing would ever change that.

"I guess this means the two of you have stopped fighting," Marco said.

"We were never really fighting," Luca said.

"Mamma was," Marco replied.

Sitting at their feet, Bravo looked up at them and barked.

"See," Marco said. "Bravo agrees with me."

Bria bent down and rubbed Bravo's ears and nuzzled her face next to his. She felt the dog's warmth and unconditional love. "That's all over with now; no more fighting."

"Until the next time," Luca joked.

"Sister B told us that it's normal for families to fight," Marco said. "As long as they all love each other, it all turns out okay."

"As usual, Sister B is right," Luca said.

"I think the four of us make a pretty good family," Marco said.

Bria looked at Luca holding her son and watched his smile grow; he was beaming. Bravo was leaning against Bria's leg and brushed his head against Luca's knee until Luca scratched Bravo's neck. Bria felt a warm sensation grow inside of her, not the fire in her belly warning her of impending disaster, but a glow spreading throughout her body.

She imagined it must be what tourists felt the first time they saw Positano's landscape. When the unreal beauty took their breath away. They knew they were as close to perfection as they'd ever get.

Bria decided right then and there that she wasn't going to let this moment pass her by. She was going to grab hold of it. She looked at Luca, Marco, and Bravo. Then at all the people in her home. This was her family, this was her life.

And she was never, ever going to let go.